FORBIDDEN TO *Love*

USA TODAY BESTSELLING AUTHOR

SIOBHAN DAVIS

Printed by Amazon
Paperback edition © September 2021

ISBN-13: 9798465959025

Editor: Kelly Hartigan (XterraWeb) editing.xterraweb.com
Proofread by: Bre Landers, Lauren Lesczynski, Brenda Parsons, Elizabeth Clinton, Aundi Marie, Megan Smith, and Amanda Marie.
Cover design by Robin Harper
Photographer: Regina Wamba
Cover Models: Steven Christiansen and Sophia Tomlinson
Formatting by CP Smith

A DARK MAFIA SECOND CHANCE FORBIDDEN ROMANCE

Natalia Mazzone has grown up knowing she is promised to a made man. As the only daughter of one of New York's most powerful mafia dons, she knows she can't refuse. It's her duty, and she would never dishonor her beloved father.

But the man she's promised to is a monster. And there is nothing but torture, pain, and heartache lying in wait.

So, she grabs happiness when she finds it—in the somewhat reluctant arms of Leonardo Messina.

Leo is her brother's best friend. A *soldato* for the Mazzone *famiglia*. A man with strong ambition and an even stronger resolve. He won't allow them to give in to temptation, so Natalia is forced to love him from afar.

Until one forbidden night changes everything, and she readily hands Leo the key to her heart.

Leo risked everything for the one woman he can never have. He doesn't regret it. It saved Natalia from a life of hell, but his actions set her on a different course.

One that doesn't involve him.

Years have passed, and his feelings remain the same. Yet he keeps his distance, dedicating himself to his new role as underboss to Bennett Mazzone, while the love of his life is married to another man.

Until a twist of fate puts Natalia in his path again, and this time, he is powerless to resist.

Mafia & Italian Glossary

Meanings are listed per the context of this book.

Amore mio – Italian for my love.

Bastardo – Italian for bastard.

Bella – Italian for beautiful.

Bella Donna – Italian for beautiful girl.

Bratva – The Russian mafia in the US.

Capo – Italian for captain. A member of a crime family who heads/leads a crew of soldiers.

Consigliere – Italian for adviser/counselor. A member of a crime family who advises the boss and mediates disputes.

Cosa Nostra – A criminal organization, operating within the US, comprising Italian American crime families.

Cuore mio – Italian for my heart.

Dolcezza – Italian for sweetness.

Don/Boss – The head of a crime family.

Famiglie – Italian for families.

Grazie – Italian for thanks/thank you.

Idiota – Italian for idiot.

Idioti – Italian for idiots.

La famiglia/famiglia – Italian for the family/family.

Made Man – A member of the mafia who has been officially initiated/inducted into a crime family.

Mafioso/Mafiosi – An official member of the mafia/the mafia.

Merda – Italian for shit.

Mob – The mafia/La Cosa Nostra/A crime family.

Principessa – Italian for princess.

Puttana – Italian for whore.

Ragazzo Mio – Italian for my handsome boy.

Soldato – Italian for soldier.

Soldati – Italian for soldiers.

Soldier – A low-ranking member of the mafia who reports to an assigned capo.

Stronzo – Italian for asshole.

Tesorino – Italian for little treasure.

Tesoro – Italian for treasure.

The Commission – The governing/ruling body of the Cosa Nostra, which sits in New York, the organized crime capital of the US.

The Five Families – Five crime families who rule in New York, each headed by a boss.

The Outfit – The Chicago division of the Cosa Nostra.

Triad – Chinese Crime Syndicate.

Underboss – The second in command within a crime family, and an initiated mafia member who works closely with, and reports directly to, the boss.

Va Bene – Italian for okay.

Note from the Author

This book is only recommended to readers aged eighteen and older due to mature content including graphic sexual scenes, violence, and cursing. This is a dark romance with dark themes. Some scenes may be triggering. I can't be more specific without ruining the story. If you are concerned about a specific trigger, you can email me: siobhan@siobhandavis.com

PART 1 – THE PAST

Chapter 1

NATALIA – AGE 17

"LET ME LOOK," Francesca says, tugging on my elbow in an attempt to pull me back from the window.

"Be careful." I step away to let my best friend sneak a peek at the five men hanging out by the pool. "Make sure they don't see you."

Frankie keeps hidden behind the curtain as she looks. "Damn." She whistles under her breath. "Mateo gets hotter every time I see him. Has he been working out more? I swear his abs are even more droolworthy."

"Don't be gross. You can't drool over my brother. There's some universal law about that, I'm sure."

"Mateo would say the same if he knew how badly you are pining for his best friend." She arches a brow, daring me to challenge her.

"Me lusting after Leo is as futile as you lusting after Mateo," I concede, staring longingly at Leo's broad shoulders and toned chest as he lies back on a lounger. Closing his eyes, he tips his head up, letting warmth from the sun beat down on his stunning face. Leonardo Messina has always been drop-dead gorgeous, but he's getting even better looking as he matures. At twenty, he is three years older than I am, and he'll never see me as anything more than his best friend's *virginal* little sister.

"True," Frankie says, flopping down on my bed. "Which is why you should agree to the double date with Vaughan. Archer says he's crazy about you."

Reluctantly dragging myself away from the window, I throw myself down on the bed beside Frankie, turning on my side so I'm facing her. "You know I'm not permitted to date." I let out a long sigh, hating that I'm denied the simple things most girls my age take for granted. I'm the only senior who hasn't even been kissed. It's pathetically embarrassing.

"No one has to know. You can say you're staying at my place. Mom won't tell. She hates you can't enjoy the normal high-school experience."

"I love your mom, but I don't want to get her or me in trouble. If Papa finds out, he'll ground me. I'll never be allowed a sleepover again." It's a miracle he even lets me spend a few nights at Frankie's apartment in the city.

"Your father adores you. You're his *principessa*. What's the worst he could do?"

I tuck my dark hair behind my ears. "Make me marry that monster the second I graduate next year." A full-body shudder works its way through me as Carlo Greco's hideously handsome face appears in my mind's eye. Acid crawls up my throat, and knots twist in my stomach like they do anytime I think of my despicable fiancé.

Frankie reaches out, taking my hand. "This sucks, Nat. You can't marry that *stronzo*. He gives me the creeps, and I hate the way he looks at you." Her face contorts unpleasantly. "You need to tell your father how he accosted you at the engagement party."

"I can't." I sit up, sighing in frustration. "Carlo is the Greco heir, and they are one of the five families. This marriage contract is a solid arrangement between our fathers. A commitment to continue doing business together. Even if I did tell him, I doubt it would make any difference. Carlo didn't touch me in a way I could complain about." A shiver creeps up my spine at the memory of how he shoved me into my father's study and pinned me against the wall. My flesh crawled as his gaze ran over me from head to toe. It was a miracle I didn't puke in his face. He wasn't shy about making his feelings clear, and he's not inclined to wait until we are married before taking my prized virginity.

I briefly squeeze my eyes shut as familiar panic attempts to strangle me.

"Yet." Frankie sits up behind me, pulling her long blonde hair back into a ponytail. "He threatened to fuck you before the wedding. That's against our revered traditions and a huge disrespect to you and your father."

"He will have little opportunity to get me alone before then, and a date isn't being set until I graduate." I'm grateful for small mercies. Every day I have without being chained to that monster as his wife is a blessing.

But I'm running out of time. The first two weeks of senior year has already flown by. This time next year, I'll be Mrs. Carlo Greco, and the thought makes me want to flay the skin from my bones.

"He's the type of man to create his own opportunities," Frankie says, concern flitting across her face. "I think you should at least tell Mateo."

My eyes pop wide. "Are you kidding? He'd blow a gasket and make things worse." My brother is utterly reckless, and he acts before he thinks. "The very last thing I need is Mateo threatening Carlo. That sick bastard would see it as a challenge." I shake my head, and my long wavy dark hair tumbles over my shoulders. "No, I can't tell anyone. I'll just have to deal with the *stronzo* myself."

I wander to the window as if on autopilot. Whenever Leo is around the house, I'm drawn to him like he's my gravity. Hiding behind the net curtain, I slowly retract it, watching as the guys get up from their loungers, making their way inside. Leo is the last to leave the pool area. He cricks his head from side to side and stretches his arms out. The movement causes all the dips and curves in his stomach to pull and tighten, and it sends a stream of liquid warmth flooding to my core.

"I can see the attraction," Frankie agrees, coming up behind me. "He's beautiful."

"He truly is."

We are both silent as we watch him stride toward the French doors leading into our living room.

Leo has this way of commanding the air when he walks. Like the particles realign to shift around his body, acknowledging his magnificence. It gives him an almost godlike presence. It's as if

Mother Nature is conceding to the power of his beauty.

Or my obsession has become a little unhealthy and I'm seeing things that don't exist.

"But it's more than the way he looks," I add, turning away from the window. "He is such a great guy. Smart, funny, charming, and honorable. He treats me with respect, and he trusts me to make good decisions. He doesn't smother me, like Mateo."

I love my only sibling. Mateo is an amazing big brother, and he regularly goes to bat for me. But he loves the criminal underworld we live in and supports the old-school traditions and rules. He refuses to see any issue with the fate lying in store for me.

It's true he's not a fan of Carlo—and he would lose it if he knew Carlo had threatened to take my virginity before marriage—but he tells me time and time again this is just the way of the Cosa Nostra. As the only daughter of the most powerful don in New York, this has always been my destiny. Written in ink while I was still a fetus growing in my mama's womb.

"Mateo would take a bullet for you," Frankie says, trailing me as I move toward my bedroom door.

"I know he would, but he babies me too much at times, and his blind support of the archaic sexist rules irritates me to no end." I open my door, and we walk side by side along the long hallway. "Especially when he's the biggest manwhore roaming the streets of New York. It's so hypocritical."

Frankie giggles. "Your brother is fucking gorgeous. It's no wonder women fall at his feet."

I pin her with narrowed eyes. "Yet you want to join them."

"Archer isn't bad in the sack, but he's only a boy," she says, referring to her boyfriend of six months. "Mateo is all man, and I heard he gave Bianca Gambino four orgasms in one night."

I poke her in the ribs with my elbow, scowling. "Oh my God. I did not need to know that. Seriously. Keep that intel to yourself."

"I just want one night." A dreamy expression ghosts over her face as we reach the top of the grand staircase. "One night to experience a real man. I'm so ready for multiple orgasms. I'm lucky if Archer gives me one."

"Be grateful you get any," I whisper as we descend the stairs, heading toward the living room.

Frankie comes from an Italian American family too. Father would not endorse our friendship if she didn't. Her father and her older brother are Mazzone *soldati*, in my father's employment. While the role of soldier is a lower-ranking position, they are well respected and expected to follow traditions.

Except Frankie is the youngest of four daughters, and there is no arranged marriage in her future. She will have to marry an Italian American, but it will be her choice. Her parents permit her to date, but they don't know she's having sex. She's supposed to remain a virgin until her wedding night too.

I'm envious at the freedom she has, even if I love her like a sister. It's hard not to feel jealous when I hear everything she is permitted to do that is denied to me.

She loops her arm through mine. "This is exactly why you should date Vaughan. I know you can't have sex with him, but there are plenty of other things you can do. You deserve to have some pleasurable experiences before you're tied to that *bastardo*."

"Stay quiet," I whisper, creeping toward the double doors to the living room. They are slightly ajar, enough to allow us to eavesdrop on the guys' conversation. "I want to hear what they're talking about."

We situate ourselves on either side of the doors and listen.

"I'm telling you, you should all tap Nicole. She let me stick it in her ass," Mateo says. "Hottest fucking sex ever."

Ew. That is seriously disgusting. I'll need to scrub my ears out later.

"She's a high-school senior," Leo says, his deep sexy voice doing weird things to my stomach.

"She's eighteen and legal. What the fuck does her age have to do with anything?" Mateo replies.

"She goes to school with your sister," Leo adds.

All the blood drains from my face. There is only one Nicole at the private all-girls academy I attend in the city. Nicole Chastain is stunning but a bona fide bitch. She hates my guts, and I wouldn't be surprised if she fucked my brother purely to get one over on me. I dig my fingernails into my palm while gritting my teeth. Frankie and I exchange a look, and I can tell her thoughts are similar to mine.

"Nicole isn't friends with Nat," Mateo clarifies. "And I think you should fuck her. You're way too uptight. You need to get laid before your blue balls strangle you."

"I got laid Saturday night. Trust me, my balls are the furthest from blue," Leo retorts, as phones ping around the room.

Pain slices across my chest at his admission. It's stupid, because he's single and free to fuck whomever he wants. I know he's no saint. He's not a walking STD like my brother, but he's had his fair share of women over the years, I'm sure. I hate thinking how some lucky women know him intimately. That they got to put their hands on him. Touch him in places I long to touch him.

"Sweet," one of the guys says. "Thanks for her number."

"Nicole is game for anything," Mateo adds. "And she didn't hesitate when I told her I was going to share her number with my friends."

"*Puttana*," Frankie mouths at me.

"She mentioned you by name, Messina. You should give her a call. Stick your grumpy dick in her ass." A round of laughter breaks out, and I have heard enough.

I stalk off, heading toward the kitchen to vent my frustration on dinner.

Frankie loyally gives chase. "They are disgusting pigs," she says, verbalizing my thoughts as I tie an apron around my waist.

"I hate the double standards." I hand her an apron as I move to the sink to wash my hands. "It's okay for them to screw anything in a skirt, but I can't even look at another man let alone kiss him or fuck him." I yank a skillet out of the cabinet, slamming it down on top of the stove. "Maybe you're right." I remove the ingredients from the refrigerator as frustration and anger simmer in my veins. "Maybe I should give Vaughan a chance."

"What are you saying?" she asks, taking the onions from my hands.

"I'm sick of being the good little Italian *principessa*. And I'm tired of waiting for Leo to notice me." My spine stiffens as I straighten up. Pinning my bestie with a wicked grin, I say, "Set up the double date. I'm going to go out with Vaughan."

Chapter 2

NATALIA

"WOW, YOU LOOK gorgeous," Vaughan says when Frankie and I reach the restaurant. Archer immediately hauls his girlfriend into his arms, and Frankie goes willingly. Vaughan leans in, kissing my cheek, before producing a single red rose from behind his back. "The color matches your lips." His smile is warm, and his inspection of my tight black knee-length dress is respectful. I know my boobs are practically spilling out of Frankie's borrowed gown, because she's smaller in the bust than me, but he's a gentleman, and his gaze doesn't linger on my ample chest.

"Thank you." I smile broadly as I bring the rose to my nose, inhaling the spicy, fruity scent emanating from the coral-red petals.

"Thank you for finally agreeing to a date," he replies, offering me his arm. "You have made all my dreams come true."

Archer pretends to gag while fixing his best friend with a grin. "Cheesy much, Fitzy?"

Frankie swats his chest. "Don't throw shade. I think it's sweet and romantic."

I loop my arm through Vaughan's. "So do I." I beam up at him, and his eyes meet mine with something akin to longing. "Thank you for being patient."

"For you, I would wait forever." He pulls me in a little tighter to his side, trapping me with a dazzling smile, showcasing his perfectly straight white teeth.

Vaughan Fitzgerald has the type of classic all-American good looks I'd expect to see in a Ralph Lauren campaign. He is tall with lean muscles, a head of glorious golden-blond hair, tan skin, and sparkling azure eyes. According to my bestie, all the girls at his mixed private school are going gaga for him. Yet somehow, he only appears to have eyes for me. Archer told Frankie he hasn't looked at another girl since meeting me at her house shortly after his best friend started dating mine. I'm not sure I believe it, but it's flattering all the same.

It's nice to have the attention of a normal, decent guy.

Archer snorts this time, and Frankie thumps him in the arm. I laugh, and I can't remember the last time I felt this happy or carefree. "You have all the right words, Vaughan."

"I mean every single one of them." His expression is sincere as he opens the door to the Thai restaurant.

Vaughan keeps his hand on my lower back as the waitress guides us to our table. I'm aware of eyes watching me as I hold my head up and stride across the room with confidence that has been drilled in me from birth.

There are many things expected of Italian women in our society, and Mama has worked hard to ensure I fulfill my duty while retaining whatever semblance of independence I can.

Rosa Mazzone has instilled in me the need to be dutiful and loyal without sacrificing the essence of who I am. Although our world reveres wives, women are still deemed inferior to men. I refuse to accept that, and I won't be trodden on. I already know my fiancé will not tolerate any signs of independence, but appearing weak will only give him further excuses to be cruel. So, I intend to be confident and strong, even in the face of adversity. No matter what that *stronzo* throws at me, I will not back down.

Dinner is a pleasant affair. The food is divine, and we laugh and talk the whole way through the meal. Vaughan is very enjoyable company. He is attentive and articulate, and I'm relaxed in his presence.

After leaving the restaurant, he takes my hand as we stroll through the streets of New York, in the direction of the movie theater. Archer and Frankie are ahead of us, and we hang back, talking privately. "Are you having a good time?" Vaughan smiles down at me.

"The best."

"Enough to want to do this again?" he inquires, lifting a brow.

A tinkling laugh escapes my throat. "The date isn't even over yet."

"I already know I want to see you again. What night are you free? I'd like to take you on a date. Just the two of us."

"I would like that, but my situation is complicated. I'm not sure when I'll be back in the city."

He stops us in the middle of the sidewalk, taking both my hands in his. "I know who your father is, Natalia, and it doesn't scare me."

"It should." Most everyone at my school avoids me like the plague because of my name. There are a few other Italian girls in my year, and we all hang around together, but other students give us a wide berth. "He would be very displeased if he knew I was on a date with you."

"Because I'm not Italian American?" He drops one of my hands, and we start walking again, picking up our pace so we don't lose our friends.

"For starters," I murmur, wondering how much he knows about our world. I should probably give it to him straight, but I like him, and I selfishly want to keep him for as long as possible.

"I can be your dirty little secret," he teases, sliding his arm around my shoulders.

"You deserve to be much more than that," I truthfully reply, tucking some wayward strands of hair behind my ear.

"How about your secret boyfriend?" His grin is mischievous.

"Let's not run before we have walked," I say, because I can't get too carried away.

"I have waited to date you a long time. I can be whatever you want me to be, and I can be patient, but I'm going nowhere."

"CAN I KISS you?" Vaughan whispers, wrapping his arm more snugly around my shoulders as we lean into one another in the back row of the theater. Beside me, Archer and Frankie are noisily making out, much to the disgust of the patrons in the row in front of us.

My heart knocks against my rib cage as I lean into my date. I am supposed to reserve my first kiss—my first everything—for my husband, but this is something I can take for me, and Carlo will never know. "Okay," I whisper back, hoping he can't hear the tremble in my voice or see how fast my chest is heaving.

Gently cupping my face, he draws me in closer, and I shut my eyes as he brushes his lips against mine ever so softly. "You are so beautiful, Natalia. The most beautiful girl I have ever seen. I am crazy for you." His lips press against mine more urgently this time, and I angle my head, kissing him back. A pleasant buzz thrums in my veins, but it's hardly fireworks. As first kisses go, it's nice, and I feel comfortable with Vaughan.

We kiss for ages while the movie plays in the background. Vaughan holds my face and the nape of my neck, but he doesn't attempt to touch me anywhere else, and it only makes me like him even more. I circle my arms around his neck, and my fingers toy with the downy hairs I find there. He moans into my mouth before slipping his tongue inside.

And then he's gone. Lips ripped from mine unexpectedly, and I blink my eyes open in confusion. Horror suffuses me as I watch my brother grab my date in a headlock and drag him out of the theater. Worst of all is the shocked expression on Leo's face as he stares at me from the end of the row. Some indecipherable emotion ghosts over his face before he scowls, gesturing for me to get up.

"Nat." Frankie grabs my elbow. "What's going on?"

"Mateo is about to rip Vaughan to pieces. Stay here," I caution when Archer makes a move to get up. "Let me handle this."

I stand and walk to where Leo is waiting for me, just inside the doors. "What the hell were you thinking?" Leo hisses when we exit the theater, walking along the corridor that leads to the stairs.

"This is none of your business," I snap, embarrassed and overheating because Leo's hand on my lower back is burning me through my clothes. I felt nothing but light warmth when Vaughan did the same thing earlier. Now, it feels like Leo is branding his mark on me as he holds me close while escorting me from the building.

His gaze roams my body, lingering briefly on my chest. My nipples instantly harden, pushing against the silky fabric of my dress. He can probably see the effect he's having on me, but I don't care. I want him to know I would much prefer to have been caught making out with him.

"The hell it isn't," he says, pulling me out of my head. "You're as much my sister as Matt's," he says, driving a dagger straight through my heart. Pain settles on my chest, making it difficult to breathe. "I care about you, and I don't want to see you getting hurt."

We step onto the escalator, and he turns to look at me. He is so close I can see the smattering of tiny freckles across the bridge of his strong nose. Heat rolls off his body in waves, washing over me, almost knocking me off my feet. I sway a little, and he takes hold of my arm while maintaining eye contact. His gray-blue eyes peer deep into mine, and it feels like I'm drowning. My heart accelerates, and butterflies swoop into my stomach as he stares at me. Warmth from his hand seeps into the exposed skin on my arm, and I'm tingly all over. My gaze drops to his plump lips, and a pulsing ache throbs down below.

I didn't feel this aroused making out with Vaughan.

One intense look from Leo, and I'm virtually melting into a puddle of frustrated hormones.

Leo's tongue darts out, wetting his lips, and his eyes lower to my mouth for a fleeting second before he looks away, clawing a hand through his brown hair. Air whooshes out of my mouth as we step off the escalator. Leo pulls me off to the side, removing his light black jacket. "Put this on," he says, in a clipped tone, thrusting the jacket at me while averting his eyes. "Mateo will lose his shit if he sees you in that dress."

"Screw my brother," I bark, throwing the jacket back at him. "I don't care what he thinks. I'm sick of his double standards." Wrenching my arm from Leo's, I stomp toward the entrance doors, desperate to find Vaughan before Mateo inflicts any damage.

"Nat!" Leo snaps, grabbing my elbow and yanking me back. "If you want to save that boy, put the damn jacket on now. Or have you forgotten how reckless your brother is and how protective he is of you?"

I hate that he's right. I snatch the jacket from him, angrily putting it on, before I race outside with Leo hot on my heels.

"This way." Leo takes my hand, pulling me in the opposite direction. His callused palm is warm against my skin, and it sinks bone-deep, spreading contentment up and down my arm. Man, I have it so bad, and I can't get distracted. I need to stop Mateo before he murders my date.

Leo pulls me around the corner of the building and down a narrow dimly lit alley.

"Fuck you, asshole," Vaughan shouts before grunting.

I run in my heels, slamming to a halt at the back of a dumpster, gasping at the sight that awaits me. Mateo has Vaughan pinned against the wall, and he's glaring at him with his raised fists, ready to inflict permanent damage. Blood coats Vaughan's nose and drips down his lips and over his chin.

"Stop!" I yell as Matty moves to punch him again. "Stop this madness." I tug at my brother's arm, but it's like yanking on a rock.

Mateo is muscle stacked upon muscle, and he isn't budging.

"I need to teach this *bastardo* a lesson," Mateo says through gritted teeth, turning his head to look at me.

"No, you don't. Let him go." I shove my face all up in my brother's. "Now, Matty," I demand. "If you want to be angry, be angry at me. Vaughan has done nothing wrong."

"Let him go, Mazzone," Leo agrees, in a lethal tone.

Mateo glares at a terrified-looking Vaughan and clenches and unclenches his fist before letting him go. Vaughan slumps against the wall, panting heavily.

"I'm so sorry," I say, reaching out to swipe at the blood dripping from his chin.

"Don't fucking touch him," Leo warns, wrapping an arm around my waist and pulling me back.

"Be grateful it's me who found you and not her fiancé," Mateo growls, pressing the muzzle of his gun to Vaughan's temple.

The poor guy looks like he wants to shit his pants. "Fiancé?" His confused gaze bounces between me and my brother. "She's seventeen. How the hell does she have a fiancé?" He looks to Mateo for answers. "And why didn't you tell me?" he adds, slanting me with a hurtful expression.

"I was trying to forget he exists, and I did tell you things are complicated," I explain. "I wanted one night to be normal. One night to pretend I have control over my life. One night to—"

Leo slaps his hand over my mouth, cutting me off mid-sentence.

"Shut your mouth, Nat." Mateo glares at me. "Or keep spouting that shit if you want me to put a bullet through his skull."

I remain quiet as tears stab my eyes. I won't let them fall. I can't, so I quietly seethe, bristling with rage under my skin.

"You tell no one about this," Mateo warns Vaughan, pressing the gun against his temple. "If I find out you breathed a word of it, I will hunt you down and slaughter you like an animal."

"I won't tell anyone. I swear," Vaughan says, his lower lip trembling.

I want to thank him for making me feel desired and giving me one night of happiness, but he can't even look at me, and I don't blame him. I'm pretty sure he'll give up all notion of dating me now.

"See that you don't." Mateo removes his gun and gives Vaughan a hefty shove. "Get lost."

Leo reaches out, grabbing Vaughan as he rushes past. "Touch her again, and I'll kill you with my bare hands." His menacing tone is one I haven't heard from him before, and it gives me chills.

Vaughan nods, still avoiding eye contact with me, and I watch with an ache in my heart as he races down the alleyway, eager to get as far away from me as he can.

Chapter 3

NATALIA

MATEO DOESN'T UTTER a word to me the entire journey home to Greenhaven. I sit in the back seat, fighting embarrassment and shame, and even being in the same car as Leo isn't helping my mood. Tonight started out so promising, but it ended in the worst possible way. Leo's words are imprinted in my brain, and I'm heartsore as well as so freaking angry. The unfairness of it all really gets to me. Leo seeing me as his pseudo little sister only adds salt to the wound.

My anxiety accelerates to coronary-inducing levels when we turn into the driveway leading to our large family home. Set on three acres of landscaped lawn, our sprawling mansion is an impressive gilded cage. Father has ensured I want for nothing—except free will. If Mateo tells Papa, there will be hell to pay. He will freak the fuck out if he hears I made out with a boy who isn't even an Italian American. He can't find out. What little freedom I have will be removed, and I'll sink into an even deeper depression.

Setting aside my swirling emotions, I sit forward, sticking my head between the two front seats. "Please don't tell Papa." My eyes plead with my brother as he looks at me through the mirror.

"You're not in any position to negotiate," he grits out through clenched teeth. "And you're lucky Enzo called me before Papa or Carlo were tipped off."

"Who is Enzo?" I figured my brother had a spy who ratted me out because our *famiglia* has contacts everywhere.

"An associate. He was working the ticket office, and he recognized you."

Of course, he did. I can barely breathe without someone reporting it. "Don't tell Angelo. Please, Matty. He will ground me for the rest of senior year." Tentatively, I reach out, touching his shoulder. "I promise I won't see Vaughan again if you promise not to tell Papa."

"I should, because that'll ensure you remain pure and avoid temptation."

I want to punch him. Viciously, until he bleeds. But I grind my teeth to the molars, clinging to the last vestiges of my patience. "I learned my lesson, Matty," I lie. "Don't take away the only freedom I have left."

Mateo parks the car in front of the stone steps leading to our front door. Tension seeps into the air as we sit in silence. The armed *soldati* guarding the front of the house briefly glance our way before they resume staring straight ahead. "I won't tell him." He turns around to level me with a somber look. "But you can't pull shit like that again. This is more than just upsetting Papa or the Greco *famiglia*. This is about your reputation, Natalia. You are ruined without your reputation."

Maybe that's what I should do. Purposely sleep with someone and make sure the monster finds out about it. I know I'd be shunned. I'd be an embarrassment, the black sheep of the family. But if it gets me out of marrying that *stronzo*, perhaps it would be worth it.

Mateo's eyes narrow as he watches me—as if he has delved into my head and heard my thoughts. Leo's intense stare bores into me, and I look away as I nod. "I know." I grip the door handle. "I won't mess up again."

"Nat." Mateo stalls me as I have one foot out of the car. "I know you're frustrated, but you have had years to accept your fate. This is the way it is for women within the *famiglia*. Virgin brides are revered, and wives are cherished. You will want for nothing. I know you are unhappy, but it will all work out. You'll see."

"That's bullshit, and you know it!" I cry out, instantly enraged. "Would you have accepted your fate if it wasn't one of power? If you had no control, whatsoever, over the rest of your life?"

"We're not talking about me, and you're acting childish. Pull your shit together."

Right now, I really want to take a swing at my brother, but what's the freaking point? Mateo is so much like my father at times it's scary. The awful thing is, I truly believe he buys into that crap. As much as he adores me, and I know he does, he still doesn't see anything wrong with the fate lying in wait for me. I don't know why I bother protesting anymore.

He will never see things my way.

I plaster a false dutiful smile on my face. "I'm going up to my room. Tell Mama I called you to come and pick me up because I felt ill."

"*Va bene*."

Leo's gaze holds a glimmer of sympathy as I exit the car, but it's gone so fast I'm not sure I didn't imagine it. I slip quietly into the house, removing my shoes and tiptoeing up the stairs to my room. I spend a restless night, tossing and turning, lamenting the futility of my life and sobbing into my pillow over my unrequited love.

The next morning, I am uncharacteristically quiet at the breakfast table, but I blame my fake illness when Mama asks me what's wrong. Truth is, I am heartsick with longing and hurt at Leo's refusal to see me as more than a sisterly figure. I'm also incredibly embarrassed over what went down last night. It's so humiliating, and I'm angry Vaughan got caught in the crosshairs. He did nothing wrong, apart from liking the wrong girl. My thoughts and my emotions veer back and forth, and I'm a certifiable mess. A black cloud has descended over me, like a shroud, and I can't summon the energy to pretend I'm not melancholy.

After pushing food around my plate, I ask to be excused and head out to walk the grounds of our estate.

Papa built a walking trail for Mama years ago, when they first moved here from our penthouse apartment in the city, and I follow the path leading around the back of the house. Armed *soldati* guard the perimeter of the property, out of sight, giving me the illusion of privacy. I tap out a message to Frankie, reassuring her I'm okay and telling her I will see her at school tomorrow.

Footsteps thud on the path behind me as I reach the entrance to our apple orchard. Mama also has a vegetable patch and an herb garden, and she grows tomatoes, peppers, and strawberries in her greenhouse. I glance over my shoulder in the direction of the approaching footfalls, and my pulse instantly quickens as I watch Leo advance.

"Hey, *dolcezza*," he calls out, smiling.

Sweetness. I equally hate and adore Leo's pet name for me. I love he calls me something no one else does, but why does it have to be something so innocent and pure and sisterly?

Leaning against a tree, I wait for him to catch up.

"Do you mind if I join you?" he asks, pinning me with those gorgeous silvery-blue eyes. A light breeze blows strands of his brown hair across his brow, and my fingers itch with a craving to touch the silky softness. A five o'clock shadow darkens the contours of his stunning face, only adding to his appeal.

"Sure." I shrug, feigning nonchalance as we walk along the path between rows of trees laden down with vibrant red apples. The sweetest scent hangs in the air, like always at this time of year, and I inhale deeply, drawing comfort from the familiarity at a time when I feel so lost. This is the middle of peak season, and our pantry is already bursting with apple jelly, apple pies, and apple strudels.

"Are you okay?" he asks, as the lingering breeze lifts the hem of my white knee-length dress.

"I'm fine. Why wouldn't I be?" I arch a brow as I look at him, skimming my hand along the bark of the trees we pass by.

"Don't do that with me, *dolcezza.* I know you were pissed last night, and I saw the wheels churning in your head. Mateo isn't the only Mazzone with a reckless streak. Please don't do anything rash."

I snort out an incredulous laugh. "When the hell would I get the opportunity to do anything rash or reckless, Leo? And don't pretend you're not prone to bouts of wild recklessness yourself. You have gone along with more of Matty's crazy schemes than anyone." The difference is Leo knows when to pull back, and he's smart enough to be responsible when he needs to be so no one can tell he's a little bit of a loose cannon too.

"We're not discussing me. This is about you. I'm worried."

I shake my head as bitterness creeps up my throat. "I'm a virtual prisoner, and very soon, I'll be exchanging one jail for another."

"I know you don't want this, and I hate that asshole is the one who has been chosen for you, but it's pointless to fight it."

Leo is usually on my side, and his defeatist talk is not what I want to hear now. My anger resurfaces in a nanosecond. Spinning around, I fix him with a sharp look. Steam is practically billowing from my ears as I pin my hands on my shapely hips while I lash out. "So, I should just let him fuck me before the wedding because he's going to be my husband soon anyway and I have to obey his every command?"

"Hell to the no." Leo frowns, and concern glimmers in his eyes. "Has something happened?" A muscle ticks in his jaw. "Did he do something?”

I gulp over the lump wedged in my throat. “Not yet, but he has made his intentions clear.”

Chapter 4

NATALIA

"IS THAT WHAT last night was about? And were you seriously going to give your virginity to that idiot?" His eyes darken, and the vein in his neck vibrates under his skin. "Vaughan." He scoffs. "What kind of a pussy name is that anyway?"

"Careful, Leo. If I didn't know better, I'd say you're jealous." A giddy smile creeps over my mouth before I can stop it.

"Don't be ridiculous. Do you have any idea how dangerous it is to even consider giving your virginity to anyone before you are married? Including Carlo. It would be so easy for him to discard you then. It would bring shame on your family, and you would be dishonored with no future. Things could turn violent and ugly. That's the reality of the situation, Nat. Mateo doesn't want that for you, and neither do I." He exhales heavily, slanting me with concerned eyes. "I'm angry you were going to risk everything for that punk kid. He could never be worthy of you."

I don't want to talk about the potential danger or the risks of being with anyone else, because Leo will completely shut himself off to the idea of an us.

To hell with the rules and tradition.

Feeling brazen, I move in closer, and our chests brush. I plant my hands on his warm, hard chest, ignoring his little speech, redirecting the conversation where I want it to go. "As opposed to risking everything for a *man*?" I tilt my head back, peering deep into his eyes, as I stretch up on tiptoes, letting my hands glide upward to curl around his neck. My heart is pounding like crazy, and butterflies are running amok in my chest, but he doesn't push me away like I expect him to.

His eyes drop to my mouth, and electricity surrounds us, crackling and potent and supercharged. Lust mixes with blood in my veins as he stares at me, as if in a daze, and it's that, combined with a wild desire to change my destiny, that has me leaning up and pressing my lips to his ear. "For you?" I whisper before my lips glide across his prickly jawline and my mouth brushes against his. His body stiffens, and I can hardly think over the rushing of blood in my ears and the *thud, thud* of my heart crashing against my chest cavity.

Snaking my arms tighter around his neck, I slant my mouth more persuasively against his, willing him to kiss me back. His lemony scent wraps around me like a comfort blanket, and I silently urge him to let go of responsibility and give in to me as my lips move against his warm, immobile mouth.

Leo pushes my shoulders, staggering away, blinking profusely, as a look of horror washes over his face.

Immense pain sits on my chest, constricting my lungs and squeezing my heart to a pulp. Agony ties my insides into knots, and it feels like I could die. Rejection mixes with shame and a boatload of hurt at the thought he doesn't feel what I feel. He doesn't desire me the same way I desire him. Pain is an invisible knife shredding strips off the pathetic organ pumping blood through my veins.

"Natalia. No." Leo shakes his head, rubbing a hand against his nape as his Adam's apple jumps in his throat. "Didn't anything Mateo said last night get through to you?!" he yells. "You can't go around kissing other men!"

"You're not just anyone, Leo." I bridge the gap between us, because it seems there's no end to my stupid bravery. I won't give up on him until I know it's completely futile. "You know how I feel about you. I know you do."

Taking my arm as I reach for him, he tenderly clasps his fingers around my slender wrist, holding me off. "This isn't happening, Nat. It can't for all the reasons I already mentioned. And you're like a little sister to me. It would be so wrong."

That's about the only thing he could say to get me to back off. No matter what I do, I am always relegated to the sister corner. Agonizing pain obliterates me from every angle, and I wish the ground could open up and swallow me. Refusing to let him see how truly devastated I am, I force my pain back down inside, steel my shoulders, and jut my chin up, leveling him with a deadly look as my injured pride overrides common sense. "I'm too sweet and innocent, is that it?" I shove at his shoulders. "I bet if I was like Nicole Chastain and I spread my legs and took it up the ass you would be beating a path to my door every night."

"Jesus, Nat." He runs a hand through his hair. "You need to stop eavesdropping."

Aggravated and risking one final attempt, I make a split-second decision, yanking my dress up over my head and tossing it aside as I stand before him in a white lacy bra and panties set. Leo gasps, grabbing fistfuls of his hair as his eyes drink their fill.

"And I need *you* to see me for who I really am." My voice is calm, belying the trembling of my limbs as I lay it all on the line. "I'm not a little girl anymore, Leo." I step toward him. "I'm all woman, and I want you. I want you to be the one to take my virginity. Not that monster. We can hide within the trees. No one will see us."

Conflict wages in his eyes, but he's struggling to tear them away from my heaving chest. My nipples are so hard they are poking through the flimsy material. The growing bulge in his black pants tells me he's aroused too. Adrenaline courses through my veins as I allow a sliver of excitement to take hold of me. He's not as immune as he'd like me to believe.

Thrusting my body flush against his, I peer up at him with hopeful, pleading eyes. "No one will know. It can be our secret. Please, Leo. Make love to me." Swallowing nerves, I slide my hand down between our bodies, placing my palm over his erection through his pants. Oh my God. He is so big and hard and all man. His cock jerks against my hand, and liquid warmth floods my panties.

A second later, Leo stumbles back as if he's been electrocuted. "Jesus, fuck, Natalia. Put your dress back on!" he snaps. "I'm not taking your virginity! Have you lost your goddamned mind?!" Dipping down, he snatches my dress, holding it out to me. His eyes blaze with a multitude of emotions. "Put that on before one of the guards see you. Your father has shot men for less."

He turns around, wringing his hands at the back of his neck while I get dressed. Humiliation crashes over me, and tears prick my eyes. My lip wobbles, and I'm struggling not to cry. The most unimaginable pain lays siege to my body, as if some invisible force is ripping me apart from the inside out.

What the hell was I thinking throwing myself at him like this?

I'm so embarrassed.

He has made it clear he doesn't want me, on more than one occasion recently. He continually rejects me, yet I continue to act like an immature fool. I basically offered myself to him on a platter, and he turned me down.

Hurt threads through me, tying me into knots.

"Are you done?" he asks, keeping his back to me.

"Yes." I croak, almost choking over the painful lump blocking my throat.

Loving someone who doesn't love you back has got to be the most agonizing thing to endure.

I thought it was bad when he wasn't aware of my feelings.

But that pales in comparison to this.

Knowing he knows and he doesn't want me is a million times

worse, and I want to die. I want to lock myself in my room, curl into a ball, and unburden myself on my already sodden pillow.

He turns around. "I don't know what's going on with you, but this isn't who you are." Leo's voice is softer as he tips my face up with a finger under my chin. "You're exquisite, *dolcezza.* So special. Kind, smart, beautiful, and compassionate. And you should remain that way."

Anger blooms inside me, and I see red. I can't appreciate his compliments because I know they aren't true—he's just trying to let me down gently. He must think I'm so naïve if he expects me to soften with those words. "You're a hypocrite!" I yell. "Mateo too. Both of you screw anything that moves, and I'm getting lectured because I dared to kiss a boy for the first time in my life and I stupidly threw myself at you!" I push him away, growling when he doesn't budge. He's like an unmovable wall of muscle, standing there with his arms crossed over his chest and his sad, slightly puzzled expression.

"You know this is the way things are. The way they have to be."

His calm reply only fuels the rage coursing through my veins. "I fucking hate it!" I roar. "And I'm not going to lie down and accept it any longer." Steely determination infiltrates my blood stream. I don't care how I achieve it, but I *am* going to get out of this arranged marriage. Papa will be disappointed if I disgrace him, but I have gone along with this charade for long enough. My entire life is at stake, and I can't sit around and do nothing any longer.

"Natalia," Leo growls, making a grab for me when I whirl around and move to walk off. "Don't do anything rash. I'm begging you. You'll only make things worse."

"Fuck off, Leo," I hiss, smothering a laugh when his eyes widen in shock. "This doesn't concern you. You have made your feelings perfectly clear. I know exactly where I stand now."

"*Dolcezza.* Please." Leo reels me into his body so my back is pressed up against his warm chest. "I don't want to see you get hurt.

You know what they do to women who don't cooperate."

"I don't care. I would rather die than marry Carlo Greco."

"I'll talk to him," he offers. "I'll warn him to back off."

I bark out a laugh. "You do that, and he'll only be more determined." I shuck out of his hold and glare at him. "Leave it alone, Leo. I'm not your responsibility. I'm not Giuliana. Your responsibility is to your actual sister, not me. I don't need you or Mateo interfering any more than you already have." Without waiting to see how he replies, I race back along the path toward the house, ready to lick my wounds in the privacy of my bedroom.

Chapter 5

NATALIA

"I CAN'T BELIEVE you stripped in front of him," Frankie says as we collect our things from our lockers at the end of the school day.

"Don't remind me. It's humiliating enough without you repeating it." I filled Frankie in, on what went down with Leo in the orchard yesterday, at lunchtime.

"I want to kick him in the junk for disregarding your feelings. Mateo too for terrorizing poor Vaughan. But maybe Leo *was* trying to protect you? He just went about it all wrong."

"I threw myself at him, and he rejected me, Frankie! I don't care whether he was trying to protect me or not. It's the most humiliating experience of my life." I slam my locker closed with more force than necessary. "A man like Leonardo Messina never turns down sex. I have to face the truth. He doesn't see me like that. I will forever be Mateo's sweet little sister in his eyes."

"He's an idiot for turning you down, and I'm not buying his reaction. You're a fucking goddess, Nat. No sane man could resist you." There is a brief pregnant pause. "At least you got some chocolates out of it."

Leo left a box of my favorite chocolates outside my door at some point yesterday. I only discovered them when I left my room for dinner. I know he had to go out of his way to pick them up from the chocolaterie in White Plains, and ordinarily, that would make me happy, but I'm too butthurt over his dismissal to swoon over the gesture. "I'd rather have had the man," I admit, because I'm still infatuated with him even though it's utterly pointless. "Whatever way you look at it, he still rejected me. Trying to sugarcoat it doesn't change that fact." Though stuffing my face with chocolate as I silently berated myself for my idiocy did help a little.

"What are you going to do?" she asks, zipping her book bag closed.

I shrug as we join the crowd in the hallway heading toward the doors. "Nothing. If flinging myself at him didn't work, nothing will."

"He needs to see you as a desirable woman, not a little girl." She ponders, rubbing her chin in contemplation as we push out through the double doors. "I know!" She grabs my arm, pulling me aside at the top of the steps. "Are your parents still going away this weekend, and is Mateo still throwing a party?"

I nod. "As far as I know, it's still on." It's not often our parents are both away, so Mateo plans to make the most of it. The weather forecast is predicting high temps this weekend, and it will be the last hurrah before the colder autumn weather sets in.

"That's it." Her eyes glint with excitement. "You are going to buy the sexiest two-piece, look hot as hell, and flirt your ass off with guys in front of him. If that doesn't get a reaction, nothing will."

"Mateo will never permit it."

She snorts. "Mateo will be drunk and fucking some piece of ass in the pool house for most of the party. A leopard doesn't change his spots. We just need to time it to perfection. We will wait until your brother has disappeared and then make our grand entrance."

Smiling, I loop my arm through hers, tugging her down the steps. "I love the way your mind works. But I'm only doing it if you're getting a sexy bikini and flirting too. We can shop online after we get our homework done." Frankie is staying at my place tonight because we have a project to finish that we are working on together.

"Girl, I'm already sold." Frankie winks.

She's the best wingwoman ever.

"Maybe I'll actually find someone to rid me of my virginity," I whisper, glancing around to ensure no one is listening. "I see the way some of Matty's friends look at me. I don't think it would take much to convince one of them to do it with me."

"You can't fuck any of those *idioti*," Frankie says, dropping my arm, as we hit the sidewalk. We turn right, heading in the direction of the parking lot where a car will be waiting, as usual. "They can't hold their piss."

"That's the whole point. My plan only works if Papa and Carlo find out."

"Mateo will murder whoever it is. Do you really want that on your conscience?"

I chew on the corner of my mouth, as nerves jangle inside me. That's the crux of my dilemma. If I do this, I would be signing someone's death warrant and potentially starting a war. Leo wasn't wrong when he outlined the risks. Am I selfish enough to go through with it knowing the consequences?

Lost in thought, I'm not watching where I'm going, and I slam into a hard chest, almost losing my balance. A muscular arm darts out, grabbing my elbow. A familiar citrusy smell wafts around me, and I curse under my breath as I look up into Leo's fierce gaze. "You need to be more observant." His deep timbre sends shivers ghosting over my skin, and I hate how I am so affected by him. Why can't my libido and my heart just get with the program?

"What are you doing here?" I ask, wrenching my arm back and grabbing the straps of my backpack.

"There was an emergency, and most of the *soldati* were called away. Your father asked me to pick you up." He cocks his head to one side, nodding at my best friend. "Hey, Frankie."

"Leonardo." She acknowledges him with a scowl and narrowed eyes.

"Come on. Let's get a move on." He glances around as he takes my bag, slinging it over one shoulder.

"Leo!" a woman with a high-pitched nasally voice screams, and I count to ten in my head as I hear her quickening footsteps behind us. "Hey, sexy," Nicole says, pushing me aside and pressing herself all up in Leo's business.

A red haze coats over my eyes, and I'm seconds from yanking her away from him when Frankie pulls me back, subtly squeezing my hand in warning.

"Watch it!" Leo snaps, stepping back a few steps, creating distance between them. "You almost knocked Natalia over."

A surge of warmth floods my chest.

"Oops." She giggles, and I want to rip her tongue from her throat so she can't make that annoying sound again. "You haven't called me." She pouts, reclaiming the distance and smashing her large fake tits into his chest. "We had fun last Friday night, and I really want to do it again." Glancing over her shoulder, she fixes me with a smug look before returning her attention to Leo.

My hands clench into balls at my side, and I want to grab her head and pound it into the sidewalk until her tiny brain leaks out.

"You're the biggest I have ever had, and I really want to fuck you again."

Leo's gaze flits to mine, and I'm not quick enough to disguise my hurt. His eyes darken as he glares at Nicole, and he opens his mouth to speak, stalling as momentary indecision appears on his face. Then his features smooth out, and he smiles, but it's not a real one. "Mateo is having a pool party this weekend. You should come. We can talk there."

Rage prickles under the surface of my skin, and I'm seething. Over my dead body is that bitch coming to my house.

"It wasn't talking I had in mind," she purrs in a gravelly voice that sounds like she's got something painful caught in her throat.

A fresh wave of pain batters me from all sides, and I avert my eyes, unable to bear it any longer.

What does she have that I don't?

How can he even bear to be near her?

She's a horrible person, and I used to think Leo was a good judge of character, but clearly, he isn't. Frankie squeezes my hand, tugging me away. We walk toward where my father's black SUV is parked as Leo shouts after us to wait for him.

Well, fuck him. I'm not staying to watch that bitch flirt with the man I'm in love with.

"Breathe, Nat," Frankie urges, clutching my hand in moral support. "She's a *puttana* and he's a *stronzo*. Fuck them both."

"It hurts," I admit, in a choked voice, fighting tears. "I offered myself to him, and he rejected me, yet he wasted no time fucking that bitch." I know he was with her the day before my date, and it was a couple of days before we had our talk in the orchard, but it only marginally lessens the blow. How could he be intimate with her? Especially after the things Mateo said about her.

I don't think I will ever understand men.

"He clearly has shit taste in women," Frankie fumes. "You're way too good for him. He isn't worthy of your love or your devotion."

"So much for our plans." I sniffle, hanging my head, wishing I had a magic wand and I could zap myself home without having to endure the car ride.

"Oh, we're still on," she confirms, stopping alongside the SUV. She glares at Leo as he strides toward us. Nicole is standing behind him, blatantly checking out his ass, and I want to gouge out her eyeballs with my sharpened nails. "With modifications," Frankie adds. "You're going to have him panting like a dog in heat, and when he comes for you—and he will—you'll reject him. Let him have a taste of his own medicine."

"I love you." I bundle my friend into a big hug, so grateful to have her in my life, always willing to fight in my corner.

We shuck out of our embrace as Leo reaches the car. He unlocks it with the key fob, and Frankie shoots daggers at the back of his head as she opens the door. Leo rounds the hood of the SUV, lifting his head as Frankie scrambles into the back seat. His eyes lock on mine, and I blast him with every ounce of repulsion I'm feeling. "You're disgusting. I hope she gave you an STD and your dick falls off."

I climb up into the car, slamming the door behind me, in case my statement was too subtle for him.

Leo slides behind the wheel and starts the engine without saying anything.

THE REST OF the week at school is a shitshow. Nicole clearly spotted my reaction on Monday, and she is enjoying taunting me about screwing my brother and his best friend. I know from previous experience the best way to deal with her is to ignore her. She loves the sound of her voice and can't stand it if someone doesn't give her the attention she craves. So, I pretend she doesn't exist. It's not easy when she's blabbing her stories every lunchtime, at the top of her lungs in the cafeteria, but I refuse to acknowledge her or let her see how much it pisses me off that Leo would sleep with her.

When I don't cave the way she intended, she resorts to stupid petty shit. Like stealing my math assignment from my bag so I get detention when I can't turn it in. Or stuffing a variety of dildos in my locker with a copy of an article describing the fifty things a virgin should know before having sex.

It's immature, and responding to it is beneath me, but I can't deny she's getting under my skin.

By the time Friday comes around, I am clinging to my sanity by my fingernails. I have had enough of that bitch to last me a lifetime, and there is no way in hell she is partying at my house tomorrow.

"You need to tell Mateo," Frankie says as we are driven home by one of Papa's *soldati* after school. She is staying the weekend with me, and we are planning a complete beauty regime tonight so I'll be epically radiant for tomorrow's pool party.

"I don't need his help," I say, slicking some gloss on my lips. "I know how to keep her out."

Frankie rubs her hands with glee. "Do tell."

"I'm going to talk to Rocco. He's in charge of the gate tomorrow, and I know he has a soft spot for me." Rocco has worked for our family for years and he has seen me grow up. He's very protective of me, and I know I can spin it so he won't let Nicole and her crew of bitches anywhere near our house, my brother, or Leo.

"Yes!" Frankie fist pumps the air, her long blonde hair swaying with the motion. "She'll up the ante next week at school."

"I know." I grin. "But I don't care. It will be worth it to keep her out."

"THAT'S ALL THE names," I say the following morning, handing the clipboard back to Rocco.

"Don't you worry about a thing, Natalia. Those nasty girls won't get past the gate. Every one of the men has the list, and security will be tight."

I expect no less. Papa is fierce about security at the house, and no one gets in or out without prior approval. "Thanks, Rocco. I knew I could rely on you." I flutter my eyelashes and flash him a wide smile. "I will save you some cannoli and apple cake." Mateo didn't ask me to cook anything because our part-time housekeeper is here and Beatrice will prepare all the food. However, I worked out a lot of my frustration in the kitchen this week, and our cabinets are overflowing with traditional Italian treats and desserts.

His features soften, as they often do around me. "*Grazie.*" He squeezes my shoulder affectionately. "You should tell Mateo what that girl is doing at school. You will get rid of her for good."

"I will take that under consideration." I know if I told my brother he would cut her loose. He gets plenty of pussy, and I know he'd be furious at some of the things she has said and done. But I don't want to run to Mateo or Leo anytime I have an issue. I can't expect them to see me as a grown woman if I need them to solve my problems.

I trot back up the stairs to Frankie, and we spend the morning doing a final pampering. When I am waxed, my fingernails and toenails are painted, and my skin is glistening from the baby lotion I slathered all over myself, I put my new bikini on and check out my reflection in the mirror.

"Holy fucking shit." Frankie's eyes pop wide when she sees me in the minuscule red and gold two-piece. The molded ruby-red cups are sculpted low on my breasts, and while my boobs are adequately supported and my nipples are covered, I'm flaunting plenty of cleavage. The gold straps are sturdy and a decent width so I don't have to worry about it snapping from the weight. The low-waisted bikini bottoms have a red panel at the front and the back and two crisscrossing gold straps on each side of my hips, which showcase *a lot* of flesh. My smooth olive skin is still tan from the summer and the tanning illuminator gel I applied last night.

"He won't be able to contain himself when he sees you," Frankie adds, winking.

We'll see.

"You look hot." I admire her green and black bikini. Frankie doesn't have my curvy hips, big boobs, or small waist, but she has a willowy figure that wouldn't look amiss on a fashion runway. Her boobs are small but perfectly formed, and the padded bikini top works perfectly to enhance her cleavage. "Archer is going to have a hard time keeping his hands to himself."

"I don't want him to keep his hands to himself," she jokes, pushing me down on the chair in front of my dressing table so she can curl my hair into soft waves.

Her boyfriend is coming over later so we have time to put our plan into action before she has to behave. Not that Frankie would ever cheat on Archer, but she loves to flirt up a storm, and I know she's looking forward to this. I am usually the demure one at these parties, so I know the guys are going to be shocked. I'm glad my bestie is here for moral support, as I'm not sure I'd be able to pull this off without her.

"If Mateo reappears, don't do anything too obvious in front of him," I remind her. While I don't think my brother would rat my bestie out to her parents, he is such a stickler for *mafioso* traditions that I can't be sure.

"I'll be careful," she promises with a devilish glint in her eyes. "If you promise not to be."

I grin at her through the mirror. "Some might say you're a bad influence on me."

"Most would say I'm a *great* influence," she protests, grinning at me in return. "I bet the guys at the pool will be lining up to thank me once they see how completely stunning you are."

She finishes my hair, and then I return the favor. We dust a light layer of bronzer over our chests, and we are party ready and raring to go.

The party is in full swing outside, but Mateo is still out by the pool, entertaining two women on his lap. I know it won't take too long before he disappears with them, so we bide our time. We drink some wine coolers we stole from the refrigerator while we sit at my window, chatting and watching the action heat up down below.

A sultry redhead is cozying up to Leo, and I gnash my teeth when she puts her hand on his bare chest and smiles seductively at him. He doesn't look that interested, but he's not pushing her away either. Every so often, his gaze skates over the growing crowd, his eyes searching. The obsessive part of me that still hankers for him imagines he is looking for me, but the more practical side of my brain says he's more than likely seeking out Nicole.

"Mateo's leaving!" Frankie squeals, jumping up and spilling some of her drink on the floor. "C'mon." She grabs my half-empty bottle, thrusts my thigh-high cover-up at me, and practically drags me to the door.

"My sandals!" I laugh, shucking out of her hand to go back for my footwear.

"Hurry up!" She hops from foot to foot, and another laugh escapes my throat.

"You're enjoying this," I say, sliding my feet into my sandals.

"Not yet I'm not." She loops my arm in hers, pulling me out of my bedroom. "But I will be soon." She flashes me a devilish grin, and I give her a quick hug, buzzing with excited nervous adrenaline. "Let's go and knock some boys flat on their asses."

Chapter 6

NATALIA

LEO IS NOWHERE to be seen when we hit the pool area, which makes things easier. However, visions of him fucking the redhead do nothing but stoke my rage up a notch.

"Get lost," Frankie says to a couple of bottle-blondes sprawled across two loungers beside a group of good-looking guys. I recognize a few of the guys as part of Mateo's extended circle, but most are new faces.

"Fuck off," one of the girls says, purposely leaning back with her arms folded behind her head, smiling smugly.

We don't have time to waste. Mateo and Leo could return at any moment and spoil my fun, so I jerk my head at Brando, calling him over. He is one of the newer *soldati*, although I have known him for years as he's part of the *famiglia*. He was initiated at thirteen, as is tradition, and he's now a fully-fledged made man.

"Miss Mazzone," he greets me formally, like we didn't regularly hang out at my house when we were kids. "What appears to be the problem?"

"Escort these girls out of my house, please. They have outstayed their welcome." I toss my hair over my shoulders, offering them a tight smile as they begin bitching and whining. Another *soldato* appears when he hears the commotion, and together, they drag the girls away.

"Boys," I say, nodding at the guys who are watching us with blatant interest. "I hope that didn't offend anyone, but I really can't have random women disrespecting me in my home."

"You're Mateo's sister," a guy with floppy dark hair and dimples says, grinning up at me.

"I'm Natalia," I say, pushing my sunglasses on top of my head before I stretch my arm out.

"Alonso," he replies, taking my hand and bringing it to his mouth. His lips brush against my knuckles, and his eyes twinkle with interest. "This is my brother Santino," he adds, still holding my hand as he nudges his head at the guy sitting on the chair beside him.

Santino is sipping a Peroni, watching me over the rim of his beer bottle, attempting indifference. He lifts his head in a silent greeting, and I smile. "These hooligans are Ezra, River, Waylon, and Milo," Alonso continues, reluctantly letting my hand go.

The guys all say hi, and I introduce Frankie.

"Can I get you beautiful ladies something to drink?" Alonso asks, unfurling to his full height. He towers over me, but that's not hard with my five-feet-five-inch frame.

"Get us some wine coolers, and we'll love you forever," Frankie coos, smiling flirtatiously at him.

"Coming right up." Alonso races off toward the tables at the back. It is stocked with an assortment of food and drinks and sheltered under the large, patterned awning.

Frankie whips her cover-up off and gracefully lies down on the recently vacated lounger, stretching her limbs and subtly arching her back, drawing attention to her cleavage. The guys stare at her with lust in their eyes. All except for Santino. His gaze is rooted on me, making my skin tingle in every place his eyes wander. Frankie stares at me, silently communicating with her eyes, telling me to stop stalling.

Nerves fire at me as my shaky fingers move to the edge of my cover-up. My mouth feels dry, and butterflies swoop into my chest, making me feel a little nauseated. I wish this was as natural for me as it is to my bestie, but I have led a pretty sheltered life, and I'm not adept at flirting or putting myself out there. But I want that to change, so I summon my lady balls and draw a brave breath. It's now or never, I remind myself, slowly pulling my cover-up over my body until it's off and I'm gripping it in my hands.

Feigning confidence, I hold my shoulders back and smile sweetly at the boys watching me. A low whistle rings out, and heat floods my cheeks as I see how they are all staring at me with their mouths hanging open, their eyes dark with desire.

"Fucking hell." Alonso slams to a halt in front of my lounger as I lie back, conscious there are plenty of other eyes watching my every move. "You are fucking beautiful, Natalia. No wonder Mateo has kept you hidden." I'm tempted to tell him I have made an appearance at previous parties, but he clearly didn't notice me.

"Thank you." I smile as I accept the cold wine cooler from his hand.

"You are gorgeous too," he tells Frankie, as he dispenses her drink.

"I like your dimples," she says. "And I'm impressed at how fast you got our drinks. If you were looking to earn brownie points, you did a good job."

Alonso practically preens under her appraising words, and I grin to myself as I take a sip of my drink.

"Hey, Nat." A guy I know as one of Mateo's close crew sinks onto the side of my lounger. "Wow. When did you get so grown up?" His hungry gaze grazes my body, lingering on my chest, and there is no disguising the growing bulge in his swim shorts.

Very soon, we are surrounded with admirers, and I'm more than a little out of my depth. But I wing it. Acting shy and demure, letting the guys do all the talking. The only one who isn't fawning over me is Santino, but every time I look in his direction, his heated gaze is pinned on me.

So, of course, he's the one I want.

He's definitely a few years older than most of the guys crowding around us. With his olive skin, dark hair, sculpted jawline, and Roman nose, he is obviously Italian American. But he's not a *soldato,* so he's either an associate or just a casual friend not affiliated with the *mafioso*. Intricate ink covers both arms, spilling over onto his impressive chest, and he's got a piercing in his nose and through one of his eyebrows. His hair is slicked back off his face, and he's sporting a stylish layer of stubble. Santino is an unusual combination of classically handsome with a side of dark edginess, and I'm intrigued. The fact he's not tripping over himself to drool at me only adds to the appeal.

I half listen to the other guys, throwing out a flirtatious laugh here and there, while Santino and I drill potent looks at one another. I don't think he's the kind of man to let something like stupid Italian traditions stop him from getting with me. But he's not the type to come to me either. I bet the man never has to chase any girl. I bet they flock to him like bees swarming a beehive.

"What the fuck are you wearing?" a man with a deep, familiar voice says, his tone carrying barely concealed anger.

Sitting up a little straighter, ensuring the girls are on full display, I eye Leo over the top of my drink. "It's called a bikini. I'm sure you're familiar with the term."

God, he's magnificent without a shirt. Broad shoulders give way to an impressive chest, tapered waist, and a solid six-pack. Biceps roll and flex in his arms as he clenches and unclenches his fists, struggling to keep his eyes on my face. His tan skin carries a light sheen, and the tantalizing line of dark hair sneaking underneath the band of his swim shorts causes saliva to pool in my mouth.

"Cover yourself up," he hisses, snatching my cover-up off the patio floor and throwing it at me.

I toss it back in his face. "You're not my father, and you don't get to tell me what to do." Taking a healthy mouthful of my wine cooler, I lie back, tipping my face up to the sun and subtly thrusting my chest forward.

"Who gave you this?" he barks, swiping the bottle from my fingers.

"I did," Alonso says, dropping his conversation with Frankie and standing. "What's the problem?"

"The problem, *stronzo*," Leo says, shoving Alonso's shoulders, "is she's seventeen and she's Mateo's little sister."

"She's all woman from what I've seen," Santino says, speaking for the first time. "And it's not like she's doing anything wrong. You need to chill the fuck out."

"This doesn't involve you, and how the fuck are you here?" Anger bristles on Leo's skin, and I watch the hostile glares being traded between both men.

Interesting.

There is some beef between them.

Now, I really want to make out with Santino, especially if it will push Leo's buttons.

"He's my brother," Alonso says, losing all good humor as he pushes his chest into Leo's. "And Mateo said I could bring whoever I wanted."

"Fuck this shit," Leo says, dragging a hand through his hair. "Get up." He leans over, reaching for my arm.

Swinging my legs over the other side of the lounger, ensuring Santino gets a good look at my body, I slowly stand and stride toward Leo with my chin held high. "Fuck you, Leo. This is my house. My pool. And I have every right to be here. If you don't like it, go complain to someone who cares." Taking a risk, I spin around and walk confidently toward Santino, my eyes pinning him in place as I silently beg him not to turn me away. Without stopping to second-guess myself, I drop down on his lap, challenging him with a heated stare.

His arms instantly band around me, and a slow smile curls up the corners of his mouth.

"Get the fuck away from him!" Leo roars, storming toward us and yanking me off Santino's lap. He jabs his finger in Santino's face as he stands. "You keep your hands off her, or I'll fucking cut them off!"

"Why, Leo?" I fix him with a glare as I wrench my arm out of his grip. "What's it to you?"

"We had this conversation last weekend," he grits out through clenched teeth. "And I'm not in the habit of repeating myself." I had expected him to fling my engagement and my status at Santino. The fact he isn't tells me he's trying to protect my reputation, although at least some of the guys at this party know who I am and who I'm promised to.

Most everyone is watching this go down now. Pretending to talk and drink while keeping one eye on the drama unfolding before their eyes.

"You made yourself perfectly clear." I place my hands on my hips, drawing attention to the copious skin on display. "As did I."

Leo's nostrils flare as his gaze automatically drifts down my body. His chest heaves and his Adam's apple bobs in his throat as he takes his time perusing me. His gaze is like a raging fire trailing over my flesh, scorching a path in every place it lands. Instant desire gushes to my core, and I hope I'm not sporting a wet patch on my bikini bottoms because that would be embarrassing in the extreme.

"Liking what you see?" I purr, moving in closer yet keeping space between our bodies.

"Stop this." He claws a hand through his hair, looking flustered with a wild glint in his eye, and I silently fist pump the air. "If you won't listen to me, I'm getting Mateo. I was on my way to update him anyway. He is going to flip out when he sees you."

"Like hell you will," I say, pushing him forcefully. He is not going to ruin this for me before I've had my fun.

Leo stumbles a little, caught off guard by the strength of my shove. Feeling brave, I push him again, and he loses his balance as he trips over the edge of the pool. With legs and arms flailing, he falls into the pool with a loud splash, showering water over everyone on this side.

I spin around, meeting Santino's amused, heated gaze. I grab his hand and tip my head back, looking up at him. "Want to get out of here?"

He flashes me a sultry smile. "I thought you'd never ask."

Chapter 7

LEO

I HAUL ASS out of the pool, shaking with anger and ready to throttle Natalia. Water sluices down my chest, leaving a wet trail behind me as I stalk toward her. Except she's fucking gone. And so is that bastard Santino. I will remove his head from his shoulders if he has laid a finger on her. "Where did they go?" I snap at Alonso, cracking my knuckles as rage festers in my tissues.

"Who?" Alonso feigns innocence, and I see red.

Wrapping my hands around his throat, I squeeze tight. "Don't play games with me, asshole. The mood I'm in, I could snap your neck by accident."

"Okay!" he chokes out, tugging at my hand.

I relax my hold so he can speak. "They went that way," he says, pointing behind us.

The orchard. Fuck.

"I'm going to get her, and you better pray your brother hasn't touched her," I growl, irritation itching at my skin.

"You've got a real hard-on for her, huh?" He dares to grin at me, and I'm all out of patience.

I punch him in the face. Harder than he probably deserves, but that's what he gets for riling me up. Blood oozes from his nose, and he cries out in pain, stumbling back and falling over the edge of Frankie's lounger.

Ignoring the whimpering idiot, I swing my gaze on Nat's best friend. "If you put her up to this, you should be ashamed of yourself. You are not helping." I lean down so no one else hears me. "She is putting herself at risk, Francesca. Do you really think Carlo would walk away, without retaliating, if she does something to disrespect him? Have you any idea how fucking dangerous that psycho is?"

I know exactly what he's capable of, and I fucking detest he is the one who has been chosen for my *dolcezza*. I would automatically hate any man who gets to spend his life with her, but my loathing for Carlo Greco goes way beyond that. He's a sick, twisted fuck, and I'm terrified of the things he will do to Nat when she becomes his wife.

Something akin to fear ghosts over Frankie's face before it's replaced with a different emotion. "I'm being a good friend. If you want to blame someone, blame yourself. You caused this." She prods her finger in my chest. "This is your fault."

Guilt pulses through my veins at her words. I know that's part of the truth. I never should have used Nicole to push Natalia away, but I need her to hate me. I can't have Nat returning my feelings because the temptation to give in and take what I want is too great. I should've known she would come out with her fists swinging. My *dolcezza* may have led a sheltered life, but she's no wallflower.

Natalia has this indomitable inner strength that drives everything she does. She's dutiful and respectful, doing what is asked of her. But her quiet determination simmers under the surface, and I'm not surprised she has reached her breaking point.

If I was promised to that psycho Greco, I would be trying everything to extract myself from the contract too. But this is not the way to go about it. She is going to ruin her reputation and risk her future and her life if she continues with this madness. It's up to me to stop it. I helped to create this mess, and now I need to fix it.

I should go straight to Mateo, but I can't leave Nat out there with that asshole Santino for a second longer. He and I have come to blows over a woman before—of a different nature—and I won't hesitate to kick his ass this time. He destroyed my cousin's faith in men when he cheated on her. Left her heartbroken in a way she has never fully recovered from. He's not going to hurt Natalia. Not under my watch.

"You!" I turn around, jabbing my finger in Alonso's direction. "Go to the pool house and get Mateo. Tell him he needs to talk to Rocco." I step closer to him. "Do not mention a word about Natalia, or I'll string you up by the balls alongside your brother."

Alonso nods, and I jog off across the lawn in the direction of the orchard.

Sweat beads on my chest and glides across my brow as I race toward the entrance to the orchard a few minutes later. I can't see them, which only fuels my anger. Hard, warm stone grazes the soles of my bare feet when I step onto the path that traverses both sides of the orchard. I can hardly hear over the thrumming in my ears, and my heart thumps frantically against my chest wall as I hurry along the path, peering left and right, wondering where the fuck they are.

A low masculine moan rings out, and I see red. When I run in the direction of the sound, my hands ball up at my sides as I prepare to inflict pain on that asshole. I push through the trees, quaking with rage as I come upon them.

Santino has Natalia pinned against a tree, and he's thrusting his hips at her as she covers her naked breasts with her hands. He is whispering in her ear while dropping kisses along her neck.

Jealousy is a feral beast. It springs to immediate life in my chest, and I want to rip his lips from his face and remove his hands so he can't taste her and touch her ever again.

Grabbing the band of his swim shorts, I forcefully yank him back away from her. Natalia shrieks, dropping her hands in shock and baring her magnificent breasts. But I don't have time to savor the view before Santino swings at me.

I duck down, driving my clenched fist into his stomach in three quick successive moves. He stands no chance against me. I have been trained in all manner of combat skills, and all he's got is some muscle mass from regular workouts at the gym. "I told you not to touch her!" I roar, slamming my head into his. He staggers back, losing his balance and falling flat on the ground.

I jump on his chest and pummel his face with both my fists. Blood spurts from his nose and a cut on his lip, but it's not enough. I want to see his face painted completely in red for daring to ever touch her. He tries to push me off, but I clasp my thighs firmly against the side of his body and continue battering his face, unleashing all the anger, jealousy, and frustration coursing through my veins.

How dare he infect her with his poisonous hands.

He isn't worthy to even speak to her, let alone touch her.

"Leo! Stop!" Natalia pleads, grabbing my elbow. "Let him go before you kill him!"

"I should kill him," I grit out, snarling in semi-satisfaction at his blood-soaked face.

"Your issue is with me. Not him."

I glare up at her. "Shut up, Nat." I know she's far from innocent in this, but he took advantage of the situation. Partly to piss me off, when I showed my hand back at the pool, and it's not like he gives a shit about our traditions. He must know Natalia is promised to a made man, and he couldn't care less about risking her reputation as long as he got his hands on her. And I get it. She's fucking gorgeous, and in that bikini, she is temptation on a platter. But that doesn't excuse it.

I climb to my feet, grabbing Natalia behind me and shielding her with my body. "Get the fuck out of here before I change my mind," I bark at the asshole.

"Fuck you." He flips me the bird as he struggles to his feet, spitting blood on the ground. Looking over my shoulder, he leers at Natalia. "Call me, doll. We can finish what we started."

Over my dead fucking body.

I gnash my teeth and move toward him, but Nat curls her arm around my waist, placing her palm on my stomach, holding me in place. "Let him go," she softly says. The asshole staggers off, and I try to rein in my anger. Nat's warm breath coasts over my exposed flesh, and I'm suddenly aware of how tight she is pressed up against me. Her bare chest is flush to my back, and her nipples are taut against my skin. Blood travels south, and my dick hardens to the point of pain.

"Leo," she whispers, her fingers tracing along the dips and curves of my abdominal wall. "On a scale of one to ten, how mad are you at me right now?"

It's hard to hold on to my anger with the lust burning through my veins, but she doesn't need to know that. "About a hundred." My voice is gruff, thick with desire, my dick attempting to poke a hole through the front of my swim shorts. I can't turn around. Not like this.

Not without reacting.

I don't want to feel this way about her.

Not when she can never be mine.

Battling my feelings is a daily challenge I have grown to accept.

I can't act on the way I feel. *We* can't.

So, I would rather love her from afar, protecting her in whatever way I can—from harm and from me.

She doesn't know how hard it was to resist her last Sunday. When she stripped down and her lips pressed against mine, I had to cage the carnal beast inside me, champing at the bit to claim her. I know if I allow myself even one taste I will be ruined forever, and I won't have the strength to stay away from her anymore.

So, I have to fight this.

For both of us, even if she seems determined to get me to cave.

"Leo." She slides out from behind me, standing in front of me, and I grind my teeth so hard pain skates along my jaw. "Look at me." She plants her small, delicate hand on my chest, and her touch sears beneath my skin, reaching deep. "Please." Her heartfelt plea spears me through the heart, and I lift my head, unable to deny her. I suck in a gasp as my eyes drink their fill. Her tits are perfection. Big and round with pert rosy nipples, and my tongue darts out, licking my lips of its own volition. My cock strains behind my swim shorts as I visualize sucking her nipples in my mouth while my hands feast on her voluptuous curves.

"I'm sorry," she adds, yanking me out of my lust-fueled daze. "I shouldn't have gone off with him." She averts her eyes, and my spine stiffens.

"Did he hurt you?" My voice is thick with pain as I tilt her beautiful face up, examining her eyes for the truth.

She shakes her head. "No. He just moved too fast."

Of course, he did, 'cause he's a jackass who wasn't thinking about her needs. Nat has been sheltered her entire life, and she is inexperienced. She needs a gentle touch and slow pace to ease her into exploring her sexuality.

One I would love to give her but can't.

One I know Greco won't offer her either.

And just like that, my anger is cranked to the max.

A primal growl rips from my throat. "I'm going to tear him limb from limb."

"No, you're not."

She moves to pull her hand away, and I slap my larger palm over hers, not ready to lose the warmth of her touch. "Did he touch you here?" Gently, I place my hand on top of her chest, over the swell of one breast, right where her heart thumps wildly against my palm. Fuck, her skin is velvety soft, and I have never wanted anyone as badly as I want her.

"I didn't let him," she whispers, peering up at me with so much adoration and longing and trust that I lose control of the tenuous hold on my emotions.

"Fuck," I hiss before I grab the nape of her neck, pull her into my body, and slant my mouth over hers. I'm a hypocrite, because there is nothing gentle or slow about this kiss. I'm devouring her mouth like I haven't eaten in years. I can't get enough of her, and I demand everything with greedy lips.

She doesn't let me down, angling her head as she kisses me back, while pressing her tantalizing chest into mine. The feel of her breasts against my bare skin undoes me, and I lose all sense of civility. Placing my hand on her lower back, I press her into me, needing her closer, closer, closer. I ravish her with my mouth as I pour all my pent-up longing into my kisses. My tongue slides easily between her lips, and when she moans into my mouth, I grind my hips against her, unable to stop myself, needing the friction to ease the overwhelming lust infiltrating my bloodstream.

I need her.

I need her so badly.

My hands freely roam her body, and we are reaching the point of no return. Nat whimpers and moans into my mouth as my hands explore her gorgeous curves, but it's still not enough. I need more. I am lost in a haze of desire. Consumed with the need to claim her. So out of my mind with fucking lust I don't think of all the reasons why this is so fucking dangerous.

She kisses me back with the same ferocity, sliding her hands up and down my chest and tilting her hips so her sweet spot rubs against where I ache for her. My *dolcezza* is so brave, grinding against my cock and clawing at my back, going after what she wants and needs.

Until she's gone, falling back, grabbing her discarded bikini top off the ground and hastily putting it on. I'm rooted to the spot, unable to act, my mind and body still lost to the touch and taste of her. The screaming in my head demands I retake her in my arms, but I ignore it, attempting to wrangle a hold on my all-consuming desire. Blood rushes to my head, and my cock leaks precum as it strains painfully behind my swim shorts.

"*Dolcezza*," I rasp, taking a step toward her as I break out of my fugue state.

"Don't, Leo." She holds up one hand. "You don't get to toy with my feelings like this. You don't get to do this just because you have some beef with Santino and now it suits your agenda."

What the ever-loving fuck did she just say? Does she seriously think this is some form of jealous revenge? "Nat. You know it's not like that."

"I know nothing of the sort."

She brushes past me, and I reach for her, my fingers meeting thin air. "Wait!" I'm rooted to the spot again, feeling conflicted and helpless as I watch her leave. I fight the urge to run after her, scoop her into my arms, and tell her how much I love her and desire her.

"You rejected me, Leo. You rejected me for *her*." Pain slices across her face, and a new wave of guilt and self-loathing crests over me.

I couldn't give two shits about Nicole Chastain. She was a mistake I will not be repeating. Though it serves me to have Nat think the opposite. Things can't develop between us. It's too dangerous. I need her to hate me. To push me away. To see I am not an option. Common sense comes flooding in, and I clamp my lips shut, folding my arms over my chest and closing off my emotions.

What the fuck have I done?

"That's what I thought," she says, spinning around and running away from me.

Crouching down, I bury my face in my hands, berating myself for being so weak. I am totally fucked now. That tiny taste has not sated my thirst for her. It has opened a void in my chest and uncaged the beast. Mateo will put a bullet in my skull if he finds out I made out with his sister. I have seen him beat the living daylights out of guys for just looking at her.

Gunfire peppers the otherwise silent air, and my heart stutters behind my chest. I'm racing after Natalia before I have even processed the motion. "Get down," I roar, spotting her in the distance, as a rain of bullets flies over her head. Nat drops to the ground on her stomach, covering her head with her hands. Cursing my stupidity at chasing after her with no shoes and no gun, I ignore the pain in my feet as I pound the pavement, exiting the orchard onto the grassy lawn.

Movement in the corner of my eye captures my attention. Horror slams into me as I spy a man with a rifle in hand making a beeline for my *dolcezza*.

Chapter 8

LEO

I PUSH MY limbs to extremes as I charge toward Natalia, already knowing I won't get to her before the man bearing down on her does. I'm conflicted on what to do. If I tell her to run, he might shoot her. Yet, if I say nothing, she's like a sitting duck. She takes the decision out of my hands, scrambling to her feet when she spots the man coming for her.

A shot rings out from the left, and Natalia screams, stumbling and swaying as she runs back in the direction of the house. One of our men, doing perimeter duty, steps forward and fires indiscriminately at the stranger; peppering the air with gunfire. The intruder drops to the grassy ground and rains a flurry of bullets at our *soldato*. I curse under my breath as he drops like a fly, dead before he hits the ground.

The intruder wastes no time giving chase to Nat, and he gains ground fast while I race to catch up to him. Grabbing her from behind, he scoops her up into his arms. I'm not too far away now, and the man hasn't noticed me yet. He's too busy trying to contain the wriggling, writhing beauty in his arms as Nat gives him hell.

That's my girl.

Ducking down, I grab the dead soldier's gun, checking the rounds and creeping toward the asshole who dares to kidnap my *dolcezza*.

The asshole makes a hissing sound when Nat sinks her teeth into his arm, but he doesn't lose his grip. I can't contain my fury when he smashes the butt of his rifle into her temple. I snarl as I visualize snapping his neck for daring to harm her. Nat's head lolls back as she instantly passes out. A strangled roar rips from my lips, destroying my element of surprise. The guy whips around, with Nat in his arms, pressing the muzzle of his gun into her head. "Make one move and I'll kill her," he threatens, his American drawl accentuated with a noticeable Italian twang.

"Touch one hair on her head, and it'll be the last thing you do," I coolly retort, pointing my gun at his skull.

"Just let us take her, and no one else has to die," he adds, his dark, beady eyes flaring with recognition. "We won't hurt her."

"News flash, asshole," I grit out. "You have already hurt her."

"We mean her no harm. Once the boss gets what he wants, he'll let her go."

"You expect me to just let her walk away with you?" I want to keep him talking while I wait for him to make a mistake—to lower his gun from her head so I can take a clear shot and get rid of the problem.

"I don't have time for this." Swinging his gun around, he fires at me.

I can't retaliate without risking injury to Natalia, so I dart sideways, throwing myself at the ground as the bullet whizzes toward me.

Pain explodes in my shoulder, and I grunt as I land heavily on the ground. Pain splinters up and down the left side of my body, and my fingers come away bloody when I touch my throbbing shoulder. Ignoring the pain, I scramble to my feet, watching the asshole run away with the girl who is my everything.

Gunfire is dying out in the background, and I hope that means we got the upper hand.

The guy continues running without looking back, assuming I'm out of action or dead. What an idiot. Every made man worth his salt knows you never turn your back on your enemy. Even if he appears to be down.

Both his hands are occupied holding Natalia as he runs, and his rifle is slung over one shoulder. I can't shoot him in the obvious places without risking serious injury to Nat, so I do the only thing I can. I shoot him in the back of his calves. One bullet in each leg, and it's enough to incapacitate him. Natalia goes flying out of his arms as he stumbles to the ground, and I curse as I run toward them.

I reclaim the distance between us before he's had the time to grab his weapon. I press my foot down hard on top of his wrist as his fingers reach for the rifle, and the sound of bone crunching is hugely rewarding. I wish I could haul this asshole in for questioning and torture, but I need to attend to Natalia, and I can't risk leaving him here for one of his goons to collect. I riddle his face with bullets and pump more in his chest, only leaving him when I'm assured he's good and dead.

Scanning my surroundings, to ensure there are no more intruders hiding in the shadows, I scoop Nat into my arms, cradling her unconscious head against my chest as I run toward the house.

"*Idiota*!" Angelo storms into the room, like a black thundercloud, leveling furious eyes on his son. He was informed of the attack immediately by one of the men at the gate, and he wasted no time chartering a helicopter to bring him and Rosa home.

Rocco enters the office, followed by Angelo's consigliere, Coppola; his underboss, Agosti; and three capos. They quietly close the door behind them. Angelo must have called his most trusted men while he was in the air, asking them to meet him here to discuss our next steps.

Don Mazzone punches Mateo in the nose before grabbing him by the shoulders and slamming him into the wall. Blood leaks from Mateo's busted nose as his father glares at him with ill-concealed frustration.

Brando and I share a look. This isn't the first time Angelo Mazzone has been angry and violent with his son, and I doubt it will be the last.

"What have I told you about throwing these parties?!" Angelo roars, keeping one hand around his son's neck while he presses the butt of his gun into Mateo's head. "When are you going to grow up and be the man I need you to be?!" Angelo presses the gun firmly into Mateo's brow. "You are a constant disappointment to me, Mateo. And my patience is wearing thin." Angelo backhands Mateo with the gun. Not enough to render him unconscious but enough to cause him pain.

He shoves Mateo away before stalking to the side table propped up against the wall and pouring himself a whiskey. Mateo slumps against the wall, his face contorted in pain and his breathing heavy.

No one speaks as we wait for the don to speak. Tension bleeds into the air, mixing with the scent of death that drifts in from the open windows. Outside, men are clearing the dead bodies from the pool area and from the front of the house.

"We lost five good men today, Mateo, and they almost got to your sister," Angelo's voice is lowered, but there's a sharp edge underscoring his tone. Angelo turns around as Mateo straightens up and his head dips low in shame. "You knew there was a threat after last Monday's ambush, yet you ignored your responsibility to party and fuck whores." He thumps his clenched fist down on top of his desk. "It ends now!" he yells, glaring at his only son and heir. He stalks toward him, gripping his chin in a tight hold. "Or I end you and consider my other options."

Shock mixes with fear in Mateo's eyes, and Brando and I shift uncomfortably.

"Yes, Mateo. You are not my only option," he adds, shoving him away.

What the actual fuck?

Is Angelo saying what I think he's saying?

It's not uncommon for dons to father illegitimate children and install them as legitimate heirs, but there have been no such rumors about Don Mazzone. While he adores his wife, Rosa, I know he has had affairs and he keeps whores on occasion. So, it's not unfathomable to consider he might have another child or two out there somewhere.

To my knowledge, he has never mentioned this to Mateo before. From the shock on his face, I can tell this is the first time he's hearing about options.

Dropping down into his seat, Angelo looks contemplative as he sips his whiskey. We stand rigidly still, awaiting instruction. I cast a quick glance at my friend. Mateo's panicked blue eyes meet mine, and I think Angelo has finally driven the point home. Looking away, I refocus on the don. Angelo smooths a hand down the front of his suit jacket, his expression giving nothing away.

"I'm sorry, Papa." Mateo shows the requisite remorse on his

face, and I know these deaths will weigh heavy on his conscience. There is nothing Mateo wants more than to earn the respect of his father and their men as a good leader and someone they can trust to succeed Angelo when the time comes. Unfortunately, that conflicts with the other part of his personality that loves the adoration, wealth, and power that comes from being the son of the number one don in New York. Mateo talks a good talk, but he struggles to live up to the expectations of his father and the ones he puts on himself. Knowing he could be ousted at any moment, in favor of some unknown option, won't help the situation.

"That is all I hear from you, and it's not enough, boy." Angelo shakes his head in disgust. "Time after time, I am having to clean up after you. One mess after another, and I am sick to death of it," he yells, jabbing his finger in Mateo's direction. Picking up his gun, he trains it at Mateo's chest. "I should just kill you now and save myself further hassle."

"It won't happen again," Mateo blurts. "I swear I will clean up my act. No more parties. No more women."

"We will talk about this again," Angelo says, effectively dismissing him when he turns his head in my direction.

I straighten up, swallowing heavily.

"I believe I have you to thank for saving my daughter." Angelo's all-seeing eyes drill into my face, and sweat collects at the back of my neck.

I nod.

"It's a shame you didn't keep the *stronzo* alive. I want to know who's behind this."

"I wanted to, sir, but it was too risky. Getting Natalia to safety was my sole priority."

He nods. "You made the right judgment call, and I'm grateful. Rosa too."

I'm hoping he'll wrap this up quickly now so I can check on my *dolcezza*. She was still unconscious when I left her with the family doctor in her bedroom. I had headed outside to locate Mateo so we could find out how the fuck these assholes got close enough to almost take Natalia. I knew we would need to have answers for Angelo before he returned.

"We had a mole," Mateo says. "He killed our other soldier at the gate and let the enemy in."

"Where is he?" Angelo barks.

"Dead," Mateo confirms. "We were taking him to the dungeon when he grabbed the gun from the waistband of my pants and shot himself in the head."

Angelo sighs, getting up and rounding the desk. He grabs his son by the neck again, spittle flying as he roars in his face. "Can't you do anything right, Mateo? I am tempted to end your miserable, pathetic ass right now." He prods the muzzle of his gun into Mateo's stomach. Mateo maintains a stoic face, but I see the pain and the fear behind his eyes.

"Don Mazzone. If I may be permitted to speak," Agosti says, pushing off the wall and walking toward Angelo.

Angelo removes his hand from Mateo's neck, waving it in the air, gesturing for his underboss to continue.

"I examined some of the dead bodies," Agosti says. "They bore the markings of the Barone." He lets that sit, without elaborating.

The Barone are made men from New Jersey with little power and control, so they take on paid gigs to flesh out their pockets. They act more like a common gang than a *mafioso* these days, and I am guessing their days are numbered. They don't seem circumspect in the work they take on, and they are pissing off a lot of the families.

"You're sure?" Angelo asks.

Agosti nods. "It was them. What do you want to do?"

Angelo picks up the phone at his desk. "I want a meeting with Greco before we take any retaliation. I want to know what that little shit Carlo has done now to warrant a target on my daughter's head."

"Wait? This was about Nat?" Mateo asks, his shame instantly transforming to fear for his sibling.

"Of course, it was. The attack at the pool was a distraction to get to your sister." Mateo curses as Angelo dials a number. Lifting his head, Angelo glares at his son. "Get the fuck out. Change into a suit, and get ready to visit the widows of the men we lost today. You will be explaining to them how you got their husbands killed."

"HE'S REALLY PISSED this time," Mateo says as we walk the long hallway outside Angelo's office.

"Did you think he wouldn't be?" Brando asks, arching a brow. While he is only eighteen and recently graduated from high school, he is sharp as a tack, and he shows lots of promise. If I need to pull a crew together for a job, I always ask if Brando is available because he's the kind of man I want to have by my side.

"It's not like it's my fault," Mateo protests. "If they were coming for Nat, nothing would have stopped them. And I'm not the one who hired the mole."

I feel for my best friend. I know he wants to fill Angelo's shoes, and he tries to be a good made man, but he just doesn't have it in him. Mateo would make a great enforcer. He loves getting his hands bloody and dirty, and he's good at that. Leadership, ownership, and decision-making ability is not in his repertoire of talents. I think, deep down, Mateo knows this too. But he doesn't want to let his father down. If what Angelo insinuated back there is true, Mateo will now have an added incentive to succeed.

"You know you have to lead by example." I remind him of something his father has tried to drill into him. "You didn't do that today, and it made it easier for the enemy to make a move. I think if you accepted that responsibility Angelo would go easier on you."

"I accept responsibility," Mateo snaps through clenched teeth. "And I don't need my supposed best friend giving me shit. I get enough of that from my father."

I slap a hand over his back. "I'm only trying to help."

"I'm going to see my sister," he huffs when we reach the stairs.

"I'll come with."

"Why?" Mateo turns to face me, eyeing me suspiciously.

"I want to make sure she's okay. He hit her pretty hard in the temple."

"I'm going back to the front gate," Brando says, as Mateo and I stare at one another, unspoken accusations and untruths stretching between us.

Brando's heels thud on the tile floor as he walks off while tension mounts between me and my best friend. "Out with it," I say when Brando closes the front door behind him with a loud clang.

"Why were you out in the orchard with my sister?" Suspicion is threaded through his tone.

I have been expecting this, and I'm torn on how to reply. I don't want Mateo to know what went down between Nat and Santino or Nat and me. The former because he would tell Angelo, and the latter because he's likely to strangle me with his bare hands. But I have to give him something plausible, so I run with an altered version of the truth.

Santino got caught in the crossfire, so he isn't alive any longer to contest this. And Alonso is so overwhelmed with grief at witnessing his brother shot down in broad daylight that he won't remember anything about the previous events. "Santino made a play for her, and he got her away before I could do anything about it. I went after him to protect her."

"Is that the truth?" Mateo asks, his gaze boring into my skull.

"It is," I lie, staring him directly in the eyes.

Silence claws through the heavy air as we face off.

"Okay," Mateo says, and I release the breath I was holding.

Chapter 9

NATALIA

"SOMETHING SMELLS DELICIOUS, Mama Rosa," Leo says, entering the kitchen.

I spin around, in a cloud of flour, glaring at him. "What are you doing up?! You should be at home resting."

Leo smirks, propping one hip against the table. "It's not the first time I've gotten shot, and it won't be the last."

I hate the truth of those words. Papa may have shielded me from a lot of the underworld, but I have always known who he is and what he does for a living. Bloody, wounded men in my house are nothing new, and I have tended to some of Mateo's and Leo's injuries in the past.

When I woke yesterday evening to find my brother and Leo sitting by my bed, waiting for me to wake up, I nearly freaked out at the sight of Leo's bloody upper torso. Though the doc had patched him up and a large white bandage covered his wound, there was so much blood, and I was terrified he had been seriously injured.

Leo explained the bullet had only grazed his shoulder and it looked worse than it was, but I knew he was lying because little beads of sweat coated his brow and he was looking pale under his tan skin. He was in pain because he refused to take the pain pills the doc had given him. Stupid man.

"That is no excuse. You won't heal if you don't rest."

"Touché, *dolcezza*. I could say the same to you. You were hurt too. What are you doing up out of bed?"

"I was bored in bed, and the pain in my head has subsided." The doc said I was lucky I didn't have a concussion. "Besides, Mama needed help. It's a big dinner." Bile swirls in my gut, and a shiver works its way through me as I contemplate our impending dinner guests. Papa invited the Greco family for dinner. They have business to discuss, and this is the usual way things work.

"*Tesorino,* we can manage without you. If you aren't well, you should go back to bed until our guests arrive." Mama cups my face, peering into my eyes with obvious concern.

"I'm fine, Mama." I kiss both her cheeks. "But I will take a break. I need to talk to Leo about something." Removing my apron, I fold it over the back of the chair as I eyeball Leo, gesturing for him to follow me.

I head out through the back hallway to the small laundry room and pull Leo inside. "What did you tell Mateo?" I ask, keeping my voice low. "He was trying to quiz me all morning over why I was in the orchard."

"I told him Santino hit on you and dragged you away and I gave chase to bring you back. What did you tell him?" Leo asks.

"Nothing. I pretended I had a really bad headache, and he left me alone."

Leo chuckles. "Cunning is not a word I would have used to describe you, until recently. You're becoming quite adept at it."

"Are you really surprised considering the world I've been brought up in?"

"You always surprise me, *dolcezza*." His adoring smile and sultry tone do wonderfully weird things to my insides. When pain wasn't hammering at my skull last night, I spent time reliving our amazing make-out session, constantly touching my lips, as if I could still feel his mouth upon mine. It took colossal willpower to break away from him when all I wanted was to let him ravish me until he owned every part of me. But I won't be disrespected by any man, and I'm still hurt he was with Nicole.

"Please don't call me that. I'm not a little girl anymore." Leo has been calling me sweetness since I was a kid, and I don't want him to see me like that anymore.

He takes a step closer, his eyes flaring with dark heat. "Trust me, I know." His deep voice sounds even deeper, and a throbbing ache takes up residence in my panties.

We stare at one another as a powerful electrical current sizzles in the air. My shirt sticks to my back, and my panties are damp between my thighs. My eyes wander to his mouth, and my lips part on a tiny exhale as potent longing trickles into every nook and cranny of my being.

Leo snaps out of it first, taking two steps back until his spine hits the wall. "Fuck, Nat. You can't look at me like that."

"Why not?" I level him with a cool stare.

"Because I'm a man who has very little self-control left when it comes to you."

I close the gap between us, pressing my chest against him. "What if I don't want you to exercise self-control?"

"Jesus, *dolcezza*." Leo grasps the nape of my neck in his meaty palms, holding my face mere millimeters from his. "You know why we can't give in to this."

"I don't care about any of that," I rasp, barely able to take a breath with him this close.

His eyes linger on my lips, and butterflies are running amok in my chest. "That's not what you said yesterday."

"I wanted to punish you for hurting and disrespecting me," I admit. Frankie would be so disappointed in me for not playing the game, but I don't think I have it in me to be anything but honest. Especially when it comes to my feelings for this man. "I wanted you to know what it's like to want something you can't have."

Leo barks out an incredulous laugh before briefly brushing his lips against mine. The groan that leaves my mouth is borderline animalistic. He tips my chin up with his finger, forcing my gaze to lock on his. "I have spent the past year wanting something I can't have. Trust me, I'm well accustomed to the feeling."

My heart careens viciously against my rib cage as his words sink bone-deep. I think he's talking about me, but I need to know. "Are you talking about me?"

He doesn't answer me immediately. He just stares at me as he holds me in an ironclad grip at my nape. Feeling more of that stupid bravery, I place one hand on his chest, careful not to touch anywhere near his sore shoulder. Leo stares at me, and I watch the conflict wash over his face. "I cannot answer that question because one of us needs to be strong." Gently, he lets go of my neck and removes my hand from his chest. "Your fiancé is on his way here, Nat. I believe that's all the reminder we need. What happened yesterday can never happen again."

"I love you," I blurt as tears sting the backs of my eyes. "I don't want to marry Carlo. I want to marry you." I grab his arm. "Please, Leo. If you have feelings for me, and I think you do, then fight for us. Fight for me."

His fingers wind into my hair, and he holds me close. "Your father would never permit you to marry a lowly *soldato*, and your marriage contract has been in place for years. If I could, I would fight to the ends of time for you, *dolcezza*. But rebelling would only get us both killed." He rests his forehead against mine. "I wish things could be different. I wish it with my whole heart. But this is our reality, and our feelings don't come into it."

A sob rips from my throat. "It hurts, Leo. I want to be with you so badly. Every time I see you, I want your arms around me and your mouth on mine. It hurts not to be with you."

"Shush, *dolcezza*." He presses a lingering kiss into my hair. "The pain will lessen in time."

I know it won't, but there is no point arguing it. I should consider this a victory because he has all but confirmed he feels the same way about me. However, he has made it clear he won't act on it. He can't be my white knight riding to the rescue. I know it would mean absolute death for him, and I could never live with that. "I don't see how I can live without you, but I love you enough to walk away to keep you safe."

His mouth comes down on mine in the softest, sweetest kiss, and it's everything. My hands rest on his shoulders while his rest on my waist as we indulge in a slow, sensual kiss I know I will remember for the rest of my life. Leo may be afraid to say the words, but I feel his heart in the tender sweep of his lips.

"I need you to promise me something," he says, pulling me into his arms when he breaks the kiss.

I wrap myself around him, placing my head on his chest, welcoming the steady vibration of his heartbeat. "Anything," I agree, my voice muffled against his chest. He smells so divine up close. All citrusy and vibrant and thrumming with life.

He lifts my head up to his. "No more flirting with other men or trying to lose your virginity before your marriage. Please, Nat," he whispers, peering deep into my eyes. "I am begging you to give up this quest because it is not the solution."

"Then what is? I don't want to marry him, Leo. He gives me the creeps."

"I will talk to Mateo and see if he can talk to Angelo again."

My eyes pop wide. "Mateo has spoken to Angelo about my marriage contract?"

He nods. "On several occasions."

"Why? He is all for the traditions and constantly telling me I need to get with the program."

"It's true he agrees with contracted marriage, but he doesn't want Carlo for you either. I think, deep down, Angelo probably doesn't want him for you too. But his hands are tied. It's a binding contract, and he can't afford to instigate a war."

"So, he'd rather sell his daughter to a monster to keep the peace."

"It sickens me, but there is nothing anyone can do."

"What if he was dead?" I blurt, articulating something I have thought about in recent weeks. "He can't marry me if he's six feet under."

"Natalia." Leo growls, glaring at me. "Do not even say what I think you're saying. He is the son of Don Greco. No one would get away with killing him and live to see another day."

"I want out of it desperately, Leo."

"I know." Tipping my head up, he dusts kisses all over my face, and I fist his shirt, drawing him closer, inhaling his scent, and siphoning his warmth and his closeness, cursing the fact I was born into the criminal underworld and I'm not free to love this man the way I want to love him.

A bloody pool forms where his injury is, and I pull back, remorseful for hurting him. "You're bleeding."

He looks down and curses.

"I didn't thank you," I say, cupping his cheek. "You saved me yesterday. You got shot protecting me. I will never forget that."

"I would take a thousand bullets for you, *dolcezza*, and you never need to thank me. Protecting you is the one thing I am permitted to do. And I am going to protect you until the day I die, even if I have to cherish you from the shadows."

A strangled sob bubbles up my throat, and tears pool in my eyes. I open my mouth to tell him I love him again, but he shakes his head, placing his hand over my mouth. "Don't," he whispers in a choked voice. "Don't say it. It hurts too much."

My heart aches. Like it physically hurts so bad it feels like it's ready to crack apart. Tears spill over my cheeks, and his eyes glimmer with unshed emotion, and that's how I know he is feeling this too. Knowing my love isn't unrequited should make me happy, but it only makes me sadder because we can never be.

Even though I want to throw caution to the wind—to spread my legs and welcome him into my body the same way he has already entered and claimed my heart—I won't because I won't take chances with his life.

"What the hell is going on here?" Mateo barks, and Leo and I jerk apart. My brother is standing in the doorway with steam practically billowing from his ears. The sharp glare he slants in Leo's direction makes me uneasy, so I swing into survival mode.

"Leo's wound is bleeding again, so I offered to patch him up." Leaning over, I grab one of Matty's pressed shirts from the hanging rail. "You don't mind if he borrows a shirt, do you?"

"Natalia." Mateo's frustrated tone tells me he isn't buying this for a second. Matty closes his eyes, and he's a little less angry when he reopens them. "Mama is looking for you. The Grecos are on their way. You need to get ready."

I swing my gaze to Leo, and he nods, telling me to go and he'll take care of this.

"Don't hurt him," I whisper in my brother's ear. "Remember he saved me yesterday and he has done nothing except loyally protect me. Don't read into things that aren't there."

I have no idea if my brother will swallow the crap I tried to feed him, but they are good enough friends that I'm not too worried. As I trudge up the stairs, the reason my heart feels like dead wood in my chest has everything to do with the reality of the situation. I was almost kidnapped yesterday, and I'm guessing it's because of who I'm engaged to. Someone wants to make Carlo pay for something, and they were going to use me to do it.

I hate that this is what my life has come to, but I cannot say I have not been prepared. It's been schooled into me for years by my parents in different ways. Mateo too. None of us may like Carlo Greco, and I'm under no illusion about the kind of marriage we will have, but I am resolved to my fate now.

I can't have Leo, and I must let him go.

There is no way of getting out of this marriage contract with the Grecos. This time next year, I will be Mrs. Carlo Greco, and I need to find a way of making peace with that.

Chapter 10

NATALIA

"THIS IS GOOD, Mama Rosa," Carlo says, smiling sweetly at my mother, while his hand moves farther up my thigh under the table. Only Mazzone *soldati* who are familiar with my mom get to call her that, but no one will call my fiancé out for his presumptuous behavior when there are more pressing matters at hand—namely, the threat to my safety.

A muscle clenches in Leo's jaw as he stands guard in one corner of the room, but he remains staring straight ahead, as if he isn't listening and watching every second of this horrendous dinner. Carlo insisted on sitting beside me, and he has spent the entire meal fawning over me while trying to touch me intimately under my dress. My wrist aches from holding his hand at bay, and my thighs ache from squeezing them together. I'm so tense it feels like all my muscles have locked up, and I can barely stomach any food.

"I'm glad you like it," Mama replies. "Natalia made the cannoli. Desserts are her speciality."

"Is that right?" my despicable fiancé says, digging his nails into my fleshy thigh while he flashes me a disarming smile. "I didn't think you could be any sweeter, *bella*."

Sweat gathers on my neck as I fake smile at him through gritted teeth.

"I think we should get married now," he announces, cutting through the other conversation at the table.

Panic sluices through my veins, and I want to beg my father not to agree, but I keep a fake smile and a cool expression plastered on my face, while I pray like I have never prayed before.

"Are you out of your mind?" Mateo snaps, leaning across the table to glare at Carlo. "It's your fault my sister's life is at risk."

"Mateo!" Papa bellows, stabbing my brother with a firm look. "Do not speak out of turn."

Don Greco smiles smugly, and I want to punch him in his stupid face. Carlo is the spitting image of his father, with his dark hair and dark eyes, so looking at my future father-in-law is like looking at my future husband when he's older. A shiver works its way through me at the thought. Carlo shares the same cold, inhuman glint in his eyes, and I wonder if I will end up like Mrs. Greco. A pale, trembling, mute mouse of a woman picking at her food with shaking hands and barely making eye contact with anyone. I can only imagine the horrors that go on in that house, and despite my earlier conviction, I want no part of it.

I'm back to rebelling against my fate and wanting out at any cost.

"And this is not your call to make either," Papa adds, turning his sharp gaze on Carlo.

"Natalia will be my wife, so I disagree. This has everything to do with me."

I wish I could wave my hand in his face and ask what about me? But what would be the point? Women get no say in our world. We are expected to do what we are told and keep our mouths shut at all times.

"Carlo. Show Don Mazzone the respect he deserves," his father says, shooting his son a warning look. "This is not dinner conversation. We will discuss it like men after we have finished this lovely meal." Carlo's father turns toward Mama. "The food has been splendid, Rosa. We thank you for your hospitality." His brow puckers. "Are you okay?" he asks, and I whip my head to my mother.

"Mama?" I query, concerned by her pale features and the glistening of sweat darkening her brow. Her eyes flutter open and shut as everyone at the table looks at her. Papa stands, moving to her side, just as she faints, falling sideways off her chair. Papa catches her before she hits the floor, and I pinch Carlo's hand, swatting it away as I stand. Leo's eyes meet mine, his gaze burning hot, his jaw clenched, and I know he saw that. But I don't care about anything in this moment but my mother.

I race to her side as Mateo approaches from the other side of the table. "Call the doctor," Papa says, eyeballing me as he gently scoops Mama into his arms. "And then come up to your mama's room."

"Maybe we should go," Don Greco says, rising.

"We have business to discuss," Papa says. "Let me get my wife settled upstairs. Finish your cannoli, and Mateo will show you to my study." He eyeballs my brother, and Mateo nods, even though I know he wants to go with Mama too. "I will meet you there shortly."

Ignoring Carlo's heated stare, I rush out of the room after my parents and head to our private living room to call our doctor.

"WHAT IS WRONG with her?" I ask a half hour later when the doc is completing his preliminary examination of Mama.

"I'm not sure," he adds, looking troubled, as he tenderly probes her stomach. "We will need to arrange some tests in the hospital, Mrs. Mazzone." He pats her hand.

She looks deathly pale, propped up in bed on a multitude of pillows. "Angelo will not like that," she rasps, her voice weak. "Can't you conduct the tests here?"

Papa keeps a full-time doctor on the payroll specifically so we avoid hospitals and drawing attention to ourselves. If we had to bring our *soldati t*o the hospital any time one of them was injured, we would be there daily, and it would claim the attention of the authorities. Which would not be good, even if Papa has cops, judges, lawyers, and other representatives of law enforcement in the palm of his hand.

"Don't worry about anything for now. I will have the results of your blood tests tomorrow, and that might tell me more." Locking his briefcase, he stands. "Stay in bed. Rest. Drink plenty of water, and make sure you eat."

"I don't have much of an appetite at the moment," Mama says. "And I already need to pee constantly."

"Why didn't you call the doctor?" I ask, growing more concerned.

"Pft." She waves her hands at me. "It is nothing to be worried about."

I wish I could share her confidence, but I have a really bad feeling about this.

He turns his face to me. "A cool cloth on her face will help with her temperature."

"Thank you." I nod at the man as he slips out of the room while I head to Mama's en suite bathroom.

"I'm worried," I tell her when I return with a cool cloth. I perch beside her on the bed, lightly dabbing the cloth over her clammy skin.

"Don't be," she says, cupping my cheek. "I'll be fine. I'm sure it's just a bug or a mild infection."

"What if it's not?"

"*Bella Donna*. I think you have enough worries without worrying about me." Unspoken words hover in the air between us. "Be careful," she adds, looking like she wants to say more.

Mama falls asleep, and after tucking the covers around her and pulling the drapes closed, I tiptoe out of her bedroom and down the stairs.

I am walking past Papa's office, staring at the closed door, when an idea forms in my head. Without stopping to think about it, I duck into the formal living room next door, quietly closing the door behind me. Striding toward the large bookshelves, I remove the dummy book on the lower shelf and stand back as the bookcase retracts on both sides, revealing the hidden tunnel. I slip inside before I change my mind.

This house has been in my papa's family for generations, and one of our ancestors built a slew of interconnected hidden tunnels between the walls of the property. There is one main tunnel that leads outside the grounds to a secret entrance, and I know Papa keeps a car there in case we ever need to flee in a hurry. When we were old enough, Papa explained about the tunnels, giving us clear instructions if the house was ever breached to use them to escape.

What Angelo didn't know is Mateo and I had found the tunnels a few years earlier, when we were playing, and we often used to sneak into this one and spy on his meetings. I haven't done this in years, and it's clear the tunnel hasn't been accessed in a long time. Cobwebs cover the ceiling, attempting to cling to my hair as I walk, so I duck down, crawling along the space with shivers creeping over every inch of my exposed skin.

Raised voices tickle my eardrums as I reach the tunnel that backs onto the bookshelves in my father's office. This shelving unit doesn't fully lock once closed and there is a tiny gap, enough to see some of what is going down in the room and enough to hear everything.

The last time Mateo and I came here, we saw our father kill two men with his bare hands. I was nine. Matty was thirteen, and it was weeks before he was initiated. He made me promise not to tell anyone what I had seen, and he forbade me from going into the tunnel again. I was scared enough I agreed without protest. For weeks, I couldn't relax in Papa's arms. Every time he hugged me, I froze as visions of him choking those men resurfaced in my mind. If Papa noticed my reticence, he never said, and gradually, I learned to block the memory from my mind.

But I never forgot.

And it was the day I realized exactly who my papa was and the kind of world we lived in.

"We have an agreement," Angelo snaps, yanking me from my head. I stay pinned in the corner, content to listen and not see.

"No one is disputing that," Don Maximo Greco says. "But this situation warrants we at least discuss modifying the terms."

"It's nonnegotiable," my father says. "Natalia is still in school, and I'm not upending her life because your son has made an enemy of one of our own."

"I don't much like your tone," Carlo says.

"Carlo!" Don Greco spews a line of Italian at his son, basically telling him to shut the fuck up.

Of course, Carlo doesn't listen. "This is not my fault. Accardi is the one going behind our back, exploring alternative options. He thinks his shit doesn't stink now he's succeeded his father and married that simpering Juliet. He parades her around like he's invincible. Like we don't know he's betraying us! And yet you sit here giving me shit. Unfucking-believable."

"Be careful, boy," Papa says. "Those are some heavy accusations to throw around, and I won't tolerate such disrespect in my own home."

"I'm speaking the truth!" Carlo yells. "Why won't you believe me? I'm telling you, it's Accardi who put the Barone up to this. He wants to take Natalia to force me into silence. I won't keep quiet, but I won't risk my future bride's life either. Which is why her marrying me now is the best choice. I can keep her safe, Don Mazzone. I won't let anyone touch her or get near her."

"You just want to get your hands on her," Mateo snarls. "This isn't about her safety at all. I see the way you look at her."

"Get used to it," Carlo snaps. "She'll be my wife soon. Whether it's now or after she graduates, it's happening."

"That is enough, Carlo." Don Greco snarls and the sound of a body crashing to the floor entices me to take a sneak peek. I can't stop the smile forming on my mouth when I see Carlo pinned to the floor, his father's foot shoved under his neck, almost choking him. "You will not disrespect Don Mazzone or me any longer. You will apologize, and keep your mouth shut unless you are spoken to."

Carlo growls, but he says nothing. His father presses his foot down harder, and a gargled sound rips from Carlo's mouth. Silently, I urge Don Greco to keep going. To choke the life from his son and do me a solid.

But nothing is ever that easy. Maximo removes his foot, fists a hand in Carlo's shirt, and yanks him to his feet. "Apologize to Don Mazzone."

Carlo has a face like thunder as he begrudgingly apologizes to my papa. Papa nods, staring at my intended with a look that would scare most men.

But Carlo is an arrogant asshole, and he thinks he can get away with anything. Though he was just apologizing to my father, he holds his stare in a way that is considered rude.

His father grunts, shoving him away. "Wait in the car, Carlo," he spits out, sounding like he's all out of patience with his son.

"But, Papa, I—"

"That wasn't a request," Don Greco roars, and I almost jump out of my skin. I huddle back in the corner, content to just listen. "Get out of my sight! I will clean up this mess you have made."

It's no wonder Mateo and Carlo don't like one another. It sounds like they share the same reckless streak and a penchant for riling their fathers up. Although, Matty wouldn't dare speak over Papa like Carlo just did. Not unless he wanted to be beaten bloody. I wonder if Maximo Greco thinks marriage to me will help tame his son or if he wants to hone the skills of the beast by giving him a permanent plaything.

Whatever the motive, that is where the comparison ends between Matty and my fiancé. My brother doesn't have dead eyes or enjoy inflicting pain on me. My brother's gaze doesn't make me feel like my skin is flaying from my bones. Matty's touch is comforting and protective where Carlo's fingers on my flesh make me want to put a bullet through my skull. The thought of his cock coming anywhere near me makes me physically ill.

A door slamming is the only indication the asshole has left the room.

"Natalia remains with her family," Angelo says, laying down the law. "We are the best qualified to keep her safe. I will assign two *soldati* to her on a permanent basis. Leo," he calls out. "You are hereby reassigned to watch over my daughter. Pick a second."

"Brando, sir," he replies without hesitation.

At any other time, I would probably celebrate at Leo being assigned as my personal bodyguard. But I don't want this. Not now I know he shares my feelings and we can't act on it. This will be the worst form of torture. For both of us.

"I don't like this," Angelo continues, and I hear the clinking of glass as he pours drinks. "Carlo needs to be taken in hand. I won't hand my daughter over unless he proves he can keep her safe—through his actions and his words. If this threat isn't eliminated by next summer, the wedding will have to be deferred. I won't entrust my daughter into your care until I'm completely assured of her safety and protection."

"You insult me, Angelo," Don Greco says, disrespecting my father by calling him by his first name.

"As you do me, Maximo," Papa replies.

"Our families have been the closest allies within the five families for decades. We agreed, many years ago, to solidify that bond through marriage. If Carlo is correct. If Accardi *is* looking for distribution routes and partners outside of New York, then our alliance is of even more importance. If you renege on our agreement, you know what it means."

"No one said anything about reneging," Papa calmly replies. "Just that it might need to be pushed out until this business is sorted. My only daughter's welfare is my primary concern."

I can't believe what I'm hearing, and while I want to believe it's the truth, I can't help wondering if there is something else at play here. I have pleaded with Papa in the past to get me out of this marriage deal, but he refused to entertain any idea of it, and he didn't seem to care what kind of man Carlo was. So, why now?

"What about the Barone?" Don Greco asks.

"I think it's time we both paid Don Barone a visit, don't you?"

Don Greco lets out a low chuckle. "A visit is most definitely in order."

They move on to talk about other stuff, and I decide to cut my losses and get out of here before Mateo or my father discovers me.

I'm picking cobwebs out of my hair when I emerge from the living room into the hallway so I'm not paying attention. Adrenaline roars through my veins, and potent fear slaps me in the face when someone clamps a hand over my mouth from behind and I'm yanked back into a hard body.

Chapter 11

NATALIA

"YOU REALLY HAVE no sense of self-preservation at all. Do you?" Carlo taunts, keeping one hand on my mouth while his free arm wraps around my waist. He nods at his two *soldati*, and they move through the open doorway into the living room I just vacated. Carlo hauls me back inside, and one of his men quietly closes and locks the door.

Blood thrums in my ears and rushes to my head as panic sets in.

"Don't scream, or you'll be sorry," he says, his mouth brushing over my earlobe as he slowly removes his hand from my mouth.

"Let me go." My voice shakes as I attempt to wriggle out of his hold.

All three men laugh, and an angry red heat crawls up my neck and onto my cheeks.

"Never," he whispers as his free hand creeps up under my dress.

"You can't be alone with me, and you can't touch me!" I gulp anxiously as bile churns in my gut at the feel of his fingers sliding up the inside of my thigh.

"Don't be such an ungrateful bitch," he hisses, and I cry out as he bites down on my earlobe. "Do you know how many women would love to be in your place? I have women lining the streets to take a ride on my cock, so this precious *principessa* routine isn't working, *dolcezza*."

My heart stutters in my chest at his words before picking up speed, thumping crazily against my chest wall, making me feel like I'm close to cardiac arrest.

"Your father underestimates me, but I suggest you don't," he adds as his fingers brush against the crotch of my lace panties.

"Please don't," I whisper, fighting tears.

"Don't do what?" he sneers, rubbing his fingers back and forth across the lace.

"Don't touch me."

"Don't touch you where?" He mocks me, and his two soldiers laugh.

"Don't touch me there," I whisper as a tear rolls down my face.

"Don't touch your pussy?" Pushing the lace aside, he probes my folds with a rough touch, and I want to die. "Don't fuck you with my fingers?" He shoves two fingers inside me with brutal force. I cry out as he spreads me, pumping his fingers in and out, and pain splinters through my core. "Or don't touch your tits?" he adds, moving his arm up and squeezing one of my breasts through my dress.

"Please stop."

"I don't think I will, *dolcezza*." Removing his hand from my pussy, he spins me around to face him, keeping one arm banded around my back as he licks my essence from his fingers. "Sweet as honey." He licks his fingers clean while staring at me with blatant need.

Aesthetically, Carlo is a very good-looking guy. Tall and toned with handsome facial features, he is deemed a good catch. He looks like a young Johnny Depp with his dark hair and sultry brown eyes, but the monster lurking behind his gaze never lets me forget he is as far removed from a handsome movie star as I can get.

There are rumors he likes to cut the girls he takes to bed and he forces them into blood play and other kinky shit. Some of the Italian girls in our small circle at school tell me over and over how lucky I am, and I hate that I have to bite my tongue from admitting the truth. Carlo Greco scares me, and he makes me sick.

Case in point.

Carlo grips my face, painfully forcing my chin to tilt so he's peering into my eyes. "Is that why Leonardo Messina calls you *dolcezza*? Has he drunk from the forbidden well?" Anger flares in his eyes as his fingers pinch my chin. Panic for Leo floods my system. What the fuck does Carlo know and how?

"Leo has been my brother's best friend since we were kids. He is basically my pseudo brother. He has called me *dolcezza* since I was a little girl. Not everyone is a sick fuck like you," I add.

My head whips back as he slaps me across the face. Pain rattles around my skull, but I don't cry, letting anger overrule all other emotions and the throbbing ache spreading across my cheek. I bring my head around to face him, pinning him with the full extent of the hatred I feel for him.

"Disrespect me again and I'll kill him," Carlo says in a lethally calm voice as his free hand trails up my body. "Disobey me and I'll kill him." He cups one breast, squeezing it tight. "You are mine, *dolcezza*. Mine to do with as I please." Tugging the top of my dress down, he slides his hand underneath the cup of my bra, fondling my bare flesh. I squeeze my eyes shut as agony twists my insides into knots. "Open your eyes," he demands, pinching my nipple, causing tears to sting the backs of my eyes. He rolls my nipple back and forth between his thumb and forefinger as he shoves his pelvis into my stomach. His disgusting erection prods at my narrow waist, and acid crawls up my throat. "If I find out Messina has touched any part of you, I will chop his dick off and feed it to him in little pieces."

He looks over my shoulder at his men. "And I'll give you to my men for a night. Let them do whatever they want. Fuck your tits, your ass, your treacherous cunt, your pouting mouth. I'll let them cut you, burn you, beat you." His hand moves from my lower back, and he pulls the bottom of my dress up, exposing my ass to his men. He squeezes one ass cheek through my lace panties and then the other before his finger traces a line through my ass crack. My eyes close of their own volition, and I'm struggling to hold on to my tears.

He slaps my ass. "Open your fucking eyes, Natalia!" he hisses. "You will do as I say, when I say it, and if you a breathe a word of this to Mateo or Leo, I will end them both." Leaning down, he suctions his mouth over the swell of one breast and sucks hard. His finger continues to rub up and down the line of my ass, and terror has done a number on me. I can't speak, can't move, and can barely breathe as he violates my body in places I have never been touched before.

Revulsion tiptoes down my spine as he sucks on my breast, bruising my skin. Lifting his head, he reviews his work, a satisfied grin tugging up the corners of his mouth. "I want you to look at that and remember what I have said." Grabbing my face, he smashes his mouth down on mine, brutalizing my lips and shoving his disgusting tongue in my mouth. "I own you, Natalia. Don't forget." He cups my crotch through my dress, squeezing tight. "This cunt is mine and mine alone. When I come for you next, you won't refuse me, or it will be Leo and your brother who will pay the price."

I BARELY SLEEP a wink that night. Concern for Mama commingles with concern for Leo and Matty and fear for myself. I played it all wrong today, and I want to scream and shout and berate myself for not being stronger. For not protesting louder. But I was scared, and I froze, intimidated by Carlo and his two leering *soldati*. I can't tell my brother because he'd lose his shit if he knows what Carlo did. Mateo is already in hot water with Papa, and I won't add to it. His temper is too fiery to risk going to him. I really want to tell Leo, but I'm afraid to because that monster warned me not to, and Carlo clearly knows things. I don't know how, but I won't risk Leo's life, so I vow to say nothing. Like I did yesterday when he asked me what was wrong.

"Natalia," Leo says, exiting the car from behind the wheel. "Wait up a minute."

I stall at the bottom of the steps to the school doors, steeling myself in preparation. "What's up, Leo? I can't be late for homeroom."

"I know something is wrong. Tell me." His eyes probe mine and I both love and hate how well he knows me.

"I'm worried about Mama," I truthfully reply.

His features soften. "I know you are. We all are, but I know there is more. What did he do to you, *dolcezza*?" My mouth turns dry as I remember Carlo taunting me with the nickname yesterday.

"Nothing," I lie, averting my eyes.

"Stop lying, Natalia. I saw his hand on your leg under the table. That bastard has no right to touch you before the wedding. You need to tell Angelo. He'll get Don Greco to rein him in."

I bark out a laugh. "Don Greco has no intention of reining his son in. Anything he said was to appease Papa. Didn't you see the pride shining in his eyes? He thinks the sun shines out of Carlo's backside. No one will tell him differently."

"Leo? What a pleasant surprise," Nicole says in her annoying voice.

"Fuck off, Nicole," Leo says without breaking eye contact with me.

"But—"

"I'm not interested." Leo glares, taking my arm and pulling me into his side as he speaks to my arch nemesis. "And I'm trying to have a private conversation, so get lost."

He's hella rude, but I can't find it in myself to care.

Nicole simmers, like a boiling kettle about to bubble over. "No one plays me for a fool," she huffs, placing her hands on her hips. "And no one picks Virgin Barbie over me." She pokes him with one bony finger. "No one." She spits on my shoes, and I'm tempted to release my anger and frustration on her pretty face, but she's nothing, and I have bigger fish to worry about.

Leo moves to retaliate on my behalf, but I hold on to his arm, subtly shaking my head. Leo straightens up, keeping his arm around my shoulder. "Natalia is worth a million of you, Nicole, and the only person who buys into that bullshit is you."

She stomps her foot, and steam practically billows from her ears. Casting one last scathing look in my direction, she spins on her heels and disappears up the steps.

"I've got to go, Leo," I say after Nicole has entered the school.

"This conversation isn't over." He removes his arm from my shoulder, and I miss his comforting warmth already. "We'll be parked in the usual spot after school."

"I'm sorry you got stuck with this."

"I'm not."

"You can't mean that. I know no *soldato* wants a babysitting gig."

He smiles, and my legs turn weak. His gray-blue eyes are awash with emotion. The dangerous kind. "There is no place else I'd rather be. You think I wanted anyone else protecting you?" He arches a brow, and my chest fills with warmth. "The greatest honor Don Mazzone could ask of me is to safeguard his only daughter." He tucks a stray strand of my hair behind my ear. "Go, *dolcezza*. Don't be late."

I'm floating on a cloud as I walk through the entrance doors, so I almost miss Nicole skulking at the side of the door, glaring at me as I pass by. I pay her no heed because she's inconsequential to me now.

That is my first mistake.

Chapter 12

NATALIA

NICOLE WASTES NO opportunity to glare at me during the school day, but I ignore her. She's a blip on my radar now. Nothing more now Leo has clearly tossed her to the curb where she belongs.

"I think you should tell your papa," Frankie whispers in the back of the library where we're supposed to be doing our homework during a free period. "I'm scared for you, Nat. He's a fucking psycho, and I'm afraid of what else he plans to do to you. He has already risked your reputation by putting his hands on you. Your father will go nuts when he hears that. Let him handle it. Please." She clasps my hands in hers, pleading with her eyes.

"I can't risk it. He knows about Leo and me." Frankie is up to speed on everything that has happened between me and my brother's best friend.

Her brow puckers. "How?"

A loud "shush" is aimed in our direction, and we whip our heads up, smiling apologetically at the boorish, matronly head librarian.

I angle my body in the chair so I'm sideways, my hair curtaining my face, as I lower my tone. "I don't know, but I'm guessing he has an insider on the payroll. One of Papa's *soldati* must be spying for him."

"That's another good reason to go to Angelo."

"I have no proof. It's only a guess, and I can't raise that topic without drawing attention to Leo and me. Papa is as likely as Carlo to put a bullet between Leo's eyes if he finds out what has transpired between us. It's too risky, Frankie."

"Then what are you going to do?"

"I don't know," I admit, gathering up my books as the bell rings. "But I'll think of something."

I GRIND TO a halt when I step into the bathroom, finding an ambush awaiting me. Nicole has rallied the troops, and five of them stand in front of me, dying to spill my blood. The door snicks shut behind me as one of her minions stands guard with her back against the only exit.

"How cliché," I drawl, narrowing my eyes at my enemy. "Though it's nothing less than I expect from you."

"You think you're so clever," Nicole hisses, stepping forward, putting her face all up in mine. "I know it was you who blocked us from the party on Saturday, and you'll pay for that."

I am wishing I had let her attend now. Perhaps she might have caught a stray bullet if she'd been present.

An ugly sneer creeps over her mouth. "I know you want him." She takes out her cell phone. "I see the way you look at him like a little fawning puppy." Titters ring out, and I clench my jaw, trying to keep my cool. "He will never want you because you wouldn't have a clue what to do with a man like Leonardo Messina." She thrusts her phone in my face, and all the blood leaches from my skin as I stare at the photo.

Leo is asleep in bed, slightly on his side, providing a good view of his upper front torso. He is clearly naked, save for a sheet pooled very low at his waist. From the angle the photo was taken, I glimpse the top of his bare ass cheek, and my cheeks flush in a combination of disgust, heartache, and jealousy.

"I will admit I was pretty taken with Mateo at first sight." Nicole prattles on while I try to wrench my gaze from the photo.

Irrespective of the circumstances, it's a beautiful picture.

Leo looks so fucking gorgeous with his tousled brown hair falling over his strong brow, long lashes fanning his cheeks, and his impressive broad chest. Dark hair covers his chest, trailing a path down his stomach and below, dipping underneath the sheet. I hate that bitch knows a side of him I will never get to experience. The unfairness of it all slaps me in the face again, and I'm destroyed on the inside. Pain presses down on my chest, making breathing difficult.

"Your brother took my anal virginity, introducing me to a whole new level of pleasure." She winks, and her cronies cackle like the malicious bitches they are. "But Leo." She whistles under her breath. "Leo takes the cake." She shoves her face in mine. "He filled every hole, and we fucked nonstop all night. He couldn't get enough of me. He pounded into me over and over and over again," she sneers, relishing the pain I'm unable to hide in my eyes. "His big cock felt incredible sliding in and out of me, and I know he'll be back for more. What he said outside? That was all for show. He's already been blowing up my phone, looking for a repeat performance."

She prods me in the chest. "You're a pathetic little princess who wouldn't have a clue what to do with a cock." More laughter rings out as my hands ball into fists at my side. "Why the fuck would he ever want you when he could have me? When I know his body intimately and all the ways he loves to be touched? I can still hear the sounds he made as my hands and my lips roamed every part of that sinful body." She licks her lips, and I'm two seconds from detonation. "I felt him between my legs for days after, and I could hardly walk straight." Her tinkling laughter grates on the last of my patience, and I'm like a kettle about to blow its top.

She plants her hands on her hips. "He doesn't want you. He never will, so who's the winner now, huh? I'll be the one bouncing on his giant cock later. I'll be the one whose finger he slides a ring on. I'll be the one having his babies. *Me*." She pushes her chest into mine. "Not you. Loser."

The gates open as a wave of red-hot anger sweeps over every part of me, and I react without thinking. Wrapping my hands around her neck, I push her toward the vanity unit, shoving her back into the edge of the counter. Her eyes shimmer with mirth, and none of her friends do anything, which is weird. But I'm too lost to my anger to consider it. The more she smirks at me, the tighter I press my hands around her neck, and in this moment, I honestly think I could squeeze all the life from her body.

That thought snaps me out of my murderous haze, and I let her go, stumbling back, staring in horror at the obvious finger marks around her neck. She jerks her head, and I'm yanked back by my hair and then let go. I slam to the ground on my back, groaning when pain shuttles up my spine. Her four friends round on me then, kicking and punching me, careful not to touch my face. I try to fight them off, but it's four against one, and I can't beat those odds.

Zoning out, I squeeze my eyes shut to hold back my tears, biting on the inside of my cheek to stop myself from crying. Abruptly, they stop, and I curl into a ball, pain wracking my body all over.

"Do it," Nicole says, and her words are followed by a low thud and a piercing scream. "You fucking bitch!" Nicole hisses at her friend. "Did you have to do it so hard?" She winches as I force my eyes to open. "I think you've broken it," she snaps, bringing her fingers to her nose, crying out in pain.

"That will get her expelled for sure," her bestie, Novah Raimond, says. "Stop bitching and whining. Your nose will heal."

"You better fucking hope it does," she barks.

The door opens as I struggle to pull myself upright. Pain spreads across my chest, cascading throughout my body, and a hiss escapes my lips.

Nicole presses her foot to my chest, pushing me back down on the floor and stepping on me. "Fucking bitch." She spits in my face. "You should know I always win." She crouches down over me, gloating. "I'm guessing your parents will go apeshit when you get expelled, and I bet you are grounded until graduation. It couldn't happen to a more deserving bitch." She slaps me across the face before straightening up. She looks like a mess. Her nose is swollen, and blood drips down over her lips and onto her chin. "We're off to the principal's office to show her what went down. Daddy makes a huge donation every year, and she'll believe what I have to say."

She waves a phone in my face, pressing a button to play the recording. The sound has been turned off so the principal can't hear her taunting me. To Mrs. Peters, it will look like I'm at fault because I made the first aggressive move. Predictably, they switched it off before my attack, so she can say her friends retaliated out of protection for her. Either way, she expects to come out of this as the victim.

What a fucking joke.

I want to tell her she's delusional. That she has no clue what she has done, but she'll learn that lesson soon enough. I guess there is no end to her stupidity. She knows who my family is. Who my father is. And doesn't she realize if I was to be expelled she wouldn't see Leo anymore?

My phone rings in my bag, and I suspect it's Leo, wondering where the fuck I am. I thought I heard it ringing during the assault, but I can't be sure.

The girls leave, their laughter ringing in my ears, long after they are gone. I hiccup and a sob travels up my throat as I haul myself to my knees. I cry out in pain as I stand, attempting to straighten up, doubling over as my ribs protest the motion. If they haven't broken them, they are at least badly bruised. Bending down to pick up my bag sends more pain crunching through my ribs, and my tears flow in earnest. I shuffle out of the door as I extract my phone with trembling fingers. Leo's name flashes on the screen, and I have never been more grateful to see it.

"Natalia! Thank fuck," he says when I answer. "Where are you?"

"Leo," I croak in between sobs.

"What's happened? Are you okay?" Rising panic lingers at the back of his cool tone.

"No," I cry. "I need you. I'm outside the bathroom beside the library. Over in the west wing."

"Hold tight. I'm coming to get you."

I press my back against the wall, letting my bag drop to the floor, as I hug my arms gently around myself and attempt to get my emotions under control. But I'm shaken. The assault was vicious, and I have done nothing to deserve it. Nicole Chastain is right up there with Carlo Greco. Both are cruel monsters with no heart or soul. What a pity I couldn't matchmake the pair and let Carlo unleash all his depravity on her.

Approaching footsteps pull me out of my head, and I lift my head, spying Leo and Brando running toward me through blurry eyes.

"Jesus, fuck, Natalia." Leo's eyes flood with concern as he drags his gaze up and down my hunched-over body. "What the hell happened?"

"I was jumped in the bathroom. They kicked me when I was down. My ribs might be broken."

"Who did this to you?" he asks as Brando reaches down to grab my bag.

"It was Nicole Chastain." My tears dry up as anger resurfaces. "I want to make her pay."

Leo's eyes darken instantly. "Don't you worry. That fucking bitch *will* pay for this."

Chapter 13

LEO

NATALIA'S DELICATE FLORAL scent wraps around me as I carry her through the empty school hallway toward the car. I hold her as close as I can without risking injury, but I want to bundle her in my arms and never ever let her go. Brando went on ahead to pull our car up to the curb at the bottom of the steps.

The sound of many raised voices can be heard as we pass by the principal's office, and it seems that little bitch wasted no time ratting Nat out. Natalia has been filling me in as we walk, telling me about the campaign of terror Nicole has been waging against her for weeks.

I feel sick that I fucked her. It was a mistake I instantly regretted. Guilt lays heavy on my heart as I hear how she's been taunting Natalia, and I know part of it is my fault because I gave her the ammunition she used to push my *dolcezza* to her breaking point.

Brando opens the back door of the car, and I carefully set Natalia inside. "I'll be there in a minute. Try and get comfortable," I say, knowing it's probably impossible if her ribs are bruised or broken. Nicole better pray they aren't broken because I will snap her conniving neck and bury her six feet under if they are. "Where is Mateo?" I ask Brando.

"He's on his way. He said to sit tight. He cursed up a storm when I told him."

"Good." I'm relying on my best friend to go nuclear so we can fix this once and for all. "Can you run to the corner store and see if they have ice. I'll stay with Nat."

"Of course," he says, striding away.

I slip into the car beside Natalia, hating how pale her skin is, her brow dotted with little beads of sweat, and her hair tangled and messy. I hate seeing her in so much pain. "Brando has gone to find ice, and Mateo is on his way. He is going to talk to the principal and smooth things over because your papa is at the hospital with Rosa. Then we will deal with Nicole."

"It wasn't just her," she pants, trying to sit up a little straighter. Pain flares across her face, and I wish I could take it away.

"We'll get the others too. Give me the names, and we'll ensure they suffer for the part they played." Gently, I tuck her hair behind her ears, removing a handkerchief from my pants pocket and wiping her clammy brow. "I need to see the damage," I softly say. "Can I unbutton your shirt to look?"

Her big blue eyes look too trusting as she nods. With careful movements, I unbutton her white school blouse, hoping she can't see how my fingers are shaking as I slowly reveal her body to me. I'm instantly appalled at the devastation on her skin. Bruising is already appearing in several places on her torso, mainly centered around her ribs on both sides, but there's an impression of a shoeprint on her chest and discoloration on her stomach. I stuff a hand in my mouth to strangle my agony, squeezing my eyes shut as I struggle to get a grip on myself. The urge to remove the rifle from the trunk and head into the school to gun down those bitches is riding me hard.

"Leo." Her melodious voice is a sensual caress over my skin, helping to ground me. "Do I look that bad?" she whispers.

My eyes snap open at that. "*Dolcezza.*" I take her hand in mine. "You look beautiful. Like always. But I cannot stand to see what those cunts have done to you. I want to go in there and riddle them with bullets until they stop breathing."

"I wouldn't oppose that plan," she says, and I can't tell if she's serious or not.

I shake my head. "No, *dolcezza.*" I bring her hand to my mouth, planting a kiss on her warm skin. "Don't say that. I know you are hurting, but that's not who you are."

"There is more darkness inside me than you realize, Leo. More hatred than I ever thought I was capable of feeling."

I don't like hearing that, but it's naïve to think she is immune to the darkness that is an inherent part of the world we inhabit. And I'm not just talking about the criminal underworld. All over America, kids are gunning one another down over stupid petty shit. It's an ugly world we live in, and I wish I could shield Natalia from the worst excesses to keep her light and her goodness intact. "I don't want that for you. You deserve better."

"I deserve you," she whispers, peering longingly at me through her gorgeous blue peepers.

"You deserve better than me, and we both know it."

"Kiss me," she whispers, threading her fingers in mine. "Please, Leo. Help me to forget this pain even if only for a minute."

This is emotional blackmail at its finest. But I can't refuse her anything in this moment. Very carefully, I maneuver myself over her, keeping my body away from hers so I don't hurt her by accident. She closes her eyes as my face draws near, and I take a moment to savor the view. Her long, thick black lashes fan across her olive-toned skin, as my fingers sweep across her smooth high cheekbones. Her plump lips part, and air trickles out of her mouth as her chest heaves in anticipation. I avoid the temptation to stare at her beautiful tits behind her white lace bra because I will never take advantage of her.

Natalia is more than the sum of how she looks. She is inherently beautiful in a way few people are. It's her goodness and the light that clings to her persona that always draws me in. Her fiery personality and sense of humor only add to the overall package.

I know I will live the rest of my life and never come close to finding anyone like her.

Because she is one of a kind. One in a million. A deity among mortal women.

I'm pretty sure I will love her until my dying breath because there is a part of me that believes we are meant for one another.

Only this world has other plans.

"Leo." Her eyes blink open. "Please."

"You don't have to beg, *dolcezza*. Queens never beg. Always remember," I say, running my thumb along her lush lower lip.

"I love you," she says, and my heart aches. I want to tell her I love her too, but it will only bring us a world of pain.

My lips slant over hers, and I kiss her tenderly, making love to her mouth as I wish I could hold her in my arms and feel the warmth of her curves against my body. But I have to be careful with her body and her heart. Her fingers wind into my hair, and I moan into her mouth as blood rushes to my cock, hardening it almost instantly. I keep my distance so she doesn't feel it, but if she looked down, she would see what she does to me. How easily she turns me on.

We kiss for a while, and it's the most amazing experience just being with her like this. Kissing with no expectation. Just enjoying the taste of her on my lips and my tongue, knowing I am helping to distract her from her pain.

Reluctantly, I break apart, a few minutes later. "We need to stop. Brando will be back any minute and Mateo could arrive at any time."

She puckers her lips, and I kiss her one last time. "God, I could kiss you for hours. Kisses have never felt so good."

"It's because you love me," she says, and I detect some of her confidence returning. "You don't have to say it for me to know, Leo. I know I'm not alone in this. I see it in your eyes. I feel it in the way you kiss me. I bask in it by the way you protect me."

"*Amore mio*, let's not torture ourselves."

She nods in understanding, and sadness surrounds her like a shroud. "I live for these moments with you, Leo. Where we can escape reality and I get to pretend this is what my life would be like if I was allowed to choose you."

Her words gut me, and I feel the same. I place my hand over my heart. "In every lifetime, I would choose you, Natalia." Taking her hand, I place it over my heart. "We may be apart, *dolcezza*, but you will always be the only woman I love."

Tears pool in her eyes, spilling onto her cheeks. "I will never love another man like I love you, Leo. I know you think I'm young and I'll change my mind, but I won't. I know what I want. I know who I love. It's you. Always you."

The weight of this conversation bears down on both of us. I caress her smooth cheek, aglow under the adoration in her eyes. She looks at me like I'm her everything, and my heart swells behind my chest. "I want you to know that shit Nicole said to you was crap. I fucked her once, and it was over fast. She was a lousy lay, and I was so bored I fell asleep straightaway." That must have been when she took the photo. Something else I want to string her up for. "When I woke in the middle of the night, I couldn't get out of there quick enough. She means nothing to me, Natalia, and I wish I had never touched her. I wish I could erase the memory and that she hadn't said any of that shit to you because I hate she used me to hurt you. I will never forgive myself for that."

"I forgive you," she says without hesitation. "And I'm not stupid. I know there have been other girls. I know there will be more. I hate it. I hate the thought of anyone else putting their hands on you, but I have no right to ask anything of you."

"Like I hate the thought of that asshole touching you." When I saw his hand on her thigh at dinner yesterday, it took every ounce of willpower I possess not to extract my gun and shoot him at the table. How fucking dare he touch her. I suspect he did something later, but Natalia refuses to tell me. I shared my suspicions with Mateo, and he is going to talk to her. We agreed that one of us will be in a room with her and him at all times so the creep has no opportunity to touch her or threaten her.

"You and me both," she says.

Silence descends. There is nothing more to be said on the subject of Carlo Greco.

The door opens, and Brando slides behind the wheel. I quickly close Nat's shirt over her exposed torso. "Got some." He turns around, handing me two medium-sized bags of ice. "Are you okay, Natalia?" he asks, concern filling his face.

"It hurts, but I'm okay. Thanks for the ice." She smiles at him, and his eyes drill into mine for a few seconds before he turns back around, minding his own business. It's one of the things I like about Brando. He doesn't get involved in shit that doesn't concern him.

Using my knife, I cut a wide strip off the end of my shirt, ignoring Nat's protests. Then I wrap the torn shirt around the ice bags and place one on either side of her ribs. Taking her hands, I place them on the bags. "Keep still and hold them there." I carefully lift her legs up onto the seat. Rolling up her school blazer, I tuck it into a ball behind her head, and that's as comfortable as I can make her. Mateo will probably blow a gasket when he sees her exposed skin, but I can't ice her ribs without leaving her shirt open.

And speak of the devil.

The back door swings open, and Mateo pokes his head in. His eyes narrow to dark pinpoints as his gaze scans his sister's injuries. "*La puttana*!" he hisses. He's immediately enraged. So much that he doesn't rip me a new one for her state of undress.

"You need to get in there, stat," I say. "Those cunts have been in the principal's office for a while."

"I will handle it." He gestures for me to get out so he can climb in beside his sister. We swap places, and I lean against the open car door, unwilling to take my eyes off her for even a second. "I'm so sorry, Natalia," he says. "You should have told me she was giving you shit." I had messaged him en route summarizing what Nat had told me.

"You think I could come to you when it was you sleeping with her that made me a target?"

Mateo has the decency to look ashamed, and I know how he feels. I'm in it with him. Mateo sighs. "I should never have touched her, knowing she was in school with you. I'm sorry. But that was even more reason to tell me."

It's rare to find Mateo so honest and remorseful. Mostly, it only happens around his sister. He loves her so much, even if he often doesn't show it in the way he should. But he genuinely adores her. I know he would get her out of the arrangement with Greco if he could. I know he worries about her being married to him. His hands are tied. A lot like Angelo's are. Though I doubt he loses much sleep over it, even if he cherishes his little girl more than most dons.

"I don't always want to be the weak girl running to her brother for help."

"I'm your brother. It's my job to protect you, and I have failed you." He exhales heavily, his sigh laden with resignation, before he leans down, kissing her brow. "Take some pain meds and try to sleep." He hands her a bottle of water and some pain pills, before getting out of the car.

"That bitch is dead," he grits out, flexing his knuckles. "I know we don't touch women, but that whore deserves to die a gruesome death for what she has done to my sister."

"I agree, but it's not worth the risk. Angelo isn't the only father with pull at this school." Nicole's father is a wealthy businessman with several ties to local, powerful politicians. If his daughter was suddenly found murdered, questions would be asked. "Let's rough her up a bit and scare the fuck out of her so she doesn't even look at Natalia again."

"Watch over her," he says, glancing over my shoulder. His gaze narrows with familiar suspicion. "And keep your fucking hands to yourself."

I flip him the bird. As if I would take advantage of his sister in that condition.

When I slide back into the car, as Brando leaves to go with Mateo, Natalia is already asleep. I prop her feet on my lap, removing her shoes gently so I don't wake her.

I stare at her, for longer than is socially acceptable, admiring her effortless beauty and the strength that emanates from her in waves, my heart throbbing with longing. I want to take care of her. To nurse her back to health. To fuss over her and let her know how much she is loved. But that can't be my role. It won't ever be, and the thought saddens me.

To distract myself, I attend to calls on my phone until Mateo and Brando reappear.

Mateo opens the back door, his features softening when he looks at his sister. "She won't be expelled. The other four girls are being kicked out, but I couldn't get them to agree to expel Nicole. The whore covered her tracks well, and Daddy is a big donor."

Well, shit. "You have a plan?"

"Hell, yeah." A smirk tugs up the corners of his mouth. "Take Natalia home, and get Brando to watch over her. I'll call the doc, and then you can meet me at the address I send you. Let's teach this little bitch a lesson she won't soon forget."

Chapter 14

NATALIA

I'M DOZING IN bed when my brother's signature rap sounds on my bedroom door, rousing me fully. "Come in," I croak, wincing as I move to sit upright in bed.

"You look like shit," Mateo says, striding through the door, carrying a tray.

"Lovely to see you too," I deadpan, biting the inside of my cheek as the pain around my ribs throbs.

He sets the tray down on my bedside table, helping to prop me up against a mountain of pillows in front of my headboard. Then he carefully sets the tray on my lap. "Mama made you chicken noodle soup. She told me what the doc said. I'm glad they didn't break any of your ribs, but bruised ribs are painful. You will need to rest up a lot, sis."

"I don't need another lecture." Mama and Papa were furious when Leo brought me home and they found out what had happened. Leo assured Papa he and Mateo had it under control, and Papa looked proud that Mateo had stepped in and handled the situation. The doctor came then with a portable X-ray unit, checking nothing was broken. I am badly bruised, and my ribs ache like a bitch, even after swallowing some heavy-duty pain meds, but it could be worse.

"What happened?"

"It's handled," Mateo says, flexing his hands, and my gaze flits to his torn knuckles and the hint of blood still hiding under his fingernails.

"Tell me. I'm not a little kid anymore. I need to know what I'm facing when I return to school next week." The doc has signed me out for the rest of the week, and I didn't protest. Frankie will come over every day after school with my homework and assignments so I don't fall behind. My GPA is good, and I don't want it to slip. Though it's probably an impossible dream, I still intend to apply to NYU to study medicine.

"I know you're not," my brother says, tucking my hair back off my face. "If I shelter you, it's only because I care."

I clasp his strong, warm hand in mine. "I know you do, Mateo, and I love you for it. But I need you to stop sheltering me. I will be by myself before too long, and I need to be prepared for the world I'm stepping into. I need you to tell me the worst of it, and I want you or Leo to teach me self-defense." I need to be able to protect myself from my future husband because I know what he plans to do to me.

Slowly, he nods, and his Adam's apple bobs in his throat. "Okay, *tesoro*. I will tell you what I can, and I will speak to Leo about training you after your ribs have healed."

"Thank you." My answering smile is grateful.

Mateo lifts the spoon, closing my hand around it. "You eat. I'll talk."

I take a sip of the delicious homemade chicken noodle soup, groaning as my taste buds explode in my mouth. Mama is the best cook. If her life had turned out different, she could have opened a restaurant.

"The four girls who attacked you have been expelled, and we paid them a little visit, in case they decided to cause more trouble. We burned their cars, knocked their fathers around a bit, and threatened their businesses." He smirks. "They were all shitting their pants. You won't hear from them again."

"And Nicole?" I ask in between mouthfuls of the delicious soup. I want her to pay as much as the others.

"Unfortunately, I couldn't get her expelled. She was too clever."

"I know that's why she didn't join in when the others were kicking me."

"Her father is a successful businessman, and he heavily donates to the school. He was arguing to have you expelled, on the grounds you started the physical fight, but the principal is no dumbass. She knows a setup when she sees one. And she knows who we are. Papa is very charitable with his donations too. Plus, the doctor's report detailed the savage beating you took, which was clearly one-sided. She knows this was Nicole's doing, but she can't be seen to pick sides, so you are both suspended this week."

I shrug, because I wouldn't have been attending school anyway, even if it pisses me off that my pristine record is now tarnished. But that's the least of my worries. "She won't stop coming after me."

Mateo smirks. "Oh, trust me. She won't even breathe funny at you."

"What did you do?"

His smirk widens, and he runs a hand through his dark hair, sending waves tumbling over his strong brow. His blue eyes glimmer, and I know he gets a thrill out of threatening people. I should probably be scared of my brother because I know his capacity for violence and cruelty, but it's never been directed at me. He's a product of our environment, our upbringing, and I won't hate him for doing what he has to do to survive and thrive. Even if I deplore the things he must do as a made man. "I always get insurance, and it came in handy now."

"Are you saying…" I consider his implication. Mateo grins. "Ugh, that is gross. And a serious invasion of those girls' privacy if you are recording them having sex with you without their permission."

He shrugs. "It served a purpose with Nicole. I had it doctored to hide my identity, and then I sent it to her father and told him if he didn't keep her in line I would release it to the school, all over the internet and the dark web, along with her contact details. Every fucking perv would be hounding her, and her reputation would be ruined. Her father can't afford the scandal, so he agreed."

I arch a brow in surprise.

"What?" He frowns.

"That was a smart way of handling it, but it's not what I was expecting."

"Are you disappointed?" he asks, his frown deepening.

"Maybe it means I'm a bad person, but I wouldn't have minded you roughing her up a little." Though Nicole didn't participate in the assault, she was the orchestrator, and I think it'll be a long time before I get the image of her gloating face out of my mind. I'm in agony from the damage they inflicted, and I would have liked those girls to feel some pain too.

Mateo fixes me with a disturbed look. "I understand why you'd want that, but I'm not sure I like my little sister thinking such dark thoughts."

I roll my eyes. "I have the same blood flowing through my veins, Matty. Don't act so surprised."

His eyes lower to my soup, and I scoop another spoonful up as Mateo continues. "If it helps you to feel better, we both wanted to beat the shit out of the bitch, but we would never have gotten away with it. Her father has connections within the police and the political system, and it could have caused some issues for Papa, so we had to be smarter about this."

I sense Leo's shrewd mind all over this plan, but I don't say anything, unwilling to insult my brother and hurt his feelings.

He leans in, grinning. "We left all of them with a permanent reminder of this day." He waggles his brows. "Trust me, none of them will give you any trouble ever again."

Relief rushes through me. Awkwardly, I lean forward, hugging my brother over my tray. My ribs protest the motion, but I'm too overwhelmed with love to care. "Thank you, Matty. I love you."

"I love you too." He kisses the top of my head. "In the future, if anyone gives you shit, including that piece of trash you're engaged to, you need to tell me."

"I will," I say, glad I'm not looking him in the face as I lie.

Mateo eases out of our embrace, cupping my face and peering deep into my eyes. "I need you to promise me, *tesoro*."

"I promise," I say, even though I know I will most likely not be able to keep my word.

"I'm going to talk to Papa about him again. See if there is any way he can get the marriage delayed while we work at finding something we can use to end the contract permanently."

Tears prick my eyes. "Really?"

Pain shimmers in his eyes. "Don't get your hopes up, Nat." He smooths his fingers over my cheek. "It's all but a done deal, and this is a long shot, but Leo and I talked about it earlier, and we are going to put a guy on Carlo. Find out what shit he's up to, and I know there is lots. If we can discover something he is doing which jeopardizes the business arrangement between us and the Grecos, Papa will listen. But it would have to be something concrete for Papa to have grounds to terminate the arrangement, and Greco is a sneaky shit, so we might not be able to outsmart him."

"But you're going to try." I swipe at the tears spilling out of my eyes. "That means so much to me, Matty. Thank you."

"You're my sister. I would go to the ends of the earth for you."

"Be careful."

He stands, peering down at me. "You too, sis." Silence engulfs us as he stares at me, looking like he's contemplating saying more. Mateo drills me with a knowing look, speaking after a couple moments of tense silence. "I know you love him, Nat. I suspect he loves you too." My heart thumps behind my chest cavity.

Are we so obvious that others can tell?

"But that shit can't happen." He pats my cheek. "Leave this up to me. If there is a way to get you out of the marriage to Greco, I will try my hardest to pull it off. You and Leo starting something could fuck it all up, so you need to stay away from him. It's too risky for both of you."

"I understand, Matty."

"Good." Crouching down, he kisses my cheek. "Finish your soup. Then sleep."

"No, Mama," I sob the following afternoon as the four of us sit in our living room, discussing the findings from the hospital tests. "Papa." I turn glassy, pleading eyes on my father. "There has to be something you can do! Specialists we can hire to cure her?"

"I would hire all the specialists in the world if it meant my Rosa would be saved," Papa says, curling his arm tighter around Mama's shoulders. "But it's too late, *principessa*. It's stage four and at a very advanced stage."

Ovarian cancer is known as the silent killer because the symptoms are often mistaken for other conditions or illnesses and it is often too late before a proper diagnosis is delivered. Which is exactly what has happened in Mama's case.

"What about chemotherapy?" Mateo asks, the strain clear as day on his face.

"Oh, *ragazzo mio*. It is too late for treatment and I don't want to spend my last weeks or months too sick to spend time with my family." Mama gets up, coming around to sit on the couch in between me and Mateo. In turn, she kisses our cheeks. "We all die eventually." A serene sort of calmness settles over her beautiful face. "My time has just come a little earlier than expected."

"How can you be so calm?" I cry out with tears streaming down my face. "Why aren't you angry?"

"I cannot change the outcome, *cuore mio*. Battling a certainty is a futile exercise. I have accepted this is the fate of my God and he has given us time to say goodbye."

"No, Mama." I sob, throwing my arms around her, ignoring the throbbing ache in my ribs. "I don't want to say goodbye. I love you. You can't leave us."

Mama hugs me close, whispering in my ear, promising me I will be all right. Papa stares straight ahead, a shellshocked look appearing at intervals in between his stoic expression. Mateo sits forward with his elbows propped on his knees and his bowed head in his hands.

"I need you to be strong, my love," Mama says, smoothing her hand up and down my hair. "You will be the woman of the house now, and I need your help to make arrangements."

A strangled cry travels up my throat, leading to another bout of crying, and then Mateo is crying too, and Mama bundles him into her other side, hugging him and whispering reassurances in his ear. My eyes lock on my father's face, and I'm startled to see tears filling his eyes.

I have never seen my papa cry, and he rarely gets emotional.

A shared understanding filters between us as Mama remains the only strong one, her assurances ringing out confidently in the room. But as Papa and I silently communicate, we know it's not the truth.

Everything isn't all right.

And nothing will ever be the same again.

Chapter 15

NATALIA

"COME SIT," MAMA says, her voice fragile and the movement of her hand sluggish as she pats the space beside her on the bed. It's been one month since her diagnosis, and she's deteriorating rapidly, much to our dismay. I begged my parents to let me be homeschooled for the rest of the semester, but Mama won't hear of it. She is insisting we lead our normal lives, and she complains if we fuss over her too much.

I race up the stairs to her bedroom every day after school, eager to spend as much time with her as I can. Every Thursday, I attend a dance class at a prestigious dance school in NYC. I used to love it, but I hate it now, as it delays me from seeing Mama. Mateo and Brando took me there today because Leo was reading to Mama.

My heart swells when my eyes find his. He's seated in a chair beside Mama's bed with a book open on his lap. Every day, Leo finds time to sit with her, and if I didn't already really fucking love him, his tender care of my dying mother would seal the deal.

He doesn't protest as she makes him read numerous classic love stories from her weathered collection. He brings her flowers from the garden and homemade treats from his mama, Paulina. His thirteen-year-old sister, Giuliana, has taken up cross-stitch lately, and she stitched a beautiful angels picture. At the bottom, it reads "Moms are angels," and the meaning is crystal clear. Mateo got it framed, and it's now on the table beside Mama's bed.

"I can take over," I tell Leo, reaching for the worn copy of *A Room with a View*.

"Read the last part before you go, Leonardo," Mama says, tapping a bony finger to the page.

Kicking off my shoes, I crawl up onto the bed, lying down beside her. Her fingers ghost over my hair as I snuggle carefully into her side.

Leo clears his throat, his eyes locked on mine for a second before his gaze lowers to the page. His deep, warm, husky voice is like a sensual caress as I close my eyes and listen to him recite the words written by E.M. Forster.

"'It isn't possible to love and part. You will wish that it was. You can transmute love, ignore it, muddle it, but you can never pull it out of you. I know by experience that the poets are right: love is eternal.'"

My eyes fly open, discovering Leo's gaze locked on mine. His chest heaves, and the urge to fling myself into his arms is almost insurmountable. The words embed deep, and I feel them worm their way into my soul. I have never believed in something as wholly as I believe in that sentiment.

Tension bleeds between us in the emotionally charged space, and the only sound is Mama's crotchety breathing.

"Read this last one," Mama says, sitting up and taking the book from Leo's hand. She flips to one of the pages she has marked, handing it back to him and pointing her finger at an underlined passage. "Go on, Leo," she prompts when he silently reads the quote without speaking.

His voice is all choked up as he reads. "'"I taught him," he quavered, "to trust in love. I said: "when love comes, that is reality." I said: "Passion does not blind. No. Passion is sanity, and the woman you love, she is the only person you will ever really understand."""

Leo stands abruptly, avoiding my gaze. "I need to go." He places the book on the bed beside me, his eyes briefly meeting mine. The pain in my heart is reflected in his gaze, and I wish I could comfort him. I don't know what Mama is playing at, but she clearly has an agenda. Leo leans down, pressing a gentle kiss to her cheek. "I will see you tomorrow, Mama Rosa."

"Remember what I said," Mama tells him, grabbing his face with more strength than she usually possesses. "You're a good man,

Leonardo. I love you."

"I love you too," he rasps, tears clouding his vision. "Until tomorrow." His eyes move to mine as I pull myself upright in the bed. "I will see you in the morning, Natalia."

I nod, watching him leave with an ache in my chest.

"He loves you," Mama says after he has closed the door. I turn my head to face her, my eyes popping wide. "And you love him." She pats my hand, smiling softly. "I know he is the boy you have been talking to me about."

I gulp over the lump wedged in my throat. I have confided in Mama a few times this past year about my fears for this arranged marriage and the depth of my feelings for another man. I didn't mention Leo by name for fear she would feel obligated to tell Papa. But I should have known Mama would work it out.

"You can't tell Papa!" I blurt. "I don't want him to hurt Leo."

"Oh, Natalia. *Cuore mio*." She pulls my head to her shoulder. "A woman should never keep secrets from her husband, but secrets of the heart, they are different." She runs her hand through my hair, and it's wonderfully soothing. "Listen to me."

I tilt my head up, staring into her face.

"I love your papa. He is a good man. A good husband. He has treated me well and loved me as best as he can. He doesn't parade his whores in front of me or society, respecting me enough to conceal that truth."

A shocked gasp rips from my mouth. "Papa has whores?" I'm not completely naïve. I know most made men have affairs and screw around, but Papa has always idolized Mama in a way that is not usual, so I thought he was different.

"Every made man takes whores, Natalia. It is the way of the *mafioso*. Carlo will sleep with other women. You need to go into your marriage with your eyes wide open. My mama didn't prepare me, and now I have run out of time to adequately prepare you."

I sit up with my back against the headboard, twisting around so I'm facing my mother.

"You know how to cook and clean, which is a trait that is rare for a woman of your position in our society. You are educated and intelligent, and you have been encouraged to be independent while remaining within the confines of our rules and traditions. The one thing I haven't taught you about is love, and I wish I had more time, but we don't."

Tears prick her eyes. "I was young and beautiful like you at seventeen. I too had a secret love." She takes the book from my hand, clutching it to her chest. "Like Lucy, in this book, I too went on holiday to Italy and found the love of my life. My own George."

Mama's grandparents lived in Italy, and she vacationed there every summer from the time she was thirteen until she was seventeen. When her parents retired to Italy, we spent a few summers there visiting both sets of grandparents. It was usually just Mama, Mateo, and me, as Papa had to work. Mama enjoyed showing us around, pointing out all the places she used to go as a young woman, but she never mentioned anything about a secret love.

"I had already been promised to your father, and our wedding date was set. Angelo scared me. He was older and more experienced than me. Already the underboss and a powerful man with many enemies. I didn't think I could ever love him, even though he always treated me with profound kindness, because I was so in love with Lorenzo."

"What happened with Lorenzo?" I'm instantly curious to learn more about this side of Mama's past I know nothing about.

"He knew who I was and that I was destined for another man. It didn't stop us from falling in love, but we never acted on it. Me, out of fear of repercussions, and him out of respect for the traditions. He was my best friend, and we spent every moment together while I stayed with my grandparents. Not being able to touch him or kiss him the way I wanted was torture, but being apart from him was worse."

"You didn't even kiss?"

Sadness crests over her face as she shakes her head. "No. We came close a lot, but one of us always held back." She palms my face. "I love your papa, Natalia, and I have had a good life. I have a beautiful home and two amazing children. I have not wanted for anything and I have only one regret." She pauses to draw a deep breath. "That I never gave in to my passion with Lorenzo. That I never allowed myself to embrace a love that was so pure."

"Mama," I gasp, shocked to hear her say such things, because it's so unexpected. "It would've been risky."

"Love is worth the risk," she says. "I wish I could tell you you don't have to marry that monster. I wish there was a way your papa could extract you from the contract, but there isn't, *tesorino*."

"I hate him, Mama," I whisper, leaning into her touch. "It won't be like the marriage you have with Papa. He wants to hurt me. To own me and do what he wants to me."

"He won't get away with mistreating you, Natalia. That is not tolerated. Wives are revered. Your father is raising his concerns with Maximo Greco, and he has already agreed that, when you marry Carlo, your bodyguard will go with you."

"What?!" Horror engulfs me.

"Not Leo." Mama is quick to reassure me. "I would never inflict such pain on my daughter, and he's too valuable to Papa. Brando will go with you. He will help to keep you safe, and I know Leo and Mateo are teaching you self-defense and how to use a gun. It will be up to you to keep yourself protected in that man's house, and I know you can do it. You're a fighter, Natalia. Carlo will not break your spirit because you won't let him."

"I will try," I say, but I'm not confident in my ability to tame the monster.

"Don't make my mistakes, Natalia," she whispers, struggling to keep her eyes open. "Don't miss out on the opportunity to experience true love and passion."

She cannot be saying what I think she's saying. "Mama? You don't mean…"

"Let yourself love him, Natalia, for however long you have together. Let Leonardo's love strengthen you before you are forced to give it all up to fulfill your duty. Be selfish now. Take something for yourself and be happy. On dark days, let the memory of his love bolster you and give you the courage to keep fighting."

I'm so stunned I can't speak for several seconds. This is not what Mama has said the previous times we spoke about my feelings for this other man. "Why are you saying this now when before you spoke to me about accepting my fate and making peace with it?"

"Life is too short to have regrets, and wasted opportunities will haunt you for the rest of your life. I wasn't brave enough or mature enough to do what I should have done, but you are, Natalia."

"What if we get caught?" I whisper.

"Don't get caught." She waggles her brows.

I bark out a laugh. "You say that like it's easy."

"It's not, but you are both clever, and he's your bodyguard now. He has an excuse to be around you." A buoyant smile graces her elegant mouth.

"Did you have something to do with that?" I inquire.

Her eyes light up. "I might have suggested Leo to your papa."

"Mama." I'm overwhelmed with love for my mother, and resenting God all over again for doing this to her. For taking her from us. Gently, I circle my arms around her neck. "I am so grateful to have you as my mother. I hope one day I can be as amazing a woman as you are. You will always be my greatest inspiration."

"You will always be my greatest achievement." She presses frail lips to my brow as a yawn slips from her mouth. Mama spends a lot of time sleeping these days. "I am so proud of you, Natalia, and wherever I am, I will always be watching over you."

"I love you, Mama," I choke out over a sob.

"I love you too." She tilts my chin up. "Be happy, *cuore mio*, but be careful too. Only take measured risks, and caution your heart to accept that it is only temporary. Make every moment count, and you will have those memories with you forever."

Chapter 16

LEO

MAMA ROSA HELD on for another month before passing away in her sleep, two nights ago, surrounded by her family. It's three weeks until Christmas, and already the ground outside the Mazzone mansion is coated in a fine layer of snow. Soft white flakes rain down on the guests as they arrive from the church and graveyard to pay their last respects to a woman who was a pillar of our community and the heart of this family.

"Poor Natalia," my mama says, coming up alongside me, as I stand by the long buffet table, laden with a glorious feast of Italian food.

My *dolcezza* is never far from my sight. Watching her fall apart in Mateo's arms at the graveyard was almost too much to bear. The need to comfort her almost overwhelming.

"Losing a parent is never easy, especially when you are on the cusp of major life changes."

"They were as close as you and Giuliana," I say, watching Nat as she stares off into space on the couch, situated between her brother and my little sister. Giuliana is snuggled into her side with her arms wrapped around Nat, looking sadder than I have ever seen her.

Angelo is in front of the fireplace, the glow of the roaring fire surrounding him like a fiery halo, as he speaks with Agosti and Maximo Greco. Carlo skulks in a corner with two of his *soldati*, his eyes burning a hole in the side of my head. Either I'm being too obvious or he knows something. Neither thought is comforting, so I tear my gaze from Natalia and focus on my mother.

"I think it's why this is hitting your sister so hard." Mom absently rubs my arm while watching her only daughter try to comfort the love of my life.

"She was crying in her bed last night," my brother admits, coming up to us with our father at his side. Frank turned sixteen recently—three days before my little sister turned fourteen—and though he's had a growth spurt these past few months, he's still a head shorter than my six-foot-two-inch frame. "I talked with her. She is terrified of something happening to either of you," he says.

"Your sister is a sensitive soul," Papa says, his expression melting as he stares at our little *principessa*.

"She has a big heart," Mama adds, leaning into my father as he slides his arm around her shoulders. She tilts her face up to his. "Joel, we should talk with her tonight."

"We will, *amore mio*." My father leans down, kissing her tenderly, and a lump forms in my throat.

Frank and I exchange looks.

My parents have a kind of love that is most unusual within the *mafioso*. They are both from Italian American families, but where Papa's family has been involved with *la famiglia* from the birth of the organization in America, Mama's family has not. Her parents were not keen on her marrying Joel Messina, fearing what it meant for her life. But my parents were deeply in love, and nothing else mattered to Mama.

As I look at them, still so in love after twenty-six years of marriage, I can't help but visualize me and Natalia in the future, staring at one another with the same adoring looks on our faces.

Reality returns, and pain slams into me, punching the air from my lungs and almost knocking me off my feet.

I could see it.

Nat and I being together for eternity.

Loving one another with the same fierce devotion as my parents.

But that is not a reality that will ever exist. For either one of us. She is already promised to another, and with my ambitious plans to climb the ranks within the organization, I know my choice might not be my own either.

"Hey." Mateo approaches with his hands shoved deep in his pockets, grief etched all over his face. "Papa wants us to join him in the study."

My eyes instantly bounce between Natalia and Carlo. The latter smirks, cocking his head to one side, and I want to rip out his insides and make him eat them. "I can't leave Natalia."

"Brando will watch her," Mateo says, his dead eyes lacking their usual spark.

"We will ensure she is protected," Papa adds, clamping a hand on my shoulder.

"We are here for you." Mama pulls Mateo into her arms. "For you and Natalia. Angelo too. Whatever you need, you let us know." Easing back, she clasps his cheeks, pressing a kiss to his brow. "Our home is your home. Always."

Mateo has been a firm feature in our household for years, in the same way everyone is familiar with me here. We have been thick as thieves from the moment we met as six-year-olds, and our families are extensions of one another.

"Thank you, Paulina." Mateo kisses her cheeks in a daze. "It means a lot to us." He thrusts out his hand toward my father. "Congratulations on your promotion, capo. It is well deserved and long overdue."

My father beams proudly as he shakes Mateo's hand. "It is my honor to serve your family." My father nods respectfully. "I have the utmost admiration and respect for your father, and you will make a wonderful don in years to come." I don't know if my father truly believes that, but no one could doubt the sincerity on his face.

"Come on. Let's not keep the boss waiting." I jerk my head to one side, casting one last glance at Natalia before we leave the room.

"I hear Frank did well last weekend," Mateo says, keeping his head low as we walk the hallway toward Angelo's study.

"So it seems." Pride laces through my words. Frank was initiated at thirteen, like we all were, and he has gradually been learning the ropes. His capo assigned him to his first serious mission last weekend, on a crew supervising a large drug shipment from Las Vegas. There was an attempted hijack, and it turned violent, but Frank kept his cool, and we didn't lose a single man or the cargo.

"He is calm under pressure," Mateo remarks as we round the corner. "That is a good trait to have in our line of work."

I nod, knowing my brother is more controlled than either of us. "All he has wanted, his whole life, is to be a *soldato* like me and Pops."

Mateo stops outside his father's study, lifting his head to look at me. There's a raw vulnerability in his expression I don't think I have ever seen. "I couldn't imagine doing what I have to do without you, Leo. You're my brother in every way that counts." In an unexpected move, he yanks me into a hug.

I hold him firmly, patting his back, choking back emotion. Mateo and I don't do this. We know what we mean to one another so it never needs to be said.

My best friend is in pain. Suffocating under agonizing grief, and he's cracked wide-open—bleeding and exposed—and I make a silent vow to be there for both Mazzone siblings. "I love you, man, and I'm here for you. Whatever you need. You and Natalia. It's yours."

"Do you think it's true?" he asks, breaking our hug. "What Papa said about me not being his only option?"

I don't want to hurt my friend, but I don't want to lie to him either. "I don't think your father would lie about that purely to back you into a corner. But if it's true, why has no one heard anything?" Illegitimate heirs are usually heavily guarded and widely known, unless Angelo has kept his other son—or sons—hidden away for a reason.

"I want to find him."

"If he exists and your father has kept him a secret all these years, I doubt there is anything you or I could do to discover his identity, but if you want to try, I'm in." I would never leave Mateo to do this alone.

He nods slowly, looking troubled as he stares off into space. "I can't believe she's gone," he whispers after a few silent beats, rubbing at his red eyes. "I'm terrified what this means. She was our rock. The beating heart of our family. Nat is falling apart. Papa is putting on a brave face, but he's lost too." He lifts his head up, thrusting his shoulders back. "I can't crumple. I need to be strong for them."

"You are. And I've got your back."

"Thanks, man." He grips my shoulder hard. "I meant what I said. This life only makes sense when you're my wingman. Someday, it will be the two of us in charge. We'll be running the show, because I could not do it without you."

"We'll be the stuff of legends." I smirk, waggling my brows. We both know I'm full of shit, but it's exactly what's needed to lighten the mood.

A familiar arrogant grin spreads over his mouth, and I'm relieved to see it. "Damn straight."

"Mateo!" Angelo calls out, obviously hearing us talking outside the door. "Come here."

We step into the room, closing the door after us. Angelo has his underboss, consigliere, and his most senior capo in the room. I'm surprised to see the new Accardi don in the room too.

Gino took over from his father when he suffered a massive heart attack and died last year. It's not unusual for heirs to ascend the throne at a young age; such is the nature of the world we live in. But all the other New York bosses—Mazzone, Greco, Maltese, DiPietro—are in their fifties and sixties, meaning Gino, at thirty-five, is the youngest don of the five families. A title I don't envy him.

"Take a seat." Angelo gestures toward the two empty seats in front of his desk, as he walks to the door and locks it. "We need to talk about the Barone."

"Have you finally confirmed who was behind the attack?" Mateo asks, sitting with his legs spread wide.

"Don Greco and I paid them a couple of visits," Angelo confirms, dropping into his seat behind the desk. "They are adamant they were hired by Accardi."

My eyes whip to Gino's. His pose is relaxed. The expression on his face is unconcerned. "You know that is untrue."

"I believe you." Angelo nods at the tall dark-haired Accardi don.

"Which means the Barone are lying," Agosti says.

"And so is Carlo," Mateo adds.

"Carlo may be telling the truth. At least what he believes to be true," Coppola, the consigliere, says.

"That is a possibility," Angelo agrees, scrubbing a hand over his chin.

"I don't trust him," Mateo says.

"You don't *like* him," Angelo replies. "Be careful your personal feelings don't interfere with business. Don't let it cloud your judgment."

Mateo clenches his jaw and grips the side of his chair. I know he's as desperate as I am to find something to pin on Carlo. We have had a guy trailing him for weeks, and he's come up empty-handed so far, which is frustrating.

Angelo sits up straighter, clearing his throat. "I made a request of Don Greco today," he informs his son. Pain flits across his face before he quickly composes it. "Your mama's last wish was that I try to get the wedding postponed until Natalia is twenty-one so she can attend NYU."

I manage to mask my surprise. Nat has confided in me about her plans to study medicine at NYU. She knows it's a pipe dream, especially because it would take years to become a qualified doctor and no don worth his salt would wait that long to marry his daughter off. But I know Natalia would be delighted to get any time at NYU, so I'm hoping Don Greco will agree.

"Why does she want to go to NYU?" Mateo asks, looking confused, and it's clear Nat hasn't confided in him.

"She wants to be a doctor," I explain, my gaze jumping from my friend to his father. "Having a qualified doctor within the family would be hugely beneficial."

"It would," Angelo agrees. "But it's no job for a woman."

I grind my teeth to the molars, wondering if *la famiglia* will ever move with the times.

"And there is no way I can get this wedding deferred indefinitely. I have no right to ask for it, except I'm appealing to Don Greco's humanity. Mama's death has hit my *principessa* hard, and she needs time to mourn."

"If he doesn't agree?" Mateo asks.

"Then she will be married next summer."

Silence descends because there is nothing else to be said on the subject that hasn't already been said.

"What are your plans for the Barone?" Agosti inquires, refocusing the discussion.

Angelo drums his fingers on top of his desk. "No one lies to my face and gets away with it. It's time we end this."

"They have been problematic for a while," Coppola supplies.

"Agreed. And while there has been no further attempt to kidnap my daughter, I don't believe the threat has passed. Removing the Barone from the equation will help me to sleep easier at night."

"I would like to talk to Don Barone before you take them out," Accardi says. "I want to know who put them up to this."

"I will agree to it with Don Greco, and I have reached out to DiPietro and Maltese. This needs a united show of strength to discourage any smaller *famiglie* from attempting to backfill the gap in the market."

"When will the attack take place?" the capo asks.

"We need two weeks to plan a coordinated attack. I will keep you updated. For now," Angelo says, standing, "we will keep this news contained to those who need to be aware. Our *soldati* will be informed a few days beforehand of a big mission, but the details will not be revealed until the night of the attack."

He must still be worried about moles within the organization. It is not unheard of and an ongoing concern, despite rigorous screening and surveillance. Curtailing the details to a small number of trusted men is smart. An operation of this size requires the utmost secrecy.

"Leave us," Angelo says, nodding at Accardi as the rest of us get up to leave.

"Leo?" he calls out as I move to follow Mateo. I turn around. "I would like it if you stayed here until after we have made our move. Brando too. Take turns guarding my daughter's room at night. I don't trust someone won't try to take advantage of our vulnerability at this time."

"We will guard her with our lives. No one is getting near Natalia."

Chapter 17

NATALIA

MY EYES STING, my throat is scraped raw, and the pain eviscerating my chest is so intense it feels like I'm dying. I cannot accept this. I cannot accept I will never see Mama again. I will never smell the lavender scent of her perfume, hear her tinkling laughter as we cook side by side, or feel the comforting warmth of her embrace. She will never whisper words of reassurance or impart her profound wisdom.

Choking sobs travel up my throat, and I cry into my sodden pillow as the door creaks open behind me. I'm too heartsick to even check who has slipped into my room and too broken to care about the state I'm in. The door closes and footsteps approach my bed as I bury my face in my pillow, sobbing my heart out.

"*Dolcezza*, don't cry," Leo whispers, climbing up on the bed behind me.

"It hurts so much, Leo," I rasp, leaning back into his warmth as he curls his body around mine.

"I know, baby." His arms wind around my waist as he holds me close. "I'm here for you."

My hands close over his as I sniffle, glancing at the clock through blurry eyes. It's almost three a.m., and I haven't slept a wink since I came to bed. "How are you still here?"

"We are sleeping here the next couple of weeks. Brando and me. To protect you around the clock."

"Why?" My spine stiffens, and I turn around in his arms. "Has something happened?"

He shakes his head as his arms band around my lower waist. "There have been no new threats. This is just precautionary. Enemies always strike when *la famiglia* is weakened. Your father wants to ensure there are extra safety measures in place to protect you."

"If it means you get to hold me every night, you won't hear me complaining."

He kisses the tip of my nose. "I don't think this is what your father had in mind, and we need to be careful. But I couldn't stand outside and listen to you crying any longer." He presses my head to his chest. "It's going to be okay, *dolcezza*." He dots kisses into my hair. "I will take care of you."

I snuggle into the warmth of his body, wrapping my arms around his back while listening to the steady rhythm of his heart. His citrusy scent envelops me in a comforting blanket, and I cling to him, siphoning some of his heat, letting it sink bone-deep. He smells like Leo. He feels like home, and his presence soothes some of my pain. "I love you," I whisper against his chest.

"I love you too," he whispers back, and my heart swells hearing those words from his lips for the first time.

Tears prick my eyes as I lift my head to stare at him, but this time, they are happy tears. "I wish I could stay in your arms forever." I slide my hands up his impressive chest.

"Brando is taking over at six," Leo whispers, sweeping hair off my face. "I will set my alarm to wake before then."

The thought of spending hours asleep in his arms is the most comforting thought I've had in a day filled with nightmares. "Kiss me first," I whisper, tipping my chin up.

He doesn't hesitate, leaning down to brush his mouth against mine. His kisses are sweet, feather-soft, and full of tender care. We cling to one another, kissing quietly and softly because Leo always knows what I need. This is not about desire. It's about comfort. We kiss a little more before we break apart, and I return my head to his chest and close my eyes. Lulled by the gentle movement of his hand against my hair and the steady beat of his heart, I fall asleep.

The next few months crawl by in a blur. Christmas comes and goes without me really feeling it. Leo's family spends the day with us, but I can't even cook with Paulina because it reminds me too much of cooking extravagant Christmas dinners with Mama, and the pain is too raw. Too fresh. Leo takes me up to my room, holding me in his arms as he reads one of Mama's books to me. That night, he slips a silver-plated diamond locket over my neck as he kisses me with all the love in his heart.

We steal plenty of hugs and kisses, but I can't even submerge myself in him because I'm too numb on the inside. I'm incapable of offering him anything more, and he makes no demands on me.

I didn't think it was possible to fall harder or deeper, but I do. Leo props me up with his unflinching support, endless patience, and his devoted love, and that's the only way I can get out of bed each day.

The only silver lining is we haven't seen the Grecos and there has been no more talk of setting a wedding date. I know I can't avoid reality forever, but I'm happy to drown in blissful ignorance for now.

"Come take a walk with me," Leo says the second Saturday in March.

"I'm not really in the mood," I reply, turning over in bed.

A shiver whips over my body as the covers are yanked off me. "Up, now, *dolcezza*."

His stern voice rouses my anger, and I bolt upright, glaring at him. "You don't get to boss me around. If I want to stay in bed, I'll stay in bed!"

"Not on my watch." He lifts me out of the bed and plants my feet on the ground. "I know you're mourning. I understand why you're depressed, but you can't lock yourself away in your bedroom forever, Nat." He bends down, lining his eyes up with mine as he tenderly cups my face. "This is not what Mama Rosa wanted for you."

I gulp over the messy ball of emotion clogging my throat. "It still hurts, Leo. It's not getting easier."

"I know, baby." He pulls me into his arms, and I go willingly. "But this isn't helping. I can't stand by and do nothing anymore."

"You haven't been doing nothing," I murmur against his chest. "You've been driving me to school, reading to me, bringing me flowers and chocolates, eating dinner with me in my room, running me baths, and forcing me out on walks." I look up at him. "Your arms around me are the only thing holding me together."

"You need to live, Natalia." He brings my fingers to his mouth, brushing his lips against my skin. "We are going for a walk after you shower, and then I'm taking you out tonight."

"You are?" I arch a brow. "Like, on a date?" He nods, smiling. "Papa and Mateo will never permit it."

"They have already approved." My brows climb higher up my hairline in disbelief, and he chuckles. "It's a secret date," he whispers in my ear. "They think you are doing dinner and the movies with Frankie."

"What about Brando?" My two bodyguards still shield me everywhere I go, even though the threat appears to be gone now. Mateo told me they took care of the people who were responsible and they wouldn't be coming after me again. Yet Papa still keeps Brando and Leo as my perpetual shadows, so everything is not as it seems.

"Brando won't say anything."

I narrow my eyes. "How can you be sure?"

Leo clasps my face in his hands. "Brando is smart, *dolcezza*. He knows I've been sleeping in your room, holding you at night. He sees the way we look at one another. He has spotted the hand-holding, the arm touches, the lingering looks."

Panic splays across my face as I think of how careless we have been. Yes, it's all been pretty innocent. Hugs and kisses and subtle touches, and we haven't progressed any further, but even that is enough for Leo to earn a bullet in his skull.

"Shush, baby. Stop panicking." Leo dusts kisses all over my face. "He won't say anything. He is loyal to your father but equally loyal to you. He is worried about you as well."

"Are you really sure?"

"One hundred percent. Ask him yourself if you don't believe me."

Eh, yeah, no thanks. "I believe you." I fling my arms around his neck, hugging him tight. "I trust you."

"Okay, good." He gently pushes me away, swatting my ass through my silk nightgown. "Get your sexy ass in the shower and meet me outside in twenty minutes."

It's a brisk spring morning when I step outside, but it's less cold than it's been recently, and I can sense the weather changing. Leo clears his throat, and I look over at him. He's wearing a warm woolen coat over jeans and thick black boots. He offers me his hand. "Come. I have something for us to do."

Intrigued, I take his hand, letting him guide me through the gardens around the back of our property. He moves toward Mama's greenhouse, and I jerk on his hand, slowing him to a halt. "Be brave, *dolcezza*." He fixes me with earnest eyes. "Do you trust me to have your best interests at heart?"

I nod immediately because I know he would never hurt me.

"Then, come."

My heart is pounding in my chest as we approach the greenhouse and I see the supplies stacked outside. Leo spins around, taking both my hands in his. "You haven't cooked anything since your mama passed. You haven't been out here or to the vegetable patch or the herb garden. You loved all these things, Nat, and Mama Rosa would want you to take joy where you used to."

"It reminds me too much of her," I admit with the usual pain in my chest.

"Isn't that all the more reason to do it?" he gently asks, squeezing my hands. "It's Mateo's twenty-second birthday next week. I know how much he would love you to bake him a cake. It would help him to stop worrying about you. Your papa too."

"We could have a little party," I blurt, my mind running with Leo's idea. "Just a few of his friends." My eyes narrow. "No girls." I don't trust myself not to launch at one of them if they even dared to throw eyes in Leo's direction. "Your family and us."

"That sounds perfect, and I know your brother would love it."

We spend the rest of the morning outside, planting tomatoes and strawberry seeds in the greenhouse and tidying up the herb garden and the vegetable patch.

Using some of the produce already there, I make a hearty soup as a late lunch with some homemade bread. I haven't had much of an appetite these past few months, and I know I have lost weight because most of my clothes are too big now.

But Leo is right.

Food was something Mama and I enjoyed together. Cooking and eating it, and I'm doing her an injustice by not taking care of myself. I need to work on my mental and physical well-being and try to find a way of living without the woman who was my greatest inspiration.

Papa and Mateo return from dealing with business and join us, and for the first time since Mama died, I feel a modicum of contentment.

"I NEED YOUR mouth," Leo whispers when we are seated in the back row of the movie theater after sharing a gorgeous meal at one of Leo's favorite Italian restaurants in the city. We had to be on our best behavior in the homey restaurant, because it was too public, but hidden in the shadowy corner of a dark theater, we can be less discreet.

Still, that doesn't mean I'm going to blow him for the first time here! We haven't even discussed taking things to the next level, but I am ready for more. My mouth hangs open as I gawk at him. His chest rumbles with laughter as he pulls my face in close to his. "Get those dirty thoughts out of your head, *dolcezza*. I meant I want to kiss you." My shoulders collapse in relief as I lean in toward him. His lips move to my ear. "Not that I'm opposed to your mouth on my cock, but I would never disrespect you by asking you to suck my dick in public."

Lust pools in my belly, and I squirm in my seat. Tingles spread up and down my spine, and my cheeks heat.

He cups my face, amusement mixing with adoration in his eyes. "When we do that, I want to be in private with you so I can worship your body the way you deserve." His smile expands as warmth explodes on my cheeks. "I'm going to make you feel so good," he purrs in my ear before pulling back and peering deep into my eyes. "But only when you are ready." He kisses the tip of my nose. "You are so precious to me, *dolcezza*. I hope you know that."

Warmth expands across my chest at his words as I press my mouth to his for a quick kiss. "I know, and you are all that to me too." I rest my forehead against his. "Thank you for being patient with me, Leo. For looking after me these past few months when I couldn't look after myself."

"I will always take care of you, my love. Always."

Chapter 18

NATALIA

"MATEO WAS IN a good mood on Saturday," Frankie says to me on Monday, as we exit the school cafeteria after lunch.

"He was. It was good to see him looking happy again." I wasn't the only one who sank into depression after Mama died. My brother is like a shell of himself. He has thrown himself into work and stopped the partying and the whoring. Papa is pleased, and that in turn pleases Mateo. But he's miserable, and I'm glad my little party helped to cheer him up. Even if it was only temporary.

"It's good to see you looking better too," my bestie adds, linking her arm through mine.

"Leo is right. I need to make more of an effort, and I'm wasting the precious little freedom I have left." While I haven't seen Carlo Greco since the day of Mama's funeral, I know it's only a temporary reprieve. I graduate in two months, and I'm sure he'll be beating a path to my door then, insisting on naming the day. Mateo told me Papa asked the Grecos if they would delay the wedding until I am twenty-one so I could attend NYU, but Don Greco declined.

Bastardo.

It took all the joy out of my acceptance to the prehealth program—which is the premed track at NYU—under the early decision application process. I found out three weeks ago I have a place. I enrolled anyway, in the hope of a last-minute miracle, but it's unlikely Carlo will permit me to attend. I expect he'll want to keep me chained to the kitchen and the bedroom, and I can't imagine I'll have many liberties.

A girl can still dream though—until the moment that dream becomes a living nightmare.

"Does that mean you are going to let things progress with Leo?" Frankie asks as we round the end of the hallway, heading toward the library.

"Yes, but I might have to convince him."

She barks out a laugh. "He's a man. They have sex on the brain constantly. I don't think it will take much persuasion."

"He's been so careful with me."

Frankie stops and tugs on my arm. "Because he loves you and he knew you were grieving. He's a good man, and I'm glad he was there for you, but you need to ride that stallion, girl, and get your fill before that fucking *stronzo* comes calling. You will only regret it if you don't."

I'm still thinking about Frankie's words twenty minutes later, instead of studying during my free period, wondering if I can reclaim my bravery and go after what I want.

What I have always wanted—Leo.

Desire laps at my skin, and I'm hot under my clothes. Liquid lust pools in my panties just imagining having sex with him. Giving Leo my virginity is something I have dreamed about for years, but now that it's a distinct possibility, I'm nervous.

Leo has been with a lot of girls, and I don't have a clue what I'm doing. Frankie is a great source of information, sharing her experiences and letting me know what guys want, but what if I'm no good at it? What if I can't give him the kind of pleasure he is used to? What if it's a big disappointment and he changes his mind about me?

I'm not sure I could cope if he turned his back on me.

Not that I truly think he would. He tells me daily he loves me, and he's always showering me with little gifts and tons of affection. I know Leo knows what he's doing and he'll make it good for me. For us. He'll show me how to please him, and the thought of learning all the ways I can turn him on helps to dispel my fears. I trust Leo. With my life. My body. My heart.

I have no need to be afraid. He will take care of me.

Just as I reach that life-changing affirmation, I'm called to the principal's office.

"Want me to come with?" Frankie asks as I gather up my stuff.

"Nah. It's probably just about NYU." Principal Peters has been very encouraging. Even offering to speak to Papa about my place at NYU. I don't know how much she knows about our rules and traditions, if anything. While it's sweet she wants to step in and support me like this, there is no way she can interfere. It wouldn't make the slightest difference.

My heart splutters in my chest when I open the principal's office to find Carlo Greco waiting for me. All the blood drains from my face, and I'm sure I'm as white as a ghost.

"Oh, Natalia. There you are." Mrs. Peters gets up out of her seat and rounds the desk, her brow puckering as she inspects my stricken face. "Are you feeling okay, Natalia? You look a little pale."

Behind her back, Carlo points his gun at her skull as he shakes his head in warning.

"I'm fine. It's just a headache. I've been studying a lot and not getting much fresh air," I blurt, trying to sound plausible.

"Your cousin is here. Apparently, there's a bit of a family emergency, and he needs to take you home."

"What emergency?" I ask, looking at Carlo, instantly panicked.

"I will explain in the car," he says, keeping his gun tucked behind his back as he stands.

I nod as rising panic crawls up my throat. Carlo grips my arm, pulling me in to his side, subtly digging the gun into my back. "Thank you for your time, Mrs. Peters. Natalia will be back at school tomorrow."

"It was lovely to meet you, Carlo," she says, a genuine smile on her face, and I guess she was taken in by his fake charm and his handsome features. "We will see you tomorrow, Natalia."

I plaster a smile on my face, nodding as I let the monster escort me from her office.

He keeps the gun pressed to my side, hidden in between our bodies as we walk the empty corridor that leads to the back of the building. "Miss me, *dolcezza*?" he asks, nuzzling his nose into my neck, and I almost barf on the spot. "Or were you too busy fucking around with Messina to care?"

"What?" I shriek, attempting to wrangle my arm from his hold. "Are you for real right now?" I glare at him. "My mother died. I've been in mourning, and for the last time, Leo is my friend. My bodyguard. Nothing more," I lie, hoping he doesn't feel how badly I'm trembling. I should have told Leo or Mateo about Carlo's threats last year because it's clear we still have a mole. Someone has been spying on us, and I doubt Carlo will accept my protests.

Fear crawls up my spine as he drags me out the back door, ensuring my bodyguards aren't aware I have left the building. Most days, only one of them sits guard in front of my school because it's not considered a big threat. For someone to take me from school, in broad daylight, is risky as fuck. But my despicable fiancé is anything but predictable.

Carlo manhandles me into the back of a blacked-out SUV. The two goons who were with him the day he assaulted me in my house are in the front. Both men turn around, leering at me in a way that turns the blood in my veins to ice.

Carlo grabs my chin hard, digging his nails in my skin. "Don't fucking lie to me, Natalia. I know that *stronzo* has been sneaking into your room at night." Snatching my wrists, he ties them with rope behind my back, and I can't stop my body from shaking uncontrollably. Fear has a vise-grip on every part of me, and I'm fucking terrified. The two assholes in the front laugh as they swivel in their seats to watch.

Carlo shoves my skirt up to my waist and pushes my panties aside, driving two fingers into my dry cunt. "Have you let him in here, *dolcezza*?" With his free hand, he grabs my chin again, hurting me. "Have his fingers been inside you? His tongue? His cock? Has he touched what is mine?"

"No!" I cry out, shaking and trembling at his vile touch. "No one has touched me there but you."

He slides his fingers in and out of me. "You do feel tight," he murmurs, adding another finger, stretching me painfully. He removes his fingers, but my relief is short-lived. In a lightning-fast move, he rips my panties, tossing the lace aside, exposing my bare pussy to the three men in the car.

Shame and fear wash over me, and I attempt to clamp my legs closed, but he digs his nails into my thighs while pushing my legs farther apart. Tears prick the backs of my eyes as I plead with him. "Please don't do this. My papa will kill you."

Carlo laughs as he keeps my thighs open with his knees, his fingers parting my folds, exposing my most intimate parts to his *soldati*. "Your papa will never know because if you tell him anything I will kill Mateo and Leo." Carlo rubs his thumb over my clit as he licks his lips while examining my vagina. "Such a pretty pussy," he says, running his finger up and down my slit. Grinning, he leans back, looking over his shoulder so his men have a better view. "What do you think?"

"So sweet," the bigger of the two men says, eye fucking me with dark beady eyes.

"You should fuck her to make sure she's pure before you marry her," the other one says, rubbing his crotch as he watches Carlo slip his finger inside my pussy while he continues to vigorously rub my clit. I'm dry as a bone, and it hurts. "If she doesn't bleed all over you, you'll know the truth."

I want to tell them they are ignorant assholes. That not every woman bleeds her first time. But I'm too terrified and too humiliated to open my mouth.

"I'm horny as fuck, and it's been over twenty-four hours since I wet my dick, so maybe you're right." Carlo grins, enjoying my abject terror.

I glimpse blonde hair outside, and it captures my attention. I react without hesitation or further thought. "If you want to get laid, you should fuck her." I jerk my head out the window. "Nicole is very experienced, and I'm sure she'd be a better fuck than a virgin," I babble, desperate to avoid his plans for me. "She loves sex. I have heard her moans through the walls of my brother's bedroom more times than I can count," I blatantly lie, knowing this nugget of information will appeal to Carlo's competitive nature.

Interest flares in his eyes. "She's your brother's whore?"

I bob my head. "I heard him say she loves it up the ass, and she's been with most all of his friends. She's into group sex," I add.

"She fuck Messina?" he asks, staring out the window, where Nicole is smoking a cigarette while talking on her phone.

I'm not sure whether a yes or a no response is what he's after, but I go with the truth, because he seems to hate Leo even more than my brother. "Yes."

He stares out the window at her as his fingers continue to explore my pussy. I wait with bated breath, praying he lets me go. I'm too terrified to even feel guilty about pawning him off on Nicole. She will probably love it and willingly open her legs for him when she sees his gorgeous face. "You want me to fuck her up? To make her pay for fucking him?"

"What? No." I shake my head, sweating buckets under my shirt. "I'm trying to give you what you want without it causing trouble. My bodyguards know I have a free period the last two classes today and that I intend to go home early to study," I lie. "If I don't show up out front in a few minutes they will come looking for me."

"What do you want to do, boss?" the stockier guy with the beady eyes asks. Neither of them has taken their gaze from my exposed cunt, and I want to gouge out their eyeballs with a fork.

"I want to fuck this bitch up," Carlo says, withdrawing his fingers and wrapping them around my hair, yanking my head back. "I want her to get a taste of married life," he adds, licking my face like he's a dog. "I want her to know all the ways I am going to hurt her and how much she's going to love it." He slants his disgusting lips over mine, thrusting his revolting tongue into my mouth. "But I need time for what I have planned," he says, pulling away from me.

He grabs my left breast through my shirt, squeezing hard. "You are lucky I'm feeling charitable and the slut is hot." He looks out the window at Nicole again, and I'm grateful her hair is curtaining her face, disguising the hideous scar transecting the right side of her face from just under her eye to below her chin. Mateo and Leo left the same mark on all the girls who assaulted me. It's not just a punishment. It acts as a permanent reminder of why they need to steer clear of me.

I know how much it must kill them to lose their flawless good looks, because they are vain to the nth degree, and looking in the mirror must devastate them. Nicole is ostracized at school now her cronies are expelled, and she literally flees the other way if she runs into me in the hallway.

I don't have it in me to feel sympathy for any of them. They brought it on themselves.

"Get the fuck out of here," Carlo growls, releasing me. He leans behind me to remove the rope from my wrists. Then he thrusts my book bag at me as I yank my skirt down. "If you breathe a word of this to anyone, and I mean *anyone*, they are dead." He pulls out his phone and pushes it in my face. "I have tabs on everyone in your life," he adds, skimming through photos of Leo, Mateo, Brando, Rocco, Papa, and Frankie.

"I won't say anything to anyone," I promise.

"Good girl." He slides his hand under my skirt, cupping my bare vagina. "And Natalia?" He licks the seam of my lips. "This cunt is mine." He digs his nails into my flesh, and I wince. "If you let anyone else touch it, I will make your life even more unbearable. If you act like trash, I will treat you like trash. I will share you with my friends and my men, and they can have you whenever they want. I will bring my whores home and make you watch while I fuck them." A smirk plays over his lips. "I'll make them pin you down and fuck you too while I fuck them."

Horror slams into me, and I'm trembling all over again. "No one has touched me, and it will stay that way," I blurt, desperate to get out of this damn car before he changes his mind and takes both of us.

"It better. Now get the fuck out. I've got a whore to ruin." He shoves me toward the door as one of the goons opens it for me, and I almost fall onto the sidewalk in my eagerness to get away.

Nicole's screams are the last thing I hear as I race through the double doors back into the hallway.

Chapter 19

LEO

"DID YOU FIND out what's wrong?" Brando asks as we watch the girls skipping down the steps in front of the school, searching for Natalia.

"She wouldn't say. Fed me some bullshit. But I'm determined to get to the truth today." I don't know what happened yesterday, but Natalia was pale and shaking when she emerged from the school building, and she retreated to her room the second we got to the house, claiming it was PMS. My intuition says it's more, and I'm determined to get to the bottom of it.

"Shit." Brando sits up straighter in his chair, his brow creasing with worry. "She looks even worse today."

Natalia barrels down the steps, visibly upset, and I'm out of the car, racing toward her before I have processed the motion. "What's happened?" I ask, gently holding her arms and peering into her gorgeous blue eyes.

"Oh my God, Leo." Tears fill her eyes, and her lower lip wobbles. "He's the worst monster, and I'm just as bad." Tears stream silently down her face as I take her bag and bundle her into my side, rushing her toward the car.

I should have known this had something to do with that bastard Greco.

If he has hurt her, I will fucking murder him. Consequences be damned.

Opening the back door, I help a trembling Natalia inside before climbing in after her. "Park around the side," I bark at Brando, unwilling to talk while we are driving. "Nat." I slide along the seat as Brando starts the engine and glides the car forward. "Talk to me. Tell me what's going on."

Her hands are visibly shaking as she looks at me. An icy shiver tiptoes up my spine at the look of sheer terror on her face. Whatever it is, it's bad. I curl my arm around her, pressing my lips to her temple. "I will fix this. Whatever has happened, I will make it all okay."

A strangled cry rips from her mouth, and she jolts out of my embrace, fixing panicked eyes on Brando. Brando pulls the car around the side of the building and cuts the engine. Turning in his seat, he stares at Natalia with nothing but concern in his eyes.

Natalia audibly gulps, her gaze flitting between me and Brando. "I need to talk to you in private, Leo," she whispers, pleading with her eyes.

I stare at her for a few seconds, wondering what exactly is going on. Silent communication passes between us, and I nod. I eyeball Brando. "Wait outside."

He obeys without hesitation, getting out and shutting the door after him.

"Tell me everything." I turn Natalia to face me, gently cupping her face. "Hold nothing back."

She's shaking and crying, and I'm petrified. With slow movements, I pull her onto my lap, wrapping my arms around her and dusting kisses on her face until she calms down a little. Enough to compose herself and put me out of my misery, because I need to know what that fuckface has done so I can plan creative ways to end his life. "Did you see the news?" she asks, and I arch a brow.

"What should I know?" I was on collection duty with Mateo this morning while Brando watched the school. I barely made it here on time, so I haven't had any opportunity to watch the news. Though if it was something important, Angelo would have had someone call us.

"Nicole Chastain was murdered," she whispers. "Her naked, mutilated body washed up on the shores of the Hudson, down at the bay, in the early hours of the morning. The police are appealing for help."

"I thought you hated her?" I ask, confused and not caring even a little bit the whore is dead.

"I did! I despised her!" she blurts, her voice rising a few octaves. "But I didn't want him to kill her! I thought he'd just fuck her, enjoy it, and maybe he'd forget about me."

All the blood drains from my body. "Back the fuck up, *dolcezza.* Explain everything."

It pours out of her like lava spewing from a volcano. All of it. Carlo's assaults. His threats. The fact someone is watching us and he knows. I cling to her as she speaks, needing her touch and her body heat to stop me from self-destructing, as she cries telling me how he has violated and disrespected her.

"You should've told me immediately yesterday when I asked what was wrong." It takes huge effort to keep my voice calm when I'm like a raging inferno inside. That bastard is a dead man walking. I am going to gut him from head to toe and feed his remains to the great whites in the Atlantic.

"I wanted to. So badly." She sobs, swiping at the tears flowing from her eyes. "But someone is watching us, and he warned me he would kill you and Mateo if I said anything to anyone. I was so scared, and…" She releases a shaky breath. "What if it's Brando? What if he's spying on us? I couldn't tell you in front of him."

My Adam's apple bobs painfully in my throat as I contemplate her words.

"Do you think it's him?" she whispers.

I exhale heavily, tightening my arms around her waist as I stare into her eyes. "My gut says it isn't. I trust Brando more than I trust most other made men. But most everyone can be bought or blackmailed, and until we know for sure, we can't rule anyone out."

"What are we going to do?" She looks to me for answers I don't have yet.

I press a fierce kiss to her lips, drinking from her, needing her to ground me before I do something completely reckless like storm over to the Greco compound and blast the whole fucking lot of them.

"Leo," she whispers against my lips. "I'm scared. And not just of Carlo. I'm scared for you if he tells anyone."

"Shush, baby." I rub at the moisture collecting on her cheeks before brushing her hair back off her gorgeous face. "I am going to take care of this. We won't say anything to Brando. We'll drive home and pretend like you are just upset over your schoolmate's murder. Then I'm going to talk to Mateo, and we are going to deal with Carlo Greco, once and for all."

"You can't kill him," she says, her eyes popping wide. "You said so yourself. It's too risky. They will come after his killer, and I can't lose you and Mateo. We need to go to Papa."

I shake my head. "We can't, Nat. If we do that, we have to come clean about everything. If he finds out the things that bastard has done to you—how he has disrespected you and tarnished your honor, he'll start a war. A bloody war where no one is safe, especially not you."

"And he would kill you," she whispers, gripping my shirt tighter. "You are right, we can't tell Papa. But what if Mateo tells him?"

"Mateo won't tell him. Mateo will want to dole out justice, in the same way I do."

Steely determination replaces her tears as she looks into my eyes. "I do want you to kill him, Leo. Hell, *I* want to kill him but not at the expense of your life or my brother's."

"We'll be careful. We will find a way of deflecting the attention from us and on to someone else."

"Do you promise?"

I take her hand, bringing it to my mouth, planting a soft kiss on her palm. "I promise, *amore mio*. The only life ending is Carlo Greco's, and we will be alive to dance on his grave."

"STOP." I PULL Mateo away from the wall, grabbing his torn knuckles before he can inflict more self-damage. "You can't help me kill that motherfucker if you have broken both of your hands."

I survey the trashed basement with a hint of envy because I haven't yet expunged my rage. I'm keeping that to unleash on the bastard who dared to put his hands on my love.

"I am going to beat the shit out of that prick until he's a bloody mess on the floor. He will be so unrecognizable by the time I'm done no one will be able to tell he was human," he snarls.

"We need a plan, and we need one quick," I say, letting him go, now his anger has cooled a little.

"Agreed." He flops down on the couch, and I sit in the chair across from him. He buries his head in his hands, and his shoulders heave. His pain is my pain, and we will make that bastard pay for what he's done to Natalia. "I can't believe she didn't tell me." He lifts his head, shaking it. "Why didn't she come to us?"

"He had her terrorized. She was afraid he was going to kill us."

"The only one dying is that prick," he snaps, cracking his shredded knuckles.

"We need to organize this carefully, and we need to cover our tracks." I run a hand through my hair, bristling with unspent anger.

"I want to grab his ass now and inflict the worst pain on him," Mateo growls.

"You think I don't?" Unspoken words filter between us. I fudged the truth a little, not wanting Mateo to direct his rage in the wrong direction.

I have decided to come clean after we take care of Greco. I know it will mean staying away from Natalia, but right now, eliminating the threat is my sole priority. Keeping her safe will always come before my own needs and wants. "I want to slice my knife into his flesh over and over and defile him in the worst way so he feels the humiliation and fear she must have felt."

Mateo's eyes burn with hatred, as he nods his agreement.

"But we have to be smart. We can't go charging over there. That will only get us killed, start a war, and leave Nat even more vulnerable."

Mateo sighs heavily. "You're right, but how do we go about this?"

“I have an idea.” I can’t keep the grin off my face at the prospect of murder and mayhem and retribution.

His eyes brighten, and he sits up straighter. “Let’s hear it.”

Chapter 20

LEO

"THAT DOUBLE-CROSSING snake," Mateo hisses under his breath, as we watch Carlo meet with the Colombian cartel, from our hiding place in the eaves of a derelict warehouse two miles from Port Newark. Down below, Carlo is finalizing a drug deal that will see him flood the streets of New York with a competitor's product, hitting all the New York families where it will hurt.

While Caltimore Holdings—the Mazzone family enterprise, started by Mateo's great-grandfather back in the nineteen twenties—has lots of different interests, our drug supply business is the most lucrative one.

Traditionally, the business was heavily focused on construction, shipping, and transportation with the usual extortion and racketeering on the side. Under Angelo's stewardship, we have branched out into the retail sector, and Mateo's family owns a number of restaurants, casinos, and seedy clubs. All are a great way to wash cash and to keep nosy do-gooder cops and FBI agents out of our hair.

Carefully, I maneuver a little to the left, ensuring I have Carlo's face in the shot as I snap pics of him with the cartel's chief representative in the US.

Saverio Salerno in Las Vegas had tipped Don Mazzone off a few months back. He'd explained a contact of his had reached out to him on behalf of the cartel, looking to open a new route through Las Vegas. The situation in Miami between the cartel and the authorities is explosive, and the cartel is looking to expand. They can hardly piss in Miami without law enforcement breathing all over them, so I'm not surprised they are exploring other options.

But Italian Americans stick together, even if we are sometimes at war among ourselves. The five families have agreements in place that divvies up districts in New York, and we all buy our supplies from the same supplier and use the same distribution channels. That way, everyone profits and we keep the peace. Until some greedy fucker decides he wants a bigger piece of the pie.

"I wonder if he is acting alone or on his father's instruction?" Mateo whispers, and I shrug because who the fuck knows what the hell Carlo is up to. We thought we were trailing him to a clandestine meeting with Gino Accardi. Carlo obviously slipped that intel to a few sources, knowing it would get around, so he was covering his tracks. He already laid the foundation a few months ago when he outright accused Accardi of shady dealings in front of his father and Don Mazzone.

Carlo shakes hands with the cartel underboss, and I nod at Mateo, hoping Frank and our cousin Ian are on guard outside and ready to swing into action. We wanted to bring Brando in on this, but until we catch the mole, we couldn't risk it. My brother and cousin are trustworthy, and both are great shots with the ability to keep their mouths closed. They were our only option because we couldn't risk coming here alone and being outnumbered.

Carlo waits for the man to leave through a side door before throwing his head back and chuckling. He rubs his hands, talking animatedly with his four *soldati*, as I spot Frank and Ian slipping into the warehouse at the back. Carlo and his men are too busy celebrating to notice. Setting the camera aside on the window ledge to retrieve later, I get into position and point my rifle at the back of the short stocky dark-haired guy. He matches Natalia's description of one of the men in the car the day Carlo showed up at her school. I wish I could prolong his death too, because he deserves to suffer, but we can't risk it.

Carlo is our main concern, and the rest should feel grateful for their quick deaths.

I give the signal when Mateo nods and Frank and Ian look up at me, and on the silent count of three, we open fire, each of us taking one man down until Carlo is the last man standing.

Predictably, he has his gun out, shooting indiscriminately as he backs up toward the side door the cartel underboss exited through. I can smell his fear from here, and it pleases me to no end.

I insisted Ian and Frank wear Kevlar vests, in case any stray bullets ended up in their chests. Mama and Aunt Cecilia would never forgive me if anything happened to them. I'm glad now as the jackass continues shooting wildly with no aim.

"Stop right there, *stronzo*," Mateo calls out, climbing to his feet as he points his rifle at Carlo's head.

"Drop the weapon and raise your hands," I add, slinging my rifle around my back and swinging down from the eaves in three fluid moves as Frank and Ian move in closer, training their guns at Carlo's skull and chest.

Carlo chuckles as his gun drops to the floor, amusement dancing over his face.

"If you think your men outside are coming to your aid, think again," I say, kicking the gun away from him. It skitters across the debris-strewn dirt floor. Removing plastic gloves from my back pocket, I pull them on, keeping my eyes on the degenerate.

"They're taking a permanent swim in the Hudson," Frank confirms, his voice and tone expressionless as he pats Carlo down for other weapons. Frank prods his gun into Carlo's temple while Ian hands me our tool bag. Dropping it on the floor, I unzip it, ensuring Carlo gets a good look inside.

Carlo's look of amusement fades, but he's still an arrogant bastard. "You won't hurt me. We all know it would start a war."

"Wrong, motherfucker." Mateo storms toward him as Ian drags over a chair. Mateo slams his fist into Carlo's face, and the force of the punch sends him sprawling to the floor. Before he can get up, I kick him in the head, and we both lay into him with our feet and our fists, rendering him bloody in record time. The pussy barely puts up a fight.

After tying him to the chair, I take his phone, slipping it into my back pocket. Then I use my knife to rip his clothes off, and he howls in pain every time my blade digs into his bare skin. Rivulets of blood trickle down his torso, and he glares at me, as if he has any power in this situation. I send Ian and Frank up to the eaves to watch both entrance points from the upstairs windows in case anyone shows up when Carlo fails to return home.

We know we can't take as much time as we would like, but we still intend to make the fucker suffer.

"Did you seriously think we would let you get away with the shit you pulled on my sister?" Mateo says, spitting in his face before he lands a hard punch to his solar plexus.

"She fucking loved it," he grunts in between pained gasps, and I pummel his face some more, enormously satisfied when one of his teeth pops out.

"You enjoy forcing yourself on women?" I snarl, pushing my face all up in his. One of his eyes is half closed, and his left cheekbone is swollen. "You're a pathetic son of a bitch."

A rough laugh escapes his mouth. "Jealous much, Messina?"

"Of a piece of filth like you? Never." I glide my knife across his lower belly, deep enough for him to feel it but not so deep that he'll die too quick.

He screams, and it's music to my ears.

Pressing my knife to his throat, I grin as I taunt him with my words. "I didn't have to force Natalia. Every touch was wanted. Every kiss desired." If Mateo, my brother, or my cousin is surprised at my admission, no one betrays the emotion. "Tell me. How does it feel to know your fiancée loves me? Enough to let me be with her in ways you could only ever dream of." I'm lying because I haven't touched Natalia inappropriately, and I intend to tell my best friend that before he shoves me in the chair after Carlo. "We've been sneaking around behind your back for months." I drag my knife down the center of his chest, stepping back as he pisses all over his legs and the floor. "Making a fool out of you all this time."

"She hates you," Mateo adds. "And I fucking loathe you." He slices his dick off in one quick thrust of his knife, and his penis flies off to the left as tears leak out of Carlo's eyes and he howls in pain. "I was never letting her marry you."

"Tell us who has been feeding you intel from inside, and we'll make this quick," I lie, extracting the blow torch.

"Fuck you and your mother."

I light the flame, blasting it over the top of his head, singeing his hair and blistering the skin on his brow.

The sounds that reverberate off the walls are animalistic, but I don't care. I want him to feel unimaginable pain before we end him. He will tell us who the mole is or die a gruesome death.

"Okay. *Va bene*," he pants with tears leaking from his eyes. The reddened skin on his forehead bubbles and blisters as he moans and cries, and trickles of blood pool between his legs. "It was Brando," he rasps, his eyes darting sideways.

Mateo and I exchange a brief look. I see my thoughts reflected in his eyes. *He's lying.* Mateo nods, and I agree. We won't get anything out of this cunt. I shrug as I light up the torch again. "Your funeral."

"You won't get away with this," he shrieks. "My father will know it was you! You'll be following me to hell."

"Nah." Mateo smirks as he slams his knife into Carlo's thigh, purposely avoiding the femoral artery.

"Unlike you, we know how to execute a plan to a satisfactory conclusion." I jerk my head to the right, gesturing at the small table where five kilos of cocaine sit in packaged bricks. No money traded hands, so it's an obvious gift. While there is no way of telling where it came from, it's existence in the place where his mutilated body will be found will be enough to cause suspicion.

"Let's gut this motherfucker," Mateo says, all out of patience. His bloodthirst is showing, and my bloodlust rushes to the surface, ready to inflict pain.

Together, we destroy him, ripping him apart with our knives, savaging into his body, every thrust a strike for Natalia and every other woman this bastard has ever hurt. When his guts are hanging out and his flesh is so torn all you can see is bones, I finish him off with the blow torch, enjoying the smell as his body burns. Mateo stops me before I reduce him to ash. We want Don Greco to suffer when he sees him because that motherfucker is every bit as sick and twisted as his son.

I call Frank and Ian down to help with the cleanup. My brother looks pale, but he says nothing, searching the ground for our shell casings, while Mateo and I strip out of our blood-soaked clothes. Ian pukes in a plastic bag, and Mateo and I grin at one another, brothers in arms. “For the record, I have kissed Natalia. Nothing more. I swear I haven’t touched her inappropriately.” I feel the need to say it before Mateo remembers and takes a swing at me.

“Not here,” he growls, narrowing his eyes at me.

I nod as I throw the five-liter bottle of water over my head, washing away the last of the blood. Then I dry off and dress in clean clothes, gathering up our ruined garments to dispose of at the incinerator later.

After we have removed all trace of evidence and checked the coast is clear, we slip out of the warehouse and head home.

Chapter 21

LEO

"YOU DID WHAT?" Angelo roars, thumping his closed fist on the desk, before whipping his gun from its holster and pointing it first at Mateo and then me. "Are you both out of your goddamned minds?"

"He hurt Natalia, Papa," Mateo says, his tone even, his expression betraying no trace of fear. Mateo has matured a lot since his mother died. I think Angelo's threat about having another option forced him to wise up too.

"He disrespected her and humiliated her," I add. "Exposing her to his men, and he would have taken it all the way if it wasn't for her quick thinking."

Pain flickers across Angelo's face, but he doesn't lower the gun, his aim alternating between us. A stream of Italian curses leaves his lips, but his anger hasn't ebbed. Not in the slightest. "You should've come to me with this!" he barks. "I would have dealt with it the appropriate way. This will start a war I don't want!"

"Only if Don Greco discovers it was us who killed Carlo," I say.

"Which he won't," Mateo supplies. "Because we were careful and we did a thorough cleanup."

"There's more," I blurt, remaining calm in the face of his father's rage.

"Sit," Angelo snaps, and we sink into chairs without hesitation.

"We caught him arranging a deal with the Columbian cartel," I say, removing the pictures from the large brown envelope in my hand. I slide them over.

Angelo finally puts the gun down on his desk to look through the pictures. We purposely waited until this morning before coming to the boss to make sure we had our ducks in a row. We stayed up all night developing the pictures in the small darkroom at my parents' apartment.

My mom is an avid photographer, and I used to love developing pictures with her when I was younger and had the time to indulge in such things.

"We don't know if he was working alone or on Don Greco's instructions," Mateo says.

Angelo's face turns troubled. "*Merda*." He is quiet as he flips through the pictures, and we hold our breath, waiting to see what he does. We have suggestions, but it is better if he draws the same conclusions himself.

"He told everyone he was meeting Accardi," I say, letting the words sit there.

Angelo glares at me, and I gulp over the ball of nerves lodged at the back of my throat. "Who else knows about this?"

"Natalia," Mateo says. "She knew we were going to handle this, and she has seen the reports on the news this morning." All the major news channels are reporting the deaths of five made men at an abandoned warehouse at Port Newark, but the news hit too late to make the newspaper headlines. I imagine it will be splashed all over the front pages tomorrow.

"No one else knows?" His eyes trap me in his gaze. "You're sure?"

"Positive," I lie, staring him straight in the eye. I want to keep Frank and Ian out of this. We know neither of them will say anything to anyone, so there is no need to involve them.

"*Va bene*." He drags a hand through his graying hair. "This is what we will do. We will act normal. I will call Don Greco to offer my condolences and my help. It won't take him long to accuse Accardi, but I cannot let Gino go down for this. It would cause untold unrest within *la famiglia*. We will feed word out onto the street about the Colombian cartel and let him connect the dots."

"We could send him some of these photos," I suggest. "I can scrub them clean of fingerprints, and I used generic film and printing supplies so it can't be traced back to me."

"No." Angelo shakes his head. "That indicates a third party in that warehouse. We want Don Greco to point the finger of blame at the Colombians."

"Won't that start a war with them?" Mateo asks.

"We can use this to our advantage. Two birds. One stone. This will rally all the families to push the Colombians away before they get a stronghold in our territory. It will get bloody, but needs must."

It's a good plan, except for one thing. "What about Natalia? The marriage contract will pass to the next in line unless the Grecos are discredited."

Angelo drills me with a deadly look that sprouts goose bumps on my arms. "I am well aware of the tradition, Messina." He breathes heavily as he thinks, and I'm afraid to move a muscle. "The suspicion should be enough to terminate the contract, but if it isn't, I will show him one of the photos. I'll tell him Accardi had a man on Carlo because he knew he was lying to cover up something."

None of us speak, but the implication is clear. If Angelo needs to throw someone under a bus to extract Natalia from a Greco marriage, he will leave Accardi to his fate.

"You tell no one about this. Ever." Angelo pins his intense stare on both of us. "We all take this secret to the grave, and you don't tell Natalia what has been agreed here today." His eyes pierce mine, and I break out into a cold sweat. All the fine hairs at the back of my neck stand to attention as I realize he knows something. Enough to have me fearing for my life.

"There is one other thing," Mateo says. "Carlo had a man on the inside who was feeding him intel."

"Who?" Angelo asks, putting his gun back in his holster.

I almost collapse in relief, but I have a feeling I'm not out of the woods yet.

"Rocco," Mateo quietly admits. We both knew Carlo was lying when he threw out Brando's name. Carlo's cell phone records identified the real culprit.

Angelo's nostrils flare as he picks up the receiver of the phone on his desk.

"He's in the dungeon," Mateo says. "We picked him up before we came to see you."

Pride shines in Angelo's eyes as he places the receiver back on the hook, and a brief smile curves the corner of his mouth. "Good, good," he says. "Let us deal with him now."

We get up to leave.

"Mateo." Angelo strides toward his son, gripping his face. He plants a firm kiss to his brow. "You did good, my son. I am proud of how you have handled yourself in recent months. Your mama would be proud of you too."

Mateo blossoms under his father's praise, and I'm happy for him.

Angelo releases his son and turns to me. "You too, Leonardo." He clamps his hand on my shoulder, squeezing hard. "I have a lot to be thankful to you for." The rest of that sentence goes unspoken, and I wonder how long it will be before he pulls me aside to say it.

We trail Angelo to the dungeon, watching as he beats one of his longest-serving *soldati* to a pulp before he puts a bullet in his skull. Natalia was fond of Rocco, and this will upset her.

Rocco knew nothing about the cartel, but we decide Greco doesn't need to know that. We now have a legitimate way of telling him what we know without using my pictures or placing anyone else at the scene.

Rocco confirmed Carlo was behind the Barone attack. Rocco gave them access that day. Apparently, Carlo wanted to have his fun with Natalia before they were married so he could decide whether she would be the right bride for him. My blood boils just thinking about the things he would have put her through if they had succeeded in kidnapping her that day.

"Find the girl," Angelo says, removing his blood-spattered shirt and dropping it to the concrete floor. He steps away from the blood pooling around his feet. Carlo kidnapped Rocco's thirteen-year-old daughter seven months ago, and he's been holding her captive ever since, forcing Rocco to spy on us. I can only imagine the state we will find the poor girl in.

Rocco was vague on the details, not confirming he was asked to spy on me and Natalia, and I know he did that for her. He has always had a soft spot for my *dolcezza*, and I'm guessing he saw his daughter in her.

Didn't stop him from dancing to the devil's tune though.

The idiot should have come to me or Mateo. We could have helped.

Rocco knew he was meeting his maker today, so I respect him for doing right by Natalia, his daughter, and his family at the end.

"And ensure his family is taken care of," Angelo adds.

"I'll make it a priority," Mateo says, moving toward the door.

I move to follow him.

"I want a word, Leonardo," Angelo calls out.

I squeeze my eyes shut before turning around. I guess we're doing this now.

"Alone, Mateo." Angelo drills a look over his shoulder at his son.

"Remember Natalia loves him, and Mama did too," Mateo says before stepping out of the room.

Angelo closes the door while I wait to hear my fate. He walks around me, coming to a standstill right in front of me, flexing his blood-coated knuckles.

I stand my ground, holding my head up and meeting his stern gaze.

"Tell me, Leonardo. Do you love my daughter as much as she loves you?" he asks, staring deep into my eyes as he pulls no punches.

I could lie, but I don't know how much he knows. If he senses I'm not being truthful, he's as likely to kill me for dishonesty as he is for the things I've done with Natalia. I figure it's best I fess up. "Yes, sir. I love her in a way I will never love any other woman. I would die for Natalia, Don Mazzone. So, if that is what you must do, I will die knowing it was for the best reason."

He stares at me, and I return it, hoping my nerve holds. Tension bleeds into the air, thicker than the substance pooling around our feet. He clamps both his hands on my shoulders, digging his fingers into the corded muscle he finds there. "I should kill you." A muscle clenches in his jaw. "Is she impure?"

I shake my head. "I did not take her virginity or touch her intimately. It's been kissing mostly, and I have been helping her come to terms with her grief. Holding her while she sleeps."

He nods his head slowly, several times, and his jaw relaxes. "I am glad to hear one of you had some sense." Letting me go, he steps back, running a hand through his hair.

"I tried to stay away from her, but she makes it difficult," I explain.

"Try harder," he says through clenched teeth. "I will extract Natalia from her obligation with the Grecos, but she must marry, Leo. I will arrange another contract. You know this is what must happen."

"I want to marry her." I decide to put all my cards on the table although I know it is futile. "I love her, and I will take good care of her. I have my own apartment now, and I have savings. I am ambitious and willing to work hard. I will ascend the ranks, and I will be able to provide her with a good life."

His face softens in a way that is rare. "You are a good man, Leonardo Messina. A product of a good upbringing and wonderful parents. Your father is a good man. A good capo." He steps toward me again, a sad expression washing over his face. "I have no doubt you will go on to do great things, and I know you would make a great husband for Natalia, but she's the daughter of a don, Leo. She must marry a don or an heir. Maybe an underboss or a consigliere." He shakes his head. "But not a capo or a *soldato*. That would be disrespectful to my daughter, and I know you don't want to disrespect her any more than you already have."

Pain stabs me through the heart as I nod. Mateo said all these things to me last night while he kept me company as I was developing the pictures. I have known all along it would come to an end, but I'm not ready to let her go. I doubt I ever will be.

"My daughter loves fiercely. She's like her mama in that regard." Grief transforms his features for a few seconds before he puts his don mask back on. "You will need to hurt her to make the point. She needs to let you go and look to the future."

"Will you let her attend NYU? It's her dream, and she needs something to focus on."

He chuckles, but it's a dry laugh. "You dare to tell me about my own daughter, son?"

I say nothing because I'm not taking it back.

"I will let her go to NYU to get her degree," he concedes, "provided you stay away from her."

The sneaky fucking bastard knows I will agree to it. "I promise I will," I say, praying I can stick to my word.

"She will be married after that, Leo."

"I understand, boss."

"*Va bene*. You may go." He looks down at his dead soldier on the ground with no discernible emotion on his face despite how much he liked the man.

I walk quickly toward the door, keen to get out of here.

"Leo?"

I silently curse as I turn around.

"Don't make me regret my decision, and you only get one pardon." He stares me down, his gaze intense and deadly. "If I discover you have touched my daughter again, I will bury you alive and not lose any sleep over it."

Chapter 22

NATALIA

IT'S BEEN SIX weeks since my life was upended, in good and bad ways. The good is I am no longer obligated to marry into the Greco *famiglia*, but Papa has told me he will be looking for another match for me. But he has agreed it won't happen until I get my undergrad degree from NYU, so I have four years of freedom to look forward to.

And four years to convince Leo he made a mistake dumping me.

I know why he did it. Mateo must have forced his hand. Blackmailed him into letting me go in exchange for his silence. Or maybe Leo's conscience got the better of him. Yet it makes no sense. I am unattached, and while we would need to continue sneaking around in secret, I thought I was worth it. Or did he mean nothing he told me?

Papa has reassigned Leo now the risk to my life has ended with the monster's death. Brando is my permanent bodyguard because there will always be threats, but the risk is low right now. Hearing it was Carlo who attempted to kidnap me, so he could act out his depraved fantasies on my innocent body, only makes me more grateful for Leo and Matty. They have saved me from a fate worse than death.

I try to remember that when I'm crying into my pillow at night, heartbroken and so lonely without Leo's strong arms to comfort me.

He is purposely keeping his distance, and it hurts so much. He failed to attend my eighteenth birthday party three weeks ago, and he didn't show up last night at my graduation.

But he can't avoid me today. It's his twenty-first birthday, and I know where he's having his party. I wasn't issued a formal invite, but I have no qualms about gate-crashing. Hence why I am currently at Frankie's apartment in the city, getting dolled up. I'm sure Mateo will throw a hissy fit when he sees the dress I'm wearing, but that's exactly why I didn't want to get ready at home.

"Ho. Lee. Shit." Frankie whistles under her breath while I check myself in the long mirror fixed to the wall of her bedroom. "There is no way he can resist you looking like that. Red looks *so good* on you."

I twirl a little, and the red chiffon layers float around my shapely hips, resting just above my knee. "Do you think it's too revealing?" I ask, pursing my lips as I scrutinize my reflection. The halter-neck straps support my bust despite the large dip in the front, which exposes a lot of my cleavage. The wide bandeau-style panel around my middle accentuates my small waist, making my hips seem curvier.

"No. It's perfect. It's seductive but classy. You look like a million dollars, Nat. Every man in the room will be salivating and clambering for your attention."

"I only want one man's attention," I say, applying another coat of red lipstick to my lips before I secure the locket Leo gave me around my neck.

"You'll have it." She reassures me while turning around so I can zip up the back of her short black minidress.

"You look beautiful." I lean in to kiss her cheek. "When is Archer getting here?"

She looks at the time on her cell phone. "Any second now."

The doorbell chimes, as if on cue, and we both smile.

"Come on." I grab my black and gold purse from the bed, grateful Frankie talked me into buying it when I was purchasing the matching strappy stiletto sandals adorning my feet. "Don't keep your man waiting."

Raucous laughter can be heard from the kitchen, where Frankie's family is eating dinner, as we pass by.

"Fuck me," a familiar male voice says when we enter the living room.

I slam to a halt at the sight of Vaughan Fitzgerald. "What are you doing here?" I blurt, surprised to see him. There is no way he can come to the party with us. Not unless he wants Leo or my brother to finish what they started in the alleyway last year.

Frankie moves toward Archer, and he pulls her into his arms, smashing his lips against hers. Their romance shows no signs of abating, and at least one of us is happy and in love. I would never begrudge that of my bestie, even if the sight of them together exacerbates my heartache and my longing for things I cannot have.

Vaughan's eyes are out on stilts as his gaze rolls over me. "You look fucking beautiful, Natalia." His eyes blaze with need, and I'm startled to see such naked desire. As far as I'm aware, he has been dating some girl from his school the past five months. I assumed he was well over his little crush on me.

"Thank you, but that doesn't answer my question."

He shrugs, stepping a little closer. "I didn't like how we left things. I thought I'd stop by and tell you there are no hard feelings." His earnest blue eyes latch on mine, and I see the truth written there.

"I don't deserve that. Not after what my brother did, but thank you." I smile graciously at him. "I should've told you I was engaged, but it's not an easy thing to just slip into a conversation, and I hated my fiancé and didn't want to marry him. I wanted to go out with you and have a good time, so that's why I said nothing."

"I don't blame you for anything that happened, Natalia." He takes another step closer, and the tops of his shoes brush against my sandals. "I heard a rumor you're no longer engaged." He flashes me a gorgeous smile, taking my hand and threading his fingers through mine. "And I'm newly single. I thought maybe we could pick up where we left off?"

He cannot be serious. Does he honestly think Mateo would approve of me dating him now, just because my engagement is over? Extracting my fingers from his, I step back, shaking my head. "That won't ever happen, Vaughan."

"Why not? I know you like me." His brow puckers in confusion. I doubt many girls say no to him, and I get it. He's hot, smart, charming, and attentive.

But he isn't the one who makes my heart race with a single look, the guy who ignites an inferno inside me with a feather-soft touch, the man who turns my heart to mush just by his mere presence.

I decide Vaughan deserves to know the truth because he took a beating for liking me, and I don't want him entertaining any notions of an us. I deliberately lower my tone and relax my facial expression, doing my best to let him down gently. "I do like you, Vaughan. You're perfect boyfriend material, but there are certain traditions in my family. Traditions that mean another fiancé will be found for me soon. But the main reason we would never work is I'm in love with someone else. Always have been. Always will be."

He peers into my eyes, and I let him see the truth of my words.

"That makes me sad for you, Natalia. No one should be forced to marry someone who isn't the person they love."

"I agree, but I am powerless to change the way things happen." I shrug, like it's not a big deal. But it's the very reason I hate that my last name is Mazzone.

"Thank you for being straight with me." He leans in, kissing me briefly on the cheek. "Take care of yourself." He glances at Archer. "I'll see myself out. Catch you later."

"Told you they'll all be falling over themselves to get to you in that dress," Frankie says, winking as she loops her arm through mine.

"I REALLY DON'T think this is wise," Brando repeats, for the umpteenth time, as he parks at the back of the nightclub in Queens where Leo's party is in full swing. I'm not worried about getting in, even though we are underage, because Papa owns this place and he gave Leo the use of it for tonight, for free, as a birthday gift. None of the staff would dare to refuse me.

"I appreciate your concern," I say, stabbing him with a "butt out" look through the mirror, "but I'm not missing Leo's party. Besides, I have to give him his gift." I don't know how much Brando knows about what went down between me and Leo, but he's no dumbass. He helped me to find and purchase Leo's gift, so I suspect he knows exactly how much I'm in love with him.

Brando sighs, getting out of the car and popping the trunk. I lean in to grab the custom leather box I had made to house Leo's gift. It has his name carved into the leather, encased in a fine border of real gold. It's stunning, and I hope he likes it as much as the gifts inside.

"I don't want to see you hurt, Natalia," Brando says, "and if you step through those doors, you *will* be upset."

All the blood drains from my face as I contemplate the meaning behind his words. Brando has never interfered in my life or tried to tell me how to live it. So, this is as close as he has come to trying to persuade me to do things his way. "I appreciate you looking out for me, Brando. I really do. But I guess I need to see this for myself."

Maybe I'm naïve, but I never even stopped to consider Leo would have moved on. We only broke up six weeks ago. Isn't he as heartbroken as me?

"Maybe we shouldn't do this," Frankie says, appearing on my other side. She and Archer clearly heard every word of our conversation.

"Nope." I slam the trunk closed. "I'm giving him his gift, and if he's in there with another woman, I want to see it with my own eyes."

Brando offers me his arm, giving in because he can see the determination on my face. "Let's go then."

Chapter 23

NATALIA

THE ROOM IS packed to the rafters, and the noise levels are headache inducing. A layer of cigarette smoke hovers in the stifling air, and lighting is extremely dim. I have never been inside this club before, and it's a total dive. Music thumps through speakers as partygoers jostle one another at the bar and swarm the heaving dance floor.

My mouth trails the ground when my gaze lands on an elevated section in the center of the room. It looks like a runway strip. The kind you see models prancing up and down on. But this is a different kind of setup. Three semi-naked strippers shimmy up and down poles, gyrating and simulating sex. They pout, as if it's an Olympic sport, sending seductive looks at the men crowding around them. Some of the men are stuffing dollar bills in their thongs while rubbing noticeable bulges in their pants.

It's fucking gross, and I'm more than a little sickened.

"Eh." Archer rubs a hand along the back of his neck as he drinks in the scene. "Maybe Brando is right. I don't think we should be here."

"We're here now. Might as well stay," I say, skimming the booths on either side of the room, looking for the birthday boy.

The instant I find him, I wish I hadn't.

Leo is at a table with some friends, but Mateo is nowhere to be seen. A skinny blonde, in a tacky gold fake-leather minidress, is perched on his lap, her plastic tits shoved all up in his face and her arms clinging to his neck. If I'm not mistaken, she is one of the college girls I got thrown out the day of Mateo's last pool party. Leo's arm is tight around her waist as he laughs at something one of his friends says.

"Shit." Frankie shoves Brando aside and takes my hand. "Do you want to go?"

I shake my head, unable to force a word out over the painful lump clogging my throat. Watching the blonde run her fingers through his hair is like a dagger through the heart. Touching his hair is something I loved to do, and I've given him plenty of scalp massages, which I know he enjoyed. Seeing someone else touch him in that way, in public, boils the blood in my veins.

"Nope." I snatch the box from Brando's hands, shoving through the crowd as I make my way toward Leo's table. I know my friends are following me, so I don't look back. The girl sees me first, flipping me the bird before pressing the side of Leo's head into her chest as she gloats at me. She clearly remembers me too.

I reach the table and slap the box down on it, capturing the attention of everyone seated there. Leo slowly turns around to face me with a cold, disinterested look on his face.

Fuck, he looks gorgeous.

It's been so long since I last saw him I had almost forgotten how completely hot he is. His hair is newly cut, and he has the front styled back off his face and the sides shorn tight. The layer of stubble on his chin and cheeks is neat, and my fingers twitch with a craving to touch it. His black button-down shirt stretches across his broad shoulders, hugging his huge biceps and the impressive chest I am familiar with. He has the sleeves rolled up to his elbows, showcasing the ink on his arms. With black pants and shoes, he looks like a dark angel and the epitome of sin.

A sin I want to indulge in repeatedly.

I want to strip him bare and lick him all over.

"What are you doing here?" he asks, dragging me away from the naughty thoughts running through my head. His eyes skim over my red dress with no show of emotion or interest, and it hurts. "I know I didn't invite you."

"You should have." I cock my head to one side and slant him with a sharp look.

"This is no place for underage virgin *principessas*," he replies, earning a round of laughter from the table.

Heat creeps up my neck and onto my cheeks as pain obliterates my insides. Why is he being so cruel? "There is no need to be rude. I only came to give you your gift." That's not exactly true. I stupidly thought I'd show up here looking too gorgeous to resist and he'd fall back into my arms.

I guess there is no end to my stupid bravery.

The blonde giggles, and I turn venomous eyes on her. The sight of her draped all over him is killing me. A heavy weight presses down on my chest, and my heart feels like it's ripping apart inside me. Sobs are building at the base of my throat, but I won't set them free. Instead, I transform the emotion into anger, letting my rage take over. I glare at the blonde as my hands ball into fists at my sides. I want nothing more than to tear her from limb to limb, before whaling on Leo, but I won't make a scene. I'm not going to disgrace myself in front of all his friends and my father's *soldati*.

Holding my head up and my shoulders back, I level Leo with a warning look. "Get rid of the whore, or I'll use the gun in this box on her."

He stares at me, and it hurts to see the cold glint in his eyes. His face lacks the warmth he usually reserves for me, and if I didn't know better, I'd say he hates me. Except I do know him. And this is a front. A wall to keep me out. Like the girl on his lap. She means nothing to him. She's a tool to keep me away. "Go get a drink," Leo says, lifting her off his lap.

She is tall and extremely skinny, her shape almost androgynous except for those ridiculous boobs. It's like he purposely set out to find someone the opposite of me. Honestly, she looks like she might topple over any second. I'd enjoy trampling her underfoot if she did.

"But, Leo!" She pouts, like she's a toddler, stomping her foot.

"Now," he growls, piercing her with a dark look.

She glares at me, looking like she wants to wring my neck, before she totters off in the direction of the bar.

"You can sit here, beautiful," a guy with short dark-blond hair says. He's sitting at the edge of the booth on the other side, patting his thigh in invitation as his gaze wanders salaciously over my body.

"She's not staying," Leo barks, dropping his cold façade and glowering at the guy.

"My father owns this club. I'll stay if I want to," I retort.

Leo regains control of himself, shrugging. "Suit yourself."

"Damn. You're Natalia Mazzone," the other guy says. His eyes trail up and down my body, and out of the corner of my eye, I spy Leo digging his nails into his thighs. I guess he's not as immune as he wants me to believe. "You're fucking beautiful. Best-looking woman in the room by a mile. I'd love to get my hands all over you, but I value breathing." He winks, shaking his head as he takes one last look before turning away from me to talk to the guy beside him. I'm guessing this is the reaction I'll get from every guy in the room because everyone is too scared to cross my brother or my father.

"Can we get this over and done with?" Leo asks, folding his arms and looking bored. "I have a date to get back to."

I'm tempted to remove the gun and shoot him with it. I even debate not giving him the gift now, but I remind myself this is all an act to push me away. I slide the box to him. "Happy birthday, Leo." Before he can stop me, I lean down and press a kiss to his cheek, uncaring I'm flashing a lot of cleavage at the men on this side of the booth. A few groans and cusses ring out, and I know I have the attention of every man at this table.

Good. I hope Leo notices and gets jealous.

His clean, citrusy scent wraps around me, and I almost fling myself at him, catching myself in time. My heart thuds painfully behind my chest, and I want to beg him to take me back. But I have more self-respect than that. I'm not groveling for any man. Ever.

"Stop it," he says through gritted teeth, his eyes lowering to my chest.

"Open it," I snap back, straightening up, letting my anger take charge again.

His Adam's apple bobs in his throat as he looks at his name engraved on the front before he opens the box, examining the gun box, thick cigars, hip flask, silver lighter, and Italian leather wallet and belt. Every piece was painstakingly chosen and customized for him by me. I've been planning this for months. Yet nobody would ever know it looking at his bland expression.

"Holy hell." The guy to Leo's right exclaims, lifting the gun from the box. "Is this what I think it is?" He opens it up, and his eyes almost bug out of his head.

"It's a Smith & Wesson Model 19, from the nineteen thirties," I confirm. "It's alleged to have once been owned by Lucky Luciano himself." I don't know if that's true, but it's definitely a collector's item. It cost a small fortune, and I used a large chunk out of the inheritance Mama left me, but it was worth it.

"I don't want it," Leo says, snatching it off his friend and placing it back in the box. Then he inserts it in the main box and hands it back to me. "I'm not accepting this."

Tears stab the backs of my eyes. "Don't be an asshole. It's a gift. Say thank you like normal people do," I snap, hating how my voice wobbles a little.

"Nat?!" My brother shouts at me from behind, and I close my eyes for a second, preparing myself for it. I set the box down on the table.

"What the hell are you doing here?" he yells, coming up alongside me and taking my elbow. "And what the hell are you wearing?" His blue eyes turn almost black with rage.

"Fuck off, Mateo." I yank my elbow out of his hold. "It's a party. I'm here to party." Turning around, I take Frankie's hand. "Let's dance." She doesn't let me down, linking her arm through mine and letting me push our way into the middle of the dance floor. Archer stands guard with Brando from the edge of the dance floor, both looking uneasy. Over their heads, I spot Mateo and Leo exchanging harsh words I know are about me.

I feel eyes all over me as I dance, but no one even brushes up against me. Everyone knows who I am, or if they didn't before, they do now, and no one will risk even talking to me. Pity. Because using Santino to make Leo jealous worked like a charm the last time, and I wouldn't have been opposed to doing that with some random hottie again.

We dance for a while, working up a sweat, but I'm not enjoying myself. I have lost sight of Leo and the blonde whore, and that cranks my anxiety up another couple of levels.

"You need to leave," Mateo says in my ear, grabbing me from behind and spinning me around. "Papa would freak if he knew you were here."

"Relax, Matty." I push off his chest. "I'm eighteen, and it's not like I can get into any trouble here. Everyone is afraid to even look at me."

"This is no place for a girl like you."

Anger resurfaces, trundling through my veins. I plant my hands on my hips and glower at my brother. "What the fuck does that mean?" I roar in his ear.

"It's a compliment, Natalia. Jeez. You're too good for a place like this, and I want you to go."

I shuck out of his hold. "I'll leave when I'm good and ready." Mateo looks over my shoulder and purses his lips. Briefly, he closes his eyes before reopening them, a look of determination clear in the depths of his blue eyes. "I know what you're doing, Nat, and it won't work. He's moved on. See for yourself." He jerks his head behind me, and acid churns in my gut.

Frankie threads her fingers through mine. "Don't look," she says. "Let's just go."

Ignoring the blood thrumming in my ears, I spin around, and the world falls apart around me. Pain slams into me, almost taking my knees out from under me. Leo is dancing with the blonde, and they are all over one another. I see his tongue as it plunges into her mouth, and his hands are splayed across her ass, squeezing and kneading her bony butt. She's grinding against him, basically dry humping him in public, not caring who sees her.

A sob bubbles up my throat, and my heart is pounding against my chest cavity, screaming to be let out. Air oozes from my mouth in heavy spurts, and I can scarcely breathe over the pain infiltrating every part of me.

Leo grabs her waist, pulling her tighter against him as he thrusts his hips into hers.

A crack forms in my heart. So loud I feel like everyone must have heard it.

His eyes dart to me, thick with lust, as he whispers something in her ear.

I stand rooted to the spot, wanting to leave but incapable of forcing my limbs to move.

Grabbing her hand, Leo tugs her through the crowd, and I watch as they disappear down a hallway, out of sight. Tears are screaming to break free as I realize where they are going and what they are planning to do. But I refuse to break down in public. I refuse to give him any more power over me.

I push my way through the crowd, holding my pain inside as I desperately flee the place.

The second I'm outside, the dam breaks, and I burst into tears, stumbling along the side of the club to get out of sight before someone sees me. I throw up when I reach the top of the parking lot, clinging to the corner of the building, while my heart shatters and my stomach heaves. I can't even move at the sound of approaching footsteps, and I'm all out of fucks to give.

"I'm sorry, Nat," Mateo says, reaching out for me. "I know you're upset, but it's better you know."

"Get the fuck away from me!" I yell, swinging around and slapping him in the face. "This is all your fault!" I say, taking the tissue Frankie hands to me and dabbing my mouth. Archer and Brando hang back. The former looks like he wishes he was anywhere but here, and the latter looks troubled. "I know you told him to do this," I hiss. Because I know Leo would never be cruel to me on purpose.

"I know you want to believe that, but I don't tell Messina what to do. You're naïve to all of this, Nat. I get that you're mad, and if you need to take that out on me, so be it." He shrugs, like the red handprint on his cheek doesn't bother him in the slightest. "But I'm not the one with my tongue down Mandy's throat and my hands on her ass. I'm not the one inside fucking her right now. That's all on Leo."

"I hate you!" I cry, wrapping my arms around myself. "And I hate him. You can both go to hell."

Chapter 24

LEO

MY PHONE PINGS with an incoming call, vibrating across the top of my bedside table, but I can't summon the strength to answer it. It's been the same this past week, and I know I need to pull myself together. Angelo has left me alone to grieve, but I'll be expected to return to work on Monday. Life must go on. Even if it was only yesterday that we buried my best friend, *my brother*, in Union Church Cemetery.

Pain splits me in two as it all returns to haunt me. If only I hadn't used Mandy to permanently push Nat away last weekend when Brando texted me to say she was on her way. If only I hadn't proceeded to get completely trashed because I knew I had hurt my *dolcezza* so deeply she would likely never speak to me again. Then I wouldn't have been so heartsick and hungover on Sunday. I wouldn't have turned Mateo down when he called and asked me to meet him in Manhattan for lunch. And he wouldn't have been alone, crossing a busy street, in broad daylight, when someone put a bullet through his skull.

Tears prick the backs of my eyes, and I squeeze them shut as my phone continues to vibrate. I'm lost. Wracked with pain and regrets. And the only person who truly understands, the one person who could offer me comfort, hates my guts.

Natalia hasn't spoken one word to me since Saturday night. At the funeral, she stuck by her father's side, stoic and so fucking beautiful in the face of so much heartache. How could God be this cruel to snatch her brother from her only six months after she lost her mama?

I know my mom has been at the house this week, helping Natalia and Angelo with the arrangements. Every day, I have wanted to go there so badly. To take Natalia in my arms, beg for forgiveness, and keep her close. I can't lose her too. But seeing the way she looked at me on Sunday, when I first showed up on their doorstep, devastated at the news Mateo had been gunned down in cold blood, I knew she wanted nothing to do with me.

And I don't blame her. What I did was reprehensible. It killed me to do it, but she hasn't let me go, and she needs to. Angelo made himself very clear. If I don't stay away from her, she will lose the opportunity to attend NYU and I'll be resting eternally in a shallow grave.

Mateo was furious when she showed up at my birthday. He made it clear I was to handle it once and for all, but he took no pleasure in hurting his sister either.

Fuck this life. I bury my face in the pillow and yell. In the background, my stupid phone keeps going until I snatch it up. "What?" I roar.

Initial silence greets me, and then Brando's placid tone tickles my eardrums. "You need to calm the fuck down and clean your shit up."

He has dropped by a couple times to check on me. So what if cleaning my apartment has been the last thing on my mind this week? Who fucking cares? "Did you seriously call me to lecture me?"

"I called because Natalia is on her way to your place right now."

My heart stutters. "What?"

"She's currently curled up in the back seat, having cried herself to sleep. But not before she blackmailed me into taking her to you."

I would love to know what she has on him to force him into doing her wishes, but that's not important. "She hates me," I say, leaning down to grab dirty clothes off my bedroom floor with one arm.

"We both know that's not true," Brando quietly replies.

"She can't come here," I say, even as an inner voice in my head yells at me to shut the fuck up.

"She needs you." Brando's words are like a dagger and a comfort blanket. "And I think you need her too."

"The boss will kill me," I mutter, stuffing the pile of clothes in the laundry basket, before I walk into the living room, surveying the mess.

"Angelo won't know. He's out of town for the weekend."

"What?" I snap. "How the hell can he leave her at a time like this?"

"Why do you think I'm taking her to you?"

"You won't tell him?"

I can almost see Brando roll his eyes. "Shut the hell up, Leo, and open your fucking windows. We'll be there in fifteen." He hangs up before I can say anything else.

I race around my small two-bedroom apartment, doing my best to tidy it up before they get here. Then I grab the quickest shower ever and change into clean sweats and a white T-shirt.

The door chimes, and I pad toward it in my bare feet, tossing the towel I was using to rub at my damp hair onto the hall table. Pressing my brow to the back of the door, I inhale deeply, knowing this is a really bad idea but powerless to stop it because I will not deny Natalia if she needs me.

And the truth be told: I fucking need her too.

The second I open the door, she throws herself at me, sobbing into my shirt, and my arms go around her without hesitation. Brando's concerned expression latches on to mine. "It's okay. I've got it from here."

"I'll wait outside in the car."

I shake my head. I know he's got a girl in the city. "I'll protect her and take care of her. You take off, and I'll call you later."

He nods, and I steer Natalia inside, closing and locking the front door. She is suctioned to my body like a limpet, crying her eyes out, and my heart is breaking all over again. Sliding my hands under her legs, I scoop her up and carry her into my living room. I sit down on the couch, cradling her to my chest, crying silent tears as she falls apart in my lap.

She didn't cry at the funeral or back at the house. Not once. Not like she did at her mother's funeral. Mama told me she has been on autopilot all week, so it's not surprising this has happened. She's been trying to block out the pain, in the same way I have. But that magnitude of pain always finds a way to break free.

I hold her tighter, letting my tears drip down my face as we both succumb to our grief. She kicks off her shoes and moves her knees up closer, snuggling into me like she wishes she could dive inside me.

I don't know how long we sit there like that, clinging to one another and crying, but eventually our tears dry up, and she moves her head, setting it on my chest. One of her hands grips my sodden shirt, and she holds me close. I rest my chin on her head, running my fingers through her hair, and this is the first moment all week where I'm not in agonizing pain. Her warmth and her touch comfort me in a way no one else can.

"I told him I hated him," she says, lifting her tear-stained face to mine. "I slapped him." Her lower lip wobbles, and tears pool in her eyes again. "I was so angry at him. At you. I took it all out on him and he died thinking I hated him. If I had known those were the last things

I would ever say to my brother—the last interaction we would ever have—I would have taken every hateful word back." Wracking sobs heave from her chest, and a tight pain slices across my chest, knowing I'm the cause of this.

"He knew you loved him, *dolcezza*. He never doubted that. And he loved you so fucking much." I hold her tight to my chest, and her body shakes against me. "I am so sorry for the things I said and the things I did. I hate myself for it. I see the look on your face every night when I close my eyes." I deserve to be haunted by her heartbreak every night for the rest of my life.

"Did you fuck her?" she whispers, sniffling.

I clasp her face, peering deep into her bloodshot eyes. "No. What I did was for show. Once you left, I got rid of her." Mandy was *not* happy about that. Though it didn't take her long to find a willing body.

"It killed me," she says, tearing another strip off my heart. "I don't know if I can ever forgive you for it, but I can't think about that now." More tears cascade down her face. "He's gone, Leo. Mateo is gone. What am I going to do without him?" Agonizing howls filter through the eerie quietness of my apartment, and I feel her pain as acutely as my own. I wish I could take it all. To free her from the devastation, but I can't. I can't even tell her I'll be here for her because I won't be. I can't be. Neither of us is strong enough to resist temptation, so returning to just being friends won't cut it anymore.

Not when our hearts are fully invested.

"I don't know, Nat," I truthfully reply, swiping at the tears coursing down her face. "I don't know how I'm going to survive without him either." Tears fill my eyes, and I let them fall. I'm not ashamed for her to see.

"It's all so pointless," she says in a soft, husky voice that is unquestionably seductive, but I know it's not on purpose.

The way Natalia speaks and moves oozes sexuality without any conscious effort on her part.

"Why are we denying what we want when we could both be dead tomorrow?" Her eyes pin mine in place, and in this moment, I can't think of a single reason why we shouldn't just give in to our desires. "I need to forget. Just for a little while," she says, brushing her mouth against mine, making her intent clear. "I think you do too."

Chapter 25

LEO

MY HANDS GRIP her head through her hair, and I pull her face closer. "*Dolcezza*," I croak. "I love you," I add before crushing my mouth to hers.

God, *this*.

This is what I've been missing these past seven weeks.

Natalia breathes life into my body with every sweep of her lips and every stroke of her tongue, and I forget everything except the way she feels pressed up against me and the taste of her on my tongue. Our kissing quickly heats, and she moves so she's straddling me, her softness pressing against where I'm so fucking hard for her. Her hands creep up under my shirt, and I grab fistfuls of her ass, grinding her against me as I cant my hips upward.

She moans into my mouth, and precum leaks from my cock. Gathering her hair around my fist, I gently tug her head back, cautioning my inner beast to go slow. She is inexperienced, and she deserves the softest touch. My lips suction to her neck as she arches it back, granting me full access. I graze my mouth up and down the column of her elegant neck as she rocks on top of me. My cock jerks behind my sweats, and the need to claim her is almost too much to bear. I push her black blouse off one shoulder, trailing my lips across her silky flesh, somehow managing to resist the urge to bite her skin and leave my mark.

"Leo," she pants, moaning as she sways on top of me. "I need more."

Fuck it. "Wrap your legs around my waist and your arms around my neck," I command in a gruff tone, struggling to leash my arousal. My lust for her is at an all-time high, and though I know this is dangerous, I don't fucking care.

She wraps her arms and legs around me, and I carry her out of the room and into my bedroom, carefully laying her down on the bed before I crawl over her, keeping myself propped up by my hands so I'm not smothering her. "What do you want?" I ask, brushing stray strands of hair off her face.

"I want you to touch me. I need it."

"Here?" I ask, gently placing my hand on her right breast, through her flimsy blouse.

She nods before taking my hand and moving it lower. "And here." She places my hand over her pussy through her black pencil skirt.

Blood rushes to my cock, and I'm straining against the front of my sweats. My dick is dying to drive into her virgin pussy and take what has always been mine.

Somehow, I find and cling to restraint. "Are you sure?" I sit back on my heels. "If we do this, there is only one way it ends."

"I know, and I want it. I want you."

"Sit up," I instruct, whipping my shirt off. I toss it on the floor, leaving me in only my sweats. Her eyes trail over my chest and down to my abs and lower, and I'm burning up under her hungry gaze. "Your turn," I say, my voice heavy with desire.

She unbuttons her blouse with shaky fingers while maintaining eye contact with me. Flinging her gorgeous hair over her shoulder, she slips the blouse off, letting it fall beside my shirt on the floor. Her chest heaves, her nipples trying to poke holes in her flimsy red lace bra. Holding my gaze, she unclips her bra, letting it fall aside.

Her tits are fucking incredible. Big, round, and perfectly formed with small, rosy-pink nipples that are as hard as my dick. I rub the pad of my thumb against one nipple and then the other, and she gasps, her cheeks flushed, her eyes almost drowsy with desire. My hands cup her breasts, and I explore them with gentle fingers before lowering my face and sucking first one and then the other into my mouth. The moans that leave her mouth are an aphrodisiac and the tenuous hold on my control snaps.

I devour her—running my hands and my mouth all over her as I push her down, grinding against her, pounding her into the bed. Her hands roam my back, and she arches against me as I suck harder on one breast. When her hands slip under the band of my sweats to grab my ass, I'm a goner.

I bolt upright and yank my sweats off, kicking them away as I stride to the bedside table, removing a condom and some lube. I set them on top of my table and return to remove Natalia's skirt, leaving her in only her matching red lace panties. My fingers toy with the sides, brushing back and forth across her hipbones. "Are you sure you want to do this?"

"Yes," she pants. "I want this."

Slowly, I drag her panties down her legs, and my eyes are like laser beams on her skin as I reveal more and more of her body. I add her panties to the clothes on the floor and spread her thighs, sitting between them, on my heels, drinking her in. To her credit, she doesn't move or flinch, but her cheeks are bright red as I stare at her most intimate parts. "You are beautiful, Natalia. You are my every wet dream come to life." Slowly, I trail my hands up her legs, starting at her calves, moving up over her knees and along her inner thighs.

Her chest is heaving, her tits jiggling with the motion. I brush against her mound, and a gasp leaves her mouth. I drape myself carefully over her, kissing her lush lips as my fingers caress her folds. "I love you," I whisper, moving my mouth down her body. "Do you trust me to look after your pleasure?" I ask, peering up at her, as I continue to stroke her gently.

"Yes, Leo. I do."

"I'm going to make you feel so good." My eyes pierce hers in a silent promise as my lips sweep across her breasts. "I want you to keep looking at me. Watch what I do to you."

She nods, desire warring with nerves. My heart swells with love, as I press a tender kiss to her hipbone, while I slide one finger inside her. Fuck. She is so tight, and her walls are clenching my finger as I slowly move it inside her. "Watch." I remind her, lowering my mouth to her clit and lapping at it with my tongue.

"Oh my God, Leo." A sultry whimper flees her mouth as her hands move to my hair. "That feels so good. Don't stop."

I smile before focusing on the task at hand. "I'm going to make you come so hard you'll scream out my name." I add another digit inside, stretching her for me. I lap at her clit with my tongue and my lips, pumping my fingers in and out of her, picking up my pace as she relaxes, and I know it feels good. My hips dry hump the mattress, as I grind my aching cock against the bed, denying the desire to thrust into her before she's ready.

Her thighs tense, her legs lift, and her hips arch as she grinds her pussy into my face, and I know she's close. I lift my head for a second. "Come for me, *dolcezza*. Come all over my face, right now." I pump my fingers faster as my mouth returns to her clit, and I suck on it hard, keeping up a relentless pace, until she screams my name, over and over, while she falls apart underneath me in the most earth-shattering way.

I stay with her, milking every last drop of her climax before I crawl back up her body, gently settling between her legs. "Taste yourself," I say, before I claim her lips and thrust my tongue into her mouth. She moans into my mouth, while grabbing me hard, her hands devouring my body in every place she can touch.

"Fuck me," she says in my ear. "Please, Leo. I need to feel you inside me."

I don't need any further encouragement, leaning across her to grab the condom.

She watches me as I rip the top off the foil packet, and I almost stop breathing when she reaches out and touches my dick. The look of awe on her face is like nothing I have ever seen. I hold still as she explores my shaft, tracing her fingers up and down my straining length, following the bulging veins and attempting to wrap her tiny hand all the way around me. Her movements are clumsy and unsure, when she strokes me, and I place my hand over hers, moving it up and down, showing her how I like it.

When she leans down and swipes her tongue over the precum beading at my crown, I almost come on the spot. A hiss escapes through my clenched teeth and she stops, looking up at me in confusion.

"Baby." I lean down and kiss her. "If you keep that up, I'm going to come in five seconds and this will be over before it's begun."

"I want to taste you," she says, her cheeks flaming in another blush. "I want you to feel as good as you made me."

"Trust me, Nat. I feel good." I ravish her mouth in a passionate kiss before breaking away to roll on the condom. She watches, and I let her help before positioning myself between her thighs and guiding my cock to her entrance. I stop and look down at her. "Are you sure this is what you want?"

"Yes, Leo," she answers without hesitation, even though I see the fear and anxiety on her face.

I sweep my hands across her belly and up along her breasts as I hold myself still. "It will hurt at first, but I'll be careful."

"Okay." Smiling shyly, she relaxes back into the bed, spreading her thighs wider, waiting for me to enter her.

I look down, seeing where we are about to join, and my heart is thumping wildly in my chest. I want her. I want her so fucking badly, but I don't move. I can't.

Trust my conscience to kick in at this very moment.

This is wrong.

She's vulnerable and hurting and not thinking clearly because this isn't right.

I can't do this. Not like this.

I can't take her virginity in a moment of desperation and vulnerability.

I won't ruin her life.

"Leo," she whispers, propping up on her elbows. "What's wrong?" she inquires, her brow creasing in worry.

Pain flattens my chest until it feels like I can't breathe. Lust battles what is right inside me until I pull back, sitting on the side of the bed, with my head in my hands. "I'm sorry, Natalia. I'm so sorry, but I can't do this with you."

"What? Why?" There is movement on the bed, and when I turn around, she has pulled her legs up to her chest, placing her hands over her pussy, protecting herself from me. Hurt is clear on her face, and I hate that I'm upsetting her again.

"I love you." I scoot up so I'm closer but still not touching her. "I love you enough not to want to ruin your future."

She opens her mouth to argue, and I silence her with a shake of my head. "I haven't been honest with you, and you deserve that much." I tell her the truth. That her father knows and he threatened me. I explain I purposely pushed her away to protect her. "I can't be close to you and not be with you, Natalia. This proves it conclusively." I gesture between us.

"What about what I want?" she whispers. "I know Mama said something to you too. She told me to grab hold of our love with both hands and to enjoy it for the short time we would have together."

"Mama Rosa said the same to me, but she didn't know Angelo would find out. That changes everything. What we want doesn't come into it. You know that." I move in a little closer, cupping her face. "I love you enough to let you go, and if you love me too, then you must do the same."

"I think I'm destined to lose everyone I love. Destined to never know a moment's happiness." She drops her eyes, refusing to look at me, and I let go of her face.

"Don't say that. I need to believe you'll be happy in order to let you go." It's the only way I can do this.

"Happiness is an illusion," she says, her voice sounding dead as she slides off the bed and retrieves her clothing. "And I'm done chasing an illusion."

I hate hearing her speak like this, but I have nothing to say to that. I'm empty.

"You're right," she says after we have silently redressed. "If we can't be together, we can't be anything."

Her words make mincemeat of my heart, but I don't deny them. "I will always love you, Nat." I get up, reeling her into my arms one last time. "There won't be a single day that goes by when you are not on my mind."

She shucks out of my hold, and the frozen, emotionless look on her face hurts me as much as her agonized, grief-stricken expression from earlier. "Goodbye, Leo. I hope you find some peace and someone amazing who showers you with love and worships the ground you walk on because you deserve to be loved like that."

I don't return the sentiment though I wish that for her too. But we both know her fate will not be of her choosing. "If you ever need me, I will always be here for you," I say, following her out of my bedroom and into the hall. Brando messaged me a few minutes ago, confirming he was outside and ready to take her home whenever she wanted to leave.

She angles her body, turning to me as her fingers grip the door handle. "That's a sweet sentiment, but we both know it's not true." Letting go of the door, she throws herself at me, hugging me close.

My arms band around her, and I pull her close, burying my head in her neck, fighting tears. Closing my eyes, I savor the feel of her in my arms, knowing this is the last time.

"Thank you for telling me the truth," she says, easing out of my embrace. She wraps her arms around herself. "I love you enough to protect you from my father. As much as I love the old bastard, I know how ruthless he is. I know it's no idle threat. I would die if you died, Leo, so I would rather live my life missing you every single second of every minute of every hour of every day, knowing you are still out there somewhere, living your life without me in it."

"*Amore mio*." I lace my fingers in hers. "*Cuore mio*." Tears fill my eyes, and my heart feels like it's about to burst, such is the intensity of the pain in my chest. "You will always be with me, and I will always be with you."

"Maybe in the next lifetime, we will get to be together," she says, smiling sadly before ripping her hand from mine and yanking the door open. "Until then," she whispers, looking at me one final time as tears roll down her face. "Stay safe, my love."

And then she leaves.

Taking every single part of my heart with her.

Chapter 26

LEO

"WAS IT THE Grecos? Have they found out?" I ask Angelo as I pace his office on Monday morning.

"No." He leans forward on his elbows, the strain showing on his face. He looks like shit and as bad as I feel. "They bought the Colombian angle, and I have men on the inside. This wasn't their doing."

"Then who?"

"Sit down, Leonardo. You're making me dizzy."

I drop into the chair in front of his desk, staring sullenly at the empty chair beside me, where Mateo would normally sit. I gulp back the lump in my throat and grip the armrests tight. "Who did this and why?"

"I think it was the Russians." He rubs his hands up and down his face.

"What beef do the Russians have with us?"

This is the first time I am hearing of any issue with the Bratva. Although I'm only a lowly *soldato*, Angelo brought Mateo and me in on a lot of high-level discussions, so it's unusual neither one of us was aware of something going down. If Mateo had known, he would have confided in me. We didn't usually keep secrets from one another. I wonder if this will change now Mateo is gone—if my access to

Angelo will be restricted.

"We found some of their guys selling product on the streets," he explains. "Sent one of them home with a message, assuming they would move out of our turf."

"Would they really take Mateo down in retaliation for that?" It seems unlikely to me.

"Five of their guys are shark fodder at the bottom of the Hudson. Maybe I killed someone's son and this was a father's revenge or it was a renegade who lost a buddy and decided to take matters into his own hands. We know how unstructured and undisciplined they are."

The Bratva are a strange mafia organization in the US. They don't have solid structures or strong leadership like the Italian *mafioso*, and it's widely known a lot of their men operate as solo agents. While they have their traditions, the same as we do, they are a wild, uncultured rabble. It's why we have never seen them as much of a threat. They lack coordination and loyal manpower.

"Whatever you are planning, I want in." My eyes bore into his. Mateo was my best friend, my brother, and I want to slaughter the man responsible for his death with my bare hands.

"I have a meeting later this morning with the other dons to discuss it. I'll let you know if anything new comes to light. If, and when, we make plans, you will be included. I give you my word." He stands, signaling the end of our conversation. Taking his jacket from the back of his chair, he folds it over his arm and comes to stand beside me. "Walk me to my car," he says, moving toward the exit. "I have something else to tell you. We have a making ceremony tonight."

"We do? Who is getting initiated?" I arch a brow as we step out into the hallway. I keep my head down, forcing myself not to seek out Natalia. I know most of the young men in our *famiglia*, and I can't think of anyone who has just turned thirteen.

"I have someone I want you to take under your wing," he adds, opening the front door. He stops on the top step, tilting his face up, basking in the early June sunshine. I quietly close the door and stand beside him, wondering what's going on. After a few beats of silence, he looks over at me. "I have another son, and I need you to help me to teach him our ways."

NATALIA

"*Natalia! Principessa!*" My father hollers up the stairs, his loud voice booming off the walls, but I ignore him, curling tighter into myself on top of my comforter, willing him to go away.

No such luck.

The door rattles as he knocks on it before walking inside a few seconds later.

I sit up, staring at him in outrage. "Papa! You can't just barge in here! I could've been undressing!"

"And you can't just ignore me." His eyes skim over my wrinkled clothing and my wan face. "We have someone special joining us for dinner. Take a shower, and clean yourself up. You're the woman of this house now, Natalia. I need you to act like it."

"My brother just died!" I cry, the words sticking in my throat. "And you're already entertaining guests, as if we haven't lost Mama and Mateo!" I fight a fresh wave of tears.

He sighs heavily, and exhaustion cloaks his face as he sits on the edge of my bed. "Princess." He clasps my hands in his. "I know you are hurting because I'm hurting too, but we can't sit around grieving all day. Life must go on. You know it is what Mateo and your mama would have wanted."

"Everywhere I look, I see reminders of them," I whisper. "I don't want to forget them, but the pain of constant reminders is killing me, Papa. I don't know how to go on when it's only you and me now. Overnight, we have lost half our family, and I feel lost too."

"Come here, *bella*." He opens his arms, and though I'm mad at my father—for this lifestyle that got Mateo killed and for forcing Leo away from me—he is the only family I have left, and I need him.

I need him to hold me and tell me it will all be okay.

So, I wrap my arms around him and let him hug me. He smooths a hand down the back of my hair. "We will get through this. *You* will get through this because you are strong like your mother. I think tonight will help too."

All the tiny hairs lift on the back of my neck at his words. "No, Papa!" I exclaim, shucking out of his embrace as I contemplate his meaning. "You said I could go to NYU! That I wouldn't have to marry until I was finished. I—"

"Shush, *principessa.*" He cuts me off before I dissolve into hysteria. "It is not a suitor. He is someone else entirely."

Air punches from my lungs in grateful relief, and now I'm intrigued. "Who is it Papa?"

He stands. "Clean yourself up and come downstairs so I can introduce you."

I take the quickest shower in the history of showers, covering my hair so it doesn't get wet as my thick locks take forever to blow-dry. Then I pull on red underwear underneath a black knee-length dress.

I used to scoff at the tradition that saw mafia wives, sisters, and daughters wearing layers of black clothing after a death in the family. Now, it's more modern to wear something black with red underwear because black symbolizes mourning, red symbolizes blood, and the contrasting colors denote revenge.

Strangely, I have found it a comfort succumbing to the tradition this past week. I trust my father to discover whoever did this to my brother and to make them pay. I'm working up the courage to ask Papa if I can be there when the culprit is tortured and killed. I want to see him suffer before we snuff out his miserable existence.

I rub some rouge into my cheeks and slick on some lip gloss and mascara before slipping my feet into my black ballet flats. Then I spritz some perfume on my wrists and my neck, and I head downstairs to meet our mystery guest.

"Ah, here she is," Papa says as I slip into our living room. He stands, walks toward me, and takes my hand, pulling me over to the stranger as he gets up from the couch.

Gosh, he is tall and extremely handsome. And oddly familiar. With dark hair, a strong nose, full lips, and expressive blue eyes, he is a very good-looking guy. The thick five o'clock shadow on his jawline and the purple shadows under his eyes suggest he hasn't had much sleep lately. He carries himself rigidly, as if he's in some pain, and I frown. Is he hurt? He looks young, but I can tell he's a bit older than me.

He eyes me curiously as I do him.

"Let's sit." Papa pulls me over to the couch opposite the man. We all sit at the same time, and there's a tension in the air I can't explain.

"Natalia, this is Bennett," Papa says, keeping his eyes trained on mine. "Bennett is my son and your brother."

I blink profusely, staring into space, sure I must have misheard him. Slowly, I turn to face my father. "What?" I blurt, thoroughly shell-shocked.

"I know this is a shock, Natalia, but a pleasant one, I hope."

I swing my gaze to Bennett, studying his features more closely, and I see the resemblance. To Papa. To me. To Mateo. His eyes contain sympathy and a healthy dose of turmoil as they connect with mine.

"How?" I ask, whipping my head back to Papa. If my father had another son he kept a secret, there can only be one reason for that. "Did Mama know you had a child with another woman?"

He nods, and his tongue darts out, wetting his lips.

Mama knew? I cannot imagine what that news must have done to her. Confusion and pain swirl in my heart, and I wrap my arms around my body, feeling a chill creep up my spine.

"My mother was Jillian Carver," Bennett says in a deep baritone voice.

"Was?" I ask, lifting my eyes to meet his.

"She died last year."

"I'm sorry," I say without hesitation. "We have that in common."

"I'm sorry for your loss too. Both of them," he replies, and this is one of the weirdest moments of my life. One of the strangest conversations.

"Did you know?" I ask him.

He shakes his head. "My mother never told me anything about my father. I had no idea I had a sister and a brother until Angelo sent men to collect me from Chicago."

"You lived in Chicago?"

"All my life." He places his hand on his right shoulder, hissing a little.

"Bennett was initiated earlier today," Papa says.

Of course, he was.

Now I know why Bennett is in pain and rubbing his shoulder where the Mazzone crest was recently imprinted. I grind my teeth to the molars. Mateo isn't even cold in his grave, and Papa is already lining up another successor.

I glare at my father, channeling all my anger and frustration in his direction.

This isn't Bennett's fault. He was as clueless as me, and now I know why he looks dazed and confused. Papa just lifted him from his life in Chicago and thrust him into the belly of the beast.

"I'm so sorry," I say, ignoring my father and looking at Bennett. "I can only imagine how confused you are."

"It's been a lot to take in," he admits, as a muscle clenches in his jaw. He cracks his knuckles and averts his eyes.

"You two need each other," Papa says, and I glare at him again, not concealing my anger. "Be careful, *principessa*," he murmurs, gripping my chin though his touch is gentle. "I have killed men for lesser looks."

I wrench out of his hold and rise, pinning him with the full extent of my rage. "Do you care about anyone, Papa?" I yell, throwing my hands around. "Or are we all just pawns in this sick game you play?

"Sit down, Natalia," he snaps. "And show me some respect. I am your father." He smacks the arm of the couch.

I walk around him and take a seat beside Bennett, reaching over and taking one of his hands in mine. I give it a reassuring squeeze as I smile at him. His eyes fill with warmth, and he squeezes my hand back. I turn my head to eyeball my father. "Don't treat me like a little girl, Papa," I say in a calm voice once I have gotten control of my anger. "And don't you dare try to treat Bennett as a replacement for Mateo."

Bennett flinches, and I hold his hand tighter. "I loved Matty," I explain, looking up at him. "And no one could ever take his place, but you're my brother too. A brother who deserves to exist in his own right, and our relationship will be ours, because we want to care for one another, not because you are trying to fill Mateo's shoes." I hope he gets the meaning behind my words.

"I have never had a brother or sister," he tells me. "I'm used to fending for myself, but I would like to get to know you."

"I would like that too." This time when he squeezes my hand, it soothes something deep inside me. I meant what I said. I can't paper over the cracks in my heart—and the soul-deep pain I know I will always feel at Mateo's loss—with anyone else, but this is an opportunity to build something new with someone who shares my DNA.

Bennett is my family now too, and I could never turn my back on him.

More than that, Bennett will need me.

He's been thrown into this life with no warning, and he will need me to help guide his path. Suddenly, I have a new purpose, and it fills me with cautious hope. Something I have not felt for a long time.

"I thought for sure you would hate me," he admits, staring into my eyes, with sincerity written all over his face. "I'm not sure I'd be as gracious if I was in your shoes."

"Nonsense. This is not your fault or mine." I drill another stern look in my father's direction. He is watching us curiously but not giving too much away. "We have been kept away from one another and denied the opportunity to form a sibling bond. That ends now. You will need my help, and that is what sisters are for."

He smiles, and it transforms his face. I bet my brother has women dropping at his feet and crawling all over him. "How old are you?" I ask.

"Twenty-one. And you're eighteen?"

Eighteen going on forty it feels sometimes, but I don't articulate that thought as I nod.

"This pleases me," Papa says, and I jerk my gaze to his.

"I'm not doing it for you," I say, my tone cold. "I'm doing it for Bennett."

"My close friends call me Ben."

I consider that for a moment, giving him my full attention. "Then I shall call you Benny."

His eyes twinkle with indecipherable emotion, and I have a feeling Benny and I are going to get along famously.

"Bennett is going to Italy for a month, next week, to your Aunt Silvie's," Papa supplies. "I want him to learn about the traditions first-hand from your Uncle Paulo and your cousins. You should go too. Explore Europe with your female cousins. Take a break from New York for a while."

I haven't been to Italy in years. When we were younger, Mama used to take us for a few weeks every summer. But since both sets of grandparents passed away, we stopped going. I don't need to consider Papa's offer for long. This is exactly what I need. Provided Leo isn't being sent on this trip. "If I go, who else will be there?" I ask, eyeballing my father.

"I will send Brando and his capo father with you. Leonardo is needed here," he adds, daring me to challenge him.

He obviously thinks I want him to go when the truth is I want to stay as far away from Leonardo Messina as possible. Saturday night finally put an end to things between us, and I am determined to lock my feelings away in a permanent lockbox and to never think of him like that again.

"Okay," I say, breathing more easily. "I will go."

Benny squeezes my hand, looking relieved. "Thank you."

No. Thank *you*, I want to say. Because I'm pretty sure this man is going to save me from myself.

Chapter 27

NATALIA

BENNETT AND I forged an instant connection from the second we met. One that was consolidated when we spent that month in Italy together. He held me together as I fell apart. Mopped the copious tears I shed for Mateo and Mama and helped to stitch my heart back together. We shared stories of our childhood, and my heart ached for all he'd had to endure with his prostitute addict mom and no father.

It evoked conflicting emotions in me.

I was so angry with Papa for abandoning him to that fate yet grateful to him for the childhood I'd had. I was loved, sheltered, and cared for in a way Ben hadn't been. He was curious to learn about the brother he never met, and reminiscing about all the amazing times I had with Mateo helped me to heal.

Ben informed me that summer that Papa was considering reneging on his agreement and marrying me off now. He was concerned I was depressed and thought a husband would be the thing to pull me out of the pit of despair I had slid back into.

As if.

I wonder if Papa knows me at all. Knows women at all.

Thank God for Ben. He convinced Papa to stick to the plan, assuring him NYU was all that was needed to help me to move forward with my life.

Things weren't one-sided though. He needed me as much as I needed him. Ben leaned on me as he struggled to adjust to a completely different life, and I helped to prop him up. We became a solid team as we both navigated new waters, and I think I may have saved him, in the same way he saved me.

In the three years that have since passed, our relationship has continued to grow despite his long absences when he is away attending to business. Benny is learning the ropes from the ground up. As one of Papa's *soldati*, he is often gone for weeks on end.

In between, we spend as much time together as we can, and I love him.

Our relationship is very different from the one I had with Matty, and I try not to compare them. Often, I wonder what would have happened if Matty had known about Ben. I think he would have felt threatened. He may even have felt the need to eliminate his competition. A shudder works its way through me at the thought.

Leo was wary of Bennett at the start. His loyalty was tested when Papa asked him to take Ben under his wing and work closely with him to teach him everything he knew. But, over time, Benny won Leo over too. And now they are close. Perhaps even closer than he was with Mateo.

If that troubles him, I wouldn't know because we rarely speak. Both of us go to huge extremes to avoid one another, and though my heart aches daily at the loss of him in my life, I know it has to be this way.

My phone pings with an incoming call, and I pick it up, smiling as Frankie's gorgeous face stares at me from my screen. I accept her FaceTime call and sit up against my headboard to talk to my bestie. "Hey, babe! You look amazing. You're all glowing and tanned and beautiful." Behind her, the sky is the clearest blue, hovering over the lapping waves of the Aegean Sea.

She laughs, raising her hand to tuck a few flyaway strands of hair behind her ear. The pretty diamond on her ring finger glints and sparkles.

"I still can't believe you are married," I say, recalling her joyous happiness two weeks ago when she said I do.

"Me either. It all happened so fast."

“It did, but it was meant to be.”

Frankie and Archer called it quits at the end of our freshman year at college. Frankie attends NYU with me—courtesy of my father’s generosity—and Archer is across the country playing ball for the California Golden Bears. The long-distance thing wasn’t working so they chose to end things amicably. She spent most of our sophomore year kissing random jocks and frat boys before she met Carlino Bianchi, at the start of our junior year, in a Manhattan club. Carlino took her home to meet his family, and the instant her eyes locked on his older brother Enrico, her heart was claimed.

Carlino was a little hurt at first when Frankie broke things off with him to date his brother, but as soon as he saw how enamored they were with one another, he found it in his heart to forgive her and to give them his blessing. It was a whirlwind romance and undoubtedly love at first sight. They were engaged within a month and married eight months later, literally one week after our junior year ended.

Frankie’s parents are over the moon she has found a nice Italian boy to settle down with. The Bianchis are part of the Maltese *famiglia* and Rico is one of their *soldati*, which means Frankie is now an official mob wife. While I’m still unattached and there has been no formal marriage contract made with any of the men who have come asking.

I am due to start my senior year in two months, so I know my reprieve is ending soon, but I fully intend to enjoy my last summer of freedom without thinking of the fate that lies in wait for me. “How is Santorini, and are you seeing anything outside of the bedroom?” I tease, pulling my knees up to my chest.

“It’s not a huge island, so it’s perfect. It means I don’t feel too guilty for spending hours tangled between the sheets with my new husband.” Her face breaks out in a wide grin. “I still get such a thrill saying that!”

“I’m so happy you are happy. Enrico is a good man, and I know he will always take care of you the way you deserve.”

“I have to pinch myself sometimes to believe this is my life. I didn’t think it was possible to feel so much joy. To feel this alive. But he has opened my eyes to a world of passion and a level of happiness I didn’t think existed.”

A pang of longing jumps up and bites me. I don’t want to be

envious of my friend because I am truly happy for her. But I remember the bursts of passion I experienced in my short relationship with Leo, and I know I won't ever be lucky enough to feel the same again. I know my future will be different from my friend's, and for a fleeting moment, I wish I could trade places with her.

The thought is gone as quickly as it enters my mind. I won't begrudge my friend her happiness. "That's all I have ever wanted for you, Frankie. You deserve it."

Her smile fades a little as she leans forward into the screen. "You deserve it too, Nat, and I want that for you so badly." Sorrow skates across her face, mirroring the expression on mine, no doubt.

"You know that's not my fate, and I have made my peace with it." That is largely true. After Mateo died and the night I almost gave my virginity to Leo, a part of me died inside. The part that was clinging to a futile dream. From then on, I embraced my destiny and my role in this world, and I shut down any other emotions. Even with Ben, and he is someone I confide a lot of things in. But he doesn't know the truths hiding in my heart or that I once swore to rebel against a future I wanted no part of.

"I hurt for you," Frankie admits, as a shadow looms behind her.

"Don't." I smile at my friend when her husband leans down to press a kiss to her neck from behind. "I am in a good place, Frankie. You shouldn't expend energy worrying about me."

I got to live my NYU dream, and it's been one of the best experiences of my life. I have thrown myself into my studies and college life. I have friends, and we go out and have fun. I have even managed a few sneaky kisses with guys in nightclubs and at frat parties, but I don't date and I haven't had sex. What is the point in risking everything for a brief attachment with someone I can never have? So, I shield my heart and protect my virtue, and I have learned to accept this is the way it will always be.

"Hey, Nat." Enrico's handsome face fills the screen. "This one misses you a lot."

I bark out a laugh. "Don't lie to me, Rico. I know what you two have been up to," I tease. "There has been no time for missing anything or anyone, and that is how it should be on your honeymoon."

"You must come over for dinner when we get back. We can tell you all about it." He winks, and I throw back my head laughing.

"I'll gladly listen to the censored version. The rest you can keep to yourselves."

We chat casually for a few more minutes before saying goodbye and ending the call.

I am sorting clothes in my closet when there is a knock on my door.

"Nat. Can I come in?" Bennett asks, and I squeal, dropping the dress in my hand onto the floor while I rush to answer the door.

I throw myself at my brother when I yank the door open, and he stumbles back a little, chuckling. "Benny! You're home early!" I hug him tight, and his arms wrap around my waist as he holds me close. "I missed you." The last time I saw him was at my twenty-first birthday party at the end of April. I ease back, holding on to his arms as I do a quick inspection. He looks uninjured and in good health. "Are you hurt any place I can't see?" Ben always comes to me when he's injured, and I personally tend to his wounds unless it's of a serious nature and he needs to see the doc.

I like looking after my brother.

In the same way I used to look after Mateo and Leo.

He shakes his head, slinging his arm over my shoulders as he saunters into the room, closing the door behind him. "I'm not home early because I'm injured."

"You're sure?" My brows crease in concern as I rake my gaze over him again. Since he got shot last year, I've been on edge every time he goes away. I cannot bear the thought of anything happening to him.

I already lost one brother.

I don't want to lose another.

"I'm sure." He presses a kiss into my hair. "What happened last year won't happen again. I never make the same mistake twice."

"I can't help worrying."

His expression turns tender as he looks at me. "I know." He brushes his fingers across my cheek. "I know how badly you miss Mateo and how much it hurt to lose him like that. I never want you to go through it again. It's why I'm going to change things, Nat. The way things have been done will change when I'm in charge. The violence and bloodshed of the past can't continue. I am going to build a new empire and modernize the Cosa Nostra in the US." He tweaks my nose. "Mark my words. Change is coming, and I will be steering that ship."

"I have no doubts about that." Pity it won't happen in time to save me from my fate, but Papa only just turned fifty-eight, and he isn't slowing down. He has no plans to retire and hand the reins to Bennett any time soon. "But violence will always be a hallmark of the world we live in, and you will always be a target."

"I know."

He readily agrees, and I love that he doesn't lie to me. I know more about the *mafiosi* now than I ever did because Benny shares things with me in a way Mateo wouldn't. I know he tones down some of the stories, but I am on this journey with him, even if he is often miles away. He doesn't treat me like a kid or a weak woman who needs to be sheltered from the truth. Ben believes knowledge is power, and he wants me to be fully versed in the things that happen so I can defend myself.

The old bastard—aka Papa—would throw a hissy fit if he knew the things Ben has told me. What he doesn't know can't hurt him.

"But I am skilled now, and I can properly defend myself," Ben continues. "And I have Leo and the guys watching my back. Nothing is going to happen to me. No one will get close enough to take me out."

"Did Leo come back uninjured?" I ask, like always. As much as I have closed my heart to my feelings for him, I still worry about Leo too. Whenever Ben comes back, I always ask if he is okay too.

"Leo is fine." Ben drills me with a look. Somehow, he understands Leo is an off-limits topic, and he never pries, even though I know he knows there is more to the story. Perhaps he asked Leo and Leo told him.

"Whatever the reason, I'm glad you're home." I snuggle into his side, heaving a sigh of contentment. The world always feels like a safer place when my brother's arms are around me.

"I won't be traveling so much in the future."

My eyes widen with hope. "You won't?"

"Angelo just promoted me to capo, and he assigned me a team of men. I'll be staying in the city, with the odd business trip required, but I'm going to be around more."

I hug him tighter. "This is the best news ever."

"I need to go apartment hunting. I was hoping you would come with me?"

"I would love that. I have a couple of months before I return to NYU, so I have time to help you to find and furnish a place."

His brow puckers, and his face glimmers with a myriad of emotions as he pulls me over to my window seat. We sit at opposite ends, staring at one another. "What is that face for?" I ask, instantly on guard.

"Has Angelo said anything to you?"

"About what?" Nerves fire at me from all angles.

"He's in talks about a marriage contract."

All the blood drains from my face. "Please tell me it's not with that perv Conti from Philly."

Papa brought the man over for dinner six months ago. He is keen to secure an alliance with the Contis, as they have some distribution routes he needs. Their don is dying, and Paulo is his successor. He was contracted to marry someone else, but it fell through, and I know Papa brought him over to see if he was agreeable to a match. He spent the entire meal leering at me, and he made my skin crawl.

I heard nothing else about it and Ben hadn't either, so I thought it was off the table, and I was hugely relieved. Paulo is pushing forty, and he has the bad combover and beer belly to prove it. All I could think at that dinner was how I would puke if he put his sweaty, stubby hands anywhere near me.

Ben shakes his head, and my breath oozes out in shuddering relief. "It's someone closer to home."

"Who?" I chew on the inside of my mouth.

"Gino Accardi."

I gasp. "No!"

"You know his wife just died in a car crash and he has twin sons. They are only three. He needs to find a new wife, and I heard last night that he approached Angelo about you."

That's why Ben came home. I knew there was a reason.

"He's ancient!" I croak.

Ben's lips curve up at the corner. "He's only thirty-eight or thirty-nine, Nat. He's hardly geriatric."

"He might as well be," I murmur, troubled over this news. It's not like I haven't known I would be married to an older man. It's usually the norm. But Gino seems older than his years, and he has always scared me a little.

"He's a decent man. Far better than any of the others Angelo was considering. And he's a don. The youngest don in our history." Admiration glistens in Ben's eyes, and I know he desires to achieve that accolade someday.

Footsteps thud up the stairs, and Ben stands. "Anyway, I wanted to give you a heads-up. Say nothing to Angelo when he informs you Don Accardi is coming for dinner."

"Ah, hell. Tonight?" I grumble, resting my head against the windowpane. "I had plans to meet my friends for dinner in the city."

"You had better unmake them," Ben says as Papa raps on my door.

Chapter 28

NATALIA

"YOU LOOK BEAUTIFUL tonight, Natalia," Gino says, lifting my hand and bringing it to his mouth. He plants a firm kiss across my knuckles. "As always."

"Thank you." I smile politely at him while inside I'm freaking out.

"She is beautiful, just like her mama." Papa stands in front of the family portrait on the wall, quietly studying the last picture taken with all of us together.

"Indeed," Gino agrees, coming to stand alongside Papa. "Rosa was stunning, and your daughter takes after her."

I barely resist the urge to gag as my eyes meet Benny's across the table.

We sit down to eat, and conversation flows easily around the table, but I'm on edge and hardly able to stomach any food. Gino is pleasant and attentive, and he smiles more than normal, which I know is his way of making me feel at ease.

After dinner, the men retire to Papa's study while I change my shoes and head outside to take a walk. I can't stay inside while I know they are discussing me, and I need to clear my head and try to work out how I feel about this.

A car is pulling up to the side of the house as I emerge, and my heart thumps wildly in my chest as Leo steps out of the vehicle. I haven't seen him since my birthday party either. I was surprised he attended, as he has avoided my birthday for years. I think he did it for his mother and Giuliana, because I know they give him a hard time for abandoning me after Mateo died.

Of course, Paulina and Giuliana know nothing of what happened between us, so it must seem unusual. Any time they broach the subject with me, I dismiss it casually, claiming we are both leading busy lives that have gone in different directions. Giuliana buys it. I'm not so sure Leo's mama does though.

I move to walk off when Leo calls out. "Wait up, *dolcezza*."

I briefly close my eyes as his dulcet tone wafts over me like a carnal breeze. Hearing his pet name for me brings a whole host of memories rushing to the surface, and just like that, my heart remembers.

Everything.

I am fooling myself if I think locking my feelings away changes anything.

I still love him.

I know I always will.

"Hey." His voice is husky, his warm breath tickling my ear as I force my eyes open.

"Leo." I do my best to keep my tone level, and I refuse to look directly at him. It hurts too much to do it.

"Is it true?"

I tilt my face up at his question. "Is what true?" It's a miracle I get the words out. Being this close to him is too much. He looks so damn good. Smells good too. He's like vintage wine that just gets better with age.

He is broader and more muscular, and he has new ink creeping up one side of his neck. He wears his hair shorter than he used to, but it's still full on top and tight at the sides. It highlights the magnificent bone structure of his face, showcasing his sculpted jawline and the light coating of facial hair covering it. His gray-blue eyes penetrate mine, and I stop breathing. I could drown in his eyes and never regret it. His eyes are the entryway to his soul, and right now, I see every emotion he wants so desperately to hide.

"Don Accardi wants to marry you?" His Adam's apple bobs in his throat as pain radiates from his eyes.

I shouldn't be pleased to know he's still hurting as much as I am, but it is good to know I'm not in this alone. That he has suffered through the years too. It helps to know it was real. Like it somehow ratifies my feelings and gives them substance.

Only a foolish woman continues to love a man who never truly loved her.

"Nothing has been formally said to me, but it appears that is the case."

He closes his eyes, and tension fills the small gap between us. Pain fills every empty part of me, and intense sorrow replaces the blood flowing through my veins as I stand beside the love of my life, unable to touch him or tell him he is still the only one.

For a long time after Leo rejected me that night, I was angry and hurt and humiliated. I cursed him a million times over. Until I moved beyond it and I realized he did it to protect me. If we had had sex that night, it would've been tarnished with pain and regret. We were both grieving my brother's loss, and it's no wonder we sought comfort in one another. It never should have gotten as far as it did, and I'm glad he stopped it. I'm glad he stopped me from making an even bigger mistake.

"I miss you," he whispers, slowly opening his eyes. Discreetly, he hooks his pinkie in mine, and my breath stutters in my throat. "I miss you so fucking much."

Drawing strength from somewhere, I step away from him. "Don't do this," I whisper back. "Don't undo years of progress."

"Don't bullshit me, *dolcezza*," he snaps. "Don't pretend like you haven't been living half a life too!"

That pisses me off. I plant my hands on my hips and glare at him. "Don't pull that crap on me, Leo. Do you think I don't know what you and Ben get up to when you're away on business or all those weekends when he staggers home reeking of booze and women?"

"Those women mean nothing to me, and there have been a lot less than you imagine. It's only sex."

My lips curl in disgust. "If that's supposed to make me feel better, newsflash, it doesn't." I prod my finger in his chest. "I haven't slept with anyone. I haven't been intimate with anyone since you."

"I'm trying to forget you! To let you go! But nothing works."

What the fuck? Does he expect me to give him a medal or something? God, I really fucking hate men sometimes.

He jams his finger in his temple. "You're in here." He slaps a hand over his heart. "And here." Stepping toward me, he takes my hands in his. His wild eyes are frantic as they probe mine. "I love you, Nat. I can't keep denying it. Run away with me. Let's disappear off the face of the earth. Ben would cover for us. I know he would. We can be together."

The words pour out of him, laced with pain and longing, and I can't take it. I can't let him ruin everything I have worked so hard to ignore. Yanking my hand from his warm palm, I shake my head. The pain in my heart is so intense I think I could be having a heart attack. It spreads across my chest, pressing down, making breathing almost impossible. I bend over, panting heavily, as I press my hands to my knees. "Why are you doing this?" I cry, even though I know the answer.

He drops to his knees on the gravel, placing his hands over mine. "I was too stupid and weak to do what I should've done three years ago. Nothing matters, Natalia, but you. Tell me what to do, and I'll do it, but don't push me away."

I straighten up, swiping at the hot tears coursing down my face. "I need you to leave me alone, Leo." My voice comes out harsh. "I need you to go back to fucking your whores and leave me to my fate." Raw pain shrouds his face, and I feel it alongside my own. It softens my edge a little. "There was a time I would have run away with you, but it's too late, Leo."

"It's not." Climbing to his feet, he takes my hands again. "I can't go on like this without you. It feels like I'm dying inside."

"You think I don't know what that feels like, Leo?" I shout as tears fill my eyes again. "You had a choice to make, and you chose it. I made my choices too. I have accepted my fate, and you need to accept that. Whatever we had can never be."

"Whatever we *have*," he corrects.

"It doesn't matter, Leo. This time next year, I will be a married woman. You need to let me go. Maybe give one of those women you fuck a chance." It kills me to say that, but I don't like thinking of him living his life alone either.

"No one will ever own my heart but you."

Ditto, I want to say, but I don't. This has gone on too long. It's a miracle Papa or Gino haven't reared their heads. "I don't want it," I lie, taking a step back. "And I don't want you saying any of these things to me again. We were over before we even began, Leo. You need to accept that and move on with your life like I am."

I don't wait for him to reply, turning around and racing back into the house.

"NO, PAPA!" I cry out later that night as I am talking with him and Ben in Papa's study. "You promised!"

"You can't go back on your word." Ben instantly jumps to defend me.

"I can and I will." He jabs his finger in the air in Bennett's direction. "A don makes decisions that will benefit the greater good. Natalia marrying Don Accardi will strengthen the five families. If you're serious about restarting The Commission, boy, you will support this decision. We need the full weight of the five behind your idea before we can broach the subject with any other *famiglia*. It will take time and planning. This union will go a long way toward solidifying the bonds within New York."

I know Ben has notions of reforming the defunct Commission, a governing body for the American *mafiosi* that was initially created by Lucky Luciano back in 1931. But I wasn't aware he had mentioned his plans to Papa. I refuse to believe it's the reason he wants me to marry Gino. Papa is old school, and he's getting old. He doesn't like change. I think he's just pandering to Ben and using that argument to win his support for this proposed contract.

Not that Ben or I need to agree to it. If Papa says it will happen, then it will happen.

"Why does it have to be now? Why can't I complete senior year and then marry him?"

"Because his boys need a mother now, *principessa*." His hand comes down on my shoulder. "You will be a wonderful Mama to Caleb and Joshua, and they need you. Gino does too. Juliet's death has devastated him."

Ben scowls while I keep my thoughts to myself. Marrying a man who has just lost his beloved, cherished wife is last on my list of things to do, but Papa has made up his mind. "Can't I marry him and continue my studies? Surely, he has a nanny?"

"His sons have just lost their mother, Natalia. He doesn't want to pawn them off on the nanny. He wants a wife to look after him and care for his children. He wants that woman to be you."

"You understand how sexist and archaic this is?" Ben's jaw is tense as he stares Papa down. "And don't spout that traditional bullshit at me. This isn't right, and you know it."

"Gino is a good man. He was a good husband to Juliet, and he will be a good husband to Natalia."

"I don't disagree, but surely, allowances can be made so Natalia can complete senior year and get her degree?" Ben continues pushing, and I love him so much for pleading my case.

"I have already asked." Papa throws his hands into the air. "I am trying to do the right thing for my daughter, and I didn't sign up for this!" His sharp gaze pins me in place. "If it isn't Accardi, it will be Conti. We were just about to finalize the contract when Juliet died and Gino approached me," he says, stalking to his liquor cabinet and pouring himself a scotch.

Acid churns in my gut at the thought of wedding that disgusting pig. Marrying Conti means moving to Philly, being away from my family and everything that is familiar. It means his lecherous greasy hands all over me, and I'd rather shoot myself than readily sign up for that fate.

Suddenly, Gino doesn't seem like such a bad option.

"Sleep on it," Papa says over his shoulder. "Make your peace with it before Gino arrives in the morning with the twins." Swirling the amber-colored liquid in his glass, he turns to face me. "This is a good match, *principessa.* And it will happen." He takes a sip of his drink while he watches me. "Remember, your duty is to this family and what you need to do. Your mama prepared you for this, and I have given you more than most fathers would. Instead of whining, count your blessings."

That statement does not dignify a reply, so I turn on my heel and flee his study for the confines of my bedroom.

Chapter 29

NATALIA

"LET'S TAKE A walk," Gino says the following morning, after introducing me to his beautiful twin boys. They are blond-haired and blue-eyed, like Juliet, and I see little of Gino in them. Joshua clings to his daddy's pants leg, not looking at me, while Caleb stares at me with childish curiosity. "Come now, Joshua." Gino pats his son on the head while prying his small arms from his leg. "Walk ahead with your brother."

Joshua shakes his head, his blond hair swaying with the motion, as he continues to cling to his Papa.

I crouch down, so I'm at his level, smiling as he slowly meets my eyes. "Do you like apples, Joshua?" He stares at me without speaking. "We have an orchard that has lots and lots of apple trees. If you come with us, you can pick some, and I can make you an apple cake. Would you like that?"

"I like apple cake!" Caleb shouts, rushing to my side. He tugs on my sleeve. "If I pick apples, will you make me cake too?"

I smile at him affectionately. "Of course, I will. I can make apple jelly too. Or apple strudel." I look up at Gino, and he's watching us with a strange expression on his face. "Or if your papa allows it, we can make chocolate-covered caramel apples."

"Please, Papa!" Caleb races to hug Gino's other leg. "Can she make us chocolate apples?"

"Be good boys, and we'll see," Gino says. "And her name is Natalia."

I straighten up, glad he didn't tell them to call me Mama. They are so little, and I wonder if they even properly understand their mother has gone to heaven or if they will remember her when they are older. My heart aches with sadness for them.

"You will need these," Ben says, appearing at the side of the house, carrying two small baskets with handles. He crouches down, smiling at the twins. "Why don't you come with me while your papa talks to Natalia. I can show you the way to the orchard."

Miraculously, both boys leave the safety of Gino's legs and rush to Ben, snatching the baskets from him. Gino nods his gratitude before they race off across the grass in the direction of the orchard.

Silence ensues, and it's uncomfortable.

Gino clears his throat as we walk at a leisurely pace. "I know you want to continue your studies, and I applaud you for that, but it simply won't work." His brown eyes bore into mine. "My sons need a mother. One who will be with them every day. They have just lost Juliet, and they are confused. I can't bring you into their lives to have you disappear every day. It will only confuse them more." He stops, touching my elbow. "My sons are my sole priority, but you will be my wife, Natalia. Your needs matter to me too. If I could align both goals, I would permit it. Perhaps you could return to finish your studies when they are older and they don't need you so much?"

"When would that be?" I ask because a lot of Italian boys remain tied to their mama's apron strings forever.

"Perhaps when they start high school?" he suggests.

It's not what I want. I want to complete my senior year now and get my initial degree, but maybe I can use this to my advantage. "If that could happen, would you be agreeable to me studying for an extended period of time?"

"Explain that?" he asks as we walk.

So, I do. Telling him how obtaining my undergraduate degree is only the first step to a full-time career as a doctor, I explain how I would have to go on to med school and a hospital residency after that.

"If I have understood correctly, you would need to complete your senior year and then go on to do another three or four years and then another few years as a resident?"

"Yes." I nod.

He looks contemplative. "I think that could work. The boys would be adults by the time you started your residency."

"You wouldn't resent your wife working long hours at a hospital?" I inquire because I think most dons would.

"You will not be chained to my side, Natalia, and I will be working long hours too. If this is what you need to agree to this marriage, then I am happy to permit it."

It feels wrong to thank him, but I want to start this marriage on the right footing. The fact he is willing to compromise and to give me some say in my future is reassuring. Perhaps, this marriage won't be too bad. "Thank you, Gino."

"I am happy we could reach an acceptable compromise." His hand moves to my face, and my eyes startle wide. "You are truly very beautiful, Natalia."

I nod my thanks, too terrified to form words. His palm is heavy on my face, and his touch doesn't elicit shivers the way Leo's touch does.

That's a good thing, my inner voice whispers in my ear.

"You will make a good wife and mother," he adds. "And I will take care of you the way a husband should, but there is one thing you must know."

I take a deep breath as I prepare for whatever he's about to say.

Pain crawls across his face as he removes his hand from me. "Juliet was the love of my life," he says, his voice cracking a little. "She will *always* be the love of my life. I promise I will look after you, Natalia. I will take care of all your needs, but I will never love you. I am not capable of loving any other woman because my heart will always belong to Juliet."

He says this like I expected him to love me. How naïve does he believe me to be? I wonder if he chose me because I look nothing like his beloved wife?

Juliet was tall with long straight blonde hair, and she was extremely slim with small breasts and a nonexistent ass. I'm shorter, curvier, with big boobs, a shapely ass, and wavy dark hair. The only thing we have in common is our blue eyes.

"I appreciate your honesty," I truthfully say, "and I don't expect love." I wish I could tell him I'm incapable of loving any other man because *my* heart will always belong to Leo. "I expect respect and kindness, and I will show you the same in return. I will be a good wife, and I will love your sons like they are my own flesh and blood." Caleb and Joshua are sweet little boys, and I don't think it will be hard to love them. "One of the reasons I want to pursue a career in medicine is because I like looking after others. Being a mother is a natural extension of that. I promise you I will care for them and protect them and cherish them."

He kisses me on the mouth, and I flinch at the unexpected contact and the tender nature of it. Undeterred, Gino grasps the nape of my neck and angles his head, deepening the kiss. Cautiously, I kiss him back, testing it out. He really shouldn't be doing this, and Papa would not be pleased. If it means Gino isn't a complete stickler for the rules and traditions, that can only be a good thing for me.

Slowly, we break apart, and he smiles, seeming pleased. My eyes lift to the window above, as if I'm pulled by some gravitational force. Leo stares down at me through the glass, pain clearly etched upon his face.

I look away before I betray any hint of emotion in front of my fiancé.

"Thank you, Natalia." Gino takes my hand, threading his fingers in mine. "I knew you were the perfect choice." We start walking again, and he keeps his hand tucked in mine.

In the distance, I spot Ben carrying Joshua on his shoulders while he holds Caleb's hand, and I smile. He is good with children. Someday, he is going to make an amazing father.

"Now, let's discuss a date, shall we?" Gino says, dragging me back into the moment.

LEO

I STARE AT the walls in my living room, bristling with rage and years of pent-up frustration. Moving boxes are stacked to one side, but I can't summon the energy to finish loading up my stuff. Ben and I are moving into a new luxury apartment in Manhattan midweek, and I should be excited to leave this shithole behind. However, I can't generate any happy thoughts or derive pleasure from anything anymore. Not now I know Natalia is marrying Gino Accardi in five weeks' time.

I want to punch Don Accardi in the face every time I think about him putting his hands and his mouth on my *dolcezza.*

I want to knee him in the balls for forcing her to defer NYU.

And I want to wring his neck for the simple fact he gets to live the rest of his life with her by his side.

I swig from my bottle of beer, seething inside. Why didn't I ask her to run away with me three years ago? Why has it taken me so long to get my head out of my ass? Why the fuck did I care about this career or pissing the boss off instead of putting her first? Now, I have lost her forever, and I have no one to blame but myself.

I know she thinks I am screwing any female with a pulse, but that is far from the truth. I have been with two women in the past three years, and both were quick fucks from behind while I closed my eyes and imagined it was my *dolcezza.* I know Ben wants to ask what the fuck is wrong with me. Women throw themselves at us wherever we go, but I can't move on.

Even if I wanted to, I can't.

Natalia is all I see when I close my eyes at night and the first image in my mind's eye when I open them in the morning. Whenever something happens, she is the first person I want to tell. Every time I'm at a family event or out with my friends, it's always her I wish was by my side.

Cutting her out of my life was like hacking off a limb or removing a vital organ. Some days, I can hardly breathe from the pain in my chest.

I have tried to keep my distance because looking at her reminds me of everything I have lost.

I shouldn't have approached her at the house last week, but I was desperate when Ben told me the news. Watching Gino kiss her destroyed me. I don't know how I'm expected to suffer this every day for the rest of my life. I can only imagine the pain and anguish I caused her when I pulled that stunt with Mandy in front of her. I'm sickened at myself, all over again, and regretting all the ways I fucked things up with Nat.

A knock at my door yanks me from my depressive inner monologue. It's late Saturday night, and I'm not expecting anyone. I know it's not Ben because he's over at Monica's place tonight. At least one of us is getting laid. Let's just say me and my hand are intimately acquainted with one another these days.

Getting to my feet, I saunter to the door, my bad mood clinging to my skin like a second layer. My eyes widen as I peek through the peephole, startled to find Natalia there. I swing the door open. "What are you doing here?" I ask, peering out into the hallway, looking for her bodyguard. Brando was reassigned a year ago. He's got too much potential to let him stay on her protection detail forever, so another *soldato* protects Nat now. "Where's Ciro?"

"I ditched the grumpy fuck," she says, barging past me into my apartment. "And I purposely left my cell phone at home and left my car at the train station."

"Why the fuck would you do that?" I stare at her like she's insane. She is the daughter of Don Mazzone and engaged to Don Accardi. That places a big target on her head. "You can't just go off the grid and tell no one, Nat! It's not safe. And please tell me you didn't take a train all alone at this time of night?"

She smirks, and I equally want to throttle her and kiss her. "I took the train and then the subway." I narrow my eyes at her, and she has the audacity to laugh. "I don't want anyone knowing I'm here, but I did send Ben a text from the station, telling him I was in safe hands and not to worry." She plucks the beer from my fingers, bringing it to her lips and drinking from it. "Got any wine?" she asks, making a face as she hands my beer back to me. "That tastes like ass."

I stare at her, dumbfounded. What is actually going on here? She slides her light trench coat off, and my mouth waters at the tight-fitting red dress clinging to her enviable curves. My dick instantly salutes her, like it's woken from a three-year hibernation. "What are you doing?" I ask, trailing her into the kitchen as I finally find my voice.

"Looking for a wineglass," she says, leaving the duh off the end.

"I mean why are you here?" I rub the back of my neck, torn between dragging her into my arms and tossing her into a cab and sending her tempting ass back home.

"Grab me a glass, and I'll tell you." She removes a chilled bottle of wine from the refrigerator while I take a glass out of the overhead cabinet. “Expecting company?” she asks, closing the fridge door with her hip.

“No.” I take the bottle from her and place it on the counter beside the glass.

“Why do you have an unopened bottle of wine in your refrigerator then?”

“Mom was over during the week, helping me pack,” I explain as I open the wine and pour her a glass, against my better judgment. I still have no clue why she is here. If anyone found out she was alone in my apartment with me, there would be hell to pay. The engagement announcement has been made, and everyone knows who she is promised to. “I bought that for her, but she didn’t end up drinking it.” I hand her the glass. “Satisfied?”

“Not yet,” she murmurs, prancing past me, sashaying her hips, and shaking that gorgeous ass in my face.

My cock swells painfully behind my jeans, and I adjust myself before I follow her into the living room. I grab another beer because mine is almost gone, and I have a feeling I will need it. I purposely sit on the chair across from her to avoid the urge to touch her. “What’s going on?”

“I hear you’re moving in with Benny.” She smooths a hand down the front of her dress. It’s low-cut, and her tits are right there, practically in my face, begging to be licked, sucked, and fucked. My cock jerks behind my zipper, and I widen my thighs for comfort. Her gaze lowers to my crotch, and red heat creeps up her chest and onto her neck. I’m not surprised she’s turned on by the evidence of my arousal. Our chemistry has always been electric. “I helped him pick the place,” she continues. “It’s nice, though not as nice as the penthouse he’s already earmarked for himself when the new development is built.”

Bennett is highly intelligent and very ambitious. He had a rough couple of years adjusting to this life, but now he has completely embraced it, he is full of plans. He talked Angelo into giving him a position at Caltimore Holdings, and he plans to rise through the ranks quickly. He’s hardworking and determined to fulfill his duty as capo and a business executive.

He has already made his mark at CH. Finding a prestigious site for sale adjacent to Central Park, he immediately met with the real estate agent and the owner. First, he charmed them. And then he charmed the Caltimore Holdings board into making a bid. A bid that was accepted because Ben dug up shit on the other interested parties and blackmailed them into pulling out. He managed to secure the site for a lot less than the asking price.

Angelo was impressed, and he readily signed off on a permanent position for him at CH. I will miss him on jobs, but I'm glad he is already making an impact. I have high hopes for Bennett Mazzone, and I know if I stick with him my star will ascend too. Now I have permanently lost Natalia, my career is all I have left, and I intend to give it my everything.

"Earth to Leo." Natalia snaps her fingers, reclaiming my attention. "Where'd you go?"

"Sorry." I drain the dregs of my old beer and set the empty bottle down on the coffee table. "I was just thinking about Ben," I admit, swiping my fresh beer. "At first, I didn't think he was built for this life, but now I know he was born for it."

She nods. "He was, and I think he will be good for *la famiglia.* He has progressive plans, and I think he will succeed."

"Why are you here?" I ask again, not wanting to get sidetracked talking about her brother.

She takes a big mouthful of wine, gulping it nervously as I sip my beer, never taking my eyes from her. Maybe she has changed her mind. I sit up straighter, my interest instantly piqued. "Have you changed your mind?" Excitement bubbles up my throat. "About running away?" I meant it, and I would do it for her.

She shakes her head, and my euphoria dies an instant death. Setting her wine down, she stands and walks over to me. She crawls onto my lap, and I let her. Her gorgeous tits are in my face, and it takes colossal willpower not to smash my face in her chest and grab handfuls of her delectable ass. I set my beer down and grip the armrests, waiting to see what she does next. Wrapping her arms around my neck, she leans down, pressing her mouth to my ear. I can see down the front of her dress and it makes concentrating hard.

"I'm getting married soon."

"I know," I growl, aggravated all over again.

"My groom has already told me he won't ever love me."

I grab her head, tilting her face to mine. "He said that to you?" I want to tear his head from his shoulders. What kind of a prick says that to the woman who has agreed to be his wife and the mother to his children?

"Yes, and I respect him for setting boundaries from the start." Her hand slides along my arm as my fingers caress her smooth silky cheek. Her touch is like a zap of electricity shooting all over my body. I'm painfully hard underneath her, and she must feel my erection digging into her ass. "He told me he'll take care of my needs."

I growl and curse under my breath, thinking about putting a bullet in his skull before their wedding day.

She ignores me, continuing to speak. "But it won't be the same as having sex with someone who loves me."

I stop breathing as I stare at her, sensing where this is going.

"I love you," she whispers, brushing her mouth against mine.

It's fleeting, but it's everything. I want to devour her. To lick, suck, and bite every inch of her skin. To worship her with my mouth, my fingers, and my cock. I want to brand every part of her body with my touch, so she never forgets how much I love her.

"And I know you love me," she adds. "We can't be together, but we can have one night."

I cannot believe she is saying this. "You need to be specific," I rasp before I get my hopes up.

"I want to know what it feels like to have sex with the man who owns my heart. I want to experience that one time. You said you would do anything for me, Leo, so I'm asking you to do this." Anxiety replaces the previous confidence on her face, and she trembles against me. She's nervous as fuck, and I know why. She kisses me sweetly. "Make love to me, Leo. Let me feel what it's like to love you in every conceivable way before I have to give myself to another man."

My *dolcezza* has balls of steel.

She's a fucking queen.

We have been here once before. When we were both drowning in grief. There have been occasions over the years when I berated myself for stopping that night, but I am glad I did. Taking her virginity when she was so vulnerable and raw would have been wrong. Especially when neither of us was thinking straight.

But this woman before me knows her mind.

She wants something for herself, and she isn't afraid to ask for it.

I want to give it to her because I want to experience it the same way she does. And I want her to take this memory and have it to comfort her on lonely nights when she misses me as much as I'll be missing her.

But above all, I want to do it because I love her and I have dreamed of this for years.

"Yes," I say, cupping her beautiful face. "It would be my absolute pleasure to make love to you."

Chapter 30

NATALIA

LEO CUPS MY face, and his expression is solemn as he peers into my eyes. "Before we do this, I need to know you are sure." He sweeps his fingers across my face, igniting a flurry of delicious tremors. "This is dangerous. If Gino finds out—"

"He won't." I cut across him. "It's a myth that girls always bleed their first time, and tons of little girls break their hymens riding horses or cycling. If he dares to challenge me, I will remind him I'm a medical student and spout a ton of statistics at him."

I'm not worried about that.

Only losing myself completely in Leonardo Messina and never being able to come back from it.

Leo's lips kick up at the corners, and my heart melts. "Always so fucking smart."

"You are so beautiful when you smile," I say, tracing my fingers through the stubble on his chin and cheeks. "And I love you so damn much."

His lips press against mine, and I close my eyes, savoring the feel of his mouth and the way he tastes. A deep sense of contentment settles in my bones as we softly kiss. His fingers wind into my hair as he pulls back. "I love you, *dolcezza*." His eyes hold mine in place. "I love you so much I don't have the words to adequately describe it." He stands, holding me up, and I wrap my legs around his waist and cling to his shoulders. "But I can show you."

"Leo," I whisper, dotting kisses all over his face as he carries me into his bedroom.

Nervous adrenaline flows through my veins as he sets me down on my feet. I came here with a plan, and I can scarcely believe he agreed. I have thought of nothing else since my conversation with Gino. Mama's wisdom played a part too. I knew I couldn't marry Gino without taking this one thing for myself.

For us.

That doesn't mean I'm not nervous because I am. I want this with him. I want it badly, but I'm scared too.

"Don't be nervous," Leo says, reading my mind. He brushes his lips against mine as his hands land on my waist. "I will take care of you. I will ensure it is good for you." He rubs my lower back through my dress. "I am going to worship every inch of you and make you feel things you have never felt before. I am going to prove how much I love you with every touch." One hand comes to my face, and he tilts my chin up. "Okay?"

I nod, smiling. "I want this with you," I whisper, dragging my fingers through his brown hair. "But I've never done it before, and I want you to enjoy it too."

His face softens as he pulls me into his arms and holds me against his warm body. "Trust me, baby. I will enjoy it because this is everything I have desired for years." We stare at one another, and the air sizzles with our usual chemistry. "You trusting me to do this means everything to me, Natalia." He pecks my lips. "I am truly honored." He kisses me again, and I'm arching into him, dying for more. "I love you."

"I love you too."

His lips seal over mine again, and he deepens the kiss while his hands run up and down my back. Angling his head, he kisses me passionately, pulling my hips into his, ensuring I feel what it's doing to him. His erection is solid against me, and lust coils in my belly. I grind against him, exploring the hard planes of his back when my hands slip under his shirt. He moans into my mouth, and I tighten my arms around him, pressing myself to him with ardent longing.

He pulls the zipper on my dress down, stepping aside to let me shuck out of it. Standing before him in my lacy red underwear, I let him drink his fill before I grab the hem of his shirt and yank it up.

My heart is beating to a new rhythm as he pulls it off, and I can only admire the view. He is broader and more ripped than the last time I saw him bare-chested with a thicker layer of dark hair that trails down under his sweatpants.

I place my hands on his chest, taking my time exploring every dip and curve.

"Fuck, Nat. You have no idea what your touch does to me," he rasps, his voice heavy with desire.

"I do," I pant when his fingers sweep up and down my sides. "Because it's like that for me too."

He unclips my bra, and I let it fall to the ground as my fingers slip under the band of his sweatpants and into his boxers. His cock is velvety soft, warm, and hard under my fingers, and saliva pools in my mouth.

Dropping to my knees, I tug on his sweats until he gets rid of the rest of his clothing, standing before me in all his naked glory. I had forgotten how big he is, and nerves fire momentarily at me again as I wonder how he's going to fit inside me. My fingers trail a path up his muscular thighs, and I cup his heavy balls, gently fondling them.

"Fuck," he hisses through clenched teeth. "That feels so good, but this is about you, baby. Get up on the bed."

I shake my head. "This isn't just about me. This is about us. If this is our only time, I want to experience everything." My fingers curl around the base of his shaft as I lean forward, my tongue lapping at the moisture crowning at the tip of his cock. I look up at him, delighted to see such raw lust blazing from his eyes. I get an enormous thrill out of knowing I'm the one putting that look on his face. "I want to taste you again. It's all I have thought about for years."

The last time we did this, I had gently explored his hard-on and tentatively tasted him. Now, I want to do it properly. I know enough to have an idea of what to do. I know Leo will guide me and show me what he likes.

Pulling his foreskin down a little, I wrap my hand around the base of his dick, stroking him in firm pumps as I lick and suck on his shaft. My tongue glides up and down his hot skin, lapping against the veins while I continue to work him with my fingers. I look up at him as I lower my mouth down over his slickened length, trying to relax my mouth and my throat so I can take him in. I gag when he hits the back of my throat, and he eases out, but I shake my head, telling him not to withdraw fully.

I find my pace, sucking him up and down as my hand strokes faster. The moans leaving his lips are borderline animalistic, and his eyes are rolling back in his head. His fingers tighten in my hair as he gently thrusts into my mouth. My panties are flooded, my core throbbing and aching with need.

"Baby." He puts his hand on top of my head. "I need you to stop. I want to be inside you the first time I come—and only after you."

His dick leaves my mouth with a loud pop, and I giggle. He smiles, lifting me up and slamming his mouth against mine. He plants a slew of drugging kisses on my lips and my face, and I'm swaying against him, almost delirious with desire. "I fucking love kissing you," he says, scooping me up and carrying me to the bed. He lays me down gently, propping my head up on the pillows. He kisses me again before pulling back. "Your mouth felt so good on me. Where the hell did you learn to do that?"

"It's not what you think," I say as he retrieves a foil packet and some lube from the drawer of his bedside table. "I haven't done that with anyone. Frankie is a big sharer, and I have watched some porn."

He chuckles as he crawls up onto the bed, tossing the supplies by my head. "Always full of surprises, *dolcezza*."

"I aim to please," I tease as he lies down on top of me, careful to keep his full weight off me.

"Now, where were we?" he purrs before his lips descend again. He kisses the shit out of me as his hands roam my body. I'm panting and writhing underneath him, more turned on than I have ever been in my life. Slowly, his mouth works its way down my body. He ravishes my breasts, fondling, sucking, and licking them. It's as if there is a hotline to my pussy, because every time he draws one of my nipples into his warm mouth, I feel it down below. My pussy is pulsing and throbbing, and I think I could come like this.

He kisses my cunt over my lace panties, and I whimper, my hips bucking up of their own volition. "I still remember how incredible you taste," he murmurs, hooking his fingers in my panties and dragging them down my legs. "You are so fucking beautiful, Natalia. Stunning." He nudges my legs apart, kissing his way up my legs and my thighs before planting his delectable mouth against my mound.

I cry out, needing more. "Leo, more. Please." I arch my back and thrust my hips up as he licks a path up and down my slit. Then he parts my folds and moves one finger inside me. I almost detonate on the spot.

"Damn, you are so wet, baby, and so tight."

"I need you, Leo." I prop up on my elbows, and the sight of him licking my pussy is so erotic it's a miracle I don't fall off the ledge.

"You will have me, I promise. But I need to make sure you're ready. Lie back and enjoy this, but watch me. I want you to watch me eating your pussy." I remember him saying something similar to me the last time and how much I blushed watching him eat me out.

He is gentle with me, kissing my clit and carefully adding another finger inside me, tenderly stroking my inner walls and coaxing my body into orgasm. I scream his name as I climax, fondling my breasts and arching my back as the most intense pleasure washes over me.

"Was that okay?" he asks, sliding up over my body.

I playfully swat his chest. "You know it was." I kiss him, aroused by the taste of me on his lips. His tongue dives into my mouth as he gently plucks at my nipples.

"I need inside you now." His gorgeous gray-blue eyes shine with love and lust as he looks at me. "Are you ready?"

I bob my head. "I have never been more ready."

I help him to roll a condom on, watching with anticipation as he lubes his dick. He settles over me again, kissing me deeply and passionately until I'm fully relaxed and my limbs sink into the bed. When I feel his cock nudge my entrance, I freeze a little. My heart is pounding, and butterflies are running amok in my chest.

He stops kissing me, lifting his head as he holds himself poised at my pussy. "This will hurt for a bit, but I will go very slow until it feels good."

"I want this, and I trust you to take care of me." I kiss him, widening my thighs and trying to relax as he pushes in a little more. He takes his time inching inside me, stretching me until I feel so full. He keeps kissing me and touching my body as he moves all the way in. There's a pinch of pain, and a hiss escapes my lips. He stops, holding himself still. "Don't stop. Just go slow," I say. He lifts my left leg, wrapping it around his waist and thrusts one final inch until he is fully seated.

"God, Nat." His voice is husky, his tone reverential. He kisses the sensitive spot just under my ear. "You feel so fucking good, baby. So good." His eyes probe mine, and I see nothing but love and devotion in his gaze. "Are you okay?"

I nod. "I'm good, Leo." Tears fill my eyes as I'm overcome with the magnitude of the moment. "This is all I have ever wanted. Make love to me."

"*Amore mio. Cuore mio.* You are my everything." He moves slowly and carefully, watching my face in between kisses, gauging my reaction and my body's response. His muscles are locked tight, and I can tell it takes effort for him to go slow. It only makes me love him even more.

Gradually, the pain subsides, replaced with pleasure and I urge him to go faster. I circle both legs around his waist, lifting my hips in sync with his thrusts, kissing him hard as he moves in and out of me. And it's heaven on earth. I have never felt anything even close to the euphoria I feel as he makes love to me, kissing and touching me and whispering loving words in my ear.

When his fingers move to my clit and he rubs me as he picks up his pace, it doesn't take too long to come, and then he's breaking that wave too, shouting my name as we fall together.

He collapses on his side, taking me with him, keeping us joined. He wipes my tears of joy from my cheeks as he dusts kisses all over my face, telling me over and over again how much he loves me. I cling to him, touching him everywhere, memorizing everything so I never forget this moment.

Although I'm sore, we make love again because I only have this one night, and I want it to last. It's even more intense the second time and more frantic as we desperately cling to one another, knowing we are on stolen time.

He flips me over, driving into me from behind, and I moan and whimper as I push back against him, going crazy with need for him. He rocks into me a little harder than before, but he is still careful with me, and his tender care of me swells my heart to bursting point.

I am so glad I gave him my virginity, and I know I will always remember this night with nothing but love in my heart.

After we come again, we explore each other intimately, touching, talking, kissing, and laughing, and I have never felt more connected to another person in my life. His soul speaks to mine, on our own special wavelength, and I know, for as long as I live, I will never love anyone as much as I love him.

Chapter 31

NATALIA

"OH, HONEY," PAULINA Messina says, dabbing at the tears in my eyes with a tissue. "Don't cry, Natalia. It's all going to be okay."

I stand in front of the mirror in my bedroom, staring at my reflection, knowing it's not.

"You are the most beautiful bride," she adds, sharing a concerned glance with Frankie. "It will be fine, you'll see." She pats my arm as I stare desolately at the vision in white in the mirror.

Gino is not who I want.

And I'm not everything he's expecting.

I don't know how he will react when he finds out.

Frankie subtly stares at me, cautioning me to get it together.

"I'm sorry," I croak, forcing a smile for Leo's mother. "I'm missing Mama and Mateo. They should be here." That's not a lie. I do wish they were here, but it's not the reason I'm crying.

"They should." Sadness is etched upon her face. "I'm going to leave you girls to talk. I'll go and check on things downstairs."

We're having the wedding reception at our house after the church ceremony. Papa hired a wedding planner, and she organized a large marquee in the garden. Beatrice, our housekeeper, hired additional cooks and waiting staff, and they are catering the wedding feast. All Italian fare, of course.

Paulina moves to leave before stopping for a second. She turns to face me, looking a little uncertain. She gently cups my face. "You are like a daughter to me, Natalia, and your happiness is important. I hate that you didn't get to marry for love." Her eyes well up, and I wonder if she knows. My mama guessed. It's not inconceivable to think Leo's mama did too. "But Gino is a good man. An honorable man, and I believe he will care for you and protect you."

"I know," I whisper, fighting more tears. Out of everyone Papa could've chosen for me to marry, Don Accardi is the best choice.

"I'm so proud of you." She presses a kiss to my brow. "And I know Mama Rosa would be too."

She slips quietly out of the room, and I kick my shoes off, sit down on the bed, and knot my hands as I attempt to regain my composure.

"Oh, Nat." Frankie slides her arms around me. "I hate this for you." Tears stream down her face. "It's so wrong. You shouldn't have to do this."

Sobs rip from my chest before I can stop them. I cling to my bestie, and I need to tell her. I have to tell someone. "Frankie," I cry, lifting my head. The pain tightening my chest is agonizing. "I have fucked up. I have fucked up so bad," I whisper.

Her eyes widen in alarm. "What do you mean? What's going on?"

My lip wobbles, and I sniffle. "I'm pregnant," I whisper.

She stares at me in shock. I didn't tell her about the night I spent with Leo. I wanted to. She's my bestie, and I know she'd have been happy for me, but I won't put Leo at risk. I couldn't tell anyone. It needed to remain a secret between us.

Until my period never arrived, and I fretted for ten days, blaming it on stress, before I grew a pair and took a test a week ago, which sealed my fate. I had to be super discreet at the pharmacy to ensure Ciro didn't see what I was buying, and I only pulled it off with the help of the nice lady behind the counter.

Her mouth opens and closes as she struggles to form words.

"Leo," I whisper, terrified in case anyone might be outside listening. "I went to him. I asked for one night, and it was the most amazing night of my life." I burst into more tears. "Until now." I place a hand over my flat stomach. "I even feel bad saying that because this baby has never been more wanted, but he will kill us!" Hysteria filters into my voice. "Gino will murder me and my baby and Leo when he finds out."

Frankie shakes herself out of her stupor. "Back up a second. How the hell did this happen? Did he not use protection?"

"He did. We used condoms both times. But no form of contraception is one hundred percent effective. I looked it up. Condoms are ninety-eight percent effective if used perfectly but on average only eighty-five percent effective because most people don't use them properly. There must have been a tear or my nail snagged it when I was rolling it on. Or maybe he stayed inside me too long after and some semen escaped when he was pulling out." I should have made him come on my stomach, especially when I'm not on the pill. It's not permitted until I'm married and I discuss contraception with my husband.

Something that is a moot point now.

"Does he know?" she asks.

I shake my head. "How can I tell him? He would want to run away, and I can't put a target on his head like that."

"I still think you should tell him. Maybe there is something he or Ben can do." Invisible wheels spin behind her eyes. "If Gino knows you're pregnant, he'll back out. He won't want to marry you."

"No, he won't, but he'll want to find out who's responsible and kill them for disrespecting him. The very last thing I can do is tell Gino. And Papa would throw a hissy fit too. I'd be bringing dishonor on his name. Neither of them would rest until they found out who knocked me up, and Leo would end up dead. I can't tell anyone, Frankie. No one can know."

She knows I'm right.

"Jesus, fuck." She rubs a soothing hand up and down my back. "What are you going to do?"

"I don't know." I glance at the clock on my nightstand, and I'm running out of time.

"How far along are you?"

"Not long." I know they calculate your due date from the date of your last period, which would be almost seven weeks.

"Maybe you can convince Gino the baby is his," she says, thinking out loud.

I'm horrified. "I can't do that! That would be unfair to Leo, Gino, and the child."

"At least everyone would be alive," she murmurs.

"I would have to get the midwife to lie when I delivered early, and how would I do that?" I shake my head. "No, I can't do that. It would be so much worse if he discovered I had lied and tried to pass another man's child off as his. We would all end up dead then anyway."

"Running away isn't seeming like such a bad idea," she quietly says. "You could go alone and leave Leo out of it."

"I'm due at the church in two hours, Frankie. If I abandon him at the altar, he will never stop hunting me down." I release a shuddering breath. "Besides, I don't have access to much money and Papa has my passport."

She hugs me, and I feel her shaking against me. "I'm scared for you, Nat." She eases back with tears in her eyes. "I think you should tell Ben. I can get him here. He'll know what to do."

"Involving him puts him at risk too. I can't do that." I know my brother would do everything in his power to find a solution, but there is none. I have thought of nothing else for the past week.

"Are you just going to think about it until you start showing? Then what?"

"I had considered a secret abortion, but I can't do it. I can't kill my baby." My hands cradle my stomach as if I can shield this new life from my heinous words. "I already love him or her."

"Maybe you will miscarry. A lot of women do with their first."

"Wishing for that is as bad as considering an abortion."

"I know." She places her hand over my stomach. "What other options are there?"

"I think my best option is to lie. Say I was raped in the city and threatened I would be killed if I told anyone. I'll tell him I was scared. Beg him not to take it out on an innocent child and ask him to send me away to give birth and then I will give my baby up for adoption." Tears spill down my cheeks as I contemplate giving Leo's baby away, but it's the best solution I have come up with.

"He might not buy it."

"I know, but he might. He has already shown he can compromise, and he kissed me when he knows it's against the rules."

"This isn't as black and white. What if he figures out it was Leo?"

"I don't think he would. Leo and I have had nothing to do with one another for years. Everyone knows we are no longer friends. No one knows I was with him that night. I think I can sell it to Gino. He might be mad he didn't get a virgin, but he needs a mother for Caleb and Joshua, and we'll be married by then. I'll be his responsibility. You know the traditions forbid divorce, so he will not have much choice."

"He could still have you killed, Nat!" she chokes out.

"He won't. He'd have Papa to answer to, and he needs me."

"But for how long?" She gets up, pacing the room in her gorgeous pink bridesmaid gown.

I get the point she's making, and it's a future concern. "I'll worry about that later."

"God, Nat." She kneels before me, taking my hands in hers. "Even if you do get him to agree, how are you going to give up your baby?"

Pain slices through me, like a red-hot blade carving chunks out of my heart. "It will destroy me, Frankie. It will kill me slowly, day by day. But there is no other choice. If it's my only way of keeping our child alive, then I will have to do it."

PART 2 – THE PRESENT

Chapter 32

NATALIA – AGE 32

"IT'S SO GOOD to see you," my sister-in-law Sierra says, enveloping me in a hug at the doorway. "Why the long faces?" she whispers in my ear, spotting the sulky expressions on Caleb's and Joshua's faces behind me.

"I'll tell you in a minute." I shuck out of her arms, gesturing at the boys to come forward. "What do you say to your aunt?"

"Hey," Caleb mumbles, shoving his hands in his pockets, staying rooted to the spot, looking like the stereotypical moody teenager. I suspect he is going to bitch and whine all weekend.

"Hi, Auntie Sierra." Joshua leans in, giving her a hug because he's too polite and too sensitive to be rude. "Where's the little dude?"

"Rowan and Romeo are in the playroom waiting for you. They have the Xbox all lined up. They were driving me crazy asking when you would get here."

"C'mon." Joshua grabs his twin, pulling Caleb into the house. Both carry their black duffels on their shoulders as they walk off in the direction of the playroom to play with my nephew and his cousin.

I drop my bag at the door, deciding to come back for it later. I need a drink, and I need it now. "Is it too early to hit the wine?" I ask, looping my arm through Sierra's slender one.

She arches a brow. "It's that bad you want to hit the bottle at noon on a Saturday?"

"I'm sure it's wine o'clock somewhere in the world," I joke as we walk down the hallway, past the living room and dining room, heading toward the large airy kitchen my brother had remodeled after Sierra and Rowan moved in.

"Well, I'm not going to indulge this early in the day, but if you need alcohol I won't judge." We step into the bright kitchen, and Sierra walks to the refrigerator as I grab a wineglass from the overhead cabinet.

Sierra pours herself a large glass of cranberry juice and a wine for me, and we take our drinks out to the sunroom. We sit down in one of the comfy wicker couches that face the majestic grounds. The French doors are open, letting in a gentle warm summer breeze, and I spot two figures jogging in the opposite direction across the manicured lawns at one side of my brother's massive estate.

Ben bought this place a few years before he reunited with Sierra and discovered she had had his son. He demolished the original house and replaced it with something that rivals The White House in sheer size. Sierra, Ben, and Rowan live in the east wing while Serena—Sierra's older sister—lives with her two children, Elisa and Romeo, in the west wing. The house is so vast it's like they're not sharing living space. They can have as much or as little privacy as they need.

"Is that Leo with Benny?" I ask, assuming it's his best friend and underboss. Leo has thrown himself into his *mafioso* duties, quickly climbing the ranks.

Papa died last year, after losing his long battle with cancer. I hate I lost both parents to that horrible disease. Where Mama went fast, I had to watch Papa struggle for years. Although we had our differences, I miss him. Yet I'm glad he is at peace now.

Ben has been in charge for some time, but he only officially became a don when Angelo died. He is transforming our world, and he has legitimized a lot of the business and brought it kicking and screaming into the twenty-first century. Gradually, he is changing things, but it's slow progress with regards to the old-school traditions.

I am so proud of him. Like I am Leo.

The irony isn't lost on me though. If I was only getting married now, there would be no voice of dissent saying I couldn't marry Leo.

It's such a crock of shit. But there is no point dwelling on all the what-ifs. It won't change a damn thing.

Sierra nods, and I take a sip of my wine. "I meant to ask," she says. "Does it bother you he is here on weekends when you are?"

"It doesn't," I lie. Truth is, it kills me to spend downtime with him. I have kept my walls up for years where Leo is concerned, and it hasn't been easy. Especially in the past few years, when he seems to look in my direction more often. I think he thinks no one is watching, but he's not always subtle, and my husband has noticed. Gino has questioned me about Leo a few times, but I always shut that shit down fast.

Gino cannot know Leo was the one, and I have stuffed my feelings for him deep down inside and ignored him for years because it's the only way I can keep him safe.

I'm so guarded now it's difficult to let anyone in.

"Are you sure?" Sierra's pretty face scrunches up in concern. She is aware there is some history between us, but I didn't go into the details. Ben doesn't even know what went down, and I need to keep it that way.

"It's fine. Don't worry." I pat her arm. "This house is a monstrosity, and it's not like I see him that much."

"How come you didn't go to Chicago this weekend?" she asks, staring at her husband's disappearing form in the distance.

"Gino is too busy." Or at least, that's the excuse he keeps feeding me. He was only supposed to be there for six months, but it's looking like he will have to stay there for another six.

The Outfit—the Italian American mafia in Chicago—is in disarray after everything that went down with their old don DeLuca and his underboss Gifoli. Both men died at a shootout in a hotel, leaving the leadership in question.

DeLuca's consigliere—Thomas Barretta—is now their acting don, but it's not a position he wants to maintain in the long-term. The Commission sent Gino there, in the capacity of acting consigliere, to work with Barretta in training and recruiting new men and identifying local candidates for the top jobs.

Ordinarily, it would pass to an heir, but there isn't one in this case. DeLuca didn't have any sons. Barretta's heir was murdered last year, and Gifoli's son is only five.

Now that The Commission is a united organization across America under the stewardship of the five families in New York and with Ben at the helm, no one questioned it when they stepped in. Ben wants things to settle down in Chicago, and while he is keen to appoint a new don and underboss, it can't be rushed. The Outfit is one of the biggest mafia organizations in the US, outside of New York, and a key territory. The Russians were sniffing around for a time, and there are other enemies who could make a move if the state isn't nailed down.

Hence why Gino has to stay there until things are solid.

The first couple of months, I flew in every second weekend with the twins. But they have duties at home, now they are initiated, and Gino is busy all the time, so it became a monthly visit. Until recently.

The last time I saw my husband was five weeks ago, and I have no clue when I will see him next. I'm annoyed with him. I'm used to coming last on his list of priorities, but his sons need him. They are at a delicate stage in their lives, and they need their father's guidance. But, as usual, Gino is happy to leave the parenting to me. Which is a joke considering he didn't even want them to call me Mama, at one point.

The boys were too young when Juliet died, and they don't remember her. I'm the only mama they have truly known, and there was nothing Gino could do to stop them from calling me that. They are my sons in every sense of the word and the main source of happiness in my life.

Caring for them saved me in the early days of my marriage when I wanted to die.

"It must get lonely," she adds, dragging me out of my head.

I shrug. "To be honest, it's not that different from when he was living in the city with us. He's a workaholic and rarely home. He made it clear before we were married that he would never love me. *Could* never love me, and he hasn't tried." I wonder if it would've made any difference if I hadn't been knocked up when I married him. A large part of me believes we would still be where we are now anyway.

"I don't even know what to say to that except it makes me sad for you."

I shrug again, swallowing a large mouthful of wine. "He hasn't been a bad husband. He doesn't shout at me or mistreat me. He ensures I have everything I need. He compliments my cooking, and I know he appreciates the relationship I have with the twins, but there is no affection between us, apart from his monthly pity fuck, and even that has dwindled."

Sex with Gino pales in comparison to that one night I had with Leo, but I don't turn him away when he comes knocking on my bedroom door. I have needs. Needs he can meet, even if it's purely clinical and not very romantic or intimate.

I imagine it's what sex must be like for Leo with all those random women and one-night stands he indulges in.

Functional but cold.

Scratching the itch without ever truly losing yourself to passion.

"Now I'm angry on your behalf." Sierra tosses her long blonde hair over one shoulder. "You're young, beautiful, compassionate, smart and fun to be with. What the hell is wrong with your husband?"

"You can't force love. He gave his whole heart to Juliet, and when she died, she took a part of him with her." My white wine feels bitter gliding down my throat. "Anyway, I'm luckier than a lot of mafia wives. Some made men are complete assholes. Treating their women as insipid arm candy at events. Beating them if they express an opinion or disagree with their point of view. Gino is attentive when we are at functions, and he likes that I have a brain and an opinion of my own. He has never raised his hand to me."

"It's all so wrong. I really hope Ben changes things."

"My brother is a progressive, and he's already fought a lot of battles, but I'm not sure that is one he will win. Marriage contracts are as old as the ages, and women being subjugated and downtrodden is all part of the control made men exert. It makes them feel like they have nine-inch dicks and they are all-powerful."

"Who's got a nine-inch dick?" Serena Lawson says, entering the sunroom with a bottle of water in her hand.

"I was speaking in general terms about made men and how powerful it makes them feel to suppress and control their wives."

Her lips narrow and a familiar anguish ghosts over her face.

"I'm sorry," I say, getting up to hug her. "I have a touch of foot-in-mouth today."

"It's fine." She returns my hug. "I know you didn't mean it personally, and you aren't wrong. Sierra got lucky with Ben because most made men are not like him. Most enjoy cracking the whip. In actual and metaphorical terms."

Serena was married to Alfredo Gifoli, the now-deceased underboss of The Outfit, and her marriage was not a happy one. When I think about everything she has endured, I feel selfish for complaining about my loveless marriage. At least Gino isn't physically or emotionally abusive.

He's just cold and distant, and he treats me like one of the paid staff a lot of the time.

"Where's Elisa?" Sierra asks her sister, looking behind her for her nine-year-old niece.

Serena sits down on the wicker couch across from us, running one hand through her dark hair. The sun beats down on us through the glass, illuminating the reddish highlights in her long hair. Where Sierra resembles their mother with her blonde hair, Serena got their father's dark hair.

"Where do you think?" Serena's hazel eyes sparkle with mirth.

"Ah." Sierra grins. "She's gone to the playroom." Sierra looks at me. "Does Caleb's bad mood have anything to do with my niece's not-so-subtle crush on him?"

I shake my head. "Not a bit. It has everything to do with him not wanting to leave his legions of adoring fangirls behind in New York. Joshua wasn't impressed either. He just hides his moods better than his brother. He's going steady with Bettina now and you'd swear they weren't going to see each other for ten years the way they could barely tear themselves apart." It's actually cute, but I can't deal with the drama.

Sierra smiles. "I'm not surprised both your sons have girls crawling all over them. They are very good-looking and sweet boys."

"I'm not sure sweet is the word I'd use to describe Caleb right now. He's acting like a typical teenager. He's been in trouble at school, and I have caught him drunk on more than a few occasions." Caleb has always been a little wild. He's the more outgoing, gregarious twin. Joshua has always been happy to stay in his brother's shadow. Joshua is sensitive and quieter, and he hasn't given us any cause for concern over the years. Unlike Caleb.

"Is this a reaction to Gino being away?" Serena asks, drinking from her bottle of water.

"I think it's a combination of things. Teenage hormones. Initiation. His dad being gone." I chew on the inside of my lip. "He's been asking about Juliet again lately."

"Auntie Natalia!" My nephew Rowan screeches, racing across the kitchen floor like he's got a bee up his butt. He flings himself into my arms, and I lift him up onto my lap. "I missed you."

He clings to my arms, and my heart melts. "I missed you too, little charmer." I ruffle his dark hair and hug him close. I adore this little guy. He is an amazing kid, and I'm so happy for Ben. Things were touch and go for a while with him and Sierra, but they worked through their differences and got married, and now they are the epitome of a happy family.

Romeo and Elisa trail into the kitchen, the latter hanging her head and looking upset. If Caleb has said or done anything to wound her little heart, I will throttle him. I warned him in the car to be gentle with her. I know it's annoying for him. She is only nine, and he just turned fourteen, but she's family, and he must treat her with kindness.

"Where are Caleb and Joshua?" I ask.

"They went to their rooms," Romeo says, bouncing over to his mama.

"To talk to their girlfriends." Elisa's lower lip wobbles.

Serena and I share a look as she climbs into her mama's lap. The poor little thing. She's too young to learn this lesson about boys.

"Who wants to go out to the playground?" I ask, knowing that will cheer them up.

"Me!" they chorus, and we all stand.

Ben had a full playground built for Rowan, shortly after he found out he had a son. Ben is extremely protective of his family and his privacy, and very few people know he lives in Greenwich or where this house is. To avoid having to go out in public, Ben has equipped his mansion with pretty much everything they could need.

The playground definitely comes in handy, especially during the summer months when the kids can play for hours while we enjoy a long dinner and a few drinks al fresco.

"Race you outside," I say, taking off through the French doors with the sound of little feet chasing after me.

Chapter 33

LEO

"THAT WAS DELICIOUS," Serena says, pushing her empty plate away. "You two should open a restaurant together." She points between Sierra and Natalia. "You'd clean up."

We are eating a late, casual dinner in the kitchen now the younger children are in bed. My brother Frank—Rowan's bodyguard—is watching the small ones over in the west wing. Natalia's sons ate dinner in record time and then asked to be excused so they could return to the Xbox. I know it must be boring for them here, and I wonder how much longer Natalia will be able to come over for weekends.

"No, thanks." Sierra crawls into Ben's lap, circling her arms around his neck.

I never thought I'd see my buddy so loved up, but he worships the ground his wife walks on. And he lives for his son. He's living the dream, and I'm happy for him, even if it's a reminder of everything I will never have.

"Sounds like too much stress. I'm happy with my little center," Sierra adds.

Ben bought his wife a building in town as a surprise wedding present and Sierra recently opened a holistic center. She's a qualified acupuncturist, and she has hired a couple of other specialists. By all accounts, business is booming.

"Gino would never agree to anything so provincial," Natalia says, gulping back wine.

I'm not sure if something has happened, but she's been drinking a lot tonight. She wears this veil of sadness that clings to her skin. It hurts my heart to see her like that. There's a hint of sarcasm in her tone, which is unusual too. Natalia is the perfect mafia wife, from what I have seen, and it's rare for her to cast dispersions on her husband.

I hate that prick.

I'm not in their company that often, but when I am, I want to rip his hands off her and riddle him with bullets.

"If I can get him to agree to anything, it will be NYU in the fall," she adds.

"You want to go back?" I ask.

"That was always the plan." She stares straight ahead, not even looking at me.

You'd think I'd be used to it by now.

From the second she got married, she put up these concrete barriers to keep me out, and they never waver. It's almost as if she can't tolerate me anymore. I'd blame it on my whoring, except she erected those walls way before I resumed fucking other women.

Not that any of my casual encounters with nameless, faceless women mean anything more than a physical release. I never go back for seconds, and the only woman I see when I close my eyes at night is my *dolcezza.*

"I thought you said he agreed you could return to your studies when the twins started high school," I say, refocusing on the conversation.

She shrugs, and a muscle flexes in her jaw. "Things change," she cryptically replies.

My eyes meet Ben's, and I see my concern mirrored in his gaze.

I'm sick of hiding in the shadows, watching her internalize everything. I hate seeing how blatantly unhappy she is. I never wanted that for her. As much as I hate Gino Accardi, I still hoped their marriage would work out and she would be content. It's obvious that's not the case, and I want to kill him for hurting her.

How does he not see the treasure he has by his side? How does he not want to spend every second of his time with her? How can he not want to worship her body, protect her heart, and nurture her soul?

I would give anything to trade places with that man just for a chance to breathe the same air as her.

She remains, to this day, the absolute love of my life.

I will never get over losing her.

I will never want any other woman.

Sierra threads her fingers through Ben's hair, and they share an intimate look as they silently communicate.

"Are you going to tell us or should we guess?" Serena smiles at her sister, before glancing sideways at Alesso.

Alesso's name is actually Alessandro, but Rowan coined his pet name when they first met, and it's stuck. Alesso is one of our most loyal *soldati*. There is no one else Ben trusted to guard his wife, even if it's a waste of Alesso's skill to assign him as Sierra's bodyguard. It's a great honor to be asked to protect the boss's family, and I don't think Alesso is unhappy at all.

Especially when he gets to share living space with Serena. I don't know if anything has happened between them, but they are close friends, and Serena has come to rely on him a lot.

My brother Frank seems content living here too and looking after Rowan. I know he misses the action, but he's unattached, and he has no plans to marry. Thank fuck my sister Giuliana is married with a baby on the way, because Mama has lost hope that either of her sons will take a bride. She regularly gets on my case, even though I have told her she is wasting her time.

I know what my reason is, but I'm unsure why my brother is so opposed to marriage. We're close enough but not that close we confide our deepest secrets and darkest fears to one another.

"It's nothing," Sierra says, sharing another look with her husband. She casts a glance at Natalia for a brief second. "We can talk about it another time."

"How about drinks on the veranda?" Ben suggests, planting his wife's feet on the ground with tender care.

"Not a chance." Serena grins over the rim of her wineglass. "Just tell us."

Sierra's pretty face startles in surprise. "You know?"

"I'm your sister, and I know the telltale signs when I see them." Her grin expands. Alesso looks confused, and Natalia moves in her seat, her eyes scrunching up.

Ben drags Sierra back onto his lap, and he's smiling as he nods at her. I know what the announcement is. Sierra took me into her confidence when she wanted to surprise Ben and needed my help. Ben places his hands over Sierra's flat stomach. "We're having a baby," he confirms, beaming like a Cheshire cat. His joy is transparent, and it's hard not to get caught up in it. He's had the biggest smile on his face since he found out.

Serena shrieks, jumping up and running around the table. She flings her arms around Sierra and Ben. "I knew it! I am so happy for you both. This is the best news."

"Congrats, guys." I salute the boss, having already hugged it out with him the other night after Sierra broke the good news to him.

Alesso stands next, hugging Sierra and shaking Ben's hand. "This is awesome news. Rowan is going to be so happy. Have you told him yet?"

Ben shakes his head. "Sierra is only six weeks pregnant. We thought we would wait a little while before telling him. Work him up to it."

"I'm sure he'll be thrilled," Sierra says, "but he's had a lot of change in his life recently, and we don't want him to feel insecure or threatened."

I look at Natalia. She hasn't said a word. She's staring off into space with the saddest expression on her face.

"Nat." Ben notices too, and I wonder if he's thinking the same thoughts as me.

Nat is thirty-two now, and she's been married to Gino for eleven years, but there have been no babies. I don't know if they have had trouble conceiving or if Gino decided he wasn't having any more kids, but it's not normal within our culture.

"Are you okay?" Ben asks, looking troubled.

Nat snaps out of it, smiling as she gets up. "Forgive me. I was a million miles away." She walks around the table, hugging her sister-in-law and then her brother. "This is fantastic news. Seeing you so happy, Benny." Her voice chokes as she slaps a hand over her chest. "It's all I have ever wanted for you." She kisses Sierra on both cheeks. "Thank you for being you. Thank you for loving my brother as well as you do. Thank you for blessing him with another child. I can't wait to meet my new niece or nephew."

We head out to the covered veranda with our drinks, settling into the comfortable couches. Sierra turns some music on low, and Ben lights the patio heater, even though it's still warm and probably in the sixties. I bet my buddy is going to fuss over his woman in a major way during her pregnancy. I don't blame him. He missed out on this when Sierra was pregnant with Rowan, and he is uber protective of his family.

With good reason.

We have plenty of enemies, and Ben is one of the most powerful mafia bosses in America. Meaning he will always be a target.

We talk and laugh, and it's a chilled-out evening. Natalia is pensive. Quieter than usual. And I wish I knew what was troubling her.

Sierra yawns, and Ben swings into action, scooping her up like she's precious cargo. "We're calling it a night. See you all in the morning."

Alesso and Serena aren't far behind them, leaving me with my *dolcezza*. It's rare we are alone together, and I'm going nowhere. "You want the rest?" I ask, lifting the almost empty wine bottle.

"Sure, why not?" Her eyes are a little glazed over, and I think she might be drunk. It's not like Natalia. She likes to have a good time at parties and events, but she is always in control.

I top off her glass and grab a fresh beer from the mini refrigerator.

Awkward silence engulfs the space between us, and I hate it. We used to be so comfortable around one another, and I hate this limbo state we exist in now. "Are you okay?" I ask, swilling some of my beer as I cross one ankle over my knee.

She barks out a laugh. "I suppose that depends on your definition."

I get up, taking my beer with me as I slide into the chair closest to her. "I'm here if you want to talk about it."

"I don't," she says after a few silent beats, swallowing another mouthful of her wine.

Maybe I should let it go, but her unhappiness is obvious. "Does this have something to do with Sierra being pregnant?"

Her blue eyes swivel to mine, blazing indignantly. "I'm delighted for my brother and his wife. They deserve to be happy."

"You do too." I set my bottle down on the coffee table, leaning forward with my elbows on my knees. "Why haven't you had babies, Natalia?"

"Why do you fuck so many whores?" she retorts, instantly silencing me.

Swiping my beer, I lean back and pour half the bottle down my throat. When I'm less agitated, I respond. "Because I'm lonely," I admit, willing her to look at me. "Because I know there isn't a wife or kids in my future and impersonal sex with women who will never mean anything more is all I am capable of."

She lifts her head, and a tight pain slices across my chest when I see the silent tears streaming down her face. "I don't want that life for you," she whispers. "You're supposed to be happy. One of us should be happy."

"A beautiful wise woman once told me happiness is an illusion." I gulp painfully over the messy ball of emotion clogging my throat. "She was right." I put my beer on the floor by my foot. Taking a risk, I reach out, brushing her tears away with my thumb.

She closes her eyes, leaning into my touch, and I cup her cheek, staring at her lips like a drowning man.

"It's still you, *dolcezza*," I whisper. "It will only ever be you."

Her eyes blink open, and she moves down the couch, as far away as she can get from me. "Don't, Leo." More tears fall down her cheeks. "Just don't. I can't hear this. I'm going to bed." She stands abruptly, knocking against the coffee table. Her glass tumbles, crashing to the ground and shattering upon impact. Wine splashes her legs and against her clothes. "Shit."

I reach her in a split-second, lifting her up and away from the broken glass. I place her back down on the ground even though my every instinct is to bundle her into my arms and love all her pain away. "Nat."

She starts openly crying, and I don't hesitate, reeling her into my arms and holding her close. Her head rests on my chest as her arms cling to my waist. I don't offer words of comfort because I have none. I don't know why she's in pain because she won't tell me. So, I do the only thing I can. I comfort her with my arms, hoping my touch is helping and not making things worse.

Chapter 34

NATALIA

"IT'S SO GOOD to see you," Frankie says, arriving fifteen minutes late to the restaurant. She is never on time, but with a capo husband and four kids under nine at home, she is incredibly busy. I'm lucky she still makes time for our monthly Sunday night meetups.

"You too." I rise from my chair to hug my best friend. "You look beautiful."

"I'm frazzled, and we both know it." She slips her coat onto the back of her chair and sits down. I pour her a glass of white wine before setting it back in the cooler. "Thanks, I need this." She gulps back a large mouthful, as I sip mine.

I indulged way too much yesterday, and I'm trying to take it easy tonight.

"Marco is teething like crazy, and I haven't had a decent night's sleep in weeks," she explains. "I have been counting down to tonight all week. I love my kids, but I definitely need this time away from them."

The waitress arrives, and we place our orders.

"Is Mrs. Caruso watching the twins?" she asks.

I nod, confirming our housekeeper is watching over my sons. "Much to their disgust. I got the whole 'I'm fourteen and we're made men' bullshit routine from Caleb. Joshua was pleading for Bettina to come over. They must think I was born yesterday. I know if I left them alone the place would be like party central when I return. And the last thing I need is Joshua knocking his sweet girlfriend up on my watch."

It's tough being a parent to twin teenage boys, even more so because they have been initiated. I'm sure if Gino was here he'd criticize me for getting Mrs. Caruso over to babysit and he would pat his sons on the back for drinking and fucking. I'm trying to keep them kids for as long as I can because there are hard times with challenging responsibilities lying in wait for them. Is it so bad to want them to remain young and carefree for as long as possible?

"They're having sex?" She almost chokes on her wine.

"Not that I know of, but the kids are all doing it so young these days."

"But she's from a good Italian family. Her parents would have drilled it in to her to protect her virtue."

"Her father is a *soldato*, and she's the youngest of six girls. While I'm sure they want her to remain a virgin until her wedding night, it's not like she's tied in the way I was."

"Joshua is a good boy. He wouldn't go there."

I bark out a laugh. "Oh, Frankie. I can't wait until your boys are teenagers. Then you'll get it. And don't you remember yourself? You were having sex with Archer when you were barely legal."

"True. That seems like a lifetime ago now."

"One husband and four kids later," I tease.

A dreamy expression materializes on her face. "I've got it good."

"You do."

I try to keep the smile on my face, but it's hard when I'm so fucking miserable.

"What's going on with you?" She takes my hand in hers.

"Same ole, same ole. My husband is still in the Windy City, and he couldn't care less about me. Every time I broach the subject of NYU, he says he has to go and hangs up on me. My life is in limbo, and it shows no signs of changing."

"He's being unfair. The deal was you could go back when the boys started high school, and they start in six weeks."

"He won't ever stop punishing me." I take a large swig of my wine. "I brought this on myself."

"Don't you dare say that." Her voice resonates with grit. "He's a fucking asshole for the way he treats you. It's been eleven years. Get the fuck over it already."

Her words bring it back, and I squeeze my eyes shut in a feeble attempt to ward off the pain. It's the same anytime I think of it. It will never get better. The pain will never truly go away. Yet I have learned to live with it for the boys and for my sanity. I was willing to work on my marriage, even if a part of me will always despise my husband, but we were doomed to fail the minute Leo knocked me up.

Instead, Gino and I came to a silent solution. We are cordial to one another, and we do what has to be done when we are in public. We put on a show, and no one can tell it's all a sham, because behind closed doors we are virtual strangers.

"Oh, Nat." Her heartfelt tone brings me back to the reality of our situation. I can't fall apart in public, and I need to get a grip. This is not who I am, and this temporary bout of melancholy ends now.

Opening my eyes, I take a few calming breaths to steady myself. I smile at my best friend. "I'm fine. I got my sons out of it, and they are my world. I love them as if I gave birth to them myself."

"I know you do. You're an amazing mother. I always knew you would be."

"Sierra is pregnant," I blurt.

"That is wonderful news. I'm happy for Ben."

"Me too. They are both over the moon."

"I know it's hard for you," she softly adds. "Like it was with me."

"I still feel bad about how I reacted when you told me you were pregnant with Gia." Shame washes over me as I think about how I blatantly ignored my bestie when she got pregnant, the year after I got married, with her firstborn. "It's one of my biggest regrets."

"Don't do that. You know I understand, and I never held it against you. My God, Natalia, it's only human to feel like that after what you've been through."

"I still hate I was so resentful. You know I didn't truly mean it."

"I know you were grieving so many things."

She lets go of my hand, and we sip our wine, both contemplative.

"I got a little drunk last night, and I almost blurted shit to Leo."

She quirks a brow. "Go on."

"I think he picked up on my mood. He asked me why I never had babies."

"And you told him?" Her mouth hangs open.

I arch a brow. "That I had an IUD fitted secretly so my husband couldn't impregnate me and how Gino thinks I'm barren because I haven't given him more kids? Of course not. I didn't answer. Instead, I asked him why he fucked whores."

She almost spits her wine out on the table. "Oh, hell, Nat." She giggles.

"He told me he's lonely and he does it because he knows he will never marry and have kids. He said it's still me. I'm the only one." My hand shakes as I lift my glass. "I wanted to throw myself at him, Frankie. I think I might have done it too, only I remembered in time why I must stay away from him."

"I've seen the way he looks at you sometimes, so I'm not surprised to hear that."

We stop talking as the waitress arrives, setting our plates down in front of us.

"I broke my wineglass in my haste to get away from him, and he lifted me out of harm's way, and then I burst out crying because even that little touch was so good." I carefully cut my chicken as I talk. "Then he hugged me, and I swear to fucking God, I have never had a hug like it."

"Only because you don't remember what his hugs felt like."

"I remember everything we shared, and every way he touched me was amazing. But this was different." I pop a piece of chicken into my mouth while Frankie cuts into her steak. "I'm starved for affection and intimacy. Honestly, if that creepy mailman brushed against me, I'd probably orgasm out of sheer neglect."

"Jesus, don't wish that on yourself. He's a perv." Frankie shudders. "When are you seeing Gino?"

"Never, I'm beginning to suspect. I wonder if he will ever return from Chicago. He seems to love it there."

"When do you need to let NYU know?"

"Next week. If I don't accept and pay my fees, I'll have to pass on my place."

"Pay it and work on him in the meantime. It's not like you don't have your own money."

Papa left his estate to Ben and a token trust fund and some personal items to me. I wasn't even pissed about it. It's the mafia way. But Ben refused to take all the money. He split the money in the bank accounts and the cash stash with me, and our old family home in Greenhaven is in both our names.

The house has been sitting idle for two years, since we packed up Papa and moved him into Ben's place, when his health declined. We can't leave it sitting there forever, and we need to decide what to do with it. We still pay the staff to manage the grounds and keep the inside clean, and we have round-the-clock security guarding the property.

I go there sometimes to walk the grounds. Mama's vegetable patch and herb garden is gone, but the orchard still thrives. Our groundskeeper maintains it, and when it's picking season, I bring the boys there and we grab baskets of apples to take home. For months, our pantry is stocked high with apple jelly and our table is laden with apple desserts and cakes. It reminds me of Mama and my youth, and it's one tradition I want to keep alive.

"I'm going to surprise Gino with a visit this week." I chew another mouthful of my chicken pasta dish. "Ben mentioned he is going to Chicago for a meeting on Wednesday, and I'm going to tag along. If I surprise my husband, rather than asking if I can come visit, he can't exactly say no. I am making him talk to me about NYU and planning to stay for an extended break. Maybe we can patch things up. At the very least, I need to get laid, and he owes me a ton of conjugal visits."

"Are you taking the twins?"

I shake my head. "They are going on that trip Don Maltese has organized for the younger initiates. They'll be gone from Tuesday to Sunday, so it's the perfect opportunity to grab some alone time with my husband."

"Maybe you can seduce a yes from him. You should stock up on sexy lingerie before you go."

I bark out a laugh. "I could get my nipples and my clit pierced, paint my body in chocolate paint, and crawl to him on my hands and knees, promising he could do whatever he wants to my body, and it still wouldn't sway my husband. He fucks me occasionally because he's not a completely heartless bastard, and, hey, he's a man. They don't usually turn down sex. But it's nothing more than a physical act. A chore. A release. I often wonder if he's as cold with the whores he fucks or if he just reserves that for me."

"I hate the unfairness of it all. If he has affairs, you should be able to fuck around too."

"In an imaginary world, I would, but in this one, that's a surefire way to earn a bullet in the back of the head." I eat another mouthful of the creamy chicken pasta. "All I care about right now is returning to NYU. I need this, Frankie, and I'm making him agree to it. I don't care what it takes; he is going to let me do this." My eyes blaze with determination as I eyeball my friend. "I need it to keep me sane, and I need to have something to look forward to because the kids are growing up fast, and before I know it, they will be reared. What the fuck do I have to look forward to then?"

Chapter 35

NATALIA

"ARE YOU SURE you don't want me to stay until you find Gino?" Ben asks as I curl my fingers around the door handle, getting ready to exit the car.

I kiss his cheek. "I know exactly where he is, thanks to you." Ben has been using digital tracking chips for years. His penchant for buying up prestigious IT firms has proven very beneficial. Not only has it helped to legitimize most of the businesses, it has given him access to a wide range of tools that help to keep his men safe. He insisted all his *soldati* and his loved ones wear one.

Gino agreed it was a good idea, and we all got the chip. What he doesn't know is Ben gave me access to the tracking app so I can always locate my family. However, I rarely check up on Gino, mainly using it to keep tabs on the boys so I know where they are, at all times, and they are safe. "I'll be fine, and I have my bodyguard."

Gino isn't as strict as some of the dons when it comes to bodyguards. When I was a girl, Papa wouldn't let me go anywhere without one. Gino trusts me not to take risks with my safety, and he knows I'm trained in self-defense and I'm proficient with a gun. I always carry a small handgun in my purse.

The rules are clear.

If I'm traveling out of state or going any place that could pose a threat, I'm to bring one of his men with me. While some went with him to Chicago, most of his *soldati* stayed behind, as it's business as usual in New York. Two guys watch our penthouse apartment around the clock, and the guys do shifts.

I'm not on personal terms with any of them, because they rotate so often, but that suits me. I don't even know the name of the guy who came with me from New York. I just told him I was surprising my husband and I needed someone to accompany me, making him promise not to call ahead.

"Okay." Ben gives me a hug. "Call me if you are staying, and I'll have your bag dropped off."

"Thanks, Benny." I'm not sure how this meeting will go, or if I'll be welcome to stay. My main aim is to have the NYU discussion and get agreement to enroll.

Ciro snorts from the front seat, and I flip him off to his face. I don't know how Ben stands that man. He was my bodyguard at one time, for about a year and a half, and it's a miracle I didn't pretend to accidentally shoot him.

Most made men are charming and well groomed. It's like Ciro deliberately set out to be the complete opposite. He's the grumpiest motherfucker I have ever met, and I swear he wears the same grubby black shirt under his suit all week. Dousing himself in cheap cologne does little to disguise the smell. Yet he loves getting his hands bloody, his instincts are sharp, and his aim never misses. Ben trusts him, and my brother doesn't make mistakes.

"I still can't believe you call the boss that." Ciro rolls his eyes, and I flip him off again.

Ben watches with a smirk on his face.

"It's not like either of us knew Benny is an Italian street name for Benzedrine when I chose to call him that." It's an amphetamine, and how were we to know? I was so naïve as an eighteen-year-old, and Bennett wasn't brought up with any knowledge of Italian traditions and ways. Leo had pointed it out to Ben, and we had a good chuckle over it. Neither of us gives a shit what anyone thinks, and the name stuck because it was already our thing.

"Good luck with your meetings," I say, opening the door.

"Thanks. I'll need it."

I know from our conversation on the plane that things are far from smooth sailing within The Outfit right now, and Ben is concerned. I wave at my brother as the car pulls away from the curb.

"I'm going over there," I explain to my bodyguard, pointing at the Italian restaurant across the street. He trails me to the lights, walking behind me as I cross the road. I check the app again to ensure I am at the right place. "Stay outside please," I tell the man, and he nods, taking up position at the side wall.

I step inside, quickly explaining to the nice woman at the front desk I'm here to surprise my husband, and she lets me wander through the large room by myself.

I find him a couple of minutes later, at a table, tucked into a corner at the back, and he's not alone. I had a suspicion Gino's reluctance for me to visit was less to do with work and more to do with *who* he was doing, and I was right.

The woman draped around him is stunning with long blonde hair and a pretty face. She looks young. Mid-twenties, if I had to guess. Her navy skirt suit and cream silk blouse are expensive, and the pearls around her neck scream old money. I duck down as they stand to leave, turning around and hiding my face so I'm not spotted.

They exit via a side door, and I follow at a discreet distance.

I watch through the glass door as Gino slides his arm around the slim blonde's shoulders, drawing her into his side, like he can't bear to have her far away. She looks up at him like he hung the stars in the sky, and I want to throw up. Gino leans down, kissing her passionately while his arms wrap around her fully. The kiss prolongs, and I'm growing angrier and more agitated as I watch.

He has never kissed me like that. Never held me so close. Never looked at me like that. Not even behind closed doors.

I gulp over the lump in my throat as I consider what this could mean for me—this woman is a threat, and I suddenly realize my life is in danger.

"What's a beautiful woman like you doing drinking all alone on a Wednesday afternoon?" a man with a smooth, deep masculine voice asks.

He takes the stool beside me at the hotel bar without invitation. I had felt his eyes on me, and I knew he'd approach at some point. It's pretty busy in here between residents having a late lunch or early dinner, groups of guys watching the game on the TV, and various businessmen and businesswomen conducting meetings over drinks in the booths at the back.

"Contemplating life and death," I truthfully reply, raising my glass of Macallan to my lips.

"Macallan 12," the stranger says, looking at the bottle sitting on the counter in front of me. "Good choice."

"Not as good as the 18, but I prefer the chocolaty, spicy taste of this vintage. The 18 is a bit too oaky for my taste."

The bartender approaches. "What can I get you, sir?"

"I'll have what she's having. Straight up too."

I should tell him to leave, but I've been sitting here for three hours, seething as I slowly get drunk, and I'm feeling a little reckless. I messaged Ben to pick me up at the Eclipse Hotel when he was en route to the airport, but I have still got a couple of hours to kill. I might as well flirt with someone who isn't my husband.

I eye him over the rim of my glass, liking what I see. His dark-blond hair is flawlessly styled, slicked back without a strand out of place. His handsome face reveals big green eyes framed by thick lashes, high cheekbones, and a full mouth. His jaw is clean-shaven and he fills out his designer suit well. He swivels in his chair to accept a glass from the bartender, and a waft of his cologne tickles my nostrils. He smells as spicy as the whisky, and maybe I'll be tempted to drink from his lips.

His eyes heat with molten lava as he clinks his glass against mine, and I know I'm not mistaking his interest. His gaze rakes over my body with zero subtlety, and I'm not sure if I applaud or abhor his confidence.

Perhaps I'll fuck him.

If my husband is as enamored with his mistress as I think he is, it's only a matter of time before Gino is plotting ways to off me so he is free to marry her. Might as well get laid before I'm buried six feet under.

"You're gorgeous." He sips from his drink as he eye fucks me.

"My husband doesn't think so." My eyes bore into his as I throw out that tidbit, waiting to see how he reacts.

"Your husband is a fucking fool."

I throw back my head, laughing. "He's a lot of things, but I'm not sure I have heard him called that before."

"You're not from here," he deduces.

"I'm not." I flash him a smile.

"In town for long?"

My smile widens. "Nope. My brother is coming to pick me up soon to take me to the airport."

"Hmm." He rubs a hand over his smooth chin. "I might need to hit the fast forward button."

"Are you always this presumptuous?" I inquire, taking another mouthful of my drink. If this was any other time, I'd kick him to the curb. But I'm blistering with rage. My skin feels like it's ready to peel off my body, and my inner voice is screaming in frustration and anger. I need physical contact to regain some control. And I want to fuck someone who isn't my husband. I want to fuck a stranger savagely and take everything out on him. So, this guy with his cocky flirtations and crass innuendos will do the job.

"When I see something I want, I go for it."

He's got balls, and I admire that. The fact he's not bothered about a little thing like a wedding ring, not so much, even if it works to my advantage. "I can see that." I trace the tip of my finger along the rim of my glass.

"I like you." He leans in closer, pressing his warm mouth to my ear. "Let's cut to the chase, beautiful. Life is short, and I want you. I've got a room upstairs. Why don't we take our drinks up there?" He eases back a little, peering into my eyes as he sweeps his fingers along my cheek.

"You want to fuck me," I say, needing him to be clear.

"I do." He lifts my hand, bringing it to his lips and pressing a kiss to my knuckles.

"I'm married."

"I know."

"Are you?"

"Does it matter?"

I jerk my hand back. "Yes." I know it might seem like double standards, but I won't be the woman who sleeps with another woman's husband.

"I'm not married." He shows me his hand, and I detect no imprint from a missing wedding band.

I shouldn't be considering this. It's risky for all kinds of reasons. But I have got zero fucks to give right now. "Okay." I gesture to the bartender for the check.

My mystery man darts in, kissing my cheek. "You won't regret it. I'll make it good for you."

Ignoring the memory those words invoke, I quirk a brow. "You'd better." I haven't gone this long without sex to be satisfied with some lackluster tangle between the sheets.

He chuckles as I remove my black credit card from my purse.

"I've got this." He hands two crisp hundred-dollar bills to the bartender. "Keep the change."

I should refuse because I can pay my own way. And I should probably ask what he does for a living or make small talk, but what's the point? I'm never going to see him again.

My heart is racing as I let him lead me out of the bar and into the lobby. Placing his hand on my lower back, he steers me toward the elevator bank. He presses the button and then backs me up against the wall, caging me in with his arms. "I have wanted you from the second you sat down," he admits, rubbing his nose against mine. "You're sexy as fuck." He kisses the corner of my mouth. "What's your name?"

"Does it matter?"

He grins, presenting me a blinding white smile. "Touché, gorgeous." His mouth descends on mine, and he kisses me confidently, not moving his arms, just casually gliding his lips against mine, in an unhurried fashion. My lips part, and his tongue slides into my mouth, awakening parts of me that have been lying dormant for a long time. I moan into his mouth as my cell pings in my purse, but I ignore it.

It's probably my bodyguard. I gave him the slip at the restaurant, knowing he would just think I'm inside with his boss. I guess he's probably figured out the truth by now. I know he won't call Gino yet because he fears a bullet in his brain. He will try to find me and only call Gino as a last resort.

I haven't decided if I want Gino to know I was there and saw him with his bit on the side or if it suits my agenda better to keep that knowledge to myself, until it's opportune to use it.

A second ping rings out, confirming the elevator has arrived, but the hottie doesn't break our lip-lock, and I'm in no rush either.

Ten seconds later, he's gone, ripped away from me by my brother.

I expel a frustrated sigh. What's a woman got to do to get laid?

Bennett thrusts the man at Ciro before rounding on me. "Do you want to tell me what you think you are doing?" His voice is lethally calm, and he has that blank expression on his face. The one I hate. It's his don persona, and right now, I need my brother. Ben takes my elbow, pulling me away from the wall.

"Hey, take your hands off her!" the guy I was just kissing demands.

"Shut your mouth." Ben wheels around and punches him in the face.

I have a mad case of déjà vu, and my heart aches, like it does every time I think of Mateo. I snap out of it before this man's death warrant is signed. "Stop overreacting, Benny. He wasn't attacking me. It was consensual."

"What the hell, asshole?" The guy glares at Ben as blood gushes from his nose.

Out of the corner of my eye, I see the woman behind the reception desk eyeing us warily. I don't want to cause a scene, any more than I have. I drill a sharp look at Ciro. "Let him go." Rummaging in my purse, I find a pack of tissues. I walk to the man I was just kissing. "I'm sorry about this." I dab at his nose before pressing the tissues into his hand. Ciro lets him go upon a nod from my brother. "It was nice to meet you," I say, stepping back. "I hope your nose isn't broken."

"Boss. What do you want me to do with him?" Ciro asks.

"Nothing," I hiss, shooting daggers at Ben's bodyguard. I swing my gaze on my brother. "This is nothing to do with him and he knows nothing. Let him go now, Benny."

Ben nods, walking over to where the two men are standing. Ciro hands Ben a black wallet.

"Hey, that's mine!" The guy's nostrils flare as he makes a swipe for his wallet. Ciro grabs both his arms, yanking them behind his back.

Ben removes his driver's license and takes a pic on his phone. Tucking the license and the wallet into the front pocket of the man's jacket, Ben narrows his eyes at him in a way that is scary. I know that face. It's when Ben readily allows all the darkness inside him to shine bright. It's been known to make grown men quake in their boots. "She was never here, and that never happened. Breathe a word of this to anyone, and I'll kill you."

The man gulps, instantly understanding the danger, and I feel like shit for placing him in this position.

"I'm sorry," I repeat before Ben takes my hand, almost dragging me outside.

My errant bodyguard is there, waiting by the car. Smart fucker clearly called my brother instead of my husband.

"Get a cab," Ben says, barking at Gino's man. "I need to speak to my sister in private."

Ciro gets into the passenger seat, beside our driver, while Ben and I climb silently into the back.

"Start talking," Ben says, through gritted teeth, as soon as the privacy screen is up.

The car glides seamlessly into the busy early evening traffic, and I stare forlornly out the window. I don't think there is much reason to keep this from my brother. So, I turn around and tell him what I discovered when I found Gino.

"That fucking bastard," he seethes. "How dare he parade his whore around town." Made men are told to revere and respect their wives. That means being discreet with their whores and mistresses, among other things.

"She's no whore." I clasp my hands on my lap. "She could be Juliet's doppelganger, and they are clearly besotted with one another. At least I know now why he has been ignoring me and refusing to let me visit."

"He was at the meeting I just left," Ben explains. "I was going to question him, but your message made me hold back. Now, I wish I hadn't."

"Don't get involved."

"You're my sister, and that cunt doesn't get to treat you like this."

"This is really nothing new, except the women he has bedded

before were always transient. This woman is different."

He turns to face me. "I know your relationship is not what you wanted, and I know it's no great love affair, but you said he treated you well. Every time you are together, it seems amicable and respectful."

A sad smile creeps over my face. "It's all an act. We are who we need to appear to be in public. We should both get Oscars."

"How bad has it been, Nat? And I want the fucking truth."

"He doesn't abuse me, if that's what you are asking. But he's neglectful, and he only cares insofar as I'm the boys' mother. They love me, and I love them. I'm the one who has raised them. That is probably the only thing that might save me now."

Ben growls. "Gino will not harm one hair on your head. I don't care who this woman is. It ends now. You're his wife, and he will treat you with the goddamn respect you deserve."

I reach out, unknotting my brother's clenched fists. "You will not mention this to him. Not until we know more." I have been stewing on this all afternoon, and I have finally made my decision. "Can you hire a PI for me? I want to get proof of his affair."

"For what gain?" Ben asks.

I shrug. "I may need it as ammunition. Before I do or say anything, I need to know who she is and what I'm dealing with."

Ben purses his lips, and his brow creases as his brain churns the idea. "Okay, but I can't let him run all over Chicago with a woman who isn't his wife. Not just because I'm liable to blow his fucking head off for mistreating you. Things are precarious and he's our main man on the ground. He needs to keep his fucking head in the game."

"Can you talk to my bodyguard? Make him keep quiet?"

"He won't tell anyone shit. You gave him the slip, and as far as he is concerned, Gino could kill him for his ineptitude."

I nod, staring absently out the window. A throbbing pain knocks on my skull, thanks to the Macallan, and I hope I manage to snatch some sleep on the plane.

"Is this why you have been so melancholy?" Ben asks, sliding over beside me. He wraps his arms around me, and I lean on him for support.

I rest my head on his shoulder. "Mostly. I had a feeling there was a woman. But it's more the futility of my life. The twins won't need me much longer, and I want to go back to NYU, but my husband refuses to speak to me about it."

"Let me handle that," Ben says.

I look up at him. "He won't take orders from you about his personal life. He might not care much about me, but I am still his wife. He won't take kindly to you butting in."

He kisses my brow. "I know how to handle Gino Accardi. Leave it up to me. I'll get his approval. Just do what you need to do to accept the place, and I'll deal with the cheating asshole."

Chapter 36

LEO

"IS THAT HANDLED?" Ben asks, as I enter his office at the Caltimore Holdings building, closing the door behind me.

"It is." I sink into a chair in front of his desk. Picking up a stress ball, I knead it in my hands. "He won't mention anything about being in Chicago. Do you want to tell me why I just split my knuckles giving the dick a personal warning?"

A muscle pops in Ben's jaw as he leans back in his chair, spinning sideways and looking out the window at New York laid bare before his feet. His sigh is heavy with exhaustion and concern. "I should, but I'm not sure I will."

I sit up straighter, almost strangling the ball in my hand. "This is about Nat," I surmise, having assumed as much when Ben told me to beat the shit out of one of Accardi's men. "I know she went to Chicago with you on Wednesday."

Ben swivels in his chair so he's facing me. All indecision is wiped from his face. "Gino is cheating on her."

Familiar rage kicks me in the gut. "That isn't anything new. We both know he's fucked around with whores behind her back for years." He isn't alone in doing it. Most of the dons have girlfriends and whores on the side. But this is Natalia we are talking about. "Why do you think I hate the fucker so much?"

Ben levels me with a lethal look. "We both know why you hate him, and it has little to do with whores."

"He doesn't treat her with respect," I snarl, throwing the ball at the window.

"And this is why I didn't want to tell you. You can't let your personal feelings get in the way."

I snort. "Are you telling me you're keeping this strictly professional?" Disbelief oozes from my tone.

He rubs at his temples, sighing again.

"I thought as much."

"No made man is permitted to disrespect his wife in such a blatant way. He's been wining and dining his lover all over Chicago, without giving a shit who sees him. It's no wonder things are a fucking mess there. He's not focused. His priorities aren't in the right place. Barretta has made it clear he wants out of the acting don role ASAP. The Russians are closing in, and the rank and file are fragmented. Loyalty is feeble. We need strong leadership. I thought Gino was the man for the job, but we may have to replace him. I can't look weak, and he's making me look weak."

My spirits perk up at that, and Ben notices.

"I don't mean take him out."

"Why not? By disrespecting Natalia, he's disrespecting you."

"I can't kill a don because he has slighted my sister, no matter how much I would love to."

"But you can if he fucks up in Chicago. This will reflect very badly on you if he can't control the situation there. The Commission entrusted this to him, and he's already sleeping on the job. Pun intended."

"I spoke to him and made it very clear he is to end it with this woman and regain control in Chicago or there will be hell to pay."

"Bet that went down well."

"Like a lead balloon, but I don't give a fuck if his feelings are hurt. I sent him to Chicago to restore order, not to find himself Juliet number two."

My eyes widen at that.

Ben opens a brown paper folder and slides a few photos across the desk toward me. With conflicting emotions, I stare at the images of Gino and the blonde.

I want to tie him to a chair and beat him bloody before slashing his skin with my blade, until there is nothing to hold his internal organs inside, for daring to cheat on someone as perfect as my *dolcezza*. Another part of me applauds him for being an idiot because this just might mean a way to extricate Natalia from her unhappy marriage. Or, at the very least, create an opportunity whereby we can be together.

I slide the photos back across the desk. "She could be Juliet's twin for sure."

"I think he's in love with her," Ben says, walking to his liquor cabinet and pouring drinks. Bourbon for him. Scotch for me. "And that's a problem."

Blood turns to ice in my veins. "You don't think…" My voice trails off because I can't even articulate the thought.

"I warned him not to do anything stupid, but I don't know. He's not acting like the man I know. He said all the right things, but I don't believe him. Natalia seems to think he will try to kill her so he is free to marry this bitch." He hands me my scotch.

"Natalia knows?"

Ben nods, retaking his seat. "She discovered them together but left before Gino spotted her."

"Who is the woman?"

"Her name is Marcella Toscana. I sicced a PI on both of them, and Philip is sending me daily reports on Gino's whereabouts from the tracking app. All I know about her so far is she comes from a distinguished family from Forest Glen. She's college educated, and she runs her own life consultancy firm. She was engaged to one of DeLuca's capos. He was shot and killed at the hotel."

"Her family is *mafioso*?"

He shakes his head, sipping his bourbon. "I don't think so though I'm waiting for that intel. It seems she was marrying in. With a name like that, there is definitely some Italian blood in her."

"Does she know he's married?"

"She does now." Ben smirks, tapping his fingers on the desk.

I arch a brow.

"I sent her family pictures with a warning to stay away." His grin expands. "I also sent her pictures of Juliet. It's only fair she knows she is just a replacement for his real true love."

I wonder if that will stop her. I whistle under my breath. "Gino will be pissed."

"Gino can go to hell."

"What are you going to do?"

He levels me with a fierce look. "Protect my sister and my family. Safeguard the business and The Commission." He drains the rest of his drink. "Whatever action I take next depends on what Don Accardi chooses to do."

I RIDE WITH Ben in the helicopter back to Greenwich later that night. I wasn't planning on staying this weekend. I want to catch up with my parents. Plus, I have drinks arranged with Brando and Alesso in the city tomorrow night, and I was planning to drop into Club H on my way home. I need to let off some steam, and Ben's Club H—short for hedonism—is my favorite of his sex clubs.

But as soon as Ben mentioned Natalia was staying at the house and she wasn't in a good mood, I made a spur-of-the-moment decision to stay over tonight. I need to check on her myself.

The helicopter deposits us on the landing pad behind the house. I grab my bag and walk with Ben across the lawn toward the impressive mansion. Ciro keeps a few paces behind us. "Are you still meeting Brando tomorrow night?" Ben asks.

"That's the plan." I might cancel, if I'm needed here, but I don't vocalize that thought.

"I want him following Natalia, and I want you to assign someone at night to watch over her apartment. Pick someone trustworthy. Set it up with Brando tomorrow." He turns to look at me, stalling as we reach the edge of the house. "I don't want her to know. She will freak out, but I need to know she's safe. I don't trust Accardi's men, but I trust Brando. He took care of her before, and he looked after Sierra last year. I know he will ensure no harm comes to her."

"*I'll* do it," I blurt. "I'll watch her during the day, and Brando can take the night duty."

Ben shakes his head. "No. I need you, and you can't be the one to do it."

Unspoken words filter between us, like always when Nat's name comes up.

Ben clamps his hand down hard on my shoulder. "I can guess what you're thinking, but don't go there. Don't make a complicated situation even more complicated."

I grind my teeth to my molars, biting back my retort. I know his intentions are coming from a good place, but I have loved Natalia for a long time, and if he thinks I'm holding back now, he's got another think coming.

Sierra greets us at the door, throwing her arms around Ben and kissing him like she didn't just see him this morning. I have rarely felt envious of their relationship, but lately, I'm beginning to crave what he has. I'm sick of meaningless sex, and I want the intimacy that comes from being with the same woman. As well as all the other benefits of being in a committed relationship. The trouble is, the only woman I want that with is already married.

To a cheating asshole who deserves to die a slow and gruesome death.

If I didn't know it would cause immeasurable problems for Ben, I would kill that motherfucker on the sly. Mateo and I got away with killing Carlo Greco, and no one found out. Don Accardi would be trickier, but I know I could pull it off.

"Hey, Leo." Serena gives me a quick hug as I step into the hallway. "This is a nice surprise. We weren't expecting you this weekend."

"I will probably have to leave tomorrow."

"We can travel to the city together," Alesso says, slapping me on the back.

"Welcome." Sierra kisses my cheek while keeping one arm around her husband. "Ben never mentioned you were coming, and we have already eaten, but we have plenty of food. Nat's been cooking up a storm the past few days."

Nat's go-to stress reliever is cooking, so I'm not surprised to hear that. "Sounds good. I'm starving." I take off in the direction of the kitchen, and Alesso keeps pace beside me. Serena walks with her sister and Ben behind us.

"I hear things have gone to shit in Chicago," he murmurs in a low voice.

While Alesso is young and technically only a *soldato*, Ben respects and trusts him, and he confides things in him the same way Angelo used to confide in me and Mateo.

"It's not looking too hot right now," I agree.

"Do you think he'll send someone else in Gino's place?"

"It's a strong possibility if Accardi continues to fuck up." Though I'm not sure who we would send. It's not like we have suitably qualified men beating down our door looking to move to Chicago, even if it's only temporary.

"I want to gut that fucker for hurting Natalia."

"You and me both, buddy," I murmur, wondering if Alesso would be up for taking the prick down. I know he doesn't care about Gino, but Alesso is loyal to Ben, through and through. Ben rescued him from a bad situation, and Alesso has never forgotten. I doubt I could convince him to go behind Ben's back on anything.

No. If anyone will be my wingman, it's Brando. He is loyal to Ben too, but we have known each other a long time, and he cares about Natalia. They were good friends growing up, and there is mutual respect between them. I think he would do it with me. I lock that away in a mental box to think about later, as I round the corner and enter the kitchen.

Natalia is at the stove, stirring something in a large pot. A half-drank glass of white wine is on the counter beside her. Her long hair is tied up in a casual bun on the back of her head, drawing attention to her elegant neck. She glances over her shoulder, offering me a timid smile. "I thought I heard your voice, and I presume you're hungry."

"Ravenous." Food is not the only thing I'm hungry for.

"Sit," she commands. "You too, Benny," she adds when Ben steps into the kitchen with his arm around Sierra.

"You're so bossy." Ben smirks.

Nat swings around, pointing a wooden spoon in her brother's direction. "You know the kitchen is my domain."

Ben shucks out of Sierra's hold and crosses to his sister. Taking the spoon from her hand, he puts it back in the pot and clasps her face, kissing both her cheeks. "Are you okay?" he asks, trying to whisper, but his words still carry.

"I'm fine." She removes his hands from her face. "You don't need to ask me a hundred times a day." She gives him a hug. "I love you, and I love how much you care, but you have your own priorities. Stop worrying about me."

"That's an impossibility," Ben says as the same words flit through my mind.

We take seats at the table, and Nat serves Ben and me with heaping plates of Mazzone meatballs and spaghetti and freshly made garlic bread. Alesso and Serena wander off to check on the kids, who should all be sleeping at this hour, while Natalia and Sierra take seats with us.

"Damn, this is so good. And it takes me back," I say in between mouthfuls.

"I remember you and Mateo devouring this any time I made it." There's a wistful smile on her face.

"Your chicken parmigiana too," I remind her. "And your apple cake. Nothing tastes as good as that melting on my tongue." *Except your pussy*, I mentally add.

Ben narrows his eyes at me as if he can read my thoughts.

"I went walking at the old house yesterday," Nat says, getting up. "Rowan and Sierra came too, and we collected some apples." She walks off, returning a minute later with a covered cake plate. She sets it down on the table and lifts the lid, revealing a scrumptious apple cake. "Leave some room," she teases, as I shovel more pasta into my mouth.

I flatten a hand against my toned stomach. "I will always have room for your apple cake." I waggle my brows. "You sure know the way to a man's heart," I blurt before stopping myself.

Her expression softens as she looks at me, and then it hardens. She harrumphs. "If it was that easy, my husband would never have fucked another woman, let alone fallen in love with one."

Tension bleeds into the air. I'm guessing everyone present at the house is aware of what has gone down. I expect no one outside of our inner circle will be privy to that news, for a variety of reasons.

"Juliet was a shit cook," she adds, gulping a large mouthful of wine. "It's the only area I have her beat. In every other way, I am lesser in Gino's eyes."

"He's a blind bastard, and he was never worthy of you. Even less so now."

"Leo." Ben's tone is clipped.

My fork drops to the table with a clang. "What?" I wave my hands in the air. "Everyone here knows it's the truth. Nat is too damn good for him, and he should be strung up by his balls for dishonoring her."

"Here, here," Sierra says, nodding in approval.

"I volunteer as tribute," I say, and Sierra giggles.

Nat slides her hand across the table, placing it on top of mine. "I love your loyalty, but there will be no bloodshed."

"Why the hell not? I know you don't love him." I'm getting all worked up, and I should just zip my lips, but I've been doing far too much of that for too long.

"He's Caleb's and Joshua's father," she quietly says. "I won't be responsible for depriving them of their papa. I know what it's like to lose a parent, and I wouldn't wish that on my worst enemy."

Chapter 37

NATALIA

LEO NODS, BUT I can tell he's not happy. I think if Ben gave him permission he would do it. He would murder Gino. Maybe I should be disgusted by the idea, but all it does is reinforce the love in my heart for Leo. I know he would kill to protect me and kill for me. I feel the walls around my heart softening, but I can't forget the risk to him from Gino. It's why I need to keep my guard up, no matter how much I long to drop it and fling myself into his arms.

"Have you heard from your sons?" he asks, picking up his fork and finishing his pasta.

"Joshua sent me a message, but I have heard nothing from Caleb. He's still pissed at me for getting him a babysitter."

Leo almost chokes on his food. "Does Gino know that?"

"He'd have to talk to me to know," I reply, sarcasm thick in my tone.

I'm not making excuses for my husband in front of my family any longer. The cards are on the table now. I have spent the past two days filling Serena and Sierra in. They know everything now except about the baby and the exact nature of my past relationship with Leo. I want to confide that in them too, but I know my sister-in-law. She's a sweet, sensitive soul, and before long, she'll blabber to Ben. Then Ben will likely want to murder both my husband and my ex-lover, and he has got enough on his plate right now. I'm already adding to his load, which I hate. His family is expanding, and this should be a happy time, yet I see the fears etched into his handsome face every time he looks at me.

It's one of the reasons I'm not falling apart. The other is I refuse to give my husband that power over me. Fuck him. And fuck that slut he's cheating with. If divorce was an option, I would gladly sign on the dotted line and let them be together if it meant I was finally free to live my life the way I want to. But divorce is not common within the *mafioso*, especially not for a don.

"You know what it means to be initiated and what happens at the making ceremony," Ben says. "They already have blood on their hands, Nat," he quietly adds. "I think you can trust them to stay home alone."

"I want them to have some normality, Benny!" I say, exasperation clear in my tone. I slurp my wine. "I know what they are involved in, and is it so wrong to want to give them some safety and stability outside their duties?"

"No, it's not wrong to want that,," Ben says. "And I can see Sierra reacting the same way you do if Rowan should choose to join *la famiglia*."

Sierra scowls, opening her mouth to protest before closing it again. I'm guessing that's an argument they will have in private. Or maybe one to set aside until Rowan is a little older. At least my brother is giving his son a choice. That is more than every other heir is granted. Yet I wonder how that will go down. Whether he chooses to initiate or not, Rowan Mazzone will always be known as the son of the most powerful mob boss in the US. It might actually be safer for him to initiate.

"But it is likely confusing them," Ben supplies, finishing his meal. "That may be where some of Caleb's animosity and wild behavior is coming from." Ben lifts Sierra onto his lap while he side-eyes my cake. "I tried talking to him last weekend, but he just clammed up."

I didn't know that. "Thanks for trying. He's shut himself off to everyone. Even Joshua. And God knows what he's getting up to this week."

"Don Maltese will keep him in line," Leo says, setting his silverware down on his empty plate. "I called him Tuesday morning before they set out and asked him to keep a special eye on Caleb and Joshua. You don't need to worry."

I stare at him in surprise. "Why would you do that?"

"They are your sons, and I wanted to help. You were clearly worried last weekend."

Gratitude fills my chest. "Thanks, Leo."

"I checked in with Rico earlier today. They are both getting on fine, so put your mind at ease."

I know Frankie had spoken to her husband before he left for the trip. But even though I know Enrico will keep a close eye on the twins, it is still hard to stop worrying. Leo checking in with him helps me to relax a little. I smile, nodding my thanks, before I get up. I fish plates and spoons from the kitchen cabinets and grab the homemade ice cream from the freezer.

Returning to the table, I plate two large slices of cake and drop a scoop of vanilla on each one. I hand them to my brother and Leo as Sierra walks over to the coffee machine to make coffee.

"God." Leo moans around his spoon. "This is almost better than sex."

Ben chuckles. "This is fucking good, but you're clearly having sex with the wrong women."

"Ben!" Sierra shouts, turning around and glaring at her husband. "Don't be mean."

And there goes my good mood. It's not like my brother to be so blatantly hurtful. He may not be privy to the specifics, but he knows what we feel for one another. Either he's tired and it slipped out or he said it on purpose to suit some agenda. Perhaps he thinks I'm going to throw myself at Leo like I did that man at the hotel. He wouldn't be wrong except I can't touch Leo without risking his life, and I won't be that selfish.

"I was thinking of visiting Mateo's grave in the morning," Leo says, deliberately changing the subject. He looks me directly in the face. "Would you like to go with me?"

I don't have to think about it. I nod. "I haven't been for a while, so yes."

"I would go too," Ben says, "but I promised the kids we would take the boat out and head to Island Beach." In the past, Ben has often come with me when I have visited the Mazzone mausoleum.

"We're all going," Sierra says, bringing a tray with coffees over to the table. "You are both welcome to join us."

"Thank you." I finish my wine. "But I think I'm going to head back to the city after the graveyard. I want to get everything ready for the twins' return on Sunday."

The guys eat their cake and drink their coffee, and then I ask to speak to Ben alone in his study.

"Did you talk to Gino about NYU?" I ask him the second the door is shut.

"I did, and you are permitted to go."

A layer of stress lifts from my shoulders, and I throw my arms around my brother. "Thank you, Ben."

"You're welcome." He kisses the top of my head before I ease out of his arms.

"How did you get him to agree?" I ask as he takes my hand, leading me to the two comfy chairs in front of the fireplace. It's summer, so there is no fire set, but it's still a relaxing space to sit and talk.

"I told him he owed you and it was the least he could do considering he's flaunting his other woman all over Chicago."

I gasp, almost spilling my wine. "You agreed you wouldn't interfere!" I cry.

"I made no such promise," he coolly replies. His blue eyes latch on to mine. "He doesn't know you know or that you were in Chicago."

I breathe easier hearing that.

"I told him I have been monitoring his movements via the app."

A laugh bubbles up my throat. "I'm betting he's considering slicing his arm open to remove the chip."

Ben chuckles. "Probably. But I put devices on his cars and in his apartment too. He's not going to outsmart me."

"Is that wise?" I know Ben heads The Commission, but Gino is still a don.

"He is fucking things up in Chicago," Ben says. "Trust me, he has more pressing concerns than a few bugs in his place."

That woman has a lot to answer for if she is responsible for Gino screwing up. But it's on him too. I have zero sympathy. "Thank you, Benny. You are the only man in my life I can truly rely on."

"You have been there for me when I needed you, and I love you. I want to take care of you." He pauses for a second to sip his drink. "I told him to end it and I wouldn't tolerate such blatant disrespect. I think he got the point."

"Do you know who she is?"

He nods, getting up to retrieve his briefcase. Silently, he hands me a brown manila folder.

I skim through it, taking in everything I need to know, before I pass it back to him. "Thanks."

"The PI will watch both of them, so try to put this out of your mind. Plan for college, and let me handle the rest."

STEPPING UP INTO the private Mazzone mausoleum, I inhale reverently as my eyes roam over the elevated family tombs. I'm not overly religious, despite my Catholic upbringing, but there is a solemnity, a comforting peace, whenever I visit my parents and my brother.

Papa had this granite mausoleum built after he became a don because he didn't want his final resting place to be in Italy like the generations before him. Inside, it's like a mini chapel with its marble walls, stained-glass windows, and triangular roof. Overhead, porcelain statues of the Virgin Mary and some angels rest on sturdy stone ledges. The three ornate tombs lie at the top of the enclosure, leaving adequate space for future additions.

I shiver as the maudlin thought lands in my brain.

Leo moves around the structure, lighting the scented candles.

I take a few minutes with Mama and Papa, setting vases of flowers on top of their tombs, before I move over to stand beside my brother's final resting place. I place my hand on the solid marble, and sadness overwhelms me. "I still miss him so much."

"Me too." Leo stands beside me. "I can't believe he's been gone fourteen years."

"In some ways, it seems like it's been longer. Yet, in other ways, it feels like it only happened yesterday."

"I know what you mean." He scrubs a hand over his prickly jawline and sighs. "I have been so conflicted since we discovered who was responsible for his death. I would rather it had been the Russians. Knowing Mateo died so Ben could come into our lives seriously fucks with my head."

"Mine too, and I know Ben is tortured over it. That man was like a father to Benny growing up, and for him to do that, even if he believed it was the only way to protect him, weighs heavy on his heart."

"Yet, if Mateo was alive, I doubt Ben would be," he quietly adds, confirming what I suspected years ago as I considered that very thing.

I don't want to continue this conversation. It makes me uncomfortable and upsets me.

And what's the point? We can't change the past.

There has been so much needless death, and I'm the last of my original family. "They are all gone now. Mama, Papa, Mateo." I sit down on the marble bench to the side, keeping my eyes locked on my brother's tomb. "It makes me unbearably sad sometimes."

"You have Ben and Sierra, Rowan, Serena, Alesso, your sons. Me." Leo reaches out, threading his fingers in mine. I look into his handsome face. "You will always have me. You are not alone."

I squeeze his hand, welcoming his touch. "Would you really have killed Gino?"

His jaw tightens. "Yes," he says in a clipped tone. "He hurt you, and he has disrespected you your entire marriage. He should pay for that." He looks away, and when he turns his head back to me, the murderous dark look is gone from his face. "But I won't do it. For the boys. They are his only saving grace."

I squeeze his hand again. "Did you hear I'm going back to NYU?"

"Ben told me." He smiles, and his entire face lights up. I get sucked into his gaze and drawn into his warm bubble. "I'm so happy for you. You are going to be the best doctor."

"You don't think I'm too old?"

"Don't be stupid." He lightly cups my face with his free hand. "You still look eighteen to me."

I snort out a laugh. "You clearly need your eyes examined."

"There is nothing wrong with my eyes." He leans in closer. "You are still the most beautiful woman I have ever seen." He brushes his thumb along my lower lip. "Your beauty is timeless, *dolcezza.* Like your inner strength."

It would be so easy to cut the distance between us and kiss him.

I want to.

I badly want to.

But I can't allow this, no matter how ardently my heart and soul beg me to reclaim the man who has always been mine.

"Mateo must be turning in his grave," I joke, removing my hand from Leo's and letting his other hand drop from my face. I stand. "He was always warning you to stay away from me."

Leo unfurls to his full height, and I can't help admiring his gorgeous form. He's so tall, broad, muscular, and manly. No wonder I always felt safe in his arms.

"Mateo was wrong. Angelo too." Leo steps up to me, and our chests brush against one another. I spot indecision in his eyes for a fleeting second. "I told him I wanted to marry you." He tucks a piece of my hair behind my ear.

My eyes pop wide. I knew Papa had threatened Leo and used me to force him into keeping his distance, but he never mentioned this. "You never told me that."

"I knew as I was asking him that he would say no, but I had to try."

"You would've married me?" I croak, my throat clogging with emotion.

"In a heartbeat," he says, pulling me into his arms.

I don't resist his embrace and readily hug him. Closing my eyes, I inhale his scent and siphon his warmth while enjoying the feel of his hard, strong body against mine. "I would have said yes," I whisper. "And I wouldn't have needed time to think about it."

His arms band tight around mine, and we hold one another, fighting our true desires, as my eldest brother watches from his earthly resting place.

Chapter 38

LEO

I SCAN THE voyeur room at Club H with disinterested eyes while sitting at the bar nursing the same scotch since I arrived a half hour ago. This is the second time I have come here in a month, and like the last time, I'm finding I'm not in the mood.

I know why.

I'm fixated on Natalia.

I can't see past her.

Even though there are gorgeous women in the room, many of them naked or semi-naked.

Even watching the action taking place behind the various glass rooms fails to arouse my flaccid cock. The place is busy tonight, and all ten rooms are full. Most all the couches in the middle of the room are occupied with people looking at the men and women fucking behind the glass walls.

Sultry music wafts in the background, but even that isn't getting my juices flowing.

I haven't seen Natalia since she drove us back to the city that Saturday from Ben's Connecticut house, but she never strays from my mind. I wanted to kiss her at the graveyard. To take her home and make love to her, replacing that sad resigned expression on her face with one of unadulterated joy.

I have moved beyond the point of no return.

I don't give a fuck about starting something with her behind Gino's back.

Not after his betrayal. He's on shaky ground with Ben, even if he has gotten his act somewhat together since Ben ripped into him. It's not like he'd be in any position to throw shade.

I would have laid it all out on the table that Saturday except Nat is keeping me at arm's length, and I must respect that.

The second that changes? The second she gives me a clear signal? I'm fucking taking it. I'm no longer a kid who thought he was a man. I'm not the same guy who made so many mistakes with her in the past.

I know what I want, and I'm done watching from the sidelines.

As soon as Nat shows me she is on the same page, I am all in.

If Gino even dares to raise a hand to hurt her, he'll have me to deal with.

Brando, and Nario—one of our most bloodthirsty and savage *soldati*—are alternating bodyguard shifts, and so far, they have managed to go undetected. When Nat starts NYU in two weeks, that may change. I'm not sure how easy it will be to keep tabs on her there and remain unnoticed. Though the tracking app is a big help. The guys report to me daily, and I feed the intel to the boss, but they know I'm their go-to person if there is any emergency. Despite what Ben said, he's got enough on his plate with running his empire and this shit in Chicago.

Natalia is mine to worry about.

Mine to covet.

Mine to love.

Out of the corner of my eye, I spy a busty redhead coming this way. Draining my drink, I slam it down on the table and stand. "Sorry, sweetheart. Not tonight," I tell Clarissa as she brushes up against me.

"You said that last time." She pouts, trekking her fingers up and down my arm. "I want a repeat."

I have no energy to explain I never go back for seconds. I just want to get out of here and go home. Watch some baseball or preseason NFL highlights on my TV and knock back a few beers. Maybe watch some porn and jerk off to images of Natalia in my head. "I'm not in the mood, but I doubt you'll be short of takers tonight." Leaning down, I kiss her cheek. "Have fun."

I walk out of the room without a second glance.

My lungs flood with relief as I hit the hallway, and I think my time frequenting Ben's sex clubs is coming to an end. Unless I'm with Nat, it no longer interests me.

I nod at one of the security guards in the hallway as I walk past the orgy room. Up ahead, a guy I recognize has a curvy blonde pinned to the wall. His hand is working under her tight black short leather dress as he kisses her. Her slim legs are encased in fuck-me knee-high boots, and she has shapely hips and a tiny waist. But her tits do me in. Fuck, they're magnificent and perfectly molded behind the strapless leather dress. I can't see her face properly, behind the mass of blonde hair and the guy sucking her mouth, but her body is to die for, and my cock twitches behind my pants for the first time tonight.

"We should go upstairs," the woman says in a slurred voice, and I freeze on the spot. All the tiny hairs lift on the back of my neck.

"Or we could visit the orgy room," the man suggests, leaning down to suck on her neck. She whimpers, throwing her head back to the wall with her eyes closed. Blood rushes to my head, and my fists ball up at my sides. "I know my friend would be down to fuck you. How do you feel about a threesome?"

Rage unlike anything I have ever felt mushrooms inside me, and I snarl.

Her pretty blue eyes startle wide, and she gasps as our gazes connect.

"If you value breathing," I growl, grabbing the asshole by the back of the shirt, "you will get your filthy fucking hands off her!" I yell, yanking him away.

Natalia squeals as I raise my clenched fist and ram it into the dickhead's face.

"Mr. Messina. Is there a problem here?" George, the security guard, asks, coming up alongside me. All the staff know who I am as I'm intimately involved in all of Ben's businesses.

"Get this asshole out of my face." I grab a fistful of the dickhead's shirt and practically throw him at George. "And revoke his membership."

"Fuck you, asshole." The man glares at me. "Don't you know who

I am? You're making a big mistake."

"I know who you are, Damiano, and I don't give a fuck. You're lucky it's me who found you and not Don Mazzone."

His brow puckers as he looks at Natalia, trying to work out why I intervened. She is clinging to the wall, looking unnaturally pale with tiny beads of sweat forming on her brow. She is trashed, and I want to pummel this asshole to the wall for even daring to look at her in that condition.

"I don't understand. Who is she?" he asks, frowning.

Thank fuck, he hasn't recognized her. No one can know she was here. If word got back to Gino, there would be hell to pay. I slap his face. "There are no names in here for a reason, *stronzo*. Forget you ever saw her. You don't mention this to anyone. You hear me?"

"You're an asshole, Messina."

"The feeling's mutual."

"Fuck this shit. This isn't the only sex club in town."

"Your loss. Our gain." I shrug, ready to be done with this bastard so I can take care of my little drunk *dolcezza*. I flip my gaze to George. "Escort Mr. Battaglia off the premises."

"Yes, sir." George drags him away, and I walk over to Natalia.

"Look at me," I say, gently lifting her face.

"I don't feel so hot," she slurs, her whiskey breath fanning across my face.

"No shit, Sherlock."

I want to tear into her and demand to know how the fuck she got in here because security is strict. I also want to know how she gave Brando the slip. I'm guessing her face was hidden behind that heavy blonde wig as she exited her apartment building and he didn't pay her too much attention. I'm still going to rip into him because she can't be roaming the streets of New York unprotected.

I'm angry. At him and her, but I can't get into it now. She's too drunk. My lecture can wait.

"Come on. Let's get you out of here." I take her arm, but she sways unsteadily, almost tumbling on her heels. Bending down, I scoop her up into my arms. "Hold on to my neck."

Her arms wrap around me as I cradle her to my chest, walking to the staff elevator. It goes all the way to the basement, so I can get her out of here undetected. "Bury your head in my shoulder," I instruct, as the elevator doors open. "And keep your face down. I don't want you captured on camera." Ben would blow a gasket if he found her here.

She mumbles something into my neck as she does what she's told. Her plump lips press against my skin, and I'm rock hard. I tell my dick to fuck off and simmer down. She is too drunk, and I won't be that lecherous prick who salivates over a vulnerable, drunk girl.

I hold her tight to my body as the elevator descends. When it stops, we step out into the brightly lit employee parking lot. I manage to maneuver my key fob from my pants pocket without dropping the precious treasure in my arms, unlock my Lexus SUV, and get Natalia buckled into the passenger seat.

I grab a light blanket, a plastic bag, and a chilled bottle of water from the cooler bucket in the back before climbing behind the wheel. I blast the AC, setting it to the coldest level, because Nat looks like she's burning up.

"Baby." I cup her face, forcing her eyes to open. "Drink this." I uncap the bottle and hold it to her lips, gently tipping it into her mouth.

"I can do it," she slurs, slapping my hand away as her fingers curl around the bottle.

Always wanting to be independent. Even when she can barely keep herself upright.

I place the blanket over her lap, positioning the plastic bag on top. I'm not convinced she won't puke before I get her back to my place, and I don't want her vomiting all over her dress. I watch her drink the water, taking it from her when she's done and situating it in the cup holder by her seat.

"Nat." I touch her face. "I need to know a few things."

Her unfocused blue eyes stare into mine. "What?"

"Were you…" I clear my throat, not wanting to ask this, but needing to. "Did you have sex with anyone at the club?"

Giggles burst from her lips, and she convulses with laughter.

"I don't see how this is remotely funny," I deadpan.

"Of course, I didn't have fucking sex!" she snaps, all humor gone as her eyes narrow to slits. "Mateo, Ben, and you all have one thing in common. You're fucking cockblockers!" she shrieks, swatting at my chest.

"We are only protecting you."

"Ha." She barks out a laugh. "That's a fucking joke."

I have rarely seen Natalia drunk, and it's unusual to hear her cursing so much.

"Do you know how long it's been since I got laid, huh? How desperate I am for some cock? How much I want to fuck all this anger and resentment from my system? How badly I want someone, *anyone*, to fuck me hard and rough me up just so I can feel something other than pain and rage?"

I try not to take her words personally. If she needs to be fucked, I will happily fuck her. Deep down, she knows that. Yet she came here tonight, preferring to fuck a stranger than come to me.

That hurts.

"Six months, Leo!" she continues. "It's been six months since that prick of a man I'm married to touched me in any way."

Fresh fury ghosts over me with a renewed desire to beat that man bloody before ending his life.

I want to say so many things to her but not while she's drunk. I need to get her to my apartment and take care of her. In the morning, we can have a serious talk. "Are you expected back home?" I ask, starting the engine. "Where are the twins?"

"They are staying over at Cristian DiPietro's house." She frowns as I drive us out of the parking lot. "He was having a party. I shouldn't have let them go. They are probably drunk, doing drugs, and fucking whores."

"Probably," I admit because that's just the way it is. "But you shouldn't worry. Don DiPietro wouldn't have left them unattended. They can't get up to too much trouble."

"He could knock her up!" she screeches as I inch out onto the road.

"Who?"

"Joshua." She moans, clutching her head. "He's so serious with Bettina."

"That doesn't mean he'll knock her up. Wearing condoms is drilled into every made man because there is no shortage of whores deliberately trying to get pregnant." I pat her knee. "Don't worry."

"But I do," she says as I take the next bend, grateful the roads aren't too busy this time of night. "And condoms aren't always reliable," she whispers. She swipes at a few errant tears running down her face.

The way she loves those boys is beautiful to behold. From the moment she married Gino, she welcomed those boys into her heart.

And their bastard father has only ever thrown it back in her face.

"I can talk to Joshua, if you like," I suggest. "Make sure he's being careful."

She turns to me with black streaks running down her face. "You would do that?"

"Of course. They are your sons, and their father is absent. They may not be part of our crew, but they are part of the New York *famiglia*, and I like to mentor the younger boys. The couple of years after you first initiate are the hardest. They might welcome someone to talk to who has been in their shoes, and they know me." I have been at family gatherings with them over the years, and everyone knows I'm Ben's number two.

"That is kind of you to offer. I'll think about it."

I nod, turning onto the next street. "I'm taking you to my place."

"No." She shakes her head. "Just take me home."

"You shouldn't be alone."

"I can't go back to your apartment, Leo. What if Ben finds out?"

Ben owns the entire apartment building, and ninety percent of the units are sold or rented out. The rest of them are kept for our personal use. It's not uncommon for us to put visitors up or to help some of our men out if they need a temporary place to stay. Traditionally, Ben's close team and personal bodyguards live in the apartments underneath his penthouse, so that's why Ciro and I still live here. Occasionally, we travel with the boss to his main residence in Connecticut, but most of the time, we live here.

If that's Natalia's only resistance, I can easily quash it. "Ben doesn't live there anymore. The only time he uses the penthouse is if he has a late night or very early morning, meeting or if Rowan and Sierra are coming up to the city for the weekend. It's only me and Ciro living there at the moment, and he won't be home for hours." I have no clue where Ciro disappears to in his downtime, because we are not close, but he rarely returns home before five a.m. on Saturday nights.

"What about the cameras?"

I tug on her blonde wig. "You're in disguise." I smirk. "And I can doctor the tape. Any other objections?"

"I'm not having sex with you," she whispers, averting her eyes and looking out the window.

That stings. I want to ask her why she was prepared to have sex with a stranger and not me, but I bite my lip and keep those words for the morning. "Natalia. Look at me," I say, as I turn onto the street that leads to the Mazzone building I live at. "I would never take advantage of you. *Never.* I am taking you to my home because you are drunk and you need someone to take care of you." I brush my fingers over her chin. "That person is me."

Tears well in her eyes as she nods. Leaning over, she kisses my cheek. "Thank you, Leo."

No, thank you, dolcezza, because I have dreamed of holding you in my arms again while you sleep, for years, and now I'm getting to do it again.

Chapter 39

NATALIA

THERE'S A MARIACHI band playing loudly in my head when I wake. Trickles of golden sunlight filter through the blinds, and I squint as my eyes try to adjust to the light. Rubbing my sore temples, I sit up, trying to ignore the screeching, thumping melody bouncing around inside my skull. Wrestling my tongue from the roof of my mouth, I almost gag on the icky taste coating my oral cavity.

Ugh. I am never drinking again, which means I am never returning to Club H. The only way I could work up the courage to go there was by pouring alcohol down my throat.

My fingers trail over the empty space beside me in the bed. It's still a little warm, so I know Leo can't have gotten up too long ago. I glance down at myself in his T-shirt, and it all comes flooding back to me.

I guess I passed out when he carried me from the car to the elevator and into his apartment. I barely made it to the bathroom before I heaved up my guts. I remember Leo holding my hair and rubbing my back as I hugged the porcelain god. I was so hot. Sweating under my leather dress. My face was on fire, and my throat was burning. My cheek was plastered to the cool tile floor when I blacked out again. The next thing I recall is being naked with Leo, fully clothed, holding me up in the shower. The cold water was like manna from heaven, and it cooled me down.

Leo increased the temperature, only to wash my hair and my body, and then he wrapped me in a fluffy towel and helped me while I brushed my teeth. He stood outside while I did my business and then carried me into his bedroom.

I rub a hand over my heart when I remember how he carefully combed and then blow-dried my hair before patting my body dry and helping me into his T-shirt and a pair of his boxers. I lift the shirt to my nose, inhaling the citrusy notes of his cologne and the fresh pine smell from whatever laundry detergent is used to wash his clothes.

My eyes dart to the bedside table, finding the half-empty bottle of water. He made me swallow some pain pills, and I shudder at the thought of how much worse my hangover would be without them. Tears prick my eyes when I remember him crawling into bed beside me and holding me in his arms.

I don't remember waking at all during the night because I was safely cocooned in his embrace.

Just like old times. After Mama died. When he comforted me on so many nights.

Just like then, last night wasn't about lust or sex. He was simply comforting me, and I love him so much for taking such good care of me.

Dragging my weary ass out of bed, I head into his en suite bathroom to freshen up before I can face him in the cold light of day. I know he has questions, and I need to give him answers. When I emerge from the bathroom, the smell of bacon lures me to the kitchen on autopilot. My belly rumbles and knots at the same time, and I'm not sure if it's a good idea to eat.

"Good morning." I enter the kitchen, wincing at the raspy sound emitting from my throat.

"How are you feeling?" Leo looks over his shoulder at me.

"Like I got trashed last night."

It's a miracle I can string a sentence together because Holy. Hell. Leo is standing in front of the stove, bare-chested and bare-footed, in only low-hanging black sweats.

And he is a sight to behold.

Has a back ever been so sexy?

When he turns around, my mouth trails the ground. He is all broad shoulders, hard muscles, and curved abs. The ink on his arms and upper chest only adds to the overall appeal. He even has those V-indents on either side of his slim hips. His body pays homage to dedicated hours spent in the gym and more than twenty years as a *mafioso*. Scars cover his chest, and I long to trace every single one with my tongue. Saliva gathers in my mouth, and a familiar ache takes up residence down below.

Leo is staring at me too. His gaze rakes up and down my bare legs, lingering a few seconds on my chest. I'm not wearing a bra, so the fact my nipples are hard as a rock is obvious in the extreme.

His eyes lift to mine, and they are dark with longing. My chest heaves and I'm torn between running into his arms and fleeing his apartment before we both do something we can't take back.

My tummy rumbles, breaking through the sexual tension, and I laugh.

"You look hot in my clothes," he says in a gruff voice. "You are too damn sexy. Go sit at the table before I decide to have *you* for breakfast."

My ovaries dance a tango while the inner devil in my ear screams at me to jump up on the island unit, spread my legs, and let him feast on me. At that thought, I scurry to the table and sit down, keeping my eyes glued to the window instead of looking at the temptation in the kitchen.

Leo comes over a few minutes later, setting a plate with eggs, bacon, and toast down in front of me. "Eat." He curls my hand around a fork before leaning down to kiss my brow.

I swoon all over again.

He walks off, returning with his food and two glasses of freshly squeezed orange juice.

I tuck in, moaning as the buttery eggs and crisp bacon hit my mouth. "This is good. I didn't know you could cook."

"Mama taught me and Frank to cook, and I have lived alone since I was twenty-one. Eating out and living off takeout got old real fast."

"I like your place." I cast my gaze around the large open-plan living space. The modern kitchen with white gloss cabinets is tucked in a corner, near the hallway to the bedrooms. The table and chairs are slotted against the window in front of the kitchen and to the side of the large living room, which stretches the length of the floor-to-ceiling windows. The view over Central Park is impressive, and it's the main reason Ben beat out his competition to purchase this site.

Unlike my brother's penthouse above, which was furnished and styled by an interior designer, Leo's place is homey with patterned rugs and cushions and an eclectic mix of furniture. Framed photos of his family and friends adorn the walls, and his bookshelf is teeming with books and knickknacks. It's neat and clean and lived in.

"Finished your inspection?" he asks, his tone teasing.

"I really like it. It has personality."

"It's perfect now you are here." He peers deep into my eyes. "There have been so many times I have visualized you sitting here, eating my food, sleeping in my bed, wearing my clothes." Emotion fills his eyes, and he is shielding nothing from me.

I gulp over the emotional lump wedged in my throat as heat creeps into my cheeks.

"Still so fucking beautiful when you blush." He reaches out, touching my face. His smile melts another layer off my heart and tears down another piece of the wall. "Eat." Removing his hand, he points at my plate. "You need to soak up the alcohol."

"I doubt there is any left in my system," I say, before shoveling more eggs in my mouth.

"I'm sorry about your dress."

I lift a brow.

"You don't remember?" he asks.

"I remember most things but not that. What about my dress?"

"I had to cut it off you. It's ruined, but I'll buy you another one."

"You don't have to do that."

"I want to." He leans in, putting his face all up in mine. "You were sexy as hell in that dress and those boots." He fingers my hair. "Not the wig though." He brings his nose to my hair and inhales. "I love your dark hair."

I place my hand on top of his. "Leo," I whisper, almost choking over the myriad of conflicting emotions I'm feeling. "Thank you for taking care of me last night."

"I love looking after you. It's never a chore." Leaning in, he kisses my lips.

It's a fleeting kiss. Only a brush of his mouth against mine. But I feel it everywhere, and it's everything.

"Eat, baby. Then we'll talk."

We eat in companionable silence, and then we clear the table together and rinse dishes side by side. It's so normal. Such a familiar couple thing. Yet Gino and I have never done this. I cook and clean up and ensure the house is spotless, the laundry is done on time, and my three men have everything they need.

"Come." Leo takes my hand, leading me into the living room. He pushes me down on the couch and sits beside me. "What were you doing at Club H last night, *dolcezza*, and how did you get in?"

"I think why I was there was obvious."

"Because you haven't been laid in six months," he says, and I cringe.

"Fuck. Did I say that?"

His lips kick up. "Yes, among other things."

"Oh, God." I bury my face in my hands.

He chuckles, sliding his arm around me as he presses a kiss to my temple. "Don't be embarrassed. You can tell me anything, even if I didn't exactly like what I was hearing."

I lift my head. "Why? What else did I say?"

"Tell me how you got in first."

"You have to promise you won't tell Ben."

"I don't like keeping secrets from your brother, but this one is a doozy. There is no way Ben can know you were there last night. He will rain bloody murder if he discovers the truth. You can trust me with this. I have already wiped all camera footage and dealt with that asshole Damiano."

My cheeks pink as I recall the wanton way I let that man touch me in the hallway. Thank fuck, Leo stopped me from taking it any further. I know I would have regretted it, and it was dangerous to consider going off with an Italian American man. I know they recognized one another, which confirms he is *mafioso*. If he had figured out who I was, I would have signed my own death warrant.

"I stole a visitor card from Ben's office when I was last at the house," I explain. "It took me two weeks to pluck up the courage to go to the club. Gino has been calling me weekly, but he's even more cold and detached. I know Ben told him to end it with that woman. I know he resents me, and every time I get off a call with him, I'm spitting blood. I seriously doubt he's ended things with her, and I am done playing the dutiful betrayed wife. Fuck him," I hiss. "Fuck him and that bitch."

Anger charges through my veins, and I'm all worked up again. "He has never fucked me right anyway, and I have needs. Needs I was no longer prepared to ignore. It's not like I can just go out and pick up a man in public, so I thought Club H was the solution. I know every member has to sign an NDA and they are not allowed to talk about what goes on at the club. I know names are generally not shared. I went in disguise, and I thought it would be safe." I chew on the corner of my lip. "Obviously, I was wrong."

"Why would you seek out a random man, in a fucking sex club of all places, instead of coming to me?"

I blink profusely, rubbing at my ears, sure I must have misheard him. "Leo, why would I come to you?"

His jaw tenses, and all the amusement dies in his eyes. "Because I fucking love you and I know you fucking love me too!" He grips my face in his large palms. "If your husband is neglecting your needs, no matter what they are, you come to me. No one else. *Me*."

"You know I can't!" I cry.

He plants a punishing kiss on my lips, and I melt against him. "Watch my lips," he says when he pulls back. "I. Don't. Care."

"You should! He'll kill you."

Laughter rumbles from his chest. "Don't insult me, *dolcezza*. If anyone is getting killed, it's that *stronzo*."

"Why me when you can have any unmarried woman without complications?" I ask, shucking out of his hold. I can't think clearly when he's touching me like this.

He links our hands. "I love you. I desire you. You're the only woman I want in my bed and in my life from now on."

Disbelief shimmers in my eyes. "I know you're not short of female company or willing bed partners."

He rests his brow against mine. "I haven't slept with anyone in two months, and I don't want to. I'm obsessed with you, Natalia, and I'm done denying what I want. What *we* want."

"What are you saying?" I whisper over his lips.

He eases back, peering deep into my eyes. "I'm saying we have suffered enough, sacrificed enough, and it ends now." He kisses me softly. "I want you, *amore mio*, and I am done resisting you. You need me, and I need you. Let's be selfish. God knows, we have waited long enough." A pregnant pause ensues. "Unless you're telling me you don't love me anymore and you don't want me. Obviously, that would change things," he quietly adds.

I should lie to protect him, but I'm tired too. It's not like years ago when I was a naïve girl who thought she was a woman and Leo was a *soldato* with little influence or power. I'm old enough now to know what I want, to go after it, and own my decision. Leo is a powerful man with loyal men who will fight for him. And there's Ben. While I don't want to drag him into this, I know my brother would not let anything happen to us.

"I still love you," I say, projecting my voice so there is no doubt. "I never stopped, Leo. I have been in love with you since I was fourteen years old. Maybe even earlier, but I didn't realize what the feeling was. There has never been any other man for me but you." I kiss him this time. "In case that isn't clear, I want you too."

He kisses me passionately, hauling my body against his warm chest and sliding his arms around my back. I fall into him, and everything I have ever felt for him comes rushing to the surface. I could drown in his taste and his touch, but before we go any further, we need to make sure we are doing the right thing.

"How?" I ask in a breathy tone, ripping my lips from his. "How will we do this?"

"We'll have to sneak around. Mainly meet here," he says in between planting open-mouthed kisses on my neck. "I'll get you a burner cell."

"We'll be lying to our family. Our friends," I say.

He lifts his head, staring solemnly into my eyes. "Yes. I don't like it, but if it's a choice between having you and having to lie to our loved ones, I will always choose you."

"It might be difficult for me to get away. I'll be at college, and I have the boys."

"I'll be busy with work, but we'll make time. Any time with you will be cherished, even if we only manage to see one another once a week."

"What about other women?" If I'm risking my life and his to enter this affair, I'm not sharing him.

"There are no other women. There is only you." He kisses the backs of my hands. "I won't be with anyone else. Why would I want to if I'm with you? You are all I have ever wanted." He kisses the tip of my nose. "I will be faithful to you, Nat. I'm not like that prick. I would never cheat on you." His eyes blaze with sincerity. "I know what I did in the past hurt you, but it was never real, and I was too weak to do what I should have done. I'm not that man anymore. You can trust me. I swear." He dots kisses all over my face. "I know I need to earn that trust, and I will prove it to you, if you just give me a chance. Give *us* this chance we never had."

Can I do this? Can I take such a huge leap of faith? Can I enter this with Leo knowing I'm hiding a big secret from him? One he may never forgive me for if he finds out?

I should tell him.

I should let him know the truth and decide then if he still wants to be with me.

But if I tell him, he will kill Gino, and that will ignite a whole chain reaction with a set of consequences that would not end well for me, him, or my brother.

Is it wrong to keep that truth locked away in my heart if it's the best way of protecting him?

Leo is waiting anxiously for an answer. Fear mixes with pain and longing on his face as he stares at me while I make my decision. I look into his gorgeous gray-blue eyes and rake my gaze over his handsome face, and I know I can't reject him. I can't do that to him or to me.

It feels like everything that has happened has been leading to this moment.

If I want to take control of my life, it starts here.

It's as simple as that.

"Yes," I say, freeing a smile. I wind my arms around his neck. "It's time to risk it all to be together. Nothing has ever felt more right or more real, and I want to do this with you."

I don't get another word out because his lips crash upon mine as he reels me into his lap, and the time for conversation is over.

Chapter 40

NATALIA

LEO CLOSES THE door behind us when he enters his bedroom, slamming me against the wall while his mouth descends on mine. Our lips and tongues explode in a frantic lust-fueled marriage as our hands feverishly explore bare flesh. His fingers slip under my shirt, gliding up my torso to cup my breasts. I whimper into his mouth, grinding against his erection, as he fondles my tits. "I have dreamed of this every night for years," he murmurs as his mouth trails along my jaw and he gently nips my skin. He brushes his thumbs across my nipples before tugging on the hard buds, sending liquid heat racing to my core.

"Leo, please." I undulate my hips, rocking against him, needing him inside me. I'm so wet I am probably leaving a damp patch on his boxers.

"Arms up," he commands, pinching my nipple.

A shiver of desire tiptoes up and down my spine. I lift my arms, and he whips the shirt off before yanking the boxers down. He kneels before me, and my pussy pulses in anticipation. Roughly shoving my thighs apart, he dives in, sliding his tongue up and down my slit before plunging it inside my throbbing walls.

I gasp, grabbing fistfuls of his hair as he devours me with his tongue before sliding three fingers inside me. I cry out, thrusting my pussy in his face, wanting him to eat me alive, because my orgasm is already building, and I know it won't take much to send me soaring skyward to heaven. "Oh, God, Leo. Don't stop," I moan, yanking on his hair. "Please don't stop."

Pinning my hips to the wall, he holds me in place as he pumps his fingers faster and sucks on my clit. When he gently bites me, I scream as I succumb to the most intense climax ever. Tears of joy leak from my eyes as I jerk and thrash against him while he keeps working his digits inside me and lapping at my sensitive bundle of nerves, until I'm sated.

Standing abruptly, he quickly sheds his sweats, stroking his hard cock while drinking me in. My chest is heaving, my thighs are shaking, and I'm wearing the biggest, dreamiest smile.

"Fuck, *dolcezza*. Look at you." He steps closer, and the tip of his cock brushes my stomach. He flicks my nipple. "You're so fucking sexy." Darting in, he smashes his mouth to mine and brutalizes my lips. I claw at his back, dragging my nails up and down his spine and roughly kneading his ass as I push my pussy against him, desperate for him to fill me up. "And *mine*," he growls before sucking on my breast in a way I know will leave a mark.

"I'm yours," I pant, arching my back as he ravages my breast. "Take me. Stamp your touch all over me."

I yelp when he throws me over his shoulder and whacks my ass. Leo throws me down on his bed and crawls over me, rolling his hips against mine as he nips and licks his way along my collarbone, over my tits, and across my stomach. I spread my legs wider, wrapping them around his back as I yank him down fully on top of me. "Fuck me," I plead, scraping my nails along his chest.

He hisses, pumping his hips and pressing his dick against my pussy. I'm so wet for him I might liquefy into a messy puddle on his bed. He claims my lips in another brutal passionate kiss, and I can't get enough of him. Without warning, he sits back on his heels, reaching across to his bedside table. "This is going to be hard and fast," he cautions, quickly sheathing his straining length. “Because I can’t wait another fucking second to bury myself inside you.”

“I want that,” I say as he lines himself up at my entrance. “I’m not a precious doll, Leo. I can take it. Fuck me hard, and take what you need.”

He slams into me in one rough thrust, and my screams commingle with moans as he slams in and out of me. I lift my hips, tightening my legs around his waist as he fucks me like a man so lost to lust he has given up all control. His fingers dig into my hips, and his hands are greedy as they roam my body.

Yanking his face to mine, I kiss him with raw need, biting on his lips and invading his mouth with my tongue.

“Jesus, fuck, Nat,” he pants, yanking my hips up higher.

My pelvis is tilted upward as he pounds into me so hard I swear his cock brushes my womb. I’m on fire. Every part of my body is doused in flames, and I never want it to end. His arms circle my back as he simultaneously sits up, bringing me with him. My legs are still wrapped around his back, and my arms encircle his neck as we fuck sitting up. His lips alternate between my mouth and my tits, and I throw my head back, moaning as pleasure hits every nerve ending in my body. I ride him as he thrusts up into me, with our arms locked around one another, and he worships my breasts and my mouth.

The pace is frenetic, our movements wild and chaotic, until he deliberately slows down. I cup his face, peering into his eyes as he holds my hips, controlling our movements. He pulls back and pushes up with teasing slow strokes, his eyes never leaving mine. “I love you,” he says, driving in deep, hitting all the right places. He slowly withdraws. “I love you so much I can’t breathe sometimes. I ache for you, Natalia. In every part of me and in every way.”

He plunges in again, and my walls tighten around him as we stare at one another. It’s wholly intimate, in a way I haven’t felt connected to another soul since the night I gave Leo my virginity. “You are the other half of my soul, Leo," I rasp as another climax builds momentum inside me. "And this is everything. *Everything*," I whisper.

He kisses me. It's hard but full of emotion, and it's almost too much. The searing-hot kisses, the agonizingly slow pace of his thrusts—hitting so deep I know he's embedding himself inside me in more than just physical ways—the love and devotion written all over his face, and the sinfully erotic touch of his hands.

"Please tell me you feel this." He moves his lips to my neck, right in that sensitive spot underneath my ear. "Tell me I'm not the only one feeling this."

"I feel it," I groan, pushing down on him as he pushes up. "God, Leo." I yank his face away from my neck, kissing him deeply. "How have I lived so long without this? Without you?"

"Never again, *dolcezza*." He slides his fingers down between our bodies. "I don't care what we have to risk. I am never being without you again." He rubs my clit, increasing speed in time with the pistoning of his hips as he rocks into me harder.

My orgasm hits me like a bolt of lightning, and I'm sparking across the sky, my limbs quivering, as I crest the heady wave of my climax. Leo carefully places me down on my back before lifting my legs up over his shoulders. Then he ruts into me, slamming his cock in and out, his chest glistening with sweat, hair tumbling sexily over his brow, as he fucks me into the mattress.

He roars out my name as he comes, and I stare at him in awe.

I love him so much.

He owns every part of me in all the ways that count.

Maybe that's why this has been the greatest sexual experience of my life.

Sex has never been this good for me, and I already know I'm going to be insatiable for him. I will never stop wanting him.

We laze around in bed, talking and kissing, before we go again. This time, Leo makes love to me, reinforcing the strength of our bond.

After, we take a shower together, and he fucks me from behind with my body pinned to the wall as he lays further claim on me.

I never want to leave his arms, but duty calls. I know the twins will be home soon, and I need to be there for them. My dress is shredded, and I can hardly show up at my apartment in Leo's clothes, so I head up to Ben's penthouse and invade Sierra's wardrobe. My sister-in-law is taller and slimmer than me, but I find a pair of leggings, a baggy T-shirt, and flip-flops that work. I can launder them and have them back before she notices they are missing.

"I don't want you to go," Leo grumbles, circling his arms around my waist from behind as I check I have everything in my purse.

"I know, babe." I hold on to his arms, leaning my head back for a kiss.

"But we'll have to get used to this," he says over my lips. "It's just my need for you is at an all-time high." He grinds his hard-on into my back.

I turn around in his arms. "I know. I just want to stay in your bed and never leave." I run my fingers through his hair. "Today has been amazing, Leo." I peer deep into his gorgeous eyes. "You rocked my world, babe."

"You rocked mine." He slaps my ass. "And there is so much more to explore," he murmurs, grazing his teeth along my neck. I have a few marks on my body, left in the throes of passion, but he was careful not to leave them in any noticeable place. And it's not like Gino is going to come home and want to fuck me anytime soon.

"I can't wait." I kiss him slow and deep before reluctantly pulling back. I rub my nose against his. "Love you," I whisper.

"Love you too." He reels me into his arms, hugging me tight.

"Shit," I hiss as a thought lands in my brain. "What about the tracking app?" Panic sluices through my veins. "What if Gino looks and locates where I am?" Hysteria bubbles up my throat.

"Relax, baby. Breathe." Leo strokes my face. "You don't need to worry about that. It doesn't pinpoint exactly where you are in the building until you are much closer. If he checks the app and calls you out on it, you can say you stayed at the penthouse because Sierra asked you to pick up some stuff for her." He runs his fingers up and down my arm.

"I can't use that excuse every time I am here."

"*Amore mio*." He cups my face. "Do you trust me to protect you?"

I nod without hesitation.

"Then don't worry. Leave this up to me. I will doctor the cameras and find out how to do the same with the tracking app. I will cover my tracks so no one will know. Let me take care of this, and you just focus on finding a way to sneak out to me again soon."

Chapter 41

NATALIA

LEO AND I have been snatching every opportune moment we can to be together in the month since we decided to have an affair. My fears about my husband discovering what I'm up to are unfounded. I sneak in and out of our building undetected, thanks to my blonde wig, and Gino's goons never even realize I am gone. My husband hasn't returned home from Chicago, and when he organized for the boys to visit him two weeks ago—before they started high school—there was no mention, from either of us, about me going.

Our sham of a marriage has never been more obvious, but I don't care.

I want him to neglect me. To forget about me. To think he is punishing me.

It just gives Leo and me more time to be together.

I emerge from the lecture hall, waving to Janice as she walks off in the opposite direction. Janice is the only other mature student in our year, and we have naturally bonded. Like me, she has a family, so we don't socialize outside of school, which suits me fine. I prefer to reserve my free time for my sons and Leo.

Serena is also studying at NYU, but she's on a different campus, so I don't see her unless we arrange to meet for lunch, which we have done a couple of times. I make a mental note to call her later to see if she wants to meet up this week.

I'm walking in the hallway, past an empty room, when an arm darts out, yanking me inside. My bag slides off my shoulder, dropping to the floor. The click of a lock has my heart thrashing against my rib cage in sheer panic. I'm about to scream bloody murder when a warm hand clamps down over my mouth and familiar gray-blue eyes come into view. I glare at Leo, and he chuckles, releasing my mouth and hauling me up against his warm, hard body. "Do you want me to drop dead of a heart attack?" I hiss, as my arms automatically wind around his neck.

"Never. I'm sorry if I scared you," he says, looking remarkably unapologetic as he unbuttons my pants.

"What are you doing here? This is reckless, Leo, and we agreed we would be careful." My breath spikes in my throat when he slides his hand into my panties and cups my pussy.

"I missed you, and I was in the neighborhood." His fingers find my folds, and he dives inside my body.

A primitive moan slips from my lips. "Leo, we could get caught," I rasp as I ride his hand, desperate for the friction.

His thumb makes swirling circles on my clit as he strokes my insides with his fingers. "No one will find us, and I'll be quick."

My hands cling to the wall, and I rest my head against his shoulder as he fingers me, increasing the pressure of his thumb until I orgasm a few minutes later, soaking his hand.

"You are so damn sexy when you come." Removing his fingers, he thrusts one into his mouth. "Hmm. You taste incredible." A wicked glint appears in his eyes. "Taste." He brings one glistening finger to my mouth, and I open without challenge. "Taste how delicious you are," he purrs, pushing his finger in and out of my mouth as the bulge in his pants strains against his zipper. Taking one of my hands, he draws it to his crotch, placing it over his hard-on. "See what you do to me? I'm going out of my mind, *dolcezza*. I'm *obsessed* with you." Yanking his finger from my mouth, he unbuckles his pants, letting them drop to the ground, along with his boxers.

I sink to my knees, lapping at the precum beading on his gorgeous cock.

"As much as I love the feel of your mouth on me, I need inside you, babe. Right this fucking second."

I'm hauled to my feet, and he rips my black pants and panties down my legs before he spins me around, pushing me against the wall, and kicking my feet apart. "Brace yourself, *amore mio*. I'm going to fuck the living daylights out of you."

A shiver works its way through me at his dark promise, and I thrust my ass up and out, stretching my legs as far as they will go. The familiar ripping sound of a foil packet builds my anticipation, and my cum is leaking down my inner thighs as my pussy throbs in anticipation.

Leo covers my mouth from behind as he thrusts inside me, and my scream is muffled against his palm. I cling to the wall, holding on for dear life, as he slams into me, his fingernails digging into my hips as he fucks me hard. His hand moves from my mouth, trailing lower to gently grip my throat. Stars explode behind my eyes, and desire swirls in my core. My inner walls hug his cock, clenching and unclenching, and our joint moans mingle with the sound of flesh slapping against flesh in the empty room.

"Going to come, babe." He grunts, flexing his hips and surging inside me. His grip on my neck tightens a little when my pussy squeezes his erection. His free hand finds my clit, and he rubs me aggressively, matching his rough thrusts. I'm scaling a massive wave, about to fall off my board, when he detonates, pounding inside me and grunting as he comes. His pleasurable moans send me over the edge, and we are falling together into bliss.

It takes me a minute to catch my breath after he removes his hand from my throat. Wrapping his body around me from behind, he stays put, brushing my hair to one side so he can place drugging kisses against my neck. "I can't get enough of you, *dolcezza*," he whispers. "This all-consuming need for you never dissipates." Winding his hand around my hair, he tips my head back. "What am I going to do with you?" He leans around, claiming my mouth in a bruising kiss, and I cling to his arm, wishing we never had to be parted.

"I'm coming over tonight, remember?" The twins have some *mafioso* thing to do, and they won't be home for hours.

"I haven't forgotten." He pulls out, and I'm instantly bereft. After dealing with the condom and tucking his dick away, he helps me to get dressed. He probes my neck with gentle fingers. "I didn't grip you too tight, did I?" He tilts his head, inspecting my neck for finger marks.

Palming his cheek, I shake my head. "No, and if I spot any bruising, I will wear a silk scarf. I often do, so no one will think anything of it." We are hiding our relationship from everyone, which is a huge source of guilt for both of us. We want nothing more than to shout about our love from the rooftops, but we can't.

"I lose control when I'm with you. I can't think but for the need to claim you, to own you," he admits, dragging my lower lip into his mouth. "Getting to love you like this is all I have ever wanted, but I don't want to place you in a precarious position. If I'm too rough, if I'm leaving too many marks, you need to tell me. I'm watching Gino's whereabouts constantly, but I don't want to fuck up."

"You won't. *We* won't." My hands land on his trim waist. Leo is kinky, and he was a regular visitor to Ben's sex clubs. I know he likes it rough, and his favorite way to take me is hard and fast. Sometimes, he puts a blindfold on me or ties my hands behind my back, but I freaking love it. I love that he doesn't treat me like I'm breakable. That he knows I can handle it. That I get as much pleasure out of it as he does.

His hand wraps around the nape of my neck, holding me in place. "There are so many things I want to do to you and *with you*, Nat." His eyes glisten with wicked promise, and my legs almost buckle as a delicious shiver skates over my skin.

"I want it all, Leo. I love the things you do to my body." I trail my hands up and down his sides. "I like seeing the imprints of your hands on my skin. It comforts me when we can't be together." I shrug because it's not a big deal. "And if it's noticeable, I can use makeup and scarves."

"You're so perfect, Nat." He grabs handfuls of my ass. "In every possible way." His cell vibrates in his pocket, and he lets go of me. He looks briefly at it before repocketing it. "I need to go." Bending down, he kisses me sweetly. "Thanks for the booty call." He smirks as he straightens up, and I swat his chest.

"You're lucky I love you." I faux glare at him as he hands me my book bag.

"Ditto, *amore mio*." He unlocks the door and opens it for me.

"Leo," a man with a gruff voice says, and I gasp as Brando pushes off the wall across from us, coming forward. "The boss is looking for you. It's urgent." His lips tip upward as his eyes light on mine. "Hey, Nat."

My mouth hangs open, and all the blood rushes to my head. I sway on my feet, and my bag slides off my shoulder again.

"Nat, I—"

"I'll handle it," Leo clips out, cutting Brando off, as he reaches down to grab my bag.

Brando nods, striding along the hallway toward the exit without another word.

"Oh my God!" I cry. Panic has a vise-grip on my heart. I bet I'm sporting the same freshly fucked look as Leo and it's obvious to Brando that we just had sex. "He'll know what we were doing in there and tell Ben!"

Leo places his hands on my shoulders, dragging me back into the room and locking the door again. He puts my bag on the ground at our feet. "Calm down, Nat. Brando knows, and he won't say anything."

"Wait? What?" My eyes pop wide. "How does he know, and why is this the first time I'm hearing about it?" I thump his chest. "I know you said you were handling things, but I need to know if someone else knows about us! It's not a carte blanche excuse to hide things from me!"

Air expels from his mouth, and he drags a hand through his hair. "Ben assigned Brando and Nario to watch you twenty-four-seven. He's not taking any chances with Gino. I didn't tell you because Ben knew you would freak out and he didn't want you to stress."

"Oh, no." I shake my head, wagging my finger in his face. "You don't get to gang up on me and call it protection. I am going to string my brother up for this!"

"*Dolcezza*." He takes my hands in his. "Ben isn't sure what is going on with Accardi. I believe you were the one who told him you thought he might try to orchestrate your death so he could be with his Juliet doppelganger. You can't say that to your brother and expect him to do nothing."

"He should have told me." I shove him away. "You should have told me when we started sleeping together!" I'm aware I'm overreacting, but seeing Brando sent the fear of God into me. Leo doesn't quite understand the risk to his life because he doesn't know about the baby or what transpired afterward. Anyone discovering we are having an affair is a big risk, and I don't like it.

"I want you to enjoy being back at college! The last thing I want is you worrying about anything." He slaps a hand over his chest. "You are mine to protect, and I won't apologize for shielding you. Is that so hard to understand?"

"I can't be kept in the dark, Leo." I try to rein in my anger. I know my brother and Leo acted with my best interests at heart, but they can't keep things from me. "I won't be treated like some helpless female."

"We don't think that." Ignoring my protests, he pulls me into his arms. "We love you, and we're just trying to keep you safe." He tilts my face up. "If anything happened to you, Nat, I would die. I mean it. I'd be following right behind you because I cannot live in this world without you any longer."

"That doesn't make it right, Leo, but I understand why you did what you did." I step out of his embrace. "Don't do it again." I fold my arms across my chest and level him with a warning look. "I assume you had to tell Brando and Nario given how frequently I visit your apartment?"

He nods. "They won't say anything. Brando because he cares for you, and Nario because he's very loyal to me. Unless Ben asks them outright, they will keep it a secret."

"I don't like it," I admit. "Already, people know."

"I couldn't not tell them."

I sigh in frustration. "I know."

He hands me my bag. "I will tell you everything from now on, if that's what you prefer."

"It is."

"Okay." My shoulders relax at the sincere expression on his face.

"Now that's sorted, let me walk you to your next class."

I'm at Leo's stove, stirring the mushroom sauce I made to go with our steaks, when Leo arrives home later that night. "Perfect timing," I say, turning around to accept his kiss.

"It smells delicious, and I love coming home to you slaving over a hot stove."

He smirks, and I slap his ass. "That's twice you have made sexist comments in one day. Don't make it a third."

He reels me in by the waist, nibbling on my ear. "You know I'm teasing." He nuzzles that sensitive spot under my ear, and I throw my head back, granting him better access. "I love you being at my place. It truly feels like a home now."

My heart melts, like it always does when he's romantic. Which is a lot, because Leo might be a feared mafioso, and he's definitely got a dark side, as well as a kinky side, but he's hella romantic with me. I circle my arms around his neck, pressing my lips softly to his. "Being here with you is everything I want and all that I need. I don't care that we can't go out. I prefer hiding away at your place, just the two of us." I wish it was permanent, and I can tell from the wistful look in his eyes he wishes that too.

His eyes fall to my neck. "You still have it," he whispers, fingering the delicate silver locket he gave me for Christmas the year I was seventeen.

"I could never bear to part with it," I admit.

"I still have the box and the gifts you gave me for my twenty-first birthday. It's one of my most treasured possessions." He kisses my brow, his look one of total adoration. "Do I have time to grab a shower before dinner?"

I shake my head. "The steak is resting, the baked potatoes and salad are already on the table, and the sauce is just done."

"You're spoiling me," he murmurs, taking two wineglasses out of the overhead cabinet.

"I like spoiling you, and you know being in the kitchen makes me happy." He pours us both a glass of red wine, bringing them over to the table as I plate up our meals. Without a word, he walks back out to the hallway, reappearing a minute later with a massive bunch of red roses and a large box of chocolates from my favorite chocolate shop.

"I haven't had these in years," I admit. "When did you find the time to drive to White Plains?"

"I didn't. I called the shop and had them delivered to me downtown."

"You're so thoughtful." I peck his lips, setting the chocolates down on the table as I walk back to the kitchen to arrange the roses in a vase.

Returning to the table, I place the vase in the center, smiling like a loon. Gino has never bought me flowers, and I'm not sure I fully understood how much it can mean to receive them until this moment. "Thank you, baby." I lean across the table to peck his lips. "I love you."

He cups my face, his features bursting with emotion. "Love you too. So much, Nat. So, so much."

We dive into our meal, talking about our day in between mouthfuls.

After, we clean up, side by side, before taking the chocolates, the bottle of red wine, and our glasses over to the couch. Leo puts Nat King Cole on, and I kick off my shoes, snuggling up beside him as we share the chocolates and sip our wine in between kisses. "I love this," I truthfully admit, placing my hand on his chest. "Just existing together. Doing the simple things but having you there by my side." I lift my face to his. "It feels like I have a true partner for the first time in my life."

"Me too." He kisses the corner of my mouth. "I agree with all of that." He idly twirls a lock of my hair around his finger. "I never wanted this before because it would never have made sense with anyone but you."

"It's the same for me. Even if I was able to set aside my feelings for you and put effort into my marriage, Gino would never have wanted this. Not with me."

"His loss is definitely my gain."

I rest my head on his shoulder, hating how temporary this is. I try to enjoy my time with Leo and just live in the moment. But there's this dark cloud hanging over my head all the time and a gnarly voice whispering in my ear that this can't last and it won't end well. A shudder works its way through me, and he bundles me in his arms. "We're not ever being separated again, Nat," he says, answering the thoughts in my head. "I told you. No matter what happens, I'm going to find a way to make this work."

I don't reply because I can't let myself hope for too much. "This is enough, Leo." The unspoken "for now" doesn't need to be articulated.

"How are things with Caleb?" he asks, and I know he's purposely changing the subject. "And did my little talk with Joshua help at all?"

We were all at Ben and Sierra's last Sunday for dinner, and Leo took the time to pull Joshua to one side to have the safe sex talk. "Joshua hasn't said anything to me," I explain, "but he thinks about things deeply, so hopefully you got through to him and he'll be careful." I didn't ask Leo if Joshua confided in him if he was having sex. I don't want to invade his privacy, and I'm not sure I want to know. As long as they are using protection, that is as much as I need to know.

"And Mr. Broody, Moody Teenager?"

My lips fight a smile, but it's fleeting as concern overshadows everything else. "Caleb is still moody and withdrawn, and I honestly don't know how to deal with him. Everything I say rubs him the wrong way. I thought after he spent the weekend with his father he might be in a better mood, but if anything, he is worse."

"It's hard being a teenager. Especially when you're part of the *famiglia*."

"I know." I sit up straighter, sighing. "I just feel so helpless. Like I'm failing him as a mother."

"You're not, babe. Just be there for him, and let him know he can always talk to you. There isn't much else you can do. You can't force him to speak. Perhaps he will come to you when he's ready."

I shrug, feeling heartsore. "I worry I'm losing them," I admit, and my voice cracks. "I love them so much."

"Shush, dolcezza." He kisses the top of my head. "You're a wonderful mother, and they love you. They are just at an age where they can't show you. They'll come through this."

Leo's phone vibrates across the table, and he reaches for it. He straightens up, accepting the incoming call. "Boss, what's up?" He stands, cursing. "What do you need me to do?" he asks as I lower my legs and slip my feet into my ballet flats. "I'll meet you at the airport," he says before hanging up.

"Trouble?" I inquire, gathering up our half-full glasses.

"You could say." He swipes the empty bottle, and I follow him into the kitchen. "The Russians just attacked three of The Outfit's warehouses. I need to go with Ben to Chicago."

Chapter 42

LEO

"FUCK, THIS IS carnage." I step out of the SUV with Ben at the plot on West Pershing Road where some of The Outfit's supply warehouses once stood. Piles of rubble and simmering ash greet us, and the scene looks like something from a movie. Several blacked-out SUVs and cherry-red fire engines are parked out front and police—whom I assume are friendlies—are cordoning off the area with official tape. A fire of this magnitude couldn't be kept away from the authorities or the media, which only adds to the problem. I can already predict tomorrow's news headlines.

Thick plumes of acrid smoke shoot into the sky and stings the backs of my eyes. We cover our mouths, walking in the direction of Gino Accardi. He is talking with an older man in uniform, and he abruptly ends the conversation when he sees us approaching.

"Don Mazzone." Gino stretches his hand out, shaking Ben's hand. "Thanks for coming so quickly." His eyes flit to mine for a second before dismissing me.

Trust me, asshole, the feeling is mutual.

I shove my hands in my pockets to avoid the urge to throttle him, reminding myself of the warning Ben imparted when we were on our private plane. He made me promise to keep my cool because he knows I'm no fan of Nat's husband and I'm prone to rash outbursts, on occasion.

"What's the damage?" Ben asks, wearing his serious don face.

"It's significant, but it could be worse." Gino glances at the men milling around the scene. "We should talk back at HQ. The fire marshal's on payroll, but I don't want to speak out in the open."

Another familiar man approaches. Thomas Barretta, acting don, carries his weariness in his gait and on his face. He nods solemnly at us. "It's good to see you both. We should talk."

"We'll meet you at the restaurant," Ben says, and we turn on our heels, back toward our car.

The Outfit has modernized in a lot of ways, but they are still old school at their core. Their HQ is in the basement of one of their Italian restaurants in midtown, and I always feel like I'm stepping onto the set of a Hollywood mobster movie whenever I'm there.

Barretta and Accardi pull up behind us when we reach the restaurant eight minutes later. It's almost one a.m., so traffic is pretty much nonexistent at this time of night.

The mood is dark when we step into the place. Several men drinking at the bar climb off their stools, nodding in respect to Ben as we walk past. Ben shakes their hands before following Accardi and Barretta to the back stairs.

We traipse downstairs and into the small office at the back.

Ben removes his jacket before sitting down on one of the battered brown leather couches. I keep my jacket on as I drop down beside him. Barretta sits across from us, looking like death warmed over. Gino moves to the liquor cabinet, fixing drinks while we make the usual bullshit small talk with Barretta.

When we all have a drink in hand, the conversation turns serious. "Tell me what you know." Ben drills a sharp look at Gino. The boss man might look composed, but he's ready to explode underneath that calm façade. Gino was skating on thin ice before this attack. That he let it happen on his watch is inexcusable. Things are falling to shit in the Windy City, and it threatens to pull everything and everyone down with it.

Gino doesn't look like a man hovering on the brink of this world and the next as he casually crosses one leg over his knee and begins explaining. Everything about the fuckface pisses me off, and I have to work hard to keep the animosity from my face. "One of our *soldati* got a tip-off that the Russians were about to imminently attack some of our warehouses, but we didn't know where. I dispatched men as quickly as I could get them mobilized, dividing them into groups, to go to all our locations. The Russians were still there when we got to the site on West Pershing Road, but it was too late to stop the blaze."

"You have them?" Ben sits up straighter. "You should have led with that."

"I interrogated them personally," Accardi says, drinking his whiskey. "They didn't give us shit, so I slit their throats and threw their bodies into the burning building."

Waves of anger roll off Ben, and he's up, out of his seat, knocking over the coffee table, as he lunges at Gino, before I have- even processed his movement. Ben jabs his gun into Accardi's temple. "I don't need much incentive to blast a fucking big hole in your head," he grits out.

Accardi presses his weapon into Ben's stomach, and I pull my gun out, pointing it at Gino's head. "It will take even less for me to pull the trigger," I say, walking right up to him. "Release Don Mazzone or his face and mine are the last faces you will ever see."

"Everyone put your weapons down." Thomas Barretta stands, clutching the arm of the couch as his leg wobbles. "Need I remind you we are all on the same side?"

"Are we though?" Ben levels a lethal stare at Accardi, his jaw tensing, before he straightens up and pulls the muzzle away from his head. I keep my weapon trained on Gino because I don't trust the fucker.

Gino withdraws his gun from Ben's stomach, placing it down on his thigh. "You might be head of The Commission, but you don't get to level accusations at me. I am still a don, and I was entrusted with this territory. That means I make the decisions and you don't get to pull rank on me."

"I have every right to question a man who would dispose of the enemy without holding them for formal interrogation."

"Don Accardi made the best decisions in the heat of the moment," Barretta says. "I was there when he questioned the men. They gave up nothing. Keeping them alive so you could personally interrogate and torture them would not have made any difference. We are getting hung up on the wrong things."

Ben and I exchange a guarded look. Something about this whole situation reeks.

Ben retracts, returning to the couch. Accardi's brown eyes meet my blue ones with equal levels of loathing and distrust.

"Messina." Ben's cold tone cuts through my stare down with Natalia's husband, and I step back, keeping my gun out as I sit down beside my boss.

"How did this happen?" Ben asks. "How are we letting the Russians run circles around us in this territory again?"

"The men are losing faith," Barretta says, palming his cheek as it spasms. "It's coming up on a year since Gifoli passed, and things are in disarray."

"Whose fault is that?" Ben asks, swirling the bourbon in his glass.

"I never wanted this gig," Barretta says. "I let you and The Commission talk me into it, but I'm done, Bennett. Last week, I was diagnosed with ALS. It's a death sentence, and I'm out of time. We need to discuss what happens next because my plane ticket to Sicily is already booked. I leave a week from Sunday."

I can't say this is a surprise because Barretta's heart hasn't been in it from the outset. He lost his will to live when his son was gunned down last year.

"I am sorry to hear that, Thomas. Truly, I am." Ben's expression conveys the truth.

Barretta nods. "This is not how I wanted to go out, but such is life."

"Barretta's loss will be another blow," Accardi says. "We need to make bold, decisive leadership decisions now. There are a few men with potential we have been working with though none of them are ready for the kind of responsibility that comes with being a don." He looks at Barretta for a second before swinging his eyes back to Ben. "I am willing to relocate to Chicago permanently. If I take charge of The Outfit as the official don, I will restore peace and order."

I snort. Can't help myself. "Because you have done such a stellar job in the time you have been here."

"The men won't bond with Gino while they know his role here is only fleeting," Barretta says.

It's a fucking bullshit statement because I watched my boss lead our men for years without the official title while Angelo was battling cancer. Our *soldati* fell in behind Ben without question because he is the kind of man who commands respect, loyalty, and trust.

Gino isn't. And therein lies the problem.

"Give him the official title and responsibility, and they will fall in behind him," Barretta continues. "This can't wait, Bennett. The time for action is now before we lose men or the Russians gain more ground. This won't be an isolated attack. They will keep coming at us until we are severely weakened."

"What about your business back in New York?" Ben asks, his facial expression giving nothing away as he stares at his brother-in-law. "The twins aren't old enough to take over yet."

"My cousin Luca will step up as acting don, reporting to me, until the twins are ready to take over," Gino coolly replies, acting as if this is already a done deal.

I'm conflicted.

The selfish side of me wants him to do this so he's permanently separated from Natalia and we can continue our relationship. The other part of me smells a rat and is distrustful. There is also the fear he will force Nat to drop out of NYU and move here to be with him. "Your sons are in school in New York, and your wife attends NYU. How will that work?" I ask, knowing Ben will haul me over the coals for it after the meeting has concluded.

"I don't see how that is any of your business," he says in a clipped tone.

"It has everything to do with your move, and it's a valid question," Ben says. "Answer it."

Slowly, Gino drags a hand through his hair. He looks at Ben, ignoring me again, like I give a fuck. "I don't propose to uproot my family or upset their routine in New York. They can visit me on the weekends and over the school breaks."

That would be perfect if I didn't suspect the fucker is up to something shady. He clearly plans to install his Juliet lookalike at his side and forget about his wife back in the city. It's what I have come to expect from him, but how could he abandon his sons when they clearly need him? There was a time I used to look up to Don Accardi, but not anymore. He was the youngest made man to become a don until Ben stole his thunder. I bet that grates on his nerves.

"I will need to talk to The Commission," Ben says. "You haven't exactly impressed us lately."

"I am well aware." He bores a hole in Ben's skull. "But I am committed to rectifying my mistakes and bringing order to the streets of Chicago. I don't see many dons lining up to take on this task."

Therein lies the crux of our issues. Ben and I discussed this on the plane. We literally don't have anyone reliable from outside Chicago who wants to step up and do this. While Chicago is a desirable territory, it comes at a high price and without guarantees. It's a lot to ask someone to step away from their own territory. To uproot their business and family for a territory that is a big risk.

It's a poisoned chalice.

Though the man who restores order will be held in high esteem, and the rewards will be great.

I very much doubt the man in front of me is the man to do that. Something else is at play here. I'm convinced of it. For now, we have no choice but to go along with it.

"I need to speak with Barretta alone." Ben stands as Gino does. "Don't leave. I will come find you before I go."

Gino shakes his hand before exiting the room.

Ben sits back down, taking another mouthful of his drink. "I want your honest opinion." Ben looks at Barretta. "What is going on in this city?"

"The events of last year have shaken the men up. They lost a lot of their colleagues at the hands of New York and The Commission. They were loyal to Gifoli, and I think they are suspecting DeLuca is dead. Then you send an outsider in and effectively tie his hands."

We need to get on top of the DeLuca news and announce his death to draw a line under him. We have been waiting for the right moment, for the right successor, and it seems time is running out.

"But you were in charge," Ben reminds him. "They know and respect you."

"They know and respect me as DeLuca's former consigliere. Your first mistake was not sending Accardi here as acting don and letting me work with him as his adviser. It's in effect how we have been operating, but without the official responsibility, the men are wary. Gino is right. You need to take strong, decisive action now. We have identified two men Gino can promote to his underboss and consigliere. Good, loyal men who the *soldati* trust. Announce DeLuca is dead. Name Gino as his permanent successor and appoint his new team." He leans forward. "Then step back, Bennett. Let him do his job without The Commission breathing down his neck at every turn."

"Do you trust him?" Ben asks. "Is there something else I'm not privy to?"

"You mean Marcella?"

It's no surprise Barretta knows. It's not like Gino has been discreet, and they work closely together.

"I know about her. I mean anything else?"

Barretta frowns. "You think Gino has an ulterior motive?"

"I'm not sure." Ben is being circumspect on purpose. Barretta is a decent man, and his relationship with Ben is solid. However, he's spent the past nine months working closely with Accardi. Loyalties can be swayed, and bought, and Barretta already has one foot in the grave. He's beyond the point of caring, and I don't feel we can put much weight behind his words or his opinions.

"I think Gino is in love and he wants to make Chicago his home." Barretta's hand shakes as he clasps his glass. "I know that is difficult for you, given the close familial ties, but this is the way of our world. Don Accardi would not be the first made man to set up home with his mistress while his wife lives in another state."

"That's not the way things are done in New York," Ben says, bristling with rage.

"You're not in New York."

No. We most certainly are not.

Ben talks briefly with Accardi after we say our goodbyes to Barretta, and then we set out for the airport.

"What did you tell him?" I ask when the privacy screen is up.

"I told him I would talk to The Commission and put it to a vote." He rubs the back of his neck.

"He's full of shit."

"I know, but my hands are tied." Ben rests his head back, closing his eyes briefly. When he straightens up, I see the plan forming in his mind's eye. "We will go along with this. Pretend we support it. I'll delay the vote for as long as I can, and we will use the time to find out what is going on. I don't trust Gino. He's up to something, and I intend to find out exactly what that is."

Chapter 43

LEO

I STEP INTO the bathroom on the plane while Ben is sleeping to check my burner cell. I know Nat will be worried, and I want to let her know we are on our way back home. It's four a.m., so I'm not expecting her to reply much less call.

Answering it quickly before it rings out and alerts Ben to my suspicious behavior, I whisper, "What's wrong?"

"It's Caleb." Her voice shakes. "He didn't come home with Joshua. They got into a fight. I stayed up, thinking he would stroll in once he cooled down, but he didn't. I woke Joshua up at one a.m. when I discovered Caleb was over at Mott Haven via the app."

Shit. That's not good. Mott Haven is South Bronx, a place notorious for murder, violence, and drugs. "Please tell me you didn't go there."

"I was going to," she admits, "but Joshua went crazy in a way I have never seen him act before. He told me he would fix it and made me promise to stay at home and not to call Gino. He left ninety minutes ago with a couple of their friends, and I haven't heard a peep from him. Now the tracker shows he's in the same neighborhood, and I'm terrified, Leo." A shuddering breath filters down the line. "What if something has happened to them?"

That place is a shithole, but Caleb and Joshua are made men, and they know how to use weapons and how to fight. I've got to trust they aren't in serious shit. "I know you are worried, but you need to keep calm and don't jump to conclusions. Joshua is a smart kid. He wouldn't have gone to handle it himself if he thought his brother was in serious trouble. Here's what I need you to do. You need to hang up with me and call Ben. Tell him what you have told me, so he can send someone to check on them. We'll be landing in forty minutes, and we'll go straight to Mott Haven."

"Call me the second you find out anything."

"I promise I will. Try not to worry," I add though I know it's pointless. "We will find them."

"ALESSO AND BRANDO have located them," Ben says, reading from his phone as Ciro drives like a maniac through the streets of New York. The city is starting to stir, but it's still early, and traffic is minimal.

"Are they okay?"

"Yes, but they're caught up in some drug shit. Alesso is holding them there until we arrive."

"That explains a lot," I murmur.

"It does. Shit." Ben rubs at his temples. "This will devastate Natalia."

"Let's just wait until we get there and see what the hell is going on."

We pull up outside the location Alesso gave us twenty minutes later, thanks to Ciro acting like he was driving in a Formula 1 race. The residential street is quiet, and it's one of the nicer parts of Mott Haven. The redbrick brownstones are well maintained, and it could be worse. It could be the Mitchel Houses where all kinds of sick shit goes down behind closed doors.

"Down here, boss," Alesso says, poking his head out from the basement door of the house in front of us.

"What are we dealing with?" Ben asks as soon as we step foot in the dark, dank space. The front room is a mess with empty beer cans, half-eaten takeout boxes, and stale pizza slices littering the coffee table. A black sheet is draped over the window, blocking out the light, as if vampires live here. A torn red leather two-seater couch is piled with crumpled clothing.

"Nothing good," Alesso cryptically says, jerking his shoulder, urging us to keep moving. "We sent Joshua's two friends home. At least the kid had the wherewithal to come with backup." Joshua is smart, and he thinks things through unlike his brother. At times, Caleb reminds me a lot of Mateo.

We walk over cracked wooden floorboards in need of repair and past a poky kitchen and a bathroom that looks like a throwback to the seventies. Alesso leads us into the bigger of the two bedrooms at the back of the place, and Ben cusses under his breath. The room has been cleared of all furniture to fit several filthy mattresses. The scent of weed is cloying in the air, and I feel it clinging to my clothes. But it's the needles and evidence of other drug use that is most alarming.

That and the prone form of Caleb Accardi being propped up in his brother's arms. Caleb's eyes are closed, his chest moving as he breathes heavily, confirming he's sleeping off the aftereffects of his drug high. Joshua's jaw is tense, and he looks worried.

"What is he taking?" Ben asks, crouching down in front of his nephews.

"Cocaine mostly," Joshua readily admits. "But I know he's taken ketamine on occasion too."

"Who are these fuckheads?" I ask, kicking at the two guys passed out on the mattress at my feet.

"Losers he met at a party. They are the ones supplying him. I told him not to do this. I said I was going to tell Uncle Ben if he came here, but he ignored me." Joshua hugs his brother tighter. "I shouldn't have let him go alone. This is getting out of hand."

Yeah, no shit, Sherlock. Natalia is going to lose it when she finds out. Joshua clearly intends to keep his father in the dark, and I can guess why.

Ben has strict rules when it comes to drug use. Our *soldati* and company employees are strictly forbidden from taking drugs or dipping into our supplies, and they must succumb to periodic random drug tests. Ben saw a lot of shit with his mom growing up, and he wants to avoid running into problems within *la famiglia.* I know Accardi shares similar views, but most of the other families are way more lenient.

We're not naïve. We know the kids do shit. It's part of growing up, but Gino would have drilled the message into his sons, and there will be hell to pay when he finds out what's been going on. No heir should be visiting a shithole like this or associating with low-level drug dealers.

"Who are they getting their stuff from?" Ben asks, straightening up and glancing around the room. All five families no longer deal on the streets. We trade high-quality drugs and supply VIP clients, mainly through our clubs and casinos. This shit here is the reason we moved out of the mass market. We don't sell to kids anymore. The high-end VIP market is just as lucrative and more aligned with our business model these days.

"The Colombians," Joshua says, and the blood freezes in my veins.

Ben looks at me, sharing my concern. The families ran those assholes out of New York many years ago. It's mainly the Irish, the Mexicans, and the Triad who supply the drugs on the streets now.

Or so we believed.

My cell pings in my pocket as Ben tells Alesso to carry Caleb to his car. I frown when I see the name flashing across the screen. I step outside to answer the call. "Jerry, what's up?"

"I'm dealing with that problem we discussed the other day," he says, choosing his words carefully. "There is something you and the boss need to hear before I resolve the issue."

"Are you at the site?"

"Affirmative."

"Okay. I'll be there in a half hour." Provided Ciro uses his Formula 1 skills and traffic hasn't built up yet.

"What is it?" Ben asks, stepping out onto the sidewalk alongside me.

"We need to head to the site in Brooklyn. The foreman is dealing with that prick who was stealing supplies. Apparently, there is something we need to hear."

"This is the day that just keeps on giving," Ben drawls, sarcasm thick in his tone, as he turns around to face Alesso. "Change of plans. Take the twins home. Tell Natalia we'll be by later to talk to them." He looks over at Brando. "I want you and Nario watching the apartment today. Caleb might try to skip out instead of answering questions. Stop him if you see him leaving."

"Sure thing, boss," Brando says.

I send a quick text to Nat letting her know we have her sons and they are on their way home. We climb in the back of our car, both of us exhausted from little sleep.

Ciro pulls into a diner and grabs us some breakfast rolls and coffee, which we eat and drink as he drives us to Brooklyn.

"What the fuck is going on?" I ask, finishing my roll and scrunching the wrapper in my hand. I drop it into the bag. "First the Russians and now the Colombians."

"I don't fucking like it. How the hell are they distributing product on the streets and we didn't know about it?"

That's a good question. One I have no answer for.

"Who is this thief?" Ben asks, finishing the shit coffee and dumping the empty cup in the bag.

I shrug. "One of the newer laborers. Jerry came to me when supplies started going missing, and I installed a few cameras. Caught the guy red-handed. I was letting him deal with it." Some asshole stealing building supplies is small fry, in the grand scheme of things. Jerry is more than equipped to deal with it, so I'm curious why we are needed.

That curiosity is sated twenty minutes later when we arrive at the oceanside site in Brooklyn. It will be twenty stories high once completed, constructed of stone and glass, and ultramodern with amazing views. It's being fitted out with high-quality fixtures and fittings with the young professional in mind. Ben has a number of these in construction in various parts of the state, and the profits add significantly to the bottom line.

Jerry leads us down to the basement. It's only a shell, but it will house a parking lot in time. A bulky guy with a bloody face sits tied to a chair in the middle of the space. A plastic sheet is laid out underneath the chair for easy cleanup.

All the top guys on our sites are trusted men who have worked with us for years. While they are not *soldati*, they know who we are and what we expect, and they are well rewarded for their hard work and their loyalty. Most of the tradesmen who work on the developments are hired locally and carefully vetted. For the most part, we keep things clean and aboveboard.

"Jimmy here thinks he has information he can trade for his life,"

Jerry explains, nodding at me and Ben.

Ben stands in front of him. "Speak."

"I'm sorry, Mr. Mazzone. I know I shouldn't have been stealing, but my old lady is sick and—"

Jerry punches him in the face, cutting him off mid-sentence. "The boss is a busy man. He didn't come here to listen to your sob story. Tell him what you know."

"If I tell you, will you let me go?" the man pleads. "Please, Mr. Mazzone. I'm begging you."

God, he's pathetic.

"Yes," Ben lies. "Proceed."

"My cousin works for Maximo Greco. He's one of his most trusted capos, and he was in the room to hear a conversation Greco had with your brother-in-law Gino Accardi."

All the hairs lift on the back of my neck.

"You have my attention," Ben says.

The man grins, displaying a mouthful of bloody teeth. The idiot actually thinks he's going to live.

"Do you know when this conversation took place?" I ask.

"Last year sometime. Maybe March?" His beady eyes scrunch up.

"Continue," Ben says.

"Apparently, Accardi pulled a gun on Greco, and it was almost a bloodbath. He accused him of killing his wife. His first wife," he corrects, "and he wanted revenge."

I have long suspected Juliet Accardi's car crash was orchestrated and she was murdered. Gino has accumulated plenty of enemies over the years, like we all have. Either Gino investigated and bought it as a tragic accident or he has spent the past eleven years trying to locate her killers.

I have a sixth sense about this, and I don't like where it is heading.

Jerry punches Jimmy in the stomach. "Spit it out, you buffoon. We don't have all day."

Jimmy coughs blood on the plastic lining coating the floor, glaring at our foreman. "Greco confirmed he was responsible for the car accident Juliet died in. He said it was retaliation for Accardi killing his son Carlo."

My stomach drops to my toes as the full horror is laid out.

"Accardi swore he hadn't killed Carlo, and Greco believed him."

"What else?" Ben asks.

"That's it. They shook hands and agreed to meet again, but my cousin wasn't at that meeting, so he doesn't know what was said."

"What's your cousin's name?" Ben quietly asks.

"Oliver Vittalo." Jimmy pulls at the restraints on his arms. "Am I free to go now?"

"I am setting you free." Ben removes his gun from the back waistband of his pants and pops a bullet through the man's skull, killing him instantly. His head whips back before falling forward. Ben walks to Jerry and shakes his hand. "You didn't hear any of that."

"Not a word, boss." Jerry nods. "I'll clean this up before the rest of the crew arrive."

Ben calls Ciro over to help while we head outside, climbing back into the car.

"Gino knows," Ben says.

"He only thinks he knows," I reply. "The only other people still alive who know what happened to Carlo Greco are you, Frank, and Natalia." I took Ben into my confidence when he first became the unofficial don. Although I had promised Angelo I would take the secret to my grave, it didn't feel right keeping it from my new boss.

Silence engulfs us for a few minutes while we both think. "Angelo always believed the Grecos bought the Colombian angle," I say. "If Greco took out Juliet, because he believed Gino killed Carlo, then they clearly discredited that theory."

"Accardi would be the natural person to blame in that scenario," Ben says, running with my train of thought. "And if that theory was discounted, it means they went looking for other guilty parties."

I can hardly force the words out of my strangled throat. "Angelo injected himself into that situation. Mateo made no secret of his hatred of Carlo, and everyone knew Natalia was terrified of him." I rest my head against the headrest. "Fuck."

"The path led back to us," Ben says.

"They have partnered to take us down," I say, extracting my cell to check the tracking app for Gino's whereabouts.

"It's all connected," Ben says. "It's got to be. The Chicago situation and this Colombian drug issue."

"They are trying to discredit you because they can't very well take you out without repercussions."

"Not at this juncture," Ben says as Ciro slides behind the wheel and starts the engine.

"Natalia needs to get out of that house," I say, waiting for the location map to load.

"Is he still in Chicago?" Ben asks, looking over my shoulder, understanding what I am doing.

"Yes." I breathe a sigh of relief, but it's minor. I won't rest until I'm holding her in my arms and I've gotten her to safety.

"Natalia can't leave." Ben eyeballs me. "It will tip Gino off. Until we know more, we can't play our hand yet."

"She's in danger," I grit out. "He has more reason to take her out now. She's a Mazzone, and she was the catalyst for this whole fucking chain of events."

"You think I don't know that?" he roars. "You think I don't want to get her a million miles away from him? Because I do. But we've got to take emotion out of it. Like I had to do with Sierra that time."

I'm instantly chastised remembering everything Ben suffered during that period. I know he knows how I feel.

"You are letting your feelings for her cloud your judgment," he says in a calmer voice. "Natalia is strong. She will want to do this the right way. She will prioritize the twins, and they will get caught in the middle of this unless we bide our time and plan a course of action."

"Nothing can happen to her, Ben." Emotion chokes my voice, but I'm beyond the point of caring.

"Nothing is going to happen to her, Leo. We will make sure of it." His eyes bore into mine. "I know about you and her."

I gulp. "How?"

"You live in my building, Messina. And Philip is on my payroll. Did you really think I wouldn't find out?"

I suspected it would be hard to pull the wool over Philip's eyes. He's a fucking tech genius and on top of everything for Ben. I can't say I'm overly surprised except Ben didn't challenge me on it. "Why didn't you say anything?"

"I was going to have a conversation with you that involved my gun in your mouth, but I took my don hat off and looked at it from a different angle." His expression softens a little. "You two love each other. You always have." His lips kick up. "Who am I to stand in the way of true love?"

"You're not mad?"

The grin slips off his mouth. "Oh, I'm plenty mad. You have placed her in even graver danger, but you have also made her very happy. It's obvious. Sierra and Serena have both commented on the change in her demeanor this past month. I want my sister to be happy, and I know her happy place is with you." He briefly glances out the window as we make our way through the streets of Brooklyn. "I understand why you felt the need to keep it a secret, but I was waiting for you to come to me. I know you would have sooner or later. And if you didn't, I would have broached the subject with you. Discussed how to get her out from under Accardi. Now, we may have lost our edge."

"I refuse to accept that. There are always options. You and I have gotten ourselves out of more scrapes and dangerous situations over the years. If anyone can do it, we can."

He nods. "You need to get over there. Fill her in. Talk to Caleb. See if he knows anything that can help. I'm going to round up the capos. Get some eyes and ears out on the streets and see what intel we can find. Then I'll set up an emergency meeting with The Commission."

"Will you tell them?"

"I can't. Not yet. Not with Greco involved. This has the potential to split The Commission apart and undo everything we have achieved the past few years. I can't let that happen. It would be fucking chaos."

"It's a mess," I agree.

"Just focus on Natalia for now. Make sure she is fully up to speed. Tell her everything. I will come over later, and we can decide what to do."

I send Nat a message to let her know I'll be there shortly. I blow air out of my mouth, contemplating how I'm going to tell the woman I love I'm indirectly responsible for her loveless marriage and the situation she is in now. I hope it's enough that I saved her back then and I will save her now.

"Would you do it again?" Ben asks. "Knowing what you know now?"

I nod without hesitation. "Absolutely. Carlo was a depraved

bastard. Her life would have been sheer hell if she had been forced to marry him. He would have ruined her, Ben. I hate that my actions led her to Gino and that she's in harm's way because of me, but at least we have a heads-up now."

"If we play our cards right, you can be together."

"That would be everything I have ever dreamed of, but I can't allow myself to hope. Right now, keeping her safe and alive must be the only goal."

Even if I have to sacrifice myself to ensure she lives.

Chapter 44

NATALIA

"COME IN." I step back from the open doorway of my penthouse apartment to let Leo inside. If I wasn't sure my husband is still in Chicago, I would tell Leo to go. Gino will freak out if he ever discovers he was here.

But screw him.

Gino is never available when I need him.

Brando brought the boys home safely, and they are currently sleeping. When he told me Caleb was mixed up with drugs, I immediately placed a call to my husband. We need to handle this together, and he needs to come home to talk with Caleb. But, of course, he didn't pick up.

He's probably too busy screwing his replacement wife to bother answering my call. My blood boils every time I think of how neglectful Gino has become. It's like no one else matters but her.

"How is Caleb?" Leo asks, shutting the door behind him.

"Asleep." I lift one shoulder, urging him to follow me across the lobby toward the living space. "He was barely coherent when Brando brought him home, so I didn't bother questioning him. I was just so relieved to see him safe." I wanted to yell at him as I hugged him, but I bit my tongue. The lecture can wait.

"Wow, someone likes beige." Leo's eyes pop wide when he enters our dreary living room.

"Juliet," I say. "It's ghastly, right?"

"Hang on here a second." He slams to a halt in the middle of our living room. "Are you telling me he hasn't let you redecorate the place since you moved in?"

"Pretty much." I shrug, having given up caring how much Gino still loves his ex-wife a long time ago. "It has been repainted, and some of the furniture has been replaced, but it has to be like for like. I spent years arguing with him at the start, begging him to let me inject some color into this place, but he refused. Why do you think I rarely host family gatherings here?"

"I just assumed it was because Angelo's and Ben's homes were much larger and it was easier to accommodate the entire family." He shakes his head as he looks around. "He's a fucking psycho," he supplies, stopping in front of the wall of family photos. His hands ball up at his sides as his gaze skims over the legacy to Juliet. "This is so wrong, Nat." He purposely moves past the small wedding photo of Gino and me, shoved at the bottom left of the wall, almost out of sight, focusing on the multitude of wedding photos of Gino and Juliet and the family pictures of the boys with both parents when they were babies. There are a few token ones of me with the boys, from over the years, but never any family ones.

Because my spot in this family has always been a placeholder.

And Gino has always wished I was invisible.

I was more of a nanny than a wife, now that I think back on it.

"This whole apartment is a shrine to Juliet." Taking his hand, I pull him away from the wall. Leo reels me into his arms, kissing me passionately. It takes iron willpower, but I break our lip-lock and push him away. "We can't! The boys could wander out here at any moment."

He presses his brow to mine, lightly holding my hips. "I hurt for the things you have had to endure, Nat. I had no idea it was this bad."

No one does because I have always hidden the true extent of the situation.

"I don't care anymore," I truthfully reply, reluctantly easing out of his hold. "I stopped letting it get to me a long time ago. The boys are my world. I put up with it for them."

I walk into the kitchen and head to the coffee machine. "Take a seat." I switch the machine on and grab the airtight container with the muffins, setting it on the table along with some plates and mugs. "I didn't sleep a wink all night. I was too worried, so I baked to stop me from driving over to Mott Haven."

"I would have spanked your ass if you went there." Leo pries the lid off the container and takes a chocolate chip muffin from the pile.

I blush as I remember Leo tying me up and spanking me with his hand and then a flogger.

His eyes flicker with lustful mirth, and I know he's remembering it too.

I pour him a coffee and sit across from him in a feeble attempt not to touch him. "Tell me what you know," I demand after he has eaten two muffins and swallowed half of his coffee. "Brando didn't say much."

He fills me in on what they found at the house in Mott Haven and what Joshua said. "Oh, God." I bury my head in my hands, fighting tears. "I knew something was wrong. He's been so moody and irritable for months. I should have pushed him to tell me. I should have—"

He walks over, taking the seat beside me, circling his arm around my shoulders. "Don't do this, *dolcezza*. It's not your fault. If you had pushed, he probably would have just pushed right back. At least you know now, and we can give him the help and support he needs."

"Why, Leo?" I pick up my head. "Why would he do this? Is the pressure of what he's expected to do responsible? Is it me and his father? Gino being so far away?"

"There's no point second-guessing the reasons. You need to talk to him and try to get him to open up."

He gets up, refilling our mugs. "I don't want to overburden you, because I know you are upset and worried about Caleb, but some other things have come to light you need to be aware of."

I welcome the distraction. "Tell me."

I don't say a word as Leo tells me it all. The Colombians. The Russians. Gino's double agenda. That they suspect Gino and Maximo Greco are working together against us. "Fuck." I get up. "I need something stronger than coffee." The situation is far more dangerous than I perceived it to be. My husband now has another reason to want me dead. I stride into the living room, toward Gino's liquor cabinet, needing alcohol to take the edge off my frayed nerves.

"I'm sorry," Leo says as I pour two glasses of Macallan.

"For what?" I hand him a glass.

"For everything."

My brow puckers in confusion. "I don't follow."

"This is my fault," he blurts. "All of it." He waves one hand around the place. "You being forced to marry Gino. Having to put up with his cruel and shitty treatment. The fact your life is in danger now."

"Stop it." I set my drink down, lacing my fingers through his. "None of this is your fault." *It's mine*, I want to say, but that would open a whole other conversation, and we have enough shit to deal with.

I know I will have to tell Leo.

If I want to be with him—and I do—I will have to tell him about the baby at some point. I don't relish the conversation, because it's going to hurt him so badly, but I know he has a right to the truth. "You saved me from a worse fate, remember?" I quietly remind him.

"But did I?"

I know it's a rhetorical question. Like I know he knows Carlo Greco would have broken me and ruined me for life. Hell, he probably would have killed me, or I'd have swallowed a load of pills to escape him. No matter how neglectful and hurtful Gino is or how dangerous the current situation is, it is not as bad as my life would have been if I'd been forced to marry the monster.

Leo drains his drink and takes his hand from mine, pacing. "I would do it again, Nat, I swear I would, but it's hard to reconcile that sentiment with how I'm feeling now because you are married to someone who wants you dead. Gino wants to make us all pay because Mateo and I killed Carlo."

The clicking of a gun sends my blood pressure sky high, and I freeze as Leo's alarmed eyes meet mine. He slowly turns around, keeping his body in front of mine.

"We wondered if Mateo acted alone or if you had helped him," Gino says. "Thank you for clearing that up." He points his gun at Leo's head, and blood thrums in my ears.

"How are you here?" I ask, carefully reaching for Leo's gun, which is tucked into the back of his waistband.

Gino must have entered the building via the rear entrance and used the staff elevator to avoid Brando and Nario because they would have warned us otherwise. His goons still keep watch outside, so I am sure they have clocked Ben's men and made Gino aware. A horrible thought races across my mind as I consider he got his *soldati* to take care of the problem, but I shake it from my mind to consider later, as I need to focus on the here and now.

Gino smirks. "Keeping tabs on me, darling wife?"

Leo growls. "You removed your tracker."

He must have found the bugs Ben planted in his car and his place too. I have been monitoring his whereabouts on the tracker every day, and it shows movement, so I'm guessing he took out his tracker and implanted it in one of his *soldati* to throw us off the scent.

"Did you fools really think you could demand I end things with Marcella and I would just comply? Ben thought he could sic a PI on both of us and I wouldn't find out. I used to respect him, but he's getting sloppy. Love can do that to a man."

Shit. He's aware of the PI too, which probably means the man is bound and gagged in a derelict building someplace or he's lying in a pool of blood with a bullet in his brain. Slowly, I remove Leo's gun, hoping it doesn't fall from my sweaty palm. "Is that your excuse?" I snap, needing to distract him.

He smirks again, cocking his weapon a second time, and I freeze as he comes closer, aiming it at Leo's chest. "Give me the gun, Natalia. Don't do anything stupid." He keeps the gun trained on Leo. "Or I'll be forced to kill your lover right in front of your eyes."

"As if you don't plan on that anyway," Leo says, grabbing my wrist as I move to step around him. He shakes his head, taking the gun and pushing me back behind the protection of his body. Leo slides the gun across the hardwood floor, and Gino kicks it away. It glides under the old velvet couch.

"I see you don't deny it," Gino says. "I suspected you might be fucking him."

"Are you really that surprised?" I jut my chin up, playing the part of the hurt wife. "You fucking lied to me!" I hiss. "You said you could never love any other woman. That Juliet would always be the love of your life."

"I was truthful when I told you that, but I was wrong. I just needed to meet the right woman and open my heart to make room for her too."

"Fuck you."

"My, my, how you have lowered your standards since I've been gone. Sleeping with the enemy and cursing like a common whore." He tut-tuts and Leo grabs hold of my arm, sensing I'm seconds from lunging at the prick, holding me in place.

"Leo is worth a million of you," I say without pausing to think. "And he's not the enemy. Greco is."

"He fucking started everything! Him and Mateo!" Gino roars, darting forward and pressing his gun to Leo's temple. "This is all your fault for messing with the order of things. If you hadn't killed Carlo,

Greco wouldn't have killed my wife!"

"How did you find out?" I ask, panicking and stalling for time. I need to do something, find something to attack Gino with, before he kills the love of *my* life.

"I always suspected Juliet had been murdered to punish me. I have spent years trying to find out who orchestrated her car accident. I had almost given up when a guy I was torturing last year told me it was the Grecos. His uncle was one of their capos, and I hunted the man down, and he told me it was true. He had been the one to mess with her car. I killed him, and then I went to kill Greco, and it all came out." He digs the muzzle of his gun in harder to Leo's brow. Leo hasn't moved a muscle, but he looks undeterred, and I'm wondering if he knows something I don't or if he has another weapon stashed someplace on his body.

I fucking hope he does because Gino is unhinged.

"At first, they believed it was the Colombians. That's the bullshit Angelo had fed them. They wanted revenge, so they spent three years looking for the guy who had met with Carlo at the warehouse that day. When they found him, he told them it wasn't him, and he had a rock-solid alibi. He had gone straight from the warehouse to a three-hour-long meeting with a crooked cop, who happened to be on the Greco payroll. The cop confirmed his alibi, and that's when they figured Angelo had lied to protect someone." A wry laugh tumbles from his chest. "They fucking thought he lied to protect *me*!" he shouts, waving the gun around.

Seizing the opportunity, I duck down and pop back up in front of Leo. I act fast so he can't stop me. Leo curses, wrapping his fingers around my arm, as if to yank me back behind him, when Gino smiles, pushing the muzzle of his gun into my head. "Don't move an inch, Messina, or I'll pull the trigger."

Leo's arms wrap around my waist from behind. "Hurt her, and you're a dead man," he promises.

"A two-for-one special." Gino grins. "This must be my lucky day."

"Or not," a familiar voice says from behind. "Put the gun down, Papa," Caleb adds, his arm extended, training his weapon at Gino. "If you hurt my mother, I will smash your fucking head in and laugh the whole time I'm doing it."

Chapter 45

NATALIA

GINO TURNS AROUND, keeping his gun pressed into my temple the whole time. “What are you doing, son?”

“Protecting and loving my mom the way you should have but never did. Give Mama to me or I’ll shoot. I mean it.” His arm is steady, and I see nothing but determination in his eyes.

“Let her go,” Leo says. “We both know it’s me you want.”

“No.” I hold on to Leo’s hands as he tries to remove them from my waist. “I won’t walk away so he can kill you.”

“Aw, how touching.” Sarcasm is thick in Gino’s tone. “And Natalia is going nowhere. You both must pay. You were in this together. You both killed my wife.”

“Are you fucking insane?” Caleb yells, walking forward with the gun still pointed at his father. “Maximo Greco killed Juliet, so why the fuck aren’t you taking it out on him?” He shoves the gun into Gino’s chest, and my heart falters. If Caleb kills his father, he will have to live with it for the rest of his life. I don’t want that for my son.

“Caleb? What the fuck? What the hell is going on here?” Joshua asks, rubbing his eyes, like he can’t believe what he’s seeing.

“Tell him, Papa.” Caleb digs his gun into Gino’s chest, and I’m scarcely breathing. The pressure of the gun at my temple has me sweating and on edge. It’s only Leo’s strong arms around my waist keeping me together. "Tell him how you made a deal with Greco, the man who killed our bio mother, instead of putting a fucking bullet straight through his heart!"

"I'm interested in that story too," Ben says, appearing behind Joshua. I almost collapse in relief when I see him with Brando, Nario, and Ciro holding up the rear. Ben pulls Joshua behind him, warning him with his eyes to stay put.

"Son. You don't have the full picture." Gino sounds way too calm for a man who has five guns trained on him.

"How about everyone puts their weapons down," Ben says, "and we talk about this."

Gino snorts. "Always with the political bullshit, Mazzone."

"I'm trying to save your life, Gino, because if you don't remove that gun from my sister's head in the next ten seconds, you're a dead man. I'm throwing you a lifeline. Take it."

Tension bleeds into the air, and I don't think Gino is going to do it when Joshua speaks up. "Don't take away the only Mama we have ever known. Please, Papa. We love Mom. Don't hurt her."

I expect Gino to throw shit at his son for being weak and letting emotion overrule logic, but he surprises me, removing the gun from my head. He still keeps it trained on me as he says, "Joshua. Get the box from the hall and collect all the guns."

Joshua runs off, returning a minute later with the brown leather box I keep scarves and gloves in. He has emptied it out, and he diligently goes around the room so everyone can put their weapons inside. Caleb is the last to resist, but Ben removes the gun from his hand, stepping in front of him. "You do not want to do this." He clamps his hand on Caleb's shoulder, and a shuddering breath leaves my son's lips. Joshua slips out of the room to hide the box out of sight before quickly returning.

Leo takes my hand, pulling me over to the other side of the room. I pull Joshua and Caleb into my arms, smothering my sobs in their shoulders. I dot kisses all over their faces, needing them to ground me.

"Let's sit," Ben says.

"This is my house," Gino snaps.

"Not anymore," Caleb says, keeping his arm around me as he glares at his father. "We don't want you here."

"I don't know what you think you know, but you're wrong," Gino says as no one makes a move to sit.

Tension is fraught in the air, and things could ignite in a split-second. No made man worth his salt only keeps one weapon on him. That show with the guns was just that.

"I heard you on the phone," Caleb spits, and I hate to see so much venom in his blue eyes. "Telling someone Greco had killed Juliet but you had come to an arrangement. An arrangement that would mutually benefit both parties."

Poor Caleb. This explains a lot about his behavior and his renewed interest in learning more about Juliet. I wish he had come to me with it.

"That's exactly why you should never eavesdrop, son. That was only half the story."

"How far does your relationship with Greco extend, and what have you promised him?" Ben asks, standing taller and leveling a look at my husband. "Don't bullshit me, Gino. I want the truth and how exactly you planned to take me down."

"Before I tell you, I want to negotiate a deal."

Leo snarls. "You're in no position to negotiate."

"Fuck you, Messina. You're just a thug who got lucky and rode Bennett's coattails all the way to the top. Everyone knows Ben is the brains behind the operation and he could run it single-handed without you."

"Enough," Ben barks. "This isn't some pissing contest, and I'm low on patience today. Say what you want to say, Accardi."

"I will tell you the deal I made with Greco and reaffirm my loyalty to you, provided I'm officially sworn in as The Outfit's don, I get to divorce your sister, and you guarantee my safety and that of my sons and my future bride." He drills a poisonous look at Leo. "You will also demote Messina to *soldato*."

"If you think that will piss me off, think again. I would happily trade my career, trade *everything*, to be with the woman I love," Leo says.

Ben sends a sharp look in Leo's direction before swinging his eyes back around to Gino. "Leave Messina out of this, and you have a deal."

Gino's harsh laugh echoes around the room, and I gulp over the ball of nerves clogging my throat. "Not a chance."

"Take the deal," Leo growls, staring at Ben, as they silently communicate. "Free Nat. I don't give a fuck whether I'm a lowly *soldato* or not."

"*I* do." Ben shoves off the wall and walks up to Gino. "I see what you're doing, and trying to weaken my position will not endear you to me."

"You know shit, Bennett." He jabs his finger over Ben's shoulder in my direction. "Why don't you ask your sister, huh? Ask her to tell you how she disrespected me?"

"Natalia has been a good wife and mother, and the only person who has been doing the disrespecting around here is you," Leo barks.

"Fuck you, Messina. I know it was you. I had my suspicions, but I could never prove it. Until you started fucking my whore wife again."

Confusion splays on Leo's face as he looks at me. I'm frozen in place, unable to move or speak as awful realization dawns.

Gino stares at Leo, frowning a little before his eyes widen. He throws back his head, laughing. "Oh my God. You don't know, do you?"

Panic has a vise-grip on my heart, and my voice is all choked up when I speak. "No, Gino. Please don't do this. Not like this! I'm begging you!"

"Natalia." Ben steps over to me, holding my arms and peering into my eyes. "What is he talking about?"

Gino clears his throat. "Shall you tell him how you shit all over our most revered traditions and lied to my face about it, or shall I?"

Briefly, I close my eyes before easing out from the protection of Leo, Ben, and my sons. I step in front of Gino, my eyes blazing, as I hold my head up. The game is up. It's going to come out now, so I might as well try to have some control over it. "How did you know?"

"The story was far-fetched, but I believed it at first."

"Yet you still treated me like shit and blamed me. Things didn't have to be like this, but you never even tried."

"Because you tricked me!" he shouts, waving his finger in my face.

Leo is beside me in a heartbeat, pulling me back. "Do that again, asshole, and I'll fucking kill you with my bare hands." He wraps protective arms around me from the side.

Ignoring him, Gino continues. "I signed up for a virgin bride not some used-up knocked-up whore."

Heavy silence fills the air, and I'm terrified to look at Leo. "You're just pissed I outmaneuvered you," I snap at Gino.

"What's going on, *dolcezza*?" Leo asks in a low tone, and my heart is ripping in two.

"I have always known you have a thing for my wife." Gino's lips kick up, as he enjoys sticking in the knife in. "You're pathetic the way you moon over her when you think no one is watching, but I've got to hand it to Natalia. She never showed you the time of day, so I didn't suspect it was you. In recent times, I've begun to wonder if I was mistaken, but your reactions today confirmed it."

Gino is going to say this in the worst possible way if I don't get the words out so I stuff my nausea and my fear down inside and turn to my lover. "I found out I was pregnant a week before my wedding."

"What?" Ben's tone is laced with disbelief.

I look between Leo's shell-shocked face and my brother's hurt one. "I wanted to tell you, but I couldn't see how that would end well."

"So, instead she married me and told me on our wedding night that she was pregnant with another man's child. The result of an assault in the city by some random rapist. He threatened her loved ones if she told anyone, and she was too scared to speak up, blah, blah."

"You were pregnant with my baby?" Leo whispers, clasping my face in his hands. "Is it true?"

I nod as a silent tear rolls down my face.

"She wanted me to send her to Italy to have the baby and give it up for adoption," Gino continues, slamming his fist into the wall, proving he is still worked up over something that happened years ago. "As if I'd ever let my wife give birth to another man's baby, rapist's or not."

Tears cascade down my cheeks as I shake all over. Leo is frozen in place, and Ben doesn't know what to think, judging by the look on his face. Caleb and Joshua too.

"I wish I had known it was yours when I aborted the bastard," Gino says with an evil grin plastered on his face. "I would have enjoyed her screams all that much more."

Chapter 46

NATALIA

LEO LUNGES AT Gino, wrapping his hands around his throat and squeezing. Gino's eyes scream amusement, not fear. "I should have put a bullet in your skull years ago," Leo growls, shoving Gino back into the wall, keeping his hands locked around my husband's neck.

"Do something!" Joshua cries, holding on to my arm and pleading with his eyes.

"Kill him," Caleb says in a cold inhuman voice. "It's what he deserves."

"No one is killing anyone." Ben steps forward, placing his hand on Leo's shoulder. "Let him go, Messina."

"Caleb is right," Leo says in a clipped tone. "He fucking deserves to die."

"Do you want the cycle to continue?" Ben asks, his voice calm and controlled. "Because that is what'll happen if I let you kill him with your bare hands. Where does it end?" Ben's intelligent gaze drills into Leo, and they silently communicate while Gino is turning a delightful shade of blue.

If it were up to me, I'd tell my lover to do it.

Gino murdered my baby, and I have never forgiven him. I never will. Though he claimed to believe my lie about the rapist, he still held it against me. He turned from a man I thought was open to compromise into a cold, hard, detached husband hell-bent on keeping me at arm's length.

That was the moment our marriage died, and I wouldn't lose any sleep if Leo killed him now.

But Joshua is trembling against me, and though Caleb spoke fighting words, I know he doesn't want his father to die. Not truly. If Leo kills Gino, he is signing his own death sentence and igniting a war because there is no doubt the Grecos will use this to their advantage.

"Benny is right." I step away from my sons and walk over to the three men. "Not like this, my love." I place my hand on Leo's arm and tug sharply on it.

Reluctantly, Leo drops his hands, standing in front of my husband and seething with unspent rage. I smooth a hand up and down Leo's back, and his arm slides around my waist as he leans into me.

"I think it's best if Gino and I continue this conversation at my office," Ben suggests, and I know this is more than wanting to defuse the situation. He's giving me time with Leo. Precious time we need because I see the hurt flaring behind Leo's eyes and how the news has shaken his entire belief system. I also need to talk to my sons. Today has been a day for a lot of revelations, and we need to discuss them.

"I want joint custody." I level Gino with a look that dares him to challenge me.

"I'm not moving to Chicago." Caleb folds his arms across his chest. "I'm staying with Mom. If I never see you again, I'll die happy."

Pain flits across Gino's face, but it's fleeting.

"The boys love their school, and their friends are here. Let them stay with me during the week, and if they want to see you on the weekends, they can fly in." I'm trying to put my feelings aside to do what is right for the twins. Caleb may feel differently in time too.

"You can forget we exist," Caleb supplies. "It's pretty much what you've done since you moved to Chicago anyway. Marry your whore, and leave us in peace."

"Watch your mouth," Gino snaps. "I am still your father."

"In name only," Caleb retorts. "Mama was the one who was here for us. It was never you."

That's not entirely true, but Gino has been neglectful of his relationship with his sons as well, and now he's paying the price. Joshua is quiet, but I know he's internalizing everything. I walk to his side, pulling him into my arms. He clings to me, pressing his chin on top of my head. Both boys are so tall they tower over me these days.

"This conversation isn't over." Gino stabs his son with a dark look. "For now, I'm going with Ben to iron out the details of our agreement. I will be back to talk to you both tomorrow."

Brando stays with us while Nario and Ciro leave with Ben and Gino after collecting their weapons. A layer of tension lifts off my shoulders with their absence. "There are muffins in the kitchen, and I made fresh orange juice," I tell my sons. "Go wait for me there. I just need a few minutes with Leo."

Joshua shucks out of my embrace, and I kiss his cheek before pulling Caleb into a hug. He's rigid in my arms, and I know he's got to be feeling so much. "I love you." I kiss his brow. "It's going to be okay."

He walks off without saying a word.

Gingerly, I step up in front of a troubled-looking Leo. "Let's talk on the balcony."

Leo trails me out of the double doors and onto the balcony that wraps around the entire side of our penthouse apartment. It's still warm for the end of September, but there's a strong enough breeze at this height, so I wrap my arms around myself to ward off the chill I feel emanating from bone-deep.

I sit down on the wicker couch, and Leo follows me. His eerie silence is worrisome, and he looks like he's carrying the weight of the world on his shoulders. "I'm sorry I never told you," I whisper, fighting the tears pricking my eyes. "I wanted to, but I was so scared."

He lifts strained eyes to mine. "I can't believe you were pregnant and you didn't tell me. I can't believe you went through all of that alone."

"I couldn't see any way out of it, Leo. I knew if I told you you'd want to run away or confront Gino, and that would have ended up with all of us dead."

"You didn't even give me a chance, Natalia. You just cut me out of the decision and then he…" He buries his face in his hands, and his shoulders heave.

"I can still feel it," I whisper, my hand going to my flat stomach. "The moment our baby was ripped away from me." Tears roll down my face. "I screamed and cried the whole time, begging Gino not to do it, but he just helped the doctor to strap me down. I swore then I would never forgive him, and I would never give him a baby. I didn't want to carry a child unless it was yours." Sobs travel up my throat, and I'm shaking all over.

He jerks his head up, in silent question, reaching out to hold me as I cry. I let him comfort me, and while I hate the way this has come out, I'm not sorry he knows now. "I had an IUD fitted in secret," I explain. "Gino was pissed when I failed to get pregnant, and he wanted to send me for tests. I told him the forced illegal abortion had probably made me sterile and investigating it would only lead to questions, so he dropped it, accepting my explanation."

"I want to kill him," Leo growls. "I have always wanted to kill him, but this?" Angry tears well in his eyes. "This is unforgivable, and he must die."

I shake my head. "No, Leo." I cup his face. "We can't dwell on the past. It's time to put it behind us and to move forward. This way, we get to be together. We have a future. A future that involves babies, if that is what you want."

"Jesus, Nat." He shucks out of my hold and stands, pacing. "How can you say that? I have only just discovered you were pregnant with my kid and that fucking asshole forced an abortion on you!" he shouts. "I can't forget that. I can't let it go. I can't even think about any other babies." He grabs fistfuls of his hair. "I need to go. I need to clear my head and think."

I stand. "Leo, please. I'm sorry." Tears stream down my face.

He walks over to me and pulls me into his arms. "I know you are," he says, his voice not quite as angry. "And I don't blame you for any of this, Nat. You were young, and you did what you thought was best. I know that. I'm angry at myself for putting you in that situation, and I hate that bastard for what he has done to you. For everything he has done to you over the past eleven years. Especially this." He eases back, kissing my brow. "This has come at me out of the blue, and I just need some time to wrap my head around it."

"I can't lose you," I croak. "Not again."

"Shush, baby." He kisses me softly. "You haven't lost me. I'm hurt, and I need time to process it, but I'm going nowhere."

I relax at his words, tightening my arms around his neck. "I love you, Leo."

"I love you too." He kisses me again before pulling back. "Don't leave the apartment until you hear from me or Ben. Brando will keep you safe. I'm going to call a locksmith to change the locks because I don't trust that fucker. Just hold tight until Ben or I come back for you."

I nod, having no issue agreeing to that. I need to speak to the boys, and I'm exhausted.

I walk Leo to the door, hugging him one last time before I close the door and slide the bolt across it.

Joshua and Caleb are sitting at the kitchen table in silence when I return. I pour myself a coffee and sit down, looking at both of my sons. "I am sorry you had to hear all of that. That you had to find out the things you did in that way."

"Is it true?" Joshua asks. "Papa has another woman in Chicago?"

I nod.

"How could he do that to you?"

"Love is complicated." I'm cryptic on purpose because I don't want to lie to them, but I can't tell them the truth either. I won't be the reason they refuse to speak to their father.

"Love is for pussies," Caleb says. "I'm never falling in love."

"You don't know what you're missing," Joshua retorts, spoken like a true lovesick teenager. He's even got the dreamy expression too. His face sobers as he turns to me. "I hate that Papa didn't show you love." He squeezes my hand. "I could see it, and it always upset me."

"Me too," Caleb says. "And what the fuck is wrong with him? You're beautiful and kind, and you make the best fucking apple cake."

I laugh, leaning in to kiss my boys on the cheeks. "You two shower me with love, and that kept me going on tough days, more than you will ever know."

"I still don't understand how Papa could cheat on you. It's disgusting and disrespectful."

God, I really hope Joshua holds on to those values.

"They all do it," Caleb says. "It's what dons do."

"Not all of them," I correct him. "Your Uncle Ben is faithful to Sierra, and a lot of made men don't have affairs or take whores."

"I'm going to be like Uncle Ben," Joshua says. "I could never cheat on Bettina."

Caleb scoffs, rolling his eyes. "She's a hot piece of ass, bro, but that's all she will ever be. It's not like you're going to marry her."

Joshua's face turns red, and I step in before this turns into a fight. "Caleb, don't speak about your brother's girlfriend like that. Or any woman, for that matter. I have brought you up to have more respect."

He rubs his nose, looking a little sheepish. "I respect *you*, Mom."

"I know, sweetheart." I clasp his hand before I take Joshua's. "You two have brought me so much joy. I love you both very much, and though things will change, that won't."

“I won’t live with him and his slut,” Caleb says, drumming his fingers on the table. “I hate him. I really fucking hate him.”

“I don’t hate him,” Joshua whispers. “He’s my dad. I love him, but how do I forgive him for this?”

“You don’t have to take sides. You can love both of us and be in both our lives. I don’t want either of you carrying any guilt or pressure. This is between your father and me to resolve, and we will resolve it.”

“Are you going to be with Leo now?” Caleb asks.

I nod. “I hope that won’t be an issue. I have loved him since I was a little girl, and now we can finally be together. But you are my sons, and you will remain my priority.”

“I just want you to be happy,” Joshua says.

“Me too,” Caleb agrees, “and if that’s with Leo, so what? Dad has been fucking someone else, so why shouldn’t you?”

I probably shouldn’t be proud, but I am.

“I like Leo,” Joshua says. “He’s a good guy and a good made man.”

“He’s not going to tell me what to do,” Caleb says, sending me a warning look. “But if he’s cool, then I’m cool.”

I look at Caleb’s bloodshot eyes, remembering we have another issue to deal with too. An issue Gino still knows nothing about. “We need to talk about the drugs.”

His entire demeanor changes. His eyes blaze, and his shoulders stiffen. “Don’t make a big deal out of something that isn’t, Mom.”

“Don’t lie,” Joshua says. “You know it’s getting out of control.”

“Like you know you’re whipped, a pussy, and a rat?” Caleb retorts.

“Mama was worried sick!” Joshua leans across the table, pleading with his eyes. “What was I supposed to do? Say nothing when I didn’t know if you were over with those assholes killing yourself?”

“You are always so dramatic.” Caleb rolls his eyes again, and I don’t like his nonchalance.

“You are going to see a counselor,” I say. “As soon as I have spoken to your father, I’m arranging an appointment for you.”

"Don't tell him." Fear spreads across Caleb's face. "He will beat me bloody if he finds out."

Air punches from my lungs. "I can't keep it from him, Caleb, but he's not going to touch you. I won't let him."

"No offense, Mom, but you have no clue how things are handled. When he finds out I've been taking shit, he's going to go crazy on my ass."

"Why do you do it?"

He shrugs, averting his eyes. "Everyone does it."

"So, this doesn't have to do with what you overheard? About Juliet?"

His jaw clenches, but he doesn't speak, and I don't think there is much point in pushing him right now. It's been a tiring day for all of us. "We will talk about this again, but promise me one thing. Promise me you won't touch any more drugs."

Caleb looks me in the eye as he says. "I promise."

I'm pretty sure my son just lied to my face, and he was very convincing doing it.

Chapter 47

LEO

"ARE NAT AND the boys okay?" I ask the following morning as I enter Ben's office at the CH building.

"Like I told you last night on the phone, they are fine. Your guy changed the locks, and I stayed over at Nat's place just in case Gino showed up. It was good. We talked for hours. They are going to move into my penthouse next week. I have movers going over there today to start packing up their stuff. My building is more secure and you're there. Until then, they are staying at my house. I don't trust Accardi not to try something." He puts down his pen, eyeballing me. "Sit."

I sink onto a chair, eyeballing him back. "Spit it out."

"It wasn't her fault."

"I know that."

"I can't believe you took her virginity and neither of you said a word to me."

"Fuck off, Ben. That had nothing to do with you, and you know it. It was between Natalia and me."

"Until you knocked her up," he snaps.

"I didn't know!" I yell. Why the hell is he giving me shit for that now? "It's a little late for the big-brother routine, don't you think? And if you're trying to make me feel bad, don't waste your energy. I'm already there." I drag a hand through my hair as I lean back in the chair. I'm tired after a restless night's sleep. "I hate Nat had to go through that alone. I hate I put her in that position."

"I know." Defeat registers on his face. "To think I used to like Accardi. Now I hate him every bit as much as I hated DeLuca."

"What's the plan?"

"The deal is made. They'll apply for a quickie divorce with joint custody, and the boys will remain in New York for school. I have scheduled a meeting with The Commission members to discuss permanently instating Accardi as The Outfit's don."

"Am I demoted?"

"Don't act stupid. I would never agree to such petty demands. He's on shaky ground with me, and he knows it."

I sit up straighter. "Yet you're giving him Chicago? Or is this all part of the play?"

Ben grins. "Of course, it is. Do you really think I'd put that prick in such a position of power after the shit he's pulled? I should put a fucking bullet in his head for disrespecting me by going behind my back and plotting with Greco to take me down."

"Why don't you? I can't see The Commission arguing after his admission."

"If I do that, I hand my ass on a platter to Don Greco. Whether he's privy to the full facts or not, he will throw it all out on the table, and it will damage our name and cause my integrity to be called into question. It doesn't matter that Carlo Greco died fourteen years ago or that Angelo was the one who conspired to keep that intel hidden, that I hadn't even been initiated then. It's a matter of honor. You can't take out an heir without just reason."

"We had just reason. He was plotting with the Colombians and trying to frame Accardi. I still have those pictures."

"I can't take that risk. Greco will call for justice. An eye for an eye." He stares at me.

"You think he'll want to kill me."

"One way or another, he is going to try that, Leo."

"I know, but he won't succeed." I haven't come this far, sacrificed all these years without the love of my life, to be gunned down now.

"The other reason is it will cause a divide in The Commission. Families will take sides, and everything we have built over the past few years will be undone like that." He snaps his fingers.

"Tell me you have a plan."

He fixes me with a wicked grin. "You bet I do." He leans forward on his elbows. "Rico has set up a meeting for me with Don Maltese. They have had beef with the Grecos over the years, and I think they will support me if the shit hits the fan."

"That's smart."

"It was actually Nat's idea." Of course, it was. My *dolcezza* is so fucking smart. "According to Rico, DiPietro isn't a fan either," Ben continues, "so if I can win both of them to my side, we have the majority. I'm going to feel Maltese out first, and if he's agreeable, I will tell him exactly what has gone down. If I have his support, I'll meet DiPietro and do the same."

"But you can't sway the vote. If Accardi doesn't get the Chicago gig, he'll renege on everything."

"I'm aware, which is why he will be voted in, but his tenure will not last long. I'm going to wait until he's comfortable and then deal with him once and for all. In the meantime, I'm going to ask Don Maltese if he'll send his heir to Chicago as Gino's right-hand man. We will make that a condition of the appointment."

"So, we have eyes and ears on him at all times." Ben nods. "It might not even come to that," I say as my mind churns ideas. "I got word last night from one of our guys. Get this. Don Greco is behind the Colombian infiltration. He's letting them use his ships and his distribution routes for a cut. And he knows they are selling to Caleb."

Ben rubs his thumb along his lower lip. "Greco's playing a dangerous game."

"He is. And if he's planning to double-cross Accardi, then he's most definitely got plans in mind for us."

"Of course, he does. I don't think Accardi has given up on taking me down either."

"So much for The Commission being a united entity. There are so many power plays going on I'm getting a headache."

"You can't change things overnight, and there will always be someone trying to take me down because they want ultimate power. As long as we are ahead of the game, they will never succeed."

"WHERE IS NATALIA?" I ask, stepping into Ben's kitchen with him later that night.

"She is with Serena in the living room." Sierra walks away from the coffee machine and comes over to hug me. "Nat told us what happened. I am so sorry, Leo." She pats her small baby bump while squeezing my hand. "I can't begin to imagine what Natalia must have been through. My heart breaks for her." Tears pool in her eyes. "For both of you."

Pain eviscerates every part of me on the inside, and I swallow over the lump in my throat. I nod, unable to find words. Ben slides up behind his wife, pulling her back into his chest. We exchange silent words over her head. Ben is trusting me to make this right with Nat and to comfort her because I know the events of the last couple of days must have brought it all to the surface for her again.

I walk off in the direction of the living room, needing to hold my woman.

"Leo." Natalia's gorgeous blue eyes pop wide when she sees me. She is sitting on the couch with Serena, drinking wine. "I wasn't expecting you."

"I know I said I needed time, but I was wrong." I stride across the room as quick as my legs will carry me and bend down to kiss her. "I just need to be with you." Taking the glass from her hand, I put it on the end table, and then I lift her up. She squeals as I hold her while plonking down in her seat, situating her on my lap. I wrap my arms around her, nuzzling her neck. "That's better."

Serena smiles softly. "I am unbelievably sorry for what happened with the baby, but I am so glad you two found your way back to one another. I'm happy you finally get to be together. You both deserve it."

"Thanks, Rena. But we're not out of the woods yet. I won't fully believe it until the divorce comes through," Nat says.

"Believe it, babe." I press a kiss to her temple. "I don't care what that fucker tries to pull. He is not taking you from me again. No one is."

She turns her head so she's staring at me, and her gaze snares me. She is so goddamn beautiful. And I can't wait to properly make her mine. "I love you." She kisses the corner of my mouth.

"Not as much as I love you." I peck her lips, conscious we have company and we need to talk.

"You two are so adorable." Serena stands, smiling wistfully. "I'm rooting for you." She walks off, leaving us alone.

"How are you holding up?" I ask, clasping her face in my hands.

"I'm doing okay."

"And the boys?"

"Joshua is sad. Caleb is so angry and refusing to accept the drugs are an issue, but at least they both want to be with me. I couldn't bear it if they'd said they wanted to go and live with their dad."

"They love you and want to protect you. That was very obvious the other day." I caress her cheek with my thumb. "Did they say anything about me?"

"Not much, but I don't think they are opposed to us. They want me to be happy."

"Good." I am planning on having a little talk with them tomorrow. "I'm sorry for walking out last night. I shouldn't have left you alone."

"I understand, Leo, and I was fine. It gave Ben and me a good opportunity to talk." Her eyes lower, and a veil of sadness glides across her face.

"All day, I kept thinking, if things had turned out differently, our kid would be ten now." Pain spears across my chest.

"I know," she whispers, burying her head in my chest. "I used to wonder whether it was a boy or a girl and whether they would look like you or me or be a combination of both of us."

I reposition her on my lap, tilting her face up because I need to be looking at her when I say this. "I know it can't make up for the pain of our loss. That we will always feel it, but I want babies with you, Nat." I open my heart and tell her everything I'm feeling. "I want everything with you. Marriage. Our own house. Filled with the twins and our kids and lots of laughter." I press my mouth to hers. "I want to give you everything you have been denied and everything your heart desires." It's not a proposal, because I want to do that right, but I'm giving her a heads-up it is on the way. As soon as she is no longer tied to that bastard.

"I thought you were never getting married."

"So did I because the only woman I have ever wanted to marry is you."

A squeal emits from the direction of the door, and we whip our heads around, to find Sierra and Ben in the doorway.

"Nosy much?" I narrow my eyes at my boss and best friend.

"We didn't mean to eavesdrop. We were just passing," Sierra says. "But, gosh! That was so romantic, Leo." She slaps a hand over her chest, and her eyes are suspiciously glossy. "One of the swooniest things I have ever heard."

"Ahem." Ben clears his throat. "I'm pretty sure I have him beat."

She swats his chest. "Don't steal Leo's thunder. He has been waiting a long time for this."

Ben lifts Sierra up into his arms. "I wouldn't dream of it, and let's give them privacy. We are retiring early. Good night." They walk off.

"That sounds like a good idea," Natalia purrs in my ear, swiveling so she's straddling me. "Maybe we should go to bed early too."

"I love the way you think." I nibble on her earlobe, and she giggles as I set her feet on the ground.

The second Nat closes the door to her bedroom, I'm on her, driving my tongue into her mouth as my lips plunder hers while I rock my hips against her pelvis.

"God, I need you. Need this," she mumbles against my neck.

"I want this every day, Nat. From now on, I don't want to be parted a single night."

"I can get behind that," she says as I drop a slew of kisses along her neck. She opens my belt and lowers the zipper on my pants, diving her hand behind my boxers to grip my cock. "Always so hard for me."

"Just thinking about your lush mouth and your tight, hot pussy has me rock hard in an instant." I shove her formfitting dress up to her waist and rip her panties off. I back her up against the wall, kissing her as I fumble with my wallet, grabbing a condom. My pants drop to my ankles, and I shove my boxers down, freeing my throbbing cock. "This will be fast, *dolcezza*, because I need inside you right now."

"I'm ready," she pants, taking my hand and bringing it to her pussy. "Feel how much I want you."

My finger slides easily inside her cunt, and I moan as her tight walls clench around me. I slam my lips down on hers as I pump my finger in and out. "I love how responsive you are."

"It's all for you, babe. Now take what is yours. Remind me we are invincible and no motherfucker is ever coming between us again."

I don't need to be told twice, so I grab the foil packet.

Nat's fingers encircle my wrist. "I have an IUD, and I'm clean. If you are too, we don't need condoms anymore."

"I'm clean." I have never gone bareback with any woman, but I still get tested regularly.

"Good." She smiles, thrusting her hips at me.

I position myself at her entrance and lift her. Her arms wrap around my neck, and she circles her legs around my waist, holding on tight. I thrust inside her in one powerful move, and she cries out. I keep her pinned to the wall and between my body as I fuck her hard. There is absolutely nothing like the feeling of being inside my woman with no barrier. Nothing beats it. Sweat rolls down my spine as I pound into her, and the muscles in my thighs get a solid workout, but all I can feel is the way her inner walls are hugging my cock in silent possession.

I kiss her and grope at her breasts through her dress while we rock against one another, moaning and whimpering.

We come together, like we have learned to do, and I collapse against her, breathing heavily, exhilarated, and already needing to do it again.

So, I do. This time, we undress fully and move to the bed, where I make slow sweet love to the woman of my dreams for hours. When I fall asleep, with a sleeping, naked Natalia curled into my side and her head on my chest, I have never felt happier, and I make a silent promise to both of us.

Gino Accardi is not going to fuck this up. I know he's got something up his sleeve, but he won't win. This time, *I'm* getting the girl, and if he interferes, I will kill him. Fuck the consequences.

Chapter 48

NATALIA

"I NEED TO speak to you both. Right now," Ben says, storming into the kitchen the next morning while we are all around the table having breakfast. Leo had called him when we got up, and Sierra said he received an early call and had to go out, but he hadn't picked up.

Leo and I trade ominous looks as we stand. He instantly clasps my hand in his, and that small gesture means so much to me. In every sense of the word, we are a team, and I love having him by my side.

My heart is all aflutter every time he is near me, and I hope the feeling never ends.

"Daddy!" Rowan frowns. "Why do you look so angry?"

Ben's features immediately smooth out, and he crouches down to his son. "I'm not angry. Just frustrated because I got some bad news at work." He kisses the top of Rowan's head. "It's nothing for you to worry about, and we're still going on our bike ride, okay?" He straightens up. "I just need to speak to Natalia and Leo first."

"Auntie Natalia," the little charmer says, eyeing our hands. "Are you and Uncle Leo getting married now?"

Sierra almost chokes on her coffee. "Rowan!"

"It's okay," Leo says. "He's just curious." He tweaks Rowan's nose and whispers something in his ear. Rowan vigorously nods his head before holding his hand up for a high-five. More whispering ensues until I notice the look on Ben's face, and I hurry Leo out of the room.

"We have a big fucking problem," Ben says the instant we step into his office and the door closes behind us.

"What has Gino done?" I ask, already knowing my husband has tried to throw a wrench in the works.

"He double-crossed us. He went to Don Greco and told him everything. Maximo called me this morning and insisted I meet him at Greenhaven." Ben rubs at his temples. "Maximo intends on raising a vote of no confidence in me as president of The Commission."

"He can't do that! You haven't done anything wrong, and you weren't even around when Carlo was killed. This is ridiculous."

"It is, but it all comes down to honor. The way he will paint it is the Mazzone heir took out the Greco heir in a cold calculated act that is against our code. There was no honor in the way Carlo died." Ben glances at Leo, and there is no denying the pride on his face. "He demands repayment."

"Mateo is dead! And Greco killed Juliet. He has already had his retribution, and the price has been paid."

"In his eyes, I haven't been punished." Leo hauls me around to his front. He pulls my back to his chest and snakes his arms around me. I hold on to his strong arms, letting his warmth and comfort soothe the edges of my frayed nerves. Ben nods. "What does he want?"

"For you to marry his eighteen-year-old granddaughter."

"What?" I splutter.

"It's that or he will kill you and have me removed from my position with The Commission."

It's a shrewd move. Bringing Leo into his family guarantees his loyalty and his silence, and it avoids war. But it's not happening. Not in my lifetime. "I thought we have Maltese and DiPietro on our side?" I say, repeating what Leo had told me last night when we were talking in bed after copious rounds of hot sex.

"We do, but it's a tied vote in a situation like this. That means it has to go to a wider vote and our business becomes known among other *famiglia*, and it would discredit me. Discredit you and Leo."

I wriggle out of Leo's arms. "This is such bullshit, and I'm fucking done." My mind whirls as ideas form in my head. "Gino is not getting away with this." I chew on my lips as I think while my brother and my lover watch me pacing. I lift my head up. “Agree to it for now, and I want extra protection on Leo. Me and the twins too.”

“Already done,” Ben says. “What exactly is your plan?”

I shoot them a wry smile. “Sit down, and I’ll explain.”

When Gino returns to New York a week later to attend the meeting with The Commission, I wait patiently outside in the car, ready to accost him as soon as it’s over. I run through my prepared speech in my head again while checking the contents of the file I intend to use when I pay a visit to Don Greco in due course, once this goes down the way I hope it does. Playing them off against one another is risky, and it could backfire if they trade notes, but that’s a risk we are willing to take.

A half hour later, Gino emerges from the building, looking like the cat that got the cream. The Commission has just told him they are ratifying his nomination for don of The Outfit, provided the heads of the other families agree at a meeting that is being convened in Chicago in two weeks. Ben got Maltese and DiPietro to agree to it before the vote, and it’s not like Greco or Gino could argue without showing their hands. They don’t know Ben has brought Maltese and DiPietro into his confidence or that they are in for a rude awakening soon.

Brando opens my car door, and I step out, holding the large white envelope in my hand. “Gino,” I call out.

He lifts his head, startled to see me here. I walk toward him with a scowl, not having to act this part. Brando and Nario flank me. “I need to speak to you.”

“I have nothing to say to you.”

Wow. He doesn’t even want to ask after his children, and there are no words for that. I waited until he had returned to Chicago to talk to him over the phone about Caleb. At least he couldn’t inflict physical damage from hundreds of miles away. He blew a gasket. Predictably blamed me. Poo-pooed my counselor proposal—not that I care. I already frog-marched Caleb to a session a few days ago, and I’m keeping a very close eye on him now. Gino hasn’t even called to check on his progress since, and I’m disgusted with him.

His new fiancée is undoubtedly a distraction, which should work in our favor.

"Well, I have plenty I want to say." I had planned on having this conversation in the car, but I can easily do it out here. I thrust the divorce papers into his chest. "I'm not signing them. Not after the stunt you pulled. Your whore will have to be content with being your bit on the side, not your wife. How long do you think she'll tolerate that?"

He laughs. "Marcella will be my wife, and she'll be a far better one than you ever were. You couldn't even bear me a child. You're defective in every way."

Beside me, Brando bristles. I grin. "I had an IUD implanted years ago, you dumb prick. Why the hell would I ever want to have a child with you?"

He raises his hand to hit me, and Nario grabs his wrist. "Touch her, and it'll be the last thing you ever do," he snarls.

"Get your hands off me."

Nario lets him go, grinning savagely as he cracks his knuckles. His reputation is well-known in New York, so Gino knows to give him a wide berth.

"All you had to do was stick to the agreement, but you couldn't even do that. Now you'll be the one to suffer." I prod him in the chest, smirking, because I know it will piss him off. "I will never divorce you, and don't even think about having me killed. Joshua and Caleb are fully aware of everything that is going on and what you have done. In time, they will probably forgive you. But not if you murder me." Leaning in, I press a traitorous kiss to his cheek. "Enjoy your whore, Gino, because that is all she will ever be."

Now that the trap is set, I turn on my heel and leave for my meeting with the PI.

"It worked like a charm," Leo says later that night when he arrives home after work. The twins and I are fully moved into Ben's penthouse now, and I can't deny how much happier I am here, even if this place needs an injection of color too. It's secure with the latest technology and high-tech cameras, and Ben has moved a number of his *soldati* into the apartments on the next level, so there is tons of backup, should we need it.

"Yeah?" I stretch up and kiss him, circling my arms around his neck. I beam at him, like I do every night when he returns home. I get a rush of butterflies the second he walks through the door, and I have to pinch myself every morning when I wake up with his strong, protective arms around my waist. I know we still have shit to wade through and the danger won't pass any time soon, but I love getting to share my life with him, and I can't keep the smile off my face. This is everything I have ever wanted, surpassing my wildest dreams.

"Yes, my little genius. Gino has already gone straight to Judge Simon, and Ben's substantial bribe will ensure the divorce is rushed through the courts in a few days." Quickie divorces are quite common in New York, but it can still take up to six weeks. Judge Simon works with all five families, and Ben knew he would make it happen much sooner, because we don't have that long to wait.

"You're sure? Because this needs to happen before the big meeting."

"We're sure." He nudges my nose. "The plan will work."

I knew reverse psychology would work on Gino, so I deliberately baited him into filing for divorce. If I had asked him to expedite it, he would have dragged his heels purely to spite me. Provided I don't contest it or any of the terms, it will be rushed through by the corrupt judge.

"This wasn't how it was supposed to go down between us." Leo slides his hands down my back to cup my ass. "I was going to do this big elaborate proposal and organize an intimate wedding, in an exotic location, with our close friends and family. I wanted to give you everything you have never had."

"We can still do that when this is dealt with." I kiss him. "All I have ever wanted is you." I press my hand over his chest, where his heart thumps steadily against my palm. "Your heart. Your soul." I place my other hand over his crotch. "Your cock."

He tugs my lower lip between his teeth. "You little minx." He swats my ass, and I jump. "You know you already own all those things." He reels me into his arms, and his expression turns tender. "Are you sure you want to do it like this? I don't want you to feel forced or like we are rushing."

"Are you kidding me right now?" Incredulity laces my tone. "I have waited a lifetime to marry you, and I'm done waiting." Gently, I cup his face. "I don't need an elaborate proposal or a fancy wedding. I just need you."

"I love you." He kisses me passionately, and I get lost in his arms.

"Ugh." Caleb groans as he strolls into the kitchen. "It's like living with horny teenagers."

Leo barks out a laugh. "Pot. Kettle. Black."

Caleb grins. "I'm allowed, but there is no excuse for you two." He pulls open the refrigerator, removing a bowl of chicken pasta. I cannot keep food in the house these days because he and his brother are eating nonstop, but you would never know it looking at their tall lean frames.

"You try living without the woman you love for more than a decade and come back and tell me you wouldn't be the damn same."

"I think it's cute," Joshua says. "And you make my mom smile. That's all that matters."

"Pussy," Caleb says over a cough, and Joshua grabs him into a headlock.

They seem to be handling things okay. Before Leo officially moved in with us, we sat them down and had a discussion about it. They know their father is living with Marcella, and while it's a big change, they both gave us the stamp of approval. It helps that Leo is a big Xbox addict too, and he has been bonding with them over violent bloody war games. He is also someone they can turn to with *mafioso* concerns, and while he would never try to replace their father, he is here for them in a way Gino isn't. It's only natural they will grow close.

I heat up some pasta for Leo, humming to myself as I sort clothes on the kitchen counter while the three men in my life enjoy a meal together, laughing and joking, and things finally feel right with the world.

Chapter 49

NATALIA

WHEN CONFIRMATION OF my divorce arrives three days later, we waste no time in heading to the city clerk's office to pick up our license. Then we return the following day to get married. Ben and Sierra, Frank, and the twins are with us in the room when the officiant declares we are man and wife. Brando, Nario, and Ciro are keeping guard outside. We wanted to invite Leo's parents and his sister and to have Serena, Alesso, and the kids and Frankie and her family here too, but it's too risky. Our plan only works if we keep the news hush-hush, for now.

I turn to my husband with tears in my eyes. "I can't believe it. You are finally mine," I choke out, grabbing his hips. "This is the happiest moment of my life."

Leo presses his forehead to mine. "I love you, Mrs. Messina. Now and always." Then he kisses me, clasping my face firmly in his hands, and no kiss has ever tasted sweeter. His kisses are passionate and unhurried, and my heart is bursting with joy.

"Get a room!" Caleb calls out, and I'm laughing as we break apart.

"You little shit." Leo grins. "Always spoiling my fun."

We accept congratulations from everyone, and then we make our way outside, via the rear staff entrance, to where our car is waiting. Leo helps me into the back seat as Brando slips behind the wheel and Nario drops into the passenger seat. The twins are heading back to Greenwich with Sierra, Ben, Ciro, and Frank. We are all staying the night with them tonight so we can share a meal and enjoy a few glasses of bubbly to celebrate.

"I'm sorry I'm not taking you to a top hotel to spend our wedding night," Leo says, bringing my hand to his lips. "I promise I will make it all up to you." He plants a kiss on my knuckles.

I lean in and kiss the corner of his mouth. "And I promise you I am perfectly happy. I don't need a luxury bridal suite or a big fancy party. I just need you." I snake my arms around his neck and plant a searing-hot kiss on his mouth.

"You have made me the happiest man alive today, *dolcezza*." He hugs me close. "I'd like to think Mateo is looking down on us and smiling. Deep down, he knew we were it for one another."

I run my hands along his smooth jawline. "I wish he had been here. Mama and Papa and Frankie too."

"I know, baby." A hint of sadness slips through his euphoria, and I know why.

"We will throw a big dinner at the penthouse for your family as soon as we can. I hate that they couldn't be here today."

"Me too, but at least Frank was there. It helped to lessen the blow, and I know Mama won't be mad. She'll be over the fucking moon I finally got married." He frees another grin. "She already loves you like a daughter, and she will be thrilled."

"I love Paulina. I love all your family."

"They are your family now too, *dolcezza*."

I smile at that thought, resting my head on his shoulder as Brando navigates our way out of the city.

"SURPRISE!" THE SMALL crowd shouts as we enter the large dining room at Ben and Sierra's house an hour later. My mouth hangs open at the sight of the transformed room. Wedding banners and photos of us throughout the years are hanging on the walls. Balloons and fresh flowers decorate the dining table, and soft candles line the mantelpiece. A gorgeous wedding cake resides on a side table along with several wrapped presents.

"Oh my God, you guys." Tears prick my eyes as Leo's mom rushes over to us, pulling both of us into a hug.

"Congratulations." Paulina squeezes us tighter. "I was so happy when Sierra called and told us to get over here for a special celebration. She only told us the good news when we arrived."

"I'm sorry, Mom." Leo presses a kiss to her cheek. "We would have told you if we could."

"It's okay, son," Joel says, coming up alongside his wife. "Frank explained, and we understand the need to keep this on the down low." He smiles at his son, clamping a hand on his shoulder, before leaning in to kiss me on the cheek. "Welcome to the family, Natalia."

"Thank you." My voice is laced with emotion. The realization I get more than Leo only recently occurred to me.

"Now I get to call you my sister for real," Giuliana says, waddling over to me with her gorgeous husband in tow. She pulls me into a hug. "This is the best news ever. I know how long you have loved each other. It warms my heart to know you are finally together." A sob travels up her throat, and she swipes at the tears welling in her eyes. "Sorry," she laughs, fanning her face. "Pregnancy hormones are no joke."

"Tell me about it." Sierra approaches with a tray, holding glasses of Cristal champagne. "I cry at the drop of a hat these days."

"Thank you for doing all this." I pull my sister-in-law into an embrace. "I love you."

"I love you too, and I'm so happy for you." She tweaks Leo's nose. "Both of you."

"We couldn't let the day pass without a proper celebration. We would have invited Frankie too if she wasn't out of town," Ben says, taking the tray from his wife. "You have done enough, Firefly. Serena too. It's time for you both to relax." Alesso drags Serena over, as if on cue. "The staff have got this, and I've got the drinks," Ben adds.

"Got any beer?" Caleb asks Ben.

He shoots me a look. "Ask your mom."

I don't want my sons drinking. They are only fourteen. But they grow up so fast in our world, and there's no point burying my head in the sand and acting like I don't know they drink. Still, I'm not going to let them get drunk or suggest it is okay. "One beer each. That's it."

Caleb opens his mouth, to protest no doubt, but he clamps it shut when Leo sends him a warning look.

"Congrats, Mama." Joshua kisses me on both cheeks. "I'm hella happy for you." He gives Leo an awkward one-armed hug. "Guess that means I get to call you stepdad now, huh?"

"You can call me whatever you want, Joshua. Whatever makes you most comfortable."

"I think I'm going to cry," Paulina says, her lower lip wobbling. "This is everything I have ever wanted for you." She yanks Leo into another hug. "I am over the moon for you, son, and I wish you both every happiness in the world."

I WAKE THE following morning to my husband's wandering hands and his erection digging into my ass. Not that I am complaining. I have never experienced this level of intimacy before, and I will never get enough. Leo loves me good, making me feel cherished in a way I have always craved. We made love for hours last night, yet my appetite for him never wanes. After a quick visit to the bathroom, I return, sans my sexy nightdress, and pounce on my hot husband, riding him until we both reach our happy place.

Sierra and Serena have prepared a massive breakfast feast for everyone, and they are all seated when we amble into the kitchen. Leo's family stayed here too last night because it was a late one. It ended up being the perfect wedding celebration, and I wouldn't have done it any differently.

"Oh my God. Mom has a hickey," Caleb says, staring at me like he's going to puke and at Leo like he wants to strangle him.

My hand subconsciously flies to my neck. "I do not!" I am going to kill him for blurting it out in front of Leo's parents.

A chorus of laughter rings out around the table.

"Shit, *dolcezza*." Leo is fighting a smirk as he pries my hands away and stares at my neck. "You actually do."

"What's a hickey?" Rowan asks, and another round of laughter breaks out.

"Your Uncle Leo is a vampire," I tease.

Rowan frowns. "He drinks your blood?"

Cue more laughter. Hell. I am making a mess of this, and I decide I'll let his parents handle this one. "I'm only joking, little charmer. Ask your dad later, and he'll explain."

"Thanks for that," Ben deadpans, flipping me the bird behind the kids' backs.

After we eat, we say goodbye to Leo's family, and then we head to Ben's study to discuss how today will go.

"You're wearing a Kevlar," Ben says, his "I'm a don and don't fucking mess with me" face perfectly intact.

"Don't attempt to argue," Leo says when he sees my mouth opening. "This is the only way we are letting you walk into Greco's house without us. It's not too much to ask."

I give in easily because I know this is hard for them. They are trusting me in a way the majority of made men, brothers, and husbands would not, and I love that they don't want to clip my wings. "It's not. I'll wear the vest, and I'll have my gun and a knife. Plus, Brando and Nario will be with me."

I want to be the one to confront Don Greco. I want to put him in his place and pay him back for the past. Besides, I don't trust he won't kill Leo if he steps foot in his house, and we need to keep Ben out of this, to protect his position and to let the ruse play out the way we need it to.

It has to be me. We all know it.

"NATALIA ACCARDI. To what do I owe this pleasure?" Maximo Greco says, failing to get up from behind his desk to greet me, when I am ushered into the office he keeps at his home.

"It's Mazzone," I say, striding across the room with Brando and Nario at my rear. I wish I could tell him it's actually Messina, but I'm waiting to drop that bomb at the most opportune time. "And we need to talk."

He arches a brow in amusement, and I can't wait to wipe that smug smile off his face. I sit down without invitation, leaning forward to slide the first envelope across his desk.

"What is this?" he asks, staring at it like it's a loaded gun. I suppose, in a way it is.

"Open it and see." I clasp my hands regally on my lap and keep my head up, letting no expression show on my face as he slides the photos out and looks at them.

A red flush creeps up his neck and onto his cheeks as he flips through the incriminating pictures. We got everything. Him meeting with the Colombians and the drug dealers peddling their shit on the streets. There are even shots of the supplies on his ships and evidence of his men unloading the cargo. "What is the meaning of this?" he roars, thumping his fist down on the desk.

"I think those photos speak for themselves, and you forced me into doing this, so spare me the self-righteousness and the bullshit threats." I narrow my eyes on him. "It wasn't that difficult for my PI to follow you or your men. You're getting sloppy in your old age." I throw a second envelope across the desk. This one contains the photos Leo took, years ago, of Carlo at the warehouse. "This is how it will go down. You will contact my brother and retract the request for Leo to marry your granddaughter. You will also give him your word that you will not raise a motion of no confidence in him as president of The Commission. You guarantee that you won't come after me, Leo, Bennett or our families, and those photos will never see the light of day," I lie.

"Refuse or attempt to double-cross us, and I will share those with my brother," I continue. "I don't think The Commission will take kindly to you doing deals with the enemy behind their backs. I'm pretty sure that would be a death sentence." I stand, smoothing a hand down the front of my skirt suit. "I will also ensure copies of those photos are delivered to the FBI and the Colombians." If it's the former, he'll go to jail. The latter and his entire family risks being slaughtered. Either way, he knows he's a dead man unless he agrees to my demands. "That will happen automatically if anything happens to me or one of my loved ones," I add as an extra incentive.

"You little—"

"Finish that sentence and we have a big problem." Nario cracks his knuckles, wearing his usual bloodthirsty face.

I turn around, giving Greco my back as a string of expletives leaves his mouth. I slip my rings on and turn to face him. "And by the way, it's Mrs. Messina now." I wave my left hand in his face. "Leo and I got married yesterday." It was our backup plan in case Greco had any other nasty surprises up his sleeve. Judging by his reaction, he's all out of ammo. Too bad for him.

Greco's eyes narrow to slits. By admitting that, I'm telling him in a none-too-subtle way that Ben already knows. His mouth curls into an ugly snarl, and his fists are clenched so tight the skin on his knuckles blanches white. I know he would love to take me out, but his hands are tied.

"One final thing." I smile down at him, gloating because there is nothing quite as satisfactory as putting this ugly little toad in his place. "You can forget about running to your pal Accardi." I throw a couple of additional photos on the desk. The first one shows Maximo deep in conversation with Caleb's dealer, and the second shot is a pic of the dealer handing shit to my son, proving Maximo went out of his way to set this up. He trapped my son into taking drugs, and I want to murder him for that fact alone. "I have just had a set of those shots delivered to Gino in Chicago. He knows what you are up to now, and I doubt he'll want to play any longer."

"Get out of my house!" he roars.

"Gladly." I flash him a wide smile. "Nice doing business with you." I blow him a kiss before straightening my shoulders and walking out with my head held high and the most self-satisfied expression on my face.

Chapter 50

LEO

IT'S BEEN TEN days since I married the love of my life, and I swear, every day I grow more and more in love with my *dolcezza*. She completes me in ways I never expected. Married life is everything I never knew I needed, and I don't take a single moment for granted.

I got laid continuously after I showed Natalia her wedding presents. I am glad I managed to pull it all off on such short notice. Sierra and Serena kept Nat occupied one day so Ben and I could hang all the framed photos on a wall in our bedroom. Everyone is represented. Her parents and Mateo, the twins, Ben and his family, my family, Serena, Alesso, Frankie, and Brando, and there are several pictures of us from when we were kids, right up to the present time. The plan is to move them to our living room when our house is built. I always want my *dolcezza* to know how much she is valued, cherished, and loved.

She cried again when the gardener I hired to grow an orchard in the vast garden behind our new house showed her his plans. We are digging the herb garden and vegetable patch ourselves, and I bought some supplies so we can get started. We spent all day last Saturday outside getting it set up. The younger kids helped too, which Nat got a kick out of.

She kissed me forever when I showed her the pictures of me and the twins now holding residence in the locket I gave her when she was seventeen. I was initially going to replace it with a more expensive one, but then I thought better of it. Nat loves it and it symbolizes our past and everything we have fought for to be here today. So, I came up with the idea of adding the photos instead.

"We all need to be on guard today," Ben says, dragging me out of my head.

We are in the back of an armored SUV en route to the building in Chicago where the biggest Italian American *mafioso* meeting is taking place. It's a big deal, with dons attending from all over the US, so security will be tight. I squeeze my wife's hand, and Nat presses in closer to my side. Ciro is driving, and Nario has his nose to the window, keeping his eyes peeled for any sign of trouble.

The twins are in another SUV behind us with Alesso and Brando. They aren't aware of the plans for their father. Something Natalia is concerned about, even if there is no other way to do this. We have to act now before he does. Hopefully, with the way we have set him and Greco off against one another, they will do us a solid and take each other out.

"Especially after we hijack the meeting and out Accardi and Greco as traitors," Ben continues. "I still don't like you are here," he adds, pinning troubled eyes on his sister.

"I was never letting my sons into that room without me."

The other heirs aren't invited, but Gino asked his sons to attend as he expects to be announced as the new don of The Outfit, and he wants to gloat. I fucking cannot wait to see him taken down. Honestly, it will make my millennium.

"And this is owed to me. After everything that man has put me through, I want to be there to witness his downfall."

It's dangerous for her to be here, but neither of us put up much of a fight, because her arguments have merit. Plus, this was all Nat's idea, and it's a genius plan. She deserves to see it through.

Accardi and Greco thought they could use what they know as leverage and that we wouldn't call their bluff. Nat suggested we play them at their own game, and it was the perfect solution. We can do it in such a way that protects me and the Mazzone name. Even if they throw accusations around, it will be too late once we divulge what they have been up to—Greco consorting with Colombians and cutting *la famiglia* out of the deal and Accardi colluding with Russians so he could claim the position of power in Chicago. I wouldn't be surprised if one of The Outfit's *soldati* kills him before he leaves the state. I would serve him right and solve that issue for us.

We know they won't go away indefinitely. That our actions today will most likely unite them in a renewed quest to take us out. But we will get to them before then. We just need to wait for the dust to settle before permanently dealing with our problem children. Greco is an easy takedown. Accardi is harder because of the twins and Nat's desire not to have him killed. I'm not sure how we will resolve it, but it's a problem for a different day.

"You have your gun?" Ben asks.

Nat nods, patting her thigh. "And my knife. Plus, I'm wearing a Kevlar, same as all of you. Don't worry, Benny. Nothing will happen to me. You need to stay focused. Let the rest of us do what we need to do, and you just worry about yourself."

I crash my lips to hers. "Damn, *dolcezza*. Your confidence really turns me on."

Ben clears his throat, grumbling. "I swear you want me to shoot you."

"Suck it up, brother-in-law." I nudge him in the ribs. "I had to endure all this and more when you and Sierra got hitched. Payback is a bitch."

He mutters under his breath, but secretly, I know he's thrilled for us. He wouldn't have offered a plot of land on his property to build our dream home otherwise. Nat and I had begun talking about buying a family home together, so Ben's timing is perfect. The estate is large enough it won't feel like we are on top of one another, and having family and friends close by will be great for Nat.

The boss travels into the city every day for work, either by helicopter or car, so we can travel with him. The commute from Greenwich isn't too bad, especially if we go by air. Ben's helicopter fits six passengers, so he has enough room to add us and the twins.

Serena has been traveling with him since she started at NYU as a mature student at the end of August. It's another thing that connects my wife and Sierra's sister. Those two get on like a house on fire, and as Serena shows no signs of moving from Ben's place, it only adds to the reasons why we should establish roots there.

We have a meeting next week with an architect to begin drawing up plans, and I can't wait. I want a place to call our own. Somewhere we can decorate together. A home we can raise lots of babies in. We haven't seriously broached that topic yet because now is not the time to consider bringing kids into the world. However, the clock is ticking, and I don't want to be too old when I become a father. Nat has had an IUD implanted for years, and it might take a while before she gets pregnant, so she has already arranged an appointment to have it removed. We can enjoy being together in the meantime while we have fun practicing.

"We're here." Ciro pulls the car into a vacant space in the parking lot at the back of the building. This place, on the city's northwest side, is one of The Outfit's largest properties, and it's been fitted out to accommodate the meeting today. Ironically, it's in Forest Glen, where Gino's fiancée is from. Backing onto Indian Woods, it is miles from any other property, so it gives us the privacy we need to conduct a meeting of this size.

It also offers our enemies ample opportunity to take potshots at us, so security has been ramped up. Dozens of The Outfit's men roam the woods and guard the perimeter of the building, but I'm still on edge. There is a lot hanging in the balance today, and there is no guarantee it will go exactly how we have planned it.

"Stay sharp," Ben says, exiting the vehicle once Ciro and Nario have confirmed it's clear. He rounds the car and opens Natalia's door, helping his sister down. I slide out behind her, my eyes instantly scanning the packed parking lot. We are cutting it close, but that's on purpose. We want to put Accardi on edge from the very start.

The twins come up to us with Alesso and Brando at the rear. They hug their mom while checking the parking lot like vultures sniffing out prey.

"Bennett." Don Maltese and Don DiPietro approach from between parked cars, trailed by a bunch of armed *soldati*. They are aware of our plans, and we have their full support. They are disgusted with the dishonorable conduct of Don Greco and Don Accardi, and it didn't take much to win their agreement.

The Maltese heir must already be in the building, having previously been confirmed as an appointed aide by The Commission. I'm sure Gino hates having a spy in his midst, and no doubt he has plans to get rid of him at the first available opportunity.

Maltese and DiPietro have become good friends and colleagues in recent times. If anything good has come out of the past few months, it's the strengthening of ties between our three families.

The three dons shake hands, and Maltese and DiPietro congratulate Natalia and me on our wedding.

"Are you ready?" Don DiPietro asks.

"Yes." Ben nods. "Let's do this."

We stride toward the entrance as a united group, and every made man is on alert, watching all angles as we approach the double doors.

The doors swing open, and Gino appears, dragging Marcella with him, flanked by four of his New York men. "What the hell took so long?" he snaps, looking on edge as he glances around.

"Watch your tone," Ben coolly replies, coming to a halt a few feet in front of him.

I shoot daggers at Marcella Toscana as she blatantly looks Natalia up and down with a derisory sneer on her face. Natalia smiles at her without a care in the world, leaning in and kissing me on the cheek. I hold her hand tighter and pull her in close, as my protective instincts ramp up.

Gino glares at us. He knows now that Nat tricked him into the quickie divorce, and he clearly hates being outsmarted by a woman. A woman he underestimated for years. Temporarily shaking off his loathing, he returns his attention to Ben. "Everyone is inside. Let's get this started."

"This is for DeLuca!" a man with a gruff voice shouts out, and all the hairs lift on the back of my neck. I shove Natalia behind my back as I withdraw my gun, glancing all around. Every other made man has their weapons out and eyes peeled as we try to locate the source of the voice.

Two shots ring out in quick succession, whizzing over our heads. "We don't recognize you as our don," a different man hollers as more shots are fired. From the elevation, I'm guessing the shooters are perched high in the trees, giving them a perfect vantage point.

We need to get the fuck out of here now.

"Get back to the cars!" Ben shouts, ducking down as bullets fly past him, embedding in Gino's chest and his fiancée's forehead. Gino roars as Marcella slumps to the ground, dead upon impact. More shots are fired, riddling his body with bullets, and it's game over for Accardi. Gino's *soldati* open fire as shots go off inside the building before men from The Outfit spill out of the doors.

Everyone in our party starts shooting, our *soldati* instantly shielding the three dons. Brando rushes to me, firing in the direction of the woods where unknown men are shooting at us. "I'll take Nat," he says. "Alesso is grabbing the twins."

"We'll cover you," Ben says, firing with weapons in both hands. Shots are coming at us from two sides now, and the odds aren't looking good.

Caleb spins around, coolly shooting a guy sneaking up on us from the side of the building. His brother is holding his own too, firing his gun at the enemy with an unnatural confidence that belies his age and his usual sensitive manner. Guess it's in their blood, and it's the one part of their upbringing where Gino wasn't remiss.

While we're distracted, Nat kicks off her shoes and takes off running toward our cars. "Go after her!" I scream at Brando while firing my weapon at the soldiers approaching from the front door.

A deafening explosion rips through the air, and the ground shakes, rippling and buckling like an earthquake has just hit. The soldiers close to the front of the building are thrown through the air as the structure ignites in a giant fireball that mushrooms high into the sky.

Screeching tires reverberate in my ears as our two SUVs pull up alongside us. More men are emerging from the trees on foot, and we need to get the fuck out of Dodge. It's clear their intention is to kill every don in the US.

"Get in," Nat screams through the lowered driver-side window. Brando hops out of the second vehicle and grabs a shell-shocked Caleb and Joshua while Ciro and Nario grab Ben and Maltese. DiPietro is on the ground with blood pumping out of his leg.

"Cover me," I yell, at no one in particular, while I crawl to DiPietro and drag him with me. He's got to be in pain, but he grits his teeth and bears it.

We all scramble into the cars, and Brando and Nat floor it out of there, veering left and right to avoid the shots chasing us, until we are out of range. Nat pulls over to let Ciro behind the wheel. She immediately climbs into the back to be with her sons and to attend to Don DiPietro's injury. Then we floor it in the direction of the airport, and if I never see Chicago again, I will welcome it.

Epilogue

LEO

IT'S BEEN TWO weeks since the bloodbath in the Windy City, and everyone is still reeling. "How did it go?" I ask Ben as he walks into his office after attending another emergency sitting of The Commission.

"Same shitshow as the last time."

"Fuck."

"What the hell am I expected to do with this?" He walks to his liquor cabinet, pouring drinks.

"I know this is a major setback, but we will rebuild. We will come back from this."

"The blowback will be felt for some time, Leo. And our enemies are closing in. This is the perfect moment for them to strike when we are on our goddamn knees."

Ben is usually one cool customer, and I have never seen him this rattled. Then again, we have just lost most every don across the US. Blown up by a motherfucking bomb set by the Sicilian DeLucas. A few of our dons weren't in attendance. Either they were running late or they hadn't bothered to show up, like Salerno from Vegas.

"I know the situation is dire, and most of the families are without their leaders, but we haven't lost the heirs or the loyal *soldati* and *capos*." Except for Don Maltese. He lost his only son to the bomb. "They will defend their territories, and everyone knows to be on guard for enemy attacks. We will train the heirs to be new leaders. The kind of leaders who will get behind your ideas, not dismiss them because they're not traditional. This could be a good thing in the long run."

"If we last that long. We are weak and vulnerable right now."

I hate hearing such defeat in his tone. I know it's the result of minimal sleep and worry for his family. Sierra is noticeably pregnant now, and he fears retaliation because DeLuca's men clearly intended for us to die that day too, and we got away. They will try again. But it's not something we need to worry about now because The Outfit is undergoing more change, and I'm sure solidifying the loyalty of the men and consolidating the territory is top of their list of priorities.

"Not us," I remind him because we haven't lost our leadership and The Commission's ruling board is intact with Ben, Maltese, and DiPietro joined by Luca Accardi and Gabriele Greco. The latter men are smarter and more accommodating than their predecessors. They understand the considerable threat to the future of the *mafioso* in the US, and they see the bigger picture. They have agreed to let the past stay in the past. That now is the time to band together instead of letting the sins of our forefathers tear us apart.

The Outfit has broken away from us, which is probably for the best. Because every other *famiglia* in America is baying for their blood. They turned on us. They turned on their own, and that is unforgivable.

"Did you get anything else from the Chicago PI?" Ben asks, handing me a scotch.

"It seems the Sicilian DeLucas came to the US six months ago. Presumably when they stopped hearing from Giuseppe and Alfredo. They infiltrated the rank and file, won their trust quickly, and got the word out who DeLuca was and who was really behind his termination."

That would be us.

"It's ironic Barretta fled to Sicily and they came here," Ben says.

"I very much doubt he's alive."

Ben nods as he takes his seat. "It was probably a relief for him. His days were numbered anyway."

"True." I doubt his death was painless, but it was probably less painful than the prolonged progression of his illness.

"I should have gone to Sicily myself last year," Ben muses, swirling his drink in his glass. "The intel we received was obviously false."

After the showdown last year, Ben hired some men to do some digging in Sicily. We wanted to find out if anyone would miss Giuseppe DeLuca or if there were any potential successors who might try to lay claim to Chicago. The findings indicated not, which clearly wasn't the truth. "Don't beat yourself up over this. We thought we had it covered. You can't be everywhere at the same time, Ben. You can't be everything to everyone."

A muscle clenches in his jaw, but he doesn't comment. After a few beats of silence, he says, "Ask Donny to stay tight with his guy on the inside of The Outfit. We need to know what they are planning."

"He wants out," I explain. "He's terrified." Accardi had beaten the man bloody when he discovered him trailing him, sending our PI to the hospital for a week. We paid Donny an extortionate sum of money to gather intel after we fled Chicago, and though he tried to refuse, we wouldn't let him. Now, he seems to have grown new balls, and he's adamant he's had enough. Even said he'd give us back the money. He wants no part of this.

"Tough shit," Ben says. "He's staying on the case whether he likes it or not."

His phone pings, and he picks it up, reading the message with a rare smile. Knocking back his bourbon, he stands. "Come on." He grabs his suit jacket. "My wife has laid down the law. I suspect your wife had a hand in it too. We're to come home early, and they're not taking no for an answer."

NATALIA

I KNOCK ON Joshua's bedroom door, waiting for him to call out before I step inside. My heart sinks when I find him lying on his bed, throwing a baseball up and down while he stares blankly at the ceiling. "Dinner will be ready soon," I say, walking across the room to sit on the edge of his bed. "Ben and Leo will be home shortly."

"I'm not hungry."

"You have to eat, Joshua." I reach out, brushing strands of messy blond hair out of his eyes. "I'm worried about you."

He lets the ball drop down onto the bed and pulls himself up against the headboard. "I hate this." He swipes at the angry tears forming in his eyes. "Why can't we go back to the penthouse? It makes no sense traveling in and out every day."

"Ben wants us all together. It's an extremely dangerous time, and it's not safe to stay in the city. This place is a fortress, and with the extra security guards and measures Ben and Leo have added, this is the safest place for us to be." My sons don't know I had to fight tooth and nail to get them to agree I could continue at NYU and the boys could continue going to their normal school. Leo wants me to switch to online classes, and Ben wants the boys to be homeschooled. I had to put my foot down, even though I know the risks.

Caleb and Joshua are suffering. They watched their father get gunned down in front of them in cold blood. Now they have been wrenched from their home and their friends. I couldn't take them out of school too. I feared what it would do to them. So, I reached a compromise with my brother and my husband. We travel to the city in Ben's helicopter every day, and a swarm of bodyguards meets us at the CH building, splitting off as we go our separate ways.

I get some strange looks on campus because of the four burly men in black suits with fierce expressions who follow me everywhere, but I can deal. If this is what my brother and my husband need for their peace of mind, I can handle it.

"I know you miss Bettina. What if I call her parents and see if they will give permission for her to come and stay this weekend?"

His eyes light up. "Yeah?"

"Yes." Ben has already done background checks on Joshua's girlfriend and her family as well as the boys' best friends, after I asked if it would be possible to let them arrange some sleepovers. I know this sucks for my sons, and I'm trying to think of ways I can make it easier on them. There is lots for them to do here with the extensive grounds, massive game room, home theater, pool, and the gym. All they are lacking is company their own age.

Any friends coming over will be required to sign NDAs, along with their parents, and they will travel on Ben's helicopter so the exact location of his house is kept a secret.

Now more than ever, we need to remain hidden.

"Thanks, Mama." He climbs across the bed, giving me a hug.

I hold him tight, kissing his head. "I know it's been a lot of change, and I know you are missing your father, but I promise it will get better."

He nods against my chest, and my heart aches for him. Where Joshua is giving in to his feelings and he's internalizing a lot, Caleb is the opposite. He is even more hardened. Closing himself off to emotion. He acts like his father isn't dead. Like the threat isn't real. And he hasn't stopped bitching and whining about being cooped up here.

Leo usually drags him out of the house when he gets home to go running on the grounds or for target practice at the new range Ben just had built at the far end of the property. Other times, Caleb works his frustration out in the gym. He has even spent a few evenings with Ben's construction workers at the site where our new home is being built. It seems pounding a few sledgehammers does wonders for his aggression.

The only saving grace is he doesn't appear to be touching drugs anymore. I hope it lasts.

"Come downstairs in twenty minutes," I say, "and drag your brother with you." I have already been in Caleb's room to convey the same message, but I got a casual shrug and a look that said leave me the fuck alone.

I walk downstairs, stepping into the kitchen, an automatic smile lighting up my face when I see my husband is home. Ben is rubbing his hands over Sierra's growing stomach while whispering in her ear. Serena appears to have disappeared. I wrap my arms around Leo from behind. "Hey there, sexy."

He spins me around, banding his arms around my back. "Stop stealing all my lines," he says before his mouth descends. Every anxiety and worry disappears as he holds me close, kissing me like it's the first time we have kissed. "How was your day?" he asks when we finally break apart.

"It was good. My afternoon classes were canceled, so Brando drove us back early. I picked up some supplies, and Sierra and I made all the family favorites for dinner." Things have been very tense lately, and the guys are working nonstop. They need a night to chill out and unwind.

"Sounds perfect." He cradles my head to his chest, and I savor the feel of his warm body and his strong arms around me.

"I have a surprise for later," I whisper coyly in his ear.

He playfully swats my ass. "You can't say that and not tell me what it is."

I press my mouth in closer to his ear. "Sierra taught me a few massage skills, and she gave me a bunch of aromatherapy oils. I plan to feed you with good food and wine, and then I'm going to massage all the stress from your body."

"Fuck, *dolcezza*." He subtly grinds his groin against me so I can feel his semi. "I can't eat a family dinner with a boner."

I giggle. "It hasn't stopped you before."

A smirk plays on his lips. "True." He kisses me deeply. "I like your plan, and after I'm nice and relaxed, I'm going to make love to my beautiful, thoughtful wife. All. Night. Long."

His teeth graze my ear, and a shiver works its way through me. "Now who isn't playing fair?" I tease, fake pouting.

His expression turns serious. "I know things are shitty right now, but you make everything better, Nat. I feel like I can take on the world with you by my side."

My heart melts, and my ovaries swoon. My husband is officially the most romantic man on this earth, and I am irrevocably and unconditionally completely head over heels in love with him. "Together we can do anything," I agree, threading our hands. "We haven't come this far to let anything come between us. Everything is going to work out."

I bring our conjoined fingers to my lips, kissing our linked knuckles. "This is our time, Leo. This is the start of something amazing, and I refuse to let anything or anyone dampen my enthusiasm for our future because we have fought to be here, and we deserve it."

"Amen to that, babe," he says before his lips descend again.

ALESSO

SERENA RACES PAST me like a whirlwind. Her gorgeous face is unnaturally pale, and her hazel eyes are wide and terror-stricken. Alarm bells ring in my ears. "Watch your brother," I tell Elisa, instantly getting up to go after the woman who has—unbeknownst to her—made mincemeat of my heart.

"Serena?" I call out, entering her bedroom through the open door. Sounds of vomiting alert me to her presence in the bathroom, and I rush to her side.

She is clutching a large brown envelope in her hand as she bends over the toilet, retching. Scraping her hair back from her face, I snatch a hair tie from the sink and tie it around her long locks. Kneeling beside her, I gently smooth my hand up and down her back as she expels the entire contents of her stomach.

When she's done, I hand her a cool cloth, and she runs it over her clammy face before wiping her mouth and slumping against the side of the tub.

"What's going on? Did something happen at college today?"

She lifts panicked eyes to mine, and my heart stutters in my chest. "Rena, please. You're scaring me." I move over in front of her. "Tell me what's wrong, and I'll fix it."

A strangled sound rips from her throat as she clutches the envelope to her chest. "They gave us our new assignments today," she says in a hoarse, lilting voice. With trembling fingers, she removes papers from the envelope, letting them drop to the ground. Picking up a small, square sheet of white card, she hands it to me.

All the blood drains from my face when I read the crudely written words.

BLOOD IN. BLOOD OUT.

"Where did you get this?"

"It was in my envelope." She gulps and tears fill her eyes. "It's them. It's the DeLucas." Tears roll down her face. "It's not over, Alesso. It's never going to be over. They are coming for me, and there isn't a damn thing you or Ben can do to stop them."

TL is releasing on November 30, 2021. More spin-off books are planned in this world including *The Accardi Twins*, slated to release in 2022. Subscribe to the author's newsletter or join her reader's group on Facebook to stay up to date with all new release news (type the below links into a browser.)

Newsletter: http://eepurl.com/dl4l5v
Reader's Group: https://smarturl.it/SiobhanSquad

If you haven't read Sierra and Bennett's romance, *Condemned to Love* is available now in ebook, paperback, and audiobook format.

#24 in the entire Amazon.com store

Multiple #1 bestseller in the US, UK, Australia, and Canada.

Her teen crush is now a ruthless killer and powerful mafia heir.

Will one life-altering night unite or destroy them?

Bennett Mazzone grew up ignorant of the truth: he is the illegitimate son of the most powerful ma-fia boss in New York. Until it suited his father to drag him into a world where power, wealth, vio-lence, and cruelty are the only currency.

Celebrating her twenty-first birthday in Sin City should be fun for Sierra Lawson, but events take a deadly turn when she ends up in a private club, surrounded by dangerous men who always get what they want.

And they want her.

Ben can't believe his ex's little sister is all grown up, stunningly beautiful, and close to being de-voured by some of the most ruthless men he has ever known. The Vegas trip is about strengthen-ing ties, but he won't allow his associates to ruin her perfection. Although it comes at a high price, saving Sierra is his only choice.

The memory of Ben's hands on her body is seared into Sierra's flesh for eternity. She doesn't re-gret that night. Not even when she discovers the guy she was crushing on as a teenager is a cold, calculating killer with dark impulses and lethal enemies who want him dead.

Understanding the risks, she walks away from the only man she will ever love, stowing her secrets securely in her heart. Until the truth becomes leverage and Sierra is drawn into a bloody war—a pawn in a vicious game she doesn't want to play.

As the web of deceit is finally revealed, Ben will stop at nothing to protect Sierra. Even if loving her makes him weak. In a world where women serve a sole purpose, and alliances mean the differ-ence between life and death, can he fight for love and win?

Available now in ebook, paperback, and audiobook format.

About the Author

Siobhan Davis *is a USA Today, Wall Street Journal*, and Amazon Top 10 bestselling romance author. **Siobhan** writes emotionally intense stories with swoon-worthy romance, complex characters, and tons of unexpected plot twists and turns that will have you flipping the pages beyond bedtime! She has sold over 1.5 million books, and her titles are translated into several languages.

Prior to becoming a full-time writer, Siobhan forged a successful corporate career in human resource management.

She lives in the Garden County of Ireland with her husband and two sons.

You can connect with Siobhan in the following ways:
Author Website: www.siobhandavis.com
Facebook: AuthorSiobhanDavis
Twitter: @siobhandavis
Instagram: @siobhandavisauthor
Tiktok: @siobhandavisauthor
Email: siobhan@siobhandavis.com

Books by Siobhan Davis

KENNEDY BOYS SERIES

Upper Young Adult/New Adult Contemporary Romance

Finding Kyler

Losing Kyler

Keeping Kyler

The Irish Getaway

Loving Kalvin

Saving Brad

Seducing Kaden

Forgiving Keven

Summer in Nantucket

Releasing Keanu

Adoring Keaton

Reforming Kent

STANDALONES

New Adult Contemporary Romance

Inseparable

Incognito

When Forever Changes

No Feelings Involved

Still Falling for You

Second Chances Box Set

Reverse Harem Contemporary Romance

Surviving Amber Springs

Dark Mafia Romance

Condemned to Love

Forbidden to Love

RYDEVILLE ELITE SERIES

Dark High School Romance

Cruel Intentions

Twisted Betrayal

Sweet Retribution

Charlie

Jackson

Sawyer

The Hate I Feel

*Drew^*

THE SAINTHOOD (BOYS OF LOWELL HIGH)

Dark HS Reverse Harem Romance

Resurrection

Rebellion

Reign

Revere

The Sainthood: The Complete Series

ALL OF ME DUET

Angsty New Adult Romance

Say I'm The One

Let Me Love You

ALINTHIA SERIES

Upper YA/NA Paranormal Romance/Reverse Harem

The Lost Savior

The Secret Heir

The Warrior Princess

The Chosen One

*The Rightful Queen**

TRUE CALLING SERIES

Young Adult Science Fiction/Dystopian Romance

True Calling

Lovestruck

Beyond Reach

Light of a Thousand Stars

Destiny Rising

Short Story Collection

True Calling Series Collection

SAVEN SERIES

Young Adult Science Fiction/Paranormal Romance

Saven Deception

Logan

Saven Disclosure

Saven Denial

Saven Defiance

Axton

Saven Deliverance

Saven: The Complete Series

Coming 2021

Release date to be confirmed

'isit www.siobhandavis.com for all future release dates. Please note lease dates are subject to change based on reader demand and the uthor's schedule. Subscribing to the author's newsletter or following er on Facebook is the best way to stay updated with planned new leases.

Made in the USA
Las Vegas, NV
26 September 2021